Praise for T. M. Logan and *Lies*

"Assured, compelling, and hypnotically readable—with a twist at the end I guarantee you won't see coming."
—Lee Child, *New York Times* bestselling author

"Just when you think things can't possibly get worse . . . they do. And then some. *Lies* is positively riveting, from the captivating first scene to the shocking twist at the end." —Sandra Brown, #1 *New York Times* bestselling author

"A tense and gripping thriller."
—B. A. Paris, bestselling author of *Behind Closed Doors*

"In this fast-paced action thriller, lies upon lies are re-vealed as a young father races against time to find the truth, prove his innocence, and save his family. You will race through this novel alongside him right up to the shocking, twisted end!"
—Wendy Walker, *USA Today* bestselling author of *All Is Not Forgotten*

"Heart-thumping suspense and the greatest twist since *Gone Girl*. I inhaled *Lies* in one day and loved every page." —Michele Campbell, author of *It's Always the Husband*

ALSO BY T. M. LOGAN

29 Seconds

LIES

T. M. LOGAN

St. Martin's Paperbacks

This is a work of fiction. All of the characters, organizations, and events portrayed in this novel are either products of the author's imagination or are used fictitiously.

First published in the United Kingdom in 2017 by Twenty7.

Published in the United States by St. Martin's Paperbacks, an imprint of St. Martin's Publishing Group.

LIES

For information, address St. Martin's Publishing Group, 120 Broadway, New York, NY 10271.

www.stmartins.com

Library of Congress Catalog Card Number: 2018013471

ISBN: 978-1-250-62142-9

Our books may be purchased in bulk for promotional, educational, or business use. Please contact your local bookseller or the Macmillan Corporate and Premium Sales Department at 1-800-221-7945, ext. 5442, or by email at MacmillanSpecialMarkets@macmillan.com.

Printed in the United States of America

St. Martin's Press hardcover edition / September 2018
St. Martin's Griffin edition / July 2019
St. Martin's Paperbacks edition / May 2020

10 9 8 7 6 5 4 3 2 1

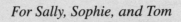

For Sally, Sophie, and Tom

Heaven has no rage like love to hatred turned . . .

—William Congreve, *The Mourning Bride*

A liar should have a good memory.

—Quintilian, *Institutio Oratoria*

PROLOGUE

I often wonder what would have happened if I hadn't seen her car that day.

If the light had been green instead of red.

If my son had been dozing, or daydreaming, or looking the other way.

If I'd been five seconds faster in the stodgy London traffic, or five seconds slower.

If, if, if.

But I did see her car.

And everything else flowed from that one moment, pulled on by gravity faster and faster until it was irresistible, unstoppable. Inevitable.

Would things have turned out differently if I'd just driven on home?

Maybe. Maybe not.

Maybe it was fate.

THURSDAY

1

My son's first word wasn't *Daddy* or *Mummy*. His first word was *Audi*. Which was strange because I'd never owned an Audi, and on my salary probably never would. But William had played with toy cars before he could walk and recognized the badges long before he could actually read the names. At the age of four (and a bit), he was already something of an expert, playing his car game as we inched along in the sluggish North London traffic, spotting badges and calling them out from his car seat in the back.

"Audi . . . Renault . . . Bimmer."

We were almost home. The traffic lights up ahead began to change, and I pulled up third in line as they turned red. In the mirror, I could see him clutching his first School Superstar certificate in both hands, as if it might blow away in the wind. A CD of kids' songs was playing low on my car stereo. *I am the music man, I come from down your way . . .*

William continued calling out cars. "Ford . . . 'nother one Ford . . . Mummy car."

I smiled. My wife—William's mum—drove a VW Golf. Every time he spotted one, he'd call it out. Not a Volkswagen. A Mummy car.

"It's a Mummy car. Look, Daddy."

My phone buzzed in the hands-free cradle: a Facebook notification.

"What was that, Wills?"

"Over there, look."

Across the divided highway, on the other side of the junction, a line of cars in the far lane filtered left onto an exit ramp. Rush hour traffic streaming through the junction, everyone on their way home. The low sun was in my eyes, but I caught a glimpse of a VW Golf. It *did* look like her car. Powder blue, five-door, same SpongeBob SquarePants sunshade suckered to the rear passenger window.

"Good spot, matey. It does look like Mummy's car."

I buzzed my window down and felt the cool city air on my face. A gap in the traffic opened up behind the Golf as it accelerated away down the exit ramp. It was a 59 registration license plate. My wife's car had a 59 plate. I squinted, trying to make out the letters.

KK59 DWD.

The number plate was hers—it wasn't *like* her car; it *was* her car. There was the familiar buzz, the little glow in my chest I still got whenever she was nearby. The VW indicated left off the exit ramp and turned into a Premier Inn. It headed into the dark entrance of an underground parking lot and disappeared from sight.

She'll be meeting a client, a work thing. Should probably leave her to it. She had been working late a lot recently.

"Can we see Mummy?" William said, excitement in his voice. "Can we can we can we?"

"She'll be busy, Wills. Doing work things."

"I can show her my certificate." William couldn't

quite pronounce the word, and it came out as *cerstiff-a-kit*.

Honking from the car behind me as the traffic lights turned green.

"Well . . ."

"Please, Daddy?" He was jigging up and down on his booster seat. "We could do a surprise on her!"

I smiled again. It was almost Friday, after all. "Yes, we could, couldn't we?"

I put the car in gear. Made a spur-of-the-moment decision that would change my life.

"Let's go and surprise Mummy."

2

I was in the wrong lane to turn right and had to get across two lanes of traffic. By the time someone had let me in—cue more furious hooting—the lights had gone red again.

"Where's Mummy whizzing off to?" William said.

"We'll catch her, don't worry."

My cell phone, in its hands-free cradle, blinked blue with the Facebook notification. I pressed the screen, and it brought up my picture of William in the school playground, clutching his first Superstar award from the reception class teacher. The post had four likes and a new comment from William's godmother, Lisa: Awww he looks so cute! ☺ What a good boy! Give him a kiss from me xx.

I hit Like below her comment.

The traffic light went green, and I turned the wheel to follow the route my wife's car had taken, down the exit ramp and left into the forecourt of the Premier Inn. Down the ramp into the underground parking lot, low concrete roof and deep shadows where the fluorescent lights didn't reach, driving slowly along the lines of parked cars.

And there it was: her VW Golf, parked next to the

elevator. Mel was nowhere to be seen. A sign on a concrete pillar read:

Parking lot for use by patrons of Premier Inn only.

There were no spaces next to her car, so I carried on around the circle and found a space in the row behind, backing in opposite an oversized white SUV that was clearly too big for the space it occupied.

"Can we go and see Mummy now?" William said. He was still clutching his "I'm a Superstar!" certificate in both hands like he was getting ready to present it to the Queen.

"Come on, then. Let's go upstairs and find her. There's an elevator."

His eyes lit up. "Can I press the button?"

The hotel lobby had dark shiny floors and anonymous décor, a single waistcoated teenager on reception. William's hot little hand gripped mine tightly as we stood looking for Mel. There was a rumpled man with a suit bag and briefcase, wearily checking out, a woman and a teenage girl behind him. An elderly Japanese couple sat in the reception area, poring over a map. But no sign of my wife.

"Where's Mummy gone?" William said in a loud stage whisper. "Come on. Let's find her."

Reception was L-shaped, with elevators and the restaurant signposted around the corner. We followed the signs, away from reception. The restaurant was mostly empty. Recessed off to the left were the elevators and a raised seating area with large black armchairs facing each other across a handful of low tables.

Mel was there. She had her back to us, but I would have recognized her anywhere, the slender curve of her neck, honey-blond hair.

Hey, there. Surprise! Wait.

She was with someone. A man, talking in animated fashion. Something made me stop. I knew the guy she was talking to.

Ben Delaney, married to one of Mel's closest friends. And he wasn't just animated—he was downright angry, his face dark with frustration. He interrupted her, pointing his finger, his voice a barely controlled growl. Mel leaned forward and put a hand on his arm. He sat back, shaking his head.

Something was wrong with this situation.

Instinctively, I moved in front of William to block his view. My first thought was to go over and check Mel was OK, but not with our son in tow. Mel was gesturing with her hands now, Ben staring at her, frowning, shaking his head.

This is not something William should see.

"Come on, Wills," I said. "Mummy's busy. Let's go back downstairs."

"Has she gone?"

"Let's wait for her in the car, matey. We'll be close by."

"Then I can show her my certificate?"

"Yup."

We got the elevator back down to the parking lot level and returned to my car. Mel's number was at the top of the favorites list on my cell phone. It went straight to voice mail.

"Hi, you've reached Mel's cell phone. Please do leave a message, and I promise I'll get back to you as soon as poss." *Beep.*

I hung up, redialed. Voice mail again. This time I left a message.

"Hi, love, it's me. Give me a call when you get

this? Just wanted to make sure you're OK . . . that everything's OK. Call me."

I sat five minutes more, starting to feel slightly foolish. I was supposed to be at home by now, running my son's bath. Drinking a nice glass of red. Thinking about making a start on tonight's marking. But instead I was here, in an underground parking lot just off the North Circular, trying to work out what the hell was going on upstairs. I wanted to check on her but didn't want to leave William. My suit shirt felt grimy and claustrophobic, a bead of sweat tracing a path down my rib cage.

So what's the plan, Stan? What if Mel isn't OK? What's up with Ben? How long are you going to sit here with one bar of cell phone reception, waiting and wondering?

There wasn't a plan. I wasn't going to do anything, just sit there and wait. Surprise my wife.

I didn't have a plan. It just happened.

3

I opened up the Angry Birds app on my iPad and passed it back to William, flicked on the radio for my own distraction. Five Live was running a piece about dating websites, featuring a series of quick interviews with women describing what they were looking for in their perfect mate. Expectations seemed to be pretty high. Their ideal man had to be at least six feet tall, in possession of a good sense of humor, a nice smile, and a six-pack. He had to be strong but not macho. Sensitive but good at DIY. Confident but not full of himself. Make decent money at work but still be around to do his share at home.

Blimey. It was exhausting just keeping track of it all.

Mel's cell phone went straight to voice mail again. I buzzed the window down and rested my elbow on the sill, absently turning the black leather bracelet on my right wrist as the radio presenter chattered on. Mel had given me the bracelet as an anniversary present: leather for three years. Now a big one was approaching—ten years—and there were already a few ideas on my list for that one. Ten was supposed to be tin, but some-one had said you could substitute diamond jewelry for tin. That was good. My plan had always been to give her a bigger diamond than I could afford as an early-career teacher when we first got—

"Daddy?"

"What's up, big man?'

"Can I get a hamster?"

"Uh, don't know, William. We'll see."

We'll see. Parents' code for *I won't mention it again, wait for you to forget.*

"Jacob P. has a hamster."

"Uh-huh."

"He's called Mr. Chocolate."

"That's a good name."

I smiled at my son in the rearview mirror as he played on the iPad. My son, the image of his mother. He was going to be a heartbreaker when he was older, that was for sure. His mother's face, her coloring, her big brown eyes.

And then there she was across the parking lot, walking quickly to her car: my pretty wife, dressed for tennis in her pink Adidas hoodie, blond ponytail tied up high.

She had her head down, a frown on her face.

Looks like she's about to cry.

I was suddenly glad we'd made this detour.

"William, I'm just going to talk to someone for a minute, OK? You stay here like a good boy, and I'll be right back."

He looked up at me with those big brown eyes. "Is it Mummy?"

"You stay here just for a minute, and don't get out, OK? Then after a minute, you can see Mummy."

"What if bad men come?"

"Bad men aren't going to come, big man. You'll be able to see me, and I'll be able to see you." I held up a finger. "One minute."

He nodded slowly but didn't look convinced.

Cell phone still in my hand, I got out and locked the car with the remote. The underground air was flat and sour in my nostrils.

Mel's VW was reversing out fast. Two lines of parked cars between me and her.

I waved. "Mel!"

The VW pulled off sharply, Mel pulling her seat belt across her chest with one hand as she accelerated hard toward the exit ramp. She hadn't seen me. Threading my way between the parked cars, I almost tripped on a low concrete divider between the rows, stumbled, shouted again, my voice flat against the low concrete ceiling.

"Mel!"

Her car disappeared up the exit ramp, and then she was gone, out into the Thursday night traffic.

4

There was a soft chime from the elevator at the far end of the parking lot. The doors slid open, and Ben emerged, briefcase in hand, cigarette between his lips. He lit up and lifted his head to exhale, seeming to spot me out of the corner of his eye as he took his cell phone out of a jeans pocket.

He had seen me, I was sure of it.

He carried on walking as if he hadn't.

"Ben!" I said, waving.

He slowed, stared at me for a second, raised a hand half-heartedly as I walked over to him. He stood by his car, a pearl-white Porsche Cayenne with the number plate W1NNR, dressed in that casual but-not-casual way you get when you spend a lot of money—designer jeans and tailored jacket. He looked at me like I was the last person he wanted to see, taking another drag on his cigarette.

There was a moment of silence, the smoke coiling lazily between us.

"Joe," he said finally, putting his briefcase down. "What are you . . . ? How's it going, big fella?"

"All good. Really good. How about you?"

"Yeah, sound. Business is booming, you know. You still setting the teaching world on fire?"

I had never been good at Awkward Guy Conversations. And Ben had never looked on me as an equal—more a bit of a runner-up, just another public-sector softie who wouldn't last five minutes in the dog-eat-dog world he inhabited.

"Something like that," I said, forcing a grin. "You just had a meeting up in the hotel?"

He opened his mouth to reply, closed it again. Tried to look past me.

"Yeah." He took another drag of his cigarette, blowing smoke from the side of his mouth. "A meeting."

"A work thing?"

"Potential client. A lead I've been warming up for a while."

"You didn't see Mel?"

"What?"

"My Mel. She was just here."

He almost flinched at the mention of her name, but caught himself. Instead, he just shook his head, dark eyes shifting toward his car.

"No, mate. Not seen her."

It was weird seeing him like this—evasive, reluctant, almost shifty—compared to his usual alpha-male demeanor. At the one and only poker game I had played at his house, he had regaled the table with a story about a former employee of his company who had quit to set up on his own, in competition with him. Ben had felt betrayed—so he had made it his personal mission to trash the guy's reputation in the industry, warning potential customers off, until the former employee's new company went bankrupt and he lost his house in the process. Ben had related the story with a trace of pride in a rival destroyed, an air of *screw with the bull and you get the horns*. It was the kind of guy he was. You didn't want to get on the wrong side of him.

"You sure you didn't see her?" I said. "I thought you were talking to her upstairs. It looked like serious stuff."

"Nope." He flicked his cigarette away. "Look, Joe, I've really got to go."

My tie suddenly felt too tight in my collar. He made to move past me, and I instinctively put a hand on his arm.

"Don't want to make a big deal out of it, Ben, I was just worried about—"

He whirled on me and grabbed two handfuls of my shirt, slamming me against the side of his SUV. He was surprisingly strong for his size, and his anger caught me off guard.

"Just leave it!" he shouted, northern inflection rising to the surface. Cigarette breath close in my face. "Just leave it alone, you big daft bastard! You have no idea! Bloody classic underachiever, that's all you are, all you've ever been."

He had anger, but I had size. At six foot two, I was six inches taller than he was. And at least forty pounds heavier.

"Leave *what* alone?" I said. "What are you talking about?"

"You're so fucking dense that you haven't seen it, have you?"

"Seen what?"

He shook his head in disbelief.

"None so blind as those that refuse to see, eh, Joe?"

With that, he pulled me forward so he could slam me back against the big Porsche again, and pain surged at the base of my skull. My hands bunched into fists, but some long-lost playground code said I couldn't hit someone smaller, shorter, lighter than I was. There was no way it could be a fair fight. Instead, I grabbed his hands and prized them away from my shirt, giving him a little shove to put some space between us.

He stumbled backward, tripped over his briefcase, and fell.

Hemmed in between two parked cars, he couldn't get his arms out to break his fall. There was a heavy wet *smack* as his head hit the concrete.

I stood over him for a moment.

He lay on his back, eyes closed, mouth open. One leg crossed under the other.

"Ben?"

He didn't move.

Get up. I need to know what you meant. And why you're so pissed off. "Ben?"

I prodded his shoe with the toe of my mine. Maybe he was faking.

"Ben, are you all right?" The world's stupidest question.

Always asked when we already know the answer.

No reaction.

Was he even breathing? I crouched down to look at him more closely.

Just move, Ben. Do something. Anything.

"Ben, can you hear me? Wake up, mate."

The first stab of panic in my stomach. There was a trickle of blood coming out of his ear.

Oh, God. Oh no.

"What's wrong with Alice's daddy?" I started at the small voice behind me and turned to see William standing there, his white school shirt untucked and sticking out from under his jumper. He peered at Ben's motionless body.

I stood up and moved to block William's view. "He, uh, he fell down, matey."

"Is he going to be all right?"

"He's fine. He's just getting his breath back."

The blood leaking from Ben's ear was dripping onto the ground, making a small pool on the gray concrete.

Oh, Jesus. What have you done?

"Blood, Daddy."

There was a little catch in his voice, a tightness that I knew all too well. My son tried to say something else, but the breath caught in his throat with an asthmatic rattle.

I said, "He's going to be fine, Wills. Are you OK?"

His chest heaved again. "Can't bre—"

I squatted down in front of my son, blocking his view. The color was draining from his face. His first asthma attack, right out of the blue when he was barely a year old, had been the most terrifying experience of my life. A panicked emergency call, running paramedics, and raw, helpless terror. The memory of that fear always returned when he had another episode.

Just like now.

He took a thin, jagged breath, like air whistling through dry reeds. Eyes wide and frightened.

Protect the boy. Get the inhaler.

"Where's your puff-puff, Wills?" I said urgently.

He shook his head, another halting, gasping breath forcing its way down his constricted windpipe as it closed to a pinhole. I scooped him up and ran to the car, diving into the glove compartment for the spare inhaler I always kept there.

It wasn't there. *Shit.*

Turning William's schoolbag upside down, I emptied the contents onto the passenger seat. Books, coloring pens, a pencil case, conkers, candy wrappers, a key ring, three toy cars, and an unwrapped lollipop stuck to a crumpled letter.

No inhaler.

Another jolt of panic.

Got to get him breathing again. Upstairs at hotel reception? No.

Time wasted. Home is the nearest, surest place.

But what about Ben?

All the details of the moment came into sharp and brilliant focus. The dark leather soles of Ben's shoes. A black Range Rover at the top of the ramp. Off in the distance, above ground, a siren. My son taking another half-strangled breath, thinner than the last. He swayed slightly on his feet, his movements slowing.

Make a choice. Make it now.

Ben still lay there, unmoving, on his back.

Protect the boy.

I should have stayed with Ben, gone upstairs to get the hotel staff, called an ambulance. Maybe driven him to hospital myself. I should have done *something.* But all I could hear was my son starting to suffocate. So I didn't. I didn't do any of those things.

Instead, I panicked.

I strapped William in and jumped into the driver's seat.

5

I ran the first two red lights as I desperately tried to remember whether there was a pharmacy, a supermarket, or a doctor's office on my route home, William heaving and wheezing beside me in the passenger seat. *Just be OK, son. Be OK. Home soon. We will make you better. Hold on.* There was a pharmacy—but it was closed. We flew past and blew through another amber traffic light as it was turning red, weaving through traffic with the honks of other drivers behind us.

"You're going to be OK, Wills. We'll be home in a minute, and we'll get you your puff-puff, OK?"

He nodded weakly but said nothing. His face was deathly pale now, eyelids drooping.

We hit a clear stretch of the North Circular, and I pushed the car harder, overtaking a van and switching lanes to pass a white SUV on the right.

Ben.

I should call the hotel. Get him some help.

Except my cell phone was nowhere to be found. It wasn't in its usual place in my jacket pocket or in my jeans. The hands-free cradle on my dashboard was empty; the glove compartment too.

I reached under the car seat as I drove. Nothing

there. It would have to wait until I could use the land-line at home.

It felt like the longest drive of my life.

Finally, I pulled the car into my driveway with a screech of tires, grabbed William, and ran into the house, to the kitchen drawer where we kept a spare inhaler—*Please be there, please be there*—and sat the boy down on a kitchen chair while he took a lungful of Ventolin. Then breathed deeply, and took another. I knelt in front of him, holding him steady, hearing his breathing slowly deepen, lengthen, as it returned to normal.

"It's OK, Will. You're OK. Does it feel better?"

He nodded solemnly. "Bit better."

A little color was returning to his cheeks, my terror receding with it. Relief flooding through me in its place.

"Just sit quiet for a minute, matey. Take it easy."

Our little-used landline phone was on the kitchen counter. Directory inquiries connected me to the hotel, and I listened as it rang six times, then put me through to an automated list of options.

The last option was to speak to a human.

"Listen," I said. "There's a man in your underground parking lot. He may be hurt. You need to send someone down there right away to help him."

"Sorry, sir, this is the Premier Inn, Redfield Way," said the voice, a young man in his late teens or early twenties. "Are you sure you have the right number?"

"Yes! There's a man down there, he fell and banged his head. His name is Ben Delaney. Can you check he's OK?"

"Is he a guest of the hotel?"

"No, but he's on your property. Can you check on him or not?"

"I'm afraid I'm not allowed to leave the front desk, sir, but my supervisor should be back in a bit. If you think an ambulance should be called for a member of the public in the meantime, you should hang up and do so immediately."

"Can't you just run down and see if he's all right? Lock the front door for two minutes and do a quick circuit of the parking lot?"

There was a pause on the other end of the line. "Is this a prank call?"

"Never mind," I said and hung up.

I grabbed a bottle of water for William, gave him a quick hug, and listened to him breathing again. His airway was getting back to normal. I put the inhaler in my jacket and picked him up.

"Where are we going, Daddy?"

"Just a quick trip out in the car before bath time."

"Are we going to go fast again?"

"Quite fast, but not as fast as before."

My imagination ran laps as I drove, new thoughts unspooling now that William's asthma emergency had passed. Going over everything I'd seen in the last hour. Trying to make some sense of it.

What did you see?

What did you actually see?

I had seen him angry, her upset. *What did he say to upset her?*

Him lying on the ground, eyes closed. Blood.

What if he's still lying there? Of course he's not.

He might be.

What if he is?

And, rising above it all, that horrible wet *smack* as Ben's head hit the concrete.

Maybe he's fractured his skull. Can you die from that? Of course you can. If you're left there and no one helps you.

Maybe there would already be police on the scene by the time I got there. Unspooling crime scene tape, putting numbered evidence markers on the ground. Floodlights. Maybe getting ready to put up one of those white tents you see on the news when the police are hiding a body from prying eyes.

My mouth was dry, and I felt off balance, like something in my life had been dislodged from its proper place, pushing everything else out of sync. Nothing was where it should be.

I left him there. Bleeding.

But going back to the hotel was still the right thing to do. It was on me to put this right; that was all there was to it. My routine Thursday evening had taken a turn for the surreal, the confusing, the downright terrifying—but there was still time to get it back on track. It was just a case of doing the right thing.

He'll be all right. Just a bump on the head. Mel will know what to do. We'll figure it out together.

More than anything, I wanted to speak to my wife, make sure she was all right after her heated encounter with Ben this afternoon. *Just let Mel be OK. Everything else we can deal with. Together.*

I wound down the window and breathed in gray city air. Turned on the radio, trying to find something to take my mind off things. Turned up the music. By the time I'd turned off the North Circular, I had half convinced myself that Ben would be OK. He'd already be home now, drinking an expensive single malt at the living room bar of his big Hampstead house. *People don't die from falling over and banging their head. They just don't. Otherwise there would be thirty murders every Saturday night in every market square, in every town in Britain.* I pulled onto the forecourt. Through the glass frontage of the hotel I could see the same waistcoated teenager as earlier behind the reception desk, talking on the phone.

The entrance to the underground parking lot gaped like an open mouth.

The barrier rose as I approached, and I drove slowly down the ramp into the dull fluorescent light below ground. Deep shadows against the concrete. I parked, leaving William in the car again, and got out. Walked up and down the four rows of cars. Went to the spot Ben's car had occupied less than an hour ago.

There was no crime scene tape. No white tent. No police.

There was nothing.

Ben and his car were gone.

6

My cell phone was gone too.

As far as I could remember, this was the last place I'd had it in my hand. Right here in this parking lot, when I'd gone to talk to Ben. Maybe I'd dropped it when things turned ugly. So where was it? I looked around, patted my jacket pockets again. Dropped to my knees and checked under the parked cars. Nothing. I walked a circle around the row of vehicles, squatted down again, squinting into the shadows. But it wasn't there. *Damn.* A twinge in my stomach. One more thing to worry about. Or maybe it was somewhere at home? I made a mental note to check later.

I called Mel three times from the landline phone when I got home. Three times it went straight to voice mail. Finally, I left a message.

"Hi, it's me. Give me a call when you get this? Just want to make sure you're OK. Thought you might be . . ." I hesitated. *Might be what?* "Call me back. Love you."

Be OK. Please be OK. Everything else I can handle, one thing at a time.

The thing with Ben was ridiculous, I decided—I

should just call him. Get to the bottom of whatever was going on—if there even *was* anything going on.

Except I couldn't call him, because all my contacts were in my cell phone, and that was lost. The address book was backed up to Mel's iPad, but she had that with her at work. The landline was useless—we hardly ever used it, and there were only about a dozen numbers stored in its memory.

And so, perched on the bathroom stool, a bottle of beer cooling my hand, there was nothing else to do except go through the usual evening routine. William was in the bath, swirling the water around with both hands, his plastic boats and animals circling him like a tiny flotilla around and around. He was talking to me about school things and how his little buddy Jonah had wet himself during assembly, and I was fending him off with lots of *Really?* and *Oh, dear* and *Uh-huh*. The long-neglected landline phone sat dark and silent on the windowsill next to me.

"When's Mummy coming back?" he said, putting bubble bath on his chin to make a white beard.

"What's that?"

"Mummy."

"She'll be home soon."

"Look at my beard, Daddy. I'm Santa."

"Good one, matey. Got a present for me?"

"It's not a proper beard. It's only bubbles really."

The sound of keys in the front door made me jump. Mel called up in her usual way.

"Mummy!" William shouted back.

"We're up here," I added.

She appeared in the bathroom doorway, and I hugged her, relief washing through me like a tide.

I kissed her cheek, tasting the familiar salty sweat mingled with perfume.

"Hey, you," I breathed into her ear.

"Hey yourself." She disentangled herself from the embrace. "Nice welcome. What's that for?"

"Thought you might need a hug."

She smiled and kissed me, her lips soft against mine.

"No more than usual." She studied me for a second, taking a drink from her water bottle. "Are *you* OK?"

"It's been a hell of an evening, but I'm all right."

"Why? What's happened?"

"It's nothing," I said, trying to summon a smile. "Tell you later. I was actually worried about you."

"About me?"

"Yes, are you OK?"

"Of course. Why wouldn't I be?"

"I saw you earlier and you seemed—"

"Mummy! Mummy!"

"What is it?" she said.

"Look, Mummy, I've got a beard!"

"Nice, William." She drank the last of her water and began refilling the bottle from the tap.

"And I had ants-ma, and me and Daddy had to come home to get my puff-puff."

"Oh, dear," she said, kneeling by the bath to stroke his cheek. "Are you OK now, darling? Was it a bad one?"

"Yes. And Daddy drove *really* fast."

She looked at me, raising an eyebrow. "Did he now?"

"He was fine once I got him on his inhaler. Thought I had one in the car, but I think I used it last time and didn't replace it. My fault, really."

Mel turned back to our son. "And how was school, William?"

"I was really *very* good, Mummy," he said slowly, pronouncing each word. "I got the Superstar award from Mrs. Green."

Mel gave him a big surprised smile. "Well, that's fantastic, William."

"For sitting nicely in assembly."

"Aren't you a good boy?"

"Yes. But Daddy isn't."

Mel raised an eyebrow at me. "Is that so?"

I shook my head, forced a smile.

Should have thought of this, talked to him about what happened.

"It *is* so," William said.

"Why has Daddy not been good?"

"William—" I started.

"This sounds interesting," my wife said.

"It was nothing, really," I said quickly, scrabbling to think up a way of deflecting what my son was about to say.

"*Not* nothing," William said.

Mel took another drink of water from the bottle, looking at me. "So why was Daddy bad, William?"

"Because he said I can't have a hamster."

I exhaled, slowly. "I didn't say that, big man, just that we'd see."

Abruptly, William stood up out of the bath, his arms outstretched.

"Towel, Daddy! Towel, towel, towel!"

I plucked him from the bath and wrapped him up in a towel that was bigger than he was.

Mel crossed her arms. "A hamster, eh?"

I shrugged. "I said we'd think about it."

She nodded, turned in the doorway. "I'm going to get a quick shower."

"Listen, Mel?"

She turned back to me. "What's up?"

"You sure you're OK?"

"Course. Why?"

"I saw you earlier and you seemed upset. Left you some messages."

She frowned, cocked her head to one side.

"My phone's out of charge. When did you see me earlier?"

"About five, at this hotel on the North Circular."

She took a sip of water from her bottle, swallowed slowly.

Then another.

And that was when everything I knew started to fall apart.

7

"A hotel?" she said.

"Near Brent Cross. I was worried about you."

She shook her head. "I wasn't at a hotel, Joe; I was at tennis. Thursday night social, same as always."

"But I saw you."

"You can't have, Joe. I wasn't anywhere near Brent Cross."

I tried to make sense of what she was saying. "You weren't?"

She laughed quickly. "Couldn't very well have lost 6–1 6–0 to Hilary Paine if I was, could I?"

"But we saw you. Your car."

"That beer's gone to your head, darling. I'm going to grab a quick shower before tea."

She turned and left.

I stared at the empty doorway for a long moment, then started to dry William's fine brown hair with the towel. The sound of the shower starting up in the master bathroom reached me from across the landing.

A lie.

I felt dizzy, disoriented, like I'd suddenly started walking up a down escalator.

A lie. Why did she lie? Why do people usually lie?

She was trying to protect me from something, or protect William, or both of us.

Do you really believe that?

No. Do you believe the alternative? No, definitely no.

I didn't know what to believe. Because what was the alternative?

Ben.

I married Mel knowing that she was independent, and I respected that, liked it about her, liked the fact that she wanted her own time, her own hobbies and friends. The same way that she respected me and knew that I was different from most of her friends' husbands in that I loved being home with William, loved spending time with the little guy. I had never regretted going down to three days a week for a couple of years after he was born so I could be there for him more before he went to school. Mel had gone back to work full-time after four months' maternity leave, but that was her choice, and I totally understood it. She brought in more than my teacher's salary anyway, she liked her job, and she was bloody good at it. We fitted together perfectly, like interlocking pieces of a puzzle.

We didn't lie to each other.

But now it felt like everything familiar was sliding away out of reach. Twelve years we had been together, nine of them married.

She was there with him, and she had lied about it.

Thinking about Ben again brought me up short. I'd been so focused on Mel and William that I had not thought about him. I had to talk to him, ask him, find out what he had to say before I broached it with Mel again.

Assuming he was OK.

You left him there. Bleeding.

"What's the matter, Daddy?" William's head emerged from the towel.

"Nothing, big man."

"You look sad."

"Not sad, Wills, just a bit tired."

He yawned, his half-dry hair sticking up in every direction. "*I'm* not tired."

"You are a little bit, aren't you? Do you want a strawberry milk before your story?"

"Yes!" He began bouncing on the spot. "Milk-shake, milkshake!" He drank it sitting at the kitchen table with his *Cars* coloring book and felt-tip pens. Next, I mixed up a strong Bloody Mary for Mel—she always had one on a Thursday, gin and tonic on a Friday—the routine of hundreds of nights. While my hands worked, my mind kept returning to it. Over and over.

A meeting. A fight. A lie.

Mel appeared in the kitchen, a towel in her hand. I handed her the Bloody Mary, kissed her on the cheek.

"Have you seen my cell phone? I think I've lost it."

"When?"

"This evening."

She shook her head, taking a long drink of the Bloody Mary. "Not seen it since it was charging on the kitchen counter this morning."

It wasn't on the kitchen table, or the dining table, or next to the landline where my charger lived. It wasn't anywhere in the living room. I ran up the stairs two at a time, checked the bedroom, bathroom, even—in desperation—checking William's bedroom to see if he'd scooped it up with his cars.

Nothing.

Mel found me rooting through the laundry basket, checking the pockets of my work trousers from earlier.

"No joy?"

"It's gone. Vanished."

She crossed her arms, leaned against the bathroom doorframe.

"What else is the matter, Joe? Is that all?"

"Not sure yet."

"What does that mean?"

I squeezed past her in the doorway and went back downstairs to the house phone in the living room. Mel's iPad had a backup of all my phone contacts, so I grabbed that too. My heart was thumping hard in my chest.

Mel's voice came down the stairs to me, high and tense. "Are you going to tell me, Joe? Let me help you, at least."

My iPad was showing nineteen notifications on Facebook.

That was weird.

Having that many notifications in one go was new to me. I was not a prolific user of Facebook in any case—*My life's not even half-interesting enough*, I'd once told Mel, which she'd said was missing the point of social media entirely. My posts were few and far between and wouldn't normally generate that many comments in a month, never mind one night. The picture of William with his school award must have hit the spot.

I ignored Facebook for the moment and went to the address book backup, found Ben's home number, and punched it in on the landline. As it connected, I went back to the iPad's home screen and hit the Facebook icon. The familiar blue and white of my timeline appeared, all the usual stuff. People going out for the night, or staying in, eating this or that, watching this or that TV show; who was already halfway gone and who was sober, who was going for an early night, and who was just getting started. As the dial tone sounded in my ear, I pressed on the notification icon to find out what people had been saying that involved me. The screen filled with a list of new updates. *Paul Coffey, Tanya Payne, and Tom Parish commented on your status.* I clicked on the top notification.

Felt the ground shifting beneath my feet.

I hung up the phone and stared at the screen.

What?

There was a status update from me. Or rather, from my account, more recent than my post about William's school award. My profile picture alongside the update.

The update was just a few words, a hashtag, and a picture.

Joe Lynch
2 hours ago
Oops! It wouldn't do to lose this
#AnniversaryPresent

The picture was a low-angle shot, the camera virtually on the ground. Taken in an underground parking lot, Ben's car registration plate visible on the right-hand side. A sign said: *Parking lot for use by patrons of Premier Inn only.*

My phone. My Facebook account was synced to my smartphone.

Oh, crap.

I clicked on the picture to enlarge it. There was something in the foreground, flared out with flash—but you could see clearly what it was. A black leather bracelet. *Looks like mine.* I dumbly looked at my wrist. Gone. *Oops! It wouldn't do to lose this.* Must have come off when I was grappling with Ben, and now it was in a photo posted on a social network with a billion users.

Next to a dark red pool of what looked like blood.

8

My throat was dry. I felt helpless, like I was toppling over and couldn't reach out to break my fall.

A message implicating me in an assault, a fight, a crime—an incident that could mean swapping my job for a prison sentence—had been seen by other people on one of the biggest social media networks in the world. It had been read, acknowledged, responded to.

My Thursday night was out there, for the whole world to see and comment on.

And there was another one, another status update from me—but not from me. From my account.

Joe Lynch

1 hour ago

I must say that the facilities at the Premier Inn NW2 are excellent. Particularly the underground parking lot. Always nice to bump into friends.

I read it, then read it again, trying to process the words. Eight likes and five comments. A message flagged to 251 people who knew me well enough to be in my extended circle of Facebook friends and acquaintances. Mates I had known since school.

Colleagues at Haddon Park Academy, the school where I worked. People who knew me, respected me. Family too. My sister, cousins, uncles, aunts. Christ, my *mother* was my friend on Facebook.

And my profile was public. I had been meaning to sort out the privacy settings for a while but had never gotten around to it, so pretty much anyone could see what was posted from my account. I scrolled down so the first comments appeared.

Tom Parish

1 hour ago

What is this Joe, TripAdvisor for parking lots? Tell me more

Karen Clarke

54 minutes ago

Eh?? Not sure what to make of this!!! You OK? xx

Andy Stamford

41 minutes ago

A bit more tonic, a bit less gin, old bean

Paul Coffey

39 minutes ago

Mel finally thrown you out mate? Knew she'd see sense lol

Tanya Payne
15 minutes ago
Who'd you bump into then? Very cryptic!! ×

Now they all knew. They had seen my post. They knew where I'd been. *Damn*. It was like suddenly realizing you lived in a goldfish bowl.

Think.

Both updates had been posted this evening. I had driven out of the Premier Inn around 5:10 P.M., and both Facebook posts had followed inside the next ninety minutes. The replies had come in the hour following that. I selected Settings from the Facebook menu, saying a silent prayer as I typed.

Please let my password work. Please don't lock me out of my account.

I held my breath.

It worked. I was in. The password was unchanged. I breathed out and went straight to my timeline, deleted the posts from earlier in the evening, and changed my password. Maybe the smart thing to do here was delete my account altogether. You couldn't hack an account that didn't exist, right? But what if posts started to appear on other accounts—about me, or Mel, or both of us?

Give it twenty-four hours, then delete the account. In the meantime, I would stay on it so I could at least see what was being said.

Next, I rang my cell phone provider to report my phone lost and get a block put on it. I poured a glass of red wine as the call handler told me a replacement should be with me by Saturday morning. My hand, holding the wine bottle, was shaking.

Life had taken another turn for the surreal.

Think. Just think for a minute. What does it all mean?

Today had been a car crash of a day. But it was slowly dawning on me that the latest turn of events at least—the hijacking of my life on social media—had at least one upside. I didn't know Ben that well, but I knew he was the kind of guy who didn't like to be challenged and couldn't bear to be beaten. In business, at home, driving in traffic, even playing bloody Pictionary, he had to win. More than that—everybody else had to lose. The fact that the messages had been posted using my phone, from the scene of this evening's altercation, could only mean one thing.

Ben was very much alive—and up to no good.

9

The possibility of Mel lying to me—about anything—had never crossed my mind. It had never troubled me for a second before. But now I couldn't think about anything else. My wife had *lied*. Did that mean she had chosen Ben over me? What did he have that I didn't have? Money, obviously. Plenty of it. A big house. Various expensive cars.

Is that it? Is that what it comes down to?

And now I had found them out, surprised him, gotten the better of him. Not really a surprise, considering I was that much bigger than he was. At school, I had been bigger, stronger, faster than most of my classmates without even really trying. I was six feet tall and nearly two hundred pounds by the age of thirteen—a man, while most of my peers were still boys—and had a blast for the next five years as everyone else tried to catch up. A lot of them, guys like Ben, never did—at least not physically. And what was his response to being on the losing end of a confrontation? To set me up, get me in trouble. To drop me right in the shit in a very public way.

That was Ben, through and through.

Ben, the technology entrepreneur, the smartphone

app developer, the school geek turned millionaire—that would be right up his street. He was the kind of guy who would roll his eyes at people who left their cell phones unlocked or didn't have the latest iPhone or who used the same password for everything. His favorite trick was picking up your phone when you weren't looking and changing the language to Korean, or Arabic, or Russian. Leaving you to navigate the settings in a foreign language to get it back to English. *Your fault for leaving it unlocked*, he'd say, grinning. *User error.*

Or maybe his messages on my Facebook account were a warning of some kind.

Mel appeared in her dressing gown, took a new bottle of red from the rack, and refilled her glass. She certainly wasn't wasting any time tonight. She pulled up a chair and sat opposite me at the kitchen table.

There was silence between us for a moment.

Finally, she said, "Are you going to tell me what's going on, Joe?"

I took a sip of my wine and placed the glass carefully back on the table. Looked her straight in the eyes.

"I think you need to tell *me* that."

"What do you mean?"

"You were at that hotel this evening, with Ben. I saw you." I hated saying it, hated hearing the words come out of my mouth, but it had to be said. "You weren't at tennis, at least not for the whole time."

She opened her mouth as if she were about to speak, closed it again, shook her head. Sighed and looked away from me.

"Tell me," I said, my heart sinking.

Please don't let it be true.

"I knew this would happen. I told him it would."

"You knew *what* would happen?"

She looked down at the table, blushing.

"Oh, God, you know me, Joe. I've never been very good at keeping secrets."

For a moment, I just stared at her, feeling the blood thrumming in my chest. It felt like all the air had been sucked from the room. When was the last time we had all been together, the Delaneys and us? A Sunday afternoon at their house at the tail end of the summer holidays, Ben showing off with his brand-new gas barbecue, Mel lingering around him, drink in hand, smiling and talking to him as if he were the most interesting man in the world.

Or was that just my imagination?

"So tell me," I said, trying to keep my voice level.

"You were right. I was there tonight."

10

"You were there, with Ben," I said.

"Yes. But it's not what you're thinking."

"And what do you think that is?"

"By the look on your face, I'd say you think I've been naughty."

"And have you?"

"No, you silly sausage." She smiled and patted my hand. Her touch was warm, reassuring. It meant everything. "We had a meeting, that's all."

"A meeting about what?"

"He rang me this morning, said it was urgent. He wanted to meet face-to-face about something work-related."

"But about what?" I said again.

"Well . . . the point is, he told me it was super-confidential. He made me promise that I wouldn't tell anyone, not even you. But I suppose I could give you a bit of the background, as long as none of it leaves this room." She held her hands up in mock surrender. "Since you caught us red-handed."

I smiled, a warm glow of relief starting to move outward from my chest.

"Go on."

She picked up her glass of wine, took a drink, set it back down between us.

"Ben thinks . . . he might have a problem inside his company. A mole. Various key bits of code have turned up in other people's apps, and he thinks someone inside is selling it on. He's narrowed it down to three possible culprits on the development team, and he wanted some advice on employment law. About how fast he could get rid of them and make sure the dismissal is watertight. He's also on the point of getting the police involved and wanted advice on that."

"Hasn't he got an HR adviser he can use internally?"

"She's married to one of the guys under suspicion."

"So he turned to you instead?"

"He wanted someone on the outside. Someone he trusted."

Mel had worked in human resources for a number of large companies since I'd known her, and she was currently with one of the big retail chains. She was often used as a troubleshooter, dealing with issues quickly and quietly before they escalated. "Dealing with," in the sense of "paying off or firing." At her previous employer, she had acquired the nickname "Machete Mel" for her style of chopping people off—figuratively—at the knees. She didn't take many prisoners.

"He couldn't wait till tomorrow?"

"He rang me this afternoon—three times—said it was urgent and wouldn't wait. You know how he is." She gave me a little smile. "Everything has to be now, now, *now*. And he insisted on face-to-face, off-site, because he's paranoid about phone conversations being recorded and didn't want to risk tipping off his guy who's selling code on. He said he learned a lesson three years ago when he dismissed an employee for gross misconduct. Do you remember that?"

"Vaguely. Matthew something."

"Matthew Goring. He saw what was coming, that meetings were happening behind closed doors. Then the whispers started, and he put two and two together, saw that he was going to get the chop. And even though he only had a couple of hours before they walked him out the front door, it was enough time to code a series of extreme pornographic images into the game app that Ben's company was developing at the time. These images were programmed to appear at various stages during the game when you unlocked a new level. Really vile stuff—women with farmyard animals, that kind of thing."

"I don't remember hearing about that."

"He's sensitive about it, as you can imagine. They discovered the images right at the last stage during final hygiene checks. If the app had gotten out there into the market, it could have sunk Ben's company. Bearing in mind the game was aimed at five- to nine-year-olds."

"Sounds like something Ben might do himself," I said.

"Exactly—he thinks the same way they do. That's why he's wary of the culprit getting wind of what's going on."

"When I saw you talking to Ben, he seemed agitated." I remembered the aggression on his face, his finger pointing. "Like he was really angry."

"Angry doesn't cover it. He was furious."

"About this thing with his member of staff ripping him off?"

She nodded. "He was telling me what he feels like

saying to him. Not in the office, of course. Ben's idea was to take him down a dark alley and have that conversation with the help of a couple of hired thugs and an iron bar."

"Blimey. Really?"

"Yup. Fortunately, I managed to talk him out of that particular course of action. Not exactly textbook HR practice."

"Good old Mel, keeping everyone on the straight and narrow."

"That's me, darling." She smiled. "But a bit less of the *old*, if you don't mind."

I sat back in my chair, smiling too, relief flooding through me in waves. *You saw what you wanted to see, Joe, and you got it 100 percent wrong. We're OK, after all. Everything's good. Everything's right where it should be.*

I held my hand up, like I was swearing an oath.

"My name is Joseph Michael Lynch, and I am officially an idiot."

My beautiful wife shook her head and smiled back at me. "It's part of your charm, darling. Always has been."

"Sorry for . . . doubting you."

"I'll let you off. Just this once."

"But why did you fib about it?"

She shrugged. "Client confidentiality."

"He's not your client, though."

"You know what I mean. I promised him I wouldn't tell anyone we'd even met."

"Not even me?"

"Not even you, Sherlock." She swatted playfully at my arm. "And now you've made me break my promise. You're such a meanie."

I slapped myself on the forehead. "Sorry, sorry, sorry. Did I mention that I was sorry?"

"You are also *very* silly. You had me worried earlier, when you were being all weird."

"I just didn't get it. When you said you weren't at that hotel, and I *knew* you were, I couldn't understand it. Couldn't bear the thought of you . . . of us . . . you know."

I looked away, my face hot.

She got up, came around the table, and sat on my lap. Kissed my cheek, nuzzling under my ear in a way that still made me forget everything else in the world.

"I'm sorry too, Joe," she breathed. "For fibbing. Shouldn't have done that."

I sat for a moment just enjoying it, her warmth, her scent, her touch. The shape of her on my lap.

"After you left the hotel," I said, "I saw Ben in the parking lot."

She stopped nuzzling my cheek. "Saw him?"

"Talked to him. Kind of. He was angry, but I guess now I know why if someone's threatening to sabotage his company."

"What did he say?"

She listened as I described my encounter with Ben, how he'd fallen and I'd had to rush off. My return to the hotel later on to check he was OK, realizing I'd lost my cell phone.

"You poor thing," she said, concern on her face. "What an evening you've had. Why don't you try Ben on the phone again? Sort things out with him."

But Ben wasn't answering, landline or cell, which I guessed was fair enough considering it was getting late on a Thursday night. Mel and I talked for another half hour about what had happened, drank more red wine, apologized to each other again. We talked about school, and work, and William and his certificate, and the weekend, and going for a meal on Saturday night. I was beyond relieved to get everything back on an even keel. To get everything back to normal after what would go down as one of the weirdest days of my life.

When the wine bottle was empty, Mel yawned and headed upstairs, and I filled the sink to do the washing-up. As I finished the dishes, I realized I hadn't told her about Ben's posts from my Facebook account. It was the one thing that didn't quite make sense. It just didn't seem to fit.

I stared at my reflection in the dark kitchen window.

Why would he have hijacked my account if every-thing Mel said was true?

FRIDAY

11

Period four on Friday was free in my schedule, and I had planned to spend it marking 7B's homework on themes and ideas in *The Coral Island*. But I was tired, and it had been a tough week, and there was still a nagging feeling—like an itch I couldn't scratch—about what had happened with Ben last night. I wanted to give him a call, ask him why he'd put those messages on my Facebook account and *Could I have my phone back, please?*

A part of me also wanted to apologize for what had happened and check that he was OK; it bothered me that he might have been hurt, and I wanted to put things straight. Just apologize to him, put it out there, say it, and move on. I didn't want it to be more awkward than it had to be when we all got together at their next dinner party, or Sunday lunch, or whenever. Ben and I weren't close; we really only knew each other through our wives, and most of my conversations with Ben were about football, the universal language invented so that men who didn't know each other very well could still talk about *something*. We'd veered into politics once, but we didn't agree on much, and I preferred not to listen to him bang on about public-sector waste and benefit cheats.

But still, it was important to Mel that we were all friends, and I wanted to make the effort for her.

I couldn't call Ben until later, at home, but I had my iPad with me. I took it out of my briefcase and opened Facebook. He hadn't posted anything today, and the two weird posts he'd put up on my account yesterday were safely deleted. I scrolled idly through recent posts on his account: the woes of Sunderland Association Football Club; a photo of the speeding fine he'd gotten for going six miles an hour over the speed limit on the A40; a link to an *Anchorman* sketch from *Saturday Night Live*. Others about the state of the economy; *Game of Thrones*; a picture of the foundations being laid for the new summerhouse in his garden; techie subjects relating to his industry. Sunderland AFC again.

I was struck by what a strange view you could get of someone's life from looking at his or her Facebook profile. I googled his name instead and got thousands of hits, starting with his company website, his LinkedIn profile, his other social media accounts, and a range of stories in the media that mentioned him.

The first was a profile of him in the *Evening Standard* from late last year, not long after he'd moved to London. It was part of a series on young entrepreneurs in the capital, "40 under 40," peopled by property developers and fashion designers, hedge fund traders, music producers, and digital millionaires like Ben. His profile drew on Ben's rags-to-riches story, which had taken him from his parents' two-bedroom terrace in Sunderland to a seven-figure mansion in one of London's most expensive neighborhoods. The son of a dockyard worker from a tough working-class area, the only kid in his school year to make it to an elite Russell Group college, a first-class degree, first company at the age of twenty-two, first million by the age of twenty-five, three consecutive number-one games in the App Store by the age of twenty-nine as he rode the new wave of demand for smartphone gaming apps. The gushing profile even made a comparison with Steve Jobs and concluded by asking Ben for the secret of his success in business.

> Delaney admits he is an obsessive.
> "I've always been able to focus on one thing to the exclusion of everything else—and I don't stop until I get it. It's what gives me an advantage. Most people get distracted. I don't. Because no one remembers the guy who comes second."

Another story—a diary piece from the *Daily Mail*'s business pages—shed a somewhat less flattering light on Ben and his business dealings. It described an incident at an "exclusive Kensington restaurant" a month ago where police had been called and arrested a man for assault and disturbing the peace. The *Mail* story gleefully named the arrested man as Alex Kolnik, thirty, a former employee of Ben's who had set up in competition with him and seen his company go bust in short order. Reading between the lines, it seemed Kolnik blamed Ben for the failure of his business and had gone to the restaurant for some payback.

Ben had mentioned it before, I remembered. *Screw with the bull and you get the horns.*

I clicked to the third page of results. More guff about Ben's company, his career, and his rise to fortune.

But there was something more interesting at the bottom of the page of results—a link to a four-year-old story in the *Sunderland Echo*, a court case involving a man named Steven Beecham, who had been up for grievous bodily harm.

It didn't seem to fit with the rest of the results. I clicked on it. Beecham had been accused of breaking a local businessman's kneecaps, ankles, and elbows with an iron bar. Beecham was alleged to have been paid by a third man—Peter Haskell—to beat up the victim following a dispute over the sale of property in Sunderland city center. The description of the injuries inflicted made for pretty grim reading, and I scrolled down the story farther, wondering why this had appeared in a Google search for Ben Delaney. A picture of the defendant walking into Newcastle Crown Court showed a huge scowling man, the shoulders and arms of his gray suit stretched taut over the muscles beneath.

His dark hair was shaved to a flattop, and there were swirls of sharp Celtic tattoos up the side of his neck.

Ben Delaney had not been involved directly with the case, but it seemed his name—along with the names of several other businessmen, investors, and high rollers—had been found in a list of contacts on one of the defendant's cell phones. Now that *was* interesting. Ben had not been called as a witness in the case but had subsequently been contacted by the *Echo* to ask if he had any comment.

Mr. Delaney said he was a member of the Mirage Casino's platinum lounge and played poker tournaments there several times a year.

He said: "I know a lot of the staff there. They know me. That's all I've got to say."

I read farther down the story.

Beecham, a doorman at the Mirage Casino on Bridge Street, Sunderland, is alleged to have told a witness that "doing some c***'s kneecaps costs £500. For a grand I'll put him in a f****** wheelchair."
The case continues.

I googled "Steven Beecham court," and a new page of results appeared: he had been found not guilty of the grievous bodily harm charge and had walked free two days later. He was pictured outside court, a death's-head grin on his face, flanked by two thick-necked friends.

The bell rang, and I checked my watch. It was time for the last lesson of the week.

SATURDAY

12

I sat poolside on a hard plastic chair and watched William's swimming class as they splashed and kicked and doggy-paddled from one side of the shallow end to the other, the smell of chlorine and wet towels hanging in the warm air. The swimming teacher stood waist-deep, urging the kids on, a T-shirt over her swimming costume to hide her modesty from the line of Saturday morning dads sitting by the side of the pool. William was not a keen swimmer but was willing to be bribed with chocolate after each lesson. We had an arrangement. I watched him kicking his little legs and felt a familiar glow of pride.

There was one kid in his group who didn't swim at all. He just walked up and down, working his arms breaststroke-style, pushing off from the bottom every so often so he could overtake all the other kids—the ones who were actually swimming. He beat them to the side every time.

"Why does that boy walk instead of trying to swim?" I asked William later, rubbing his back with the towel.

"Ryan?"

"The lad with the blond curly hair."

"That's Ryan."

"Yeah, him. He never actually swims."

William nodded, studying his wrinkled fingers. "His mummy is the teacher, and she says she doesn't mind."

"Doesn't she want him to learn?"

"She says he can do it however he wants."

"Oh. But how's he going to get better at swimming?"

"His mummy says it doesn't matter 'cause he'll always have arm bands to keep him safe anyway."

I looked over at Ryan the curly-haired boy, being dried with a towel by his curly-haired mother. She was beaming at him, smiling encouragement, chatting as she dressed him.

What lies we tell our children, I thought. *But why not?* I hoped for Ryan's sake that he'd always have someone there to catch him when he fell.

William was quiet in the car, his need for activity sated for the time being. Small boys were like puppies. Both needed lots of exercise every day and had basically two gears: *go* and *stop*. They had to be walked every day; otherwise they'd go stir-crazy and start tearing the house up.

His next engagement today was a fifteen-minute drive to Dollis Hill for a five-year-old's birthday party. Jacob Pendlebury, one of his school classmates. A wall of noise greeted us as we stepped into the hallway and handed our coats to Jacob's father. He gave me a *welcome to the madhouse* smile, eyebrows raised, as we went through to the living room and William took his place, cross-legged on the floor, with a dozen other kids. Parents were arrayed around the edge of the room on a collection of sofas and kitchen chairs. The entertainer was a loud-voiced woman dressed as a jester who did magic tricks and got the birthday boy to join in as her assistant. She was good, but the cacophony of small children in a confined space was eventually too much for my mild Saturday morning hangover. After half an hour, I sneaked out toward the kitchen, following the warm smells of home baking and fresh coffee.

There was a petite dark-haired woman in the kitchen—her face vaguely familiar from the school playground—carefully putting five candles on a Manchester United cake. Of course. We were in North London, so of course it made sense that Jacob Pendlebury was a Man U fan. Growing up in Berkshire, I had supported Chelsea. Small boys supported winning teams. It took a few years to get used to the idea of supporting a local team that was consistently, miserably average.

"The jester's very good," I said.

She stopped planting candles and smiled.

"She is, isn't she? We booked her for my daughter's birthday a couple of years ago, and Jacob always wanted to have his turn."

"Thanks for the invite."

"That's no problem at all."

"I'm William's dad, by the way."

She nodded, returning her attention to the cake. "I know. We're friends on Facebook."

I felt a spasm of unease. *That's why her face looked familiar.* How many people were there who knew me, even slightly, whom I'd friended on Facebook and then forgotten about? Some were actual friends in the old-fashioned sense of the word, but many were little more than vague acquaintances. Like this woman in her kitchen in Dollis Hill, with whom I had probably exchanged six words before today.

"Really?" I managed. "I don't really use it that much, to be honest."

"Did you find that thing you were looking for the other night?"

"What thing was that?"

"That bracelet. You posted a picture of it."

"Oh, that. Yes. Found it." I felt my face getting warm. "Silly, really; I don't think alcohol and social media are a good mix."

"I'm rubbish at Facebook. Hardly ever post anything myself."

"I know what you mean."

She stood back from the cake and looked at me again. "So, technically, I'm more of a stalker really."

I wonder what she really *thinks about those posts from Thursday night?*

"Well," I said, "Facebook's certainly good for stalking too."

She pointed at my chest. "I like your T-shirt, by the way."

I smiled and looked down at the navy T-shirt, a speech bubble with white text inside: I'M SILENTLY CORRECTING YOUR GRAMMAR.

"My wife got it for me—kind of an in-joke with English teachers. Grammar is becoming a bit of a lost art these days, with textspeak and social media and what have you."

There was a burst of shouts and clapping and then a disappointed wail from the other room, and we both turned toward the noise.

"Better go and see what's up," I said, grabbing the opportunity to get away.

I returned to the living room, where a game of pass the parcel had ended in tears for two little girls in dresses and plaits, both of whom had a hand on the parcel when the music stopped. The rest of them, William included, stared in fascination as the two girls screwed their faces up and competed to see who could cry the loudest.

I avoided talking to Jacob's mum again when the children trooped into the dining room for birthday lunch. As always happened at these parties, they all reached first for the Hula Hoops and chocolate fingers, leaving the carrot sticks and cherry tomatoes untouched in the middle of the table.

Mel was in the kitchen when we got back home. Drinking coffee and dressed for tennis again. She kissed me and handed me a cup, asked me about the party, and how was swimming, and did William manage a length of the pool? A normal Saturday. Normal stuff happening. Not for the first time, I wondered if I had just dreamed the whole of Thursday evening: Ben and my wife, the hotel parking lot, the aftermath. All just a dream, a fiction conjured from fitful sleep.

"A courier came," Mel said, indicating a small plastic-wrapped package on the kitchen countertop.

I opened it. A replacement cell phone sent out on the insurance. *God forbid we should ever have to go offline for more than twenty-four hours.* I took the phone out of its box and unspooled the power cable.

"Your phone didn't turn up, then?" Mel asked.

"Nope."

"You sure it's not in the house somewhere?"

"Pretty sure."

"Wills has started getting a bit obsessed with phones and gadgets, remote controls, that sort of thing. He puts them in with his cars. Maybe you should go and have a look."

I plugged the new phone in to start charging it. "Bit late now."

"Have you tried calling it?"

It occurred to me that in Thursday night's panic, I had not even tried once to call my cell to see if anyone answered. And now it had been disconnected.

"You're right. That's the first thing I should have done. Wasn't thinking straight. Think I was distracted by the Facebook stuff."

She frowned. "What Facebook stuff?"

"A couple of weird posts on my account, from my cell phone."

"You think Ben did that?"

"Don't see who else it could have been."

She picked up her phone and went to Facebook. "What did he post?"

"Oh, I deleted them the other night. Just some stuff about seeing me at the Premier Inn. A bit weird."

"Maybe it wasn't him. Maybe your account got hacked."

There was something odd in the tone of her voice. Something slightly unnatural.

"Maybe," I said.

"Sounds weird, though."

William appeared in the doorway, three cars in each hand. "Can you play airport parking lot with me, Daddy?"

Airport parking lot involved bringing all his toy cars downstairs—maybe a couple of hundred, although I'd never counted—and lining them up in rows on the living room floor, according to make and model. The end result resembled an airport parking lot in miniature, hence its name.

"Need to have lunch first, big man. Then I'll play."

He held out one hand. "You can do Bimmers if you want."

I took the three little BMWs from him, the metal warm from his small fingers.

"Thanks, matey."

He trotted off back to the living room.

Mel said, "You should change your password on Facebook."

"Done that already."

"You OK?" she asked.

"Of course." I smiled. "Why wouldn't I be?"

"I mean about the Facebook thing, someone posting as you. It happened to Marie at work last year; really shook her up. Getting fraped, they call it."

"Fraped?"

"Facebook raped."

I shook my head. "Never heard that one before. Who thinks this stuff up?"

"Are you OK, though?"

"It's no big deal. Really."

"I thought I might go for a few sets at the tennis club this afternoon," she said. "You boys are all right together, aren't you?"

"Sure. We still on for tonight?"

The phone rang on the countertop next to me, the landline for once. I picked it up.

"Hello?"

Silence.

"Hello?" I said again.

"I need to speak to Mel. Is she there?"

It was Beth, Ben's wife, a wobble in her voice like she was trying to hold it together and only just managing. Mel mouthed a silent question at me. *Who?*

I realized I was still holding the three toy BMWs and put them down on the kitchen counter.

"Beth? Are you OK?"

"No. I don't know." She paused, and I thought I heard a half sob in the silence. "Can I speak to Mel, please?"

I handed the phone to my wife. "Hi. Melissa speaking."

She turned away from me and took the phone into the conservatory. I was about to follow her when William appeared at my side again.

"Daddy, can you get my cars down?"

"Which ones, Wills?"

"Um, all of them?"

I followed him to his bedroom and brought down the two wicker boxes of cars. They were heavy, and I had to carry them one at a time. When I returned to the conservatory, Mel was putting the home phone back in its cradle. She was frowning. She looked downcast, genuinely worried.

"What's up?" I said. "Beth didn't sound good."

Mel looked away from me. She blinked, checked her cell phone, put it back in her pocket.

"Mel, what is it?"

She tucked a stray strand of hair behind her ear, the way she always did when she was agitated or stressed.

"She wants to come over. It's about Ben."

13

If there was one word to describe Beth Delaney on a normal day, it would be *serene*. She had a calmness, a quiet elegance about her that never seemed to waver. I couldn't recall a single time when I'd seen a ripple of anxiety disturb the perfection.

Until today.

Today, her eyes were shadowed dark from lack of sleep, and she looked brittle, like fine china that might shatter at the slightest touch. Tall and willowy, dressed in a cream turtleneck and gray trousers that accentuated her long legs; dark hair falling to her shoulders, only the subtlest of makeup to disguise the fact that she was working hard to hold herself together.

I had met her maybe half a dozen times over the past year, at dinner parties and barbecues, since she and Ben had left Manchester and bought the big house in Hampstead. She was beautiful, for sure, but never wanted to talk about herself, and I had never managed to break down her reserve to find out anything meaningful beyond it. So even after a year, I knew little about her, beyond the basics. She and Ben had a daughter, Alice, a very levelheaded fourteen-year-old who had babysat for William a few times. Mel knew

Beth from school and had stayed in touch through college, before jobs and careers took them to different parts of the country.

Their friendship from school had stayed strong despite—or maybe because of—the differences between them: Mel the extrovert, the leader, the sporty alpha female; Beth the clever, kind, quiet counterpoint, but just as much an achiever in her own way. They had stayed in contact in the years since, and when she and Ben moved to London, Mel insisted we have them over for dinner and help them get settled in. Ben had invited me to join his fortnightly poker game, where I had gone once, lost £75 in two hours, and decided poker wasn't the game for me.

We sat in the conservatory at the back of our house, the three of us. A freshly made cup of apple and elderflower caffeine-free tea infusion sat steaming, untouched, on the table in front of Beth. She didn't drink regular tea or coffee. No caffeine. No meat, no dairy, no sugar, no nonorganic either.

She looked as if she were going to begin to speak, then closed her eyes, took a deep breath, let it out. Then another. She seemed to be meditating.

Mel put a comforting hand on her arm.

"It's all right, Bee. It's going to be all right. Just take your time."

Beth glanced at me for a second, dropping her gaze as if she were embarrassed.

Mel said, "Do you want Joe to go somewhere else?"

In normal circumstances, I would have taken the hint and made myself scarce. But these weren't normal circumstances, and I wanted to hear what Ben might have told her in the last thirty-six hours. She was torn between a desire for privacy—to keep this wives only—and the desire to avoid causing offense. On a normal day Beth would rather die than give offense.

"No, it's fine," she said in a small voice. "It's fine."

"What happened, Beth?" I said as gently as I could manage.

Mel shot me a sharp look that said, *Let me handle this.* "Take your time, Bee," she said.

Beth took a sip of herbal tea, setting the cup carefully back down on the glass-topped table as if she were worried both might shatter with the slightest force.

"It's Ben. He's . . . I don't know." She always spoke quietly, and I'd never heard her raise her voice. But today she was almost whispering.

"Nothing goes further than this room, Bee. You're among friends here. We're on your side."

Beth crossed her arms tightly across her stomach, shoulders hunched.

"I just can't work out what I did wrong," she said. "What I did to set him off."

"Tell us what's happened, Bee."

"It's like a nightmare. Like Jekyll and Hyde."

"Take your time."

"OK. So two nights ago, Ben came home really late. I was in bed asleep, and he woke me up. He never normally tells me when he's getting home, but this was out of the ordinary; it was almost midnight. He was drunk, I think. Goodness knows how he managed to drive home. You've never seen him like that. Sometimes he gets . . ." She tailed off.

Mel sat forward, her voice soft. "How does he get, Bee?"

"Sometimes when he's upset with things at work,

he gets drunk, and when he's really drunk, he gets angry. He breaks things."

"At work or home?"

"At our house," she said in a small voice. "At home."

"What else does he do?"

"How do you mean?"

"Does he hurt you as well?"

Just like my Mel. Straight to the point.

Beth closed her eyes, her chin quivering.

"Has he done this before?" I asked.

She looked away, lips clamped together. A tear ran down her cheek, and she wiped it away quickly with the heel of her hand.

"This last year, since we left Manchester and moved to London, a lot of the time he's seemed so distant. Angry sometimes. Refuses to talk to me about it. Mood swings, all the time. One minute, he's absolutely fine. The next minute . . ."

"But has he hurt you before?" I said.

Beth nodded, taking the tissue Mel offered her.

I felt the ache in my back from where Ben had slammed me against his car. He was pretty strong for a smaller guy. I supposed domestic violence was more common than people thought, but I had never actually known anyone who'd been an abuser. *Jesus.*

And another thought, which made my anger flare: *Did he take his anger out on Mel too, when they met on Thursday evening?*

Her voice quiet, Mel said, "What happened after he came back, Bee?"

"I heard him moving around, slamming doors, breaking things. I thought he'd come up, but he didn't. So I just lay there waiting, waiting. I couldn't move."

Mel got up and sat next to Beth on the couch, put an arm around her shoulders.

"Try not to worry. You and Alice are both OK, that's the main thing."

"What a mess, Mel. Oh, God, what a mess."

I tried to catch Mel's eye, but she wouldn't look at me. Beth dabbed at her cheeks with another tissue.

"Next morning, his Aston Martin was gone. And some of his clothes, an overnight bag, and a laptop."

"Oh, Bee, you poor thing. I can't imagine what it's been like. Have you tried calling him?"

Beth nodded. "Twenty times at least. He's not been answering his cell phone. I waited for him to come home all yesterday, worried sick. I checked work, he wasn't there and had missed various meetings. Called his mum; she hadn't heard from him. I waited up half the night for him last night, but no sign of him. And then today I suddenly thought, I wasn't sure I *want* to be there when he finally gets home. So I called you."

Mel said, "What time did Ben get home on Thursday night?"

"About a quarter to midnight."

"I don't understand this."

"Neither do I. When he's done this before, it's been triggered by work problems. But he seemed quite happy about the way things were going with the company."

"No, I don't understand how he can go from being fine and talking business, to getting drunk and storming out of his house a few hours later."

Beth frowned. "How do you mean, talking business?"

"His company."

"When were you talking to him about his company?"

"Thursday night, after work."

"You saw him?" Beth said, her voice rising slightly.

"Yes," Mel said. "Before I went to tennis. He seemed OK then."

Not entirely true, I thought.

"I saw him too," I added. "We both did."

Beth sat up straighter, frowning first at me and then at Mel. "Why?"

Mel gave her friend a summary of what she'd told me last night, leaving out the details of my encounter with Ben.

"But if you left him just after 5:00 P.M.," Beth said, "that still leaves seven-plus missing hours. Where was he? Where did he go?"

"What did Ben actually say that night, when he came home?" I asked slowly. "It might help us find him, help him, if we know what was bothering him."

Beth blew her nose delicately and dabbed at her reddened eyes with a tissue.

"He didn't say much. Just came in, got his stuff, and left. The only thing I heard was actually about you."

"Me?" Mel and I said in unison.

Beth pointed at me. "Joe."

"Really?" said Mel, a little too quickly. "In what . . . context?"

"Bad things."

"Really?" I tried to sound surprised.

"Like he wanted to hurt you."

"Oh. That's weird."

"Why would he say that?" Beth said, her gaze unwavering. "Did you two have a falling out?"

"Well, we did have a bit of a—"

"Joe reversed into his Porsche as he was leaving," Mel cut in, talking over me. "Not on purpose, obviously, just one of those things. But Ben wasn't best pleased, was he, Joe?"

I stared at her for a moment.

Why did you lie? And then it clicked. *To protect you, idiot.*

Mel gave me one of her no-nonsense looks. "Was he, Joe?" she repeated.

"No. He wasn't happy," I said.

"He does love that car," Beth said, dabbing at her eyes with a fresh tissue. "Even more than the Morgan. It's his favorite."

"What did Ben actually say on Thursday night?"

Beth took a sip of her herbal tea, setting the mug down delicately on the coaster as if she were scared of making any noise at all. "It was something like, 'Joe effing Lynch. Time you were put in your effing place.' Or words to that effect. He was downstairs, and I was in the bedroom. Then I heard the door slam, and he was gone."

I had never heard Beth swear. Not once. Instead she said *effing* and *blummin'* and *Lord* and *blimey* like a little old lady. But somehow it made it more chilling, more real, to hear Ben's threats relayed in such an understated way.

"Jesus, Beth, are you serious?"

She nodded, lips pursed together.

"Do you think he might come here, to our house?" Mel said.

Beth shrugged. I tried to remember whether I'd locked the front door behind her when she'd arrived.

"I don't know where he'll go; I really have no idea at this point. He might have gone for good, for all I know."

"I'm sure he hasn't, Bee. He'll be back."

"It wouldn't be the first time."

"He's done it before?"

"Only for a few days. Work was getting on top of him, and he just had to let off some steam. Last time, he drove home to Sunderland, blew some money in the casinos. A couple of nights in a hotel with his phone switched off. Then he came back."

"Sorry, Bee, I had no idea."

"It's not the sort of thing you shout about on Facebook."

"No, of course. Well, I'm sure he'll be back this time as well," Mel said, trying to sound upbeat.

"I hope so."

"He's probably just letting off steam, like you said. It'll be OK."

"Maybe." Beth didn't sound convinced. "But there's something else."

"How do you mean?"

"The things he took with him . . ."

"Clothes and an overnight bag, you said."

"That wasn't all."

Mel said, "What else, Bee?"

"One of the reasons why I'm so worried. Especially with what he said about Joe."

"Tell us."

Beth's next words froze me in my chair. "One of his guns is gone."

14

"He has guns?" I said, trying to keep my voice level.

Beth nodded. Took another sip of herbal tea. "Shotguns, mostly."

"What does he shoot?"

"Wood pigeons and ducks," Beth said. "Clays as well. He's a pretty good shot. Has quite a collection of sporting guns." She smiled a small smile. "I think he fancies himself shooting grouse on the Glorious Twelfth. He's always wanted to be a member of the landed gentry, wear Barbour coats and Hunter boots. He bought me a gun to encourage me to shoot, even though I've been a vegetarian since before we got married. I couldn't imagine anything worse."

It felt like the temperature had just dropped a few degrees in our conservatory. Ben was out there somewhere, furious, with a shotgun for company. I imagined him turning up on our doorstep. Staring at him down the barrel.

"Wait here a minute," I said, standing up. I checked the conservatory door, kitchen door, and front door were all locked before picking William up from the living room floor and carrying him back into the kitchen on my hip.

"Do you want a cookie, Wills?"

He nodded solemnly, and I handed him two ginger-snaps from the cookie jar. I sat him down at the kitchen table, where I could keep an eye on him from the conservatory, and rejoined Mel and Beth.

There was an awkward silence for a moment, punctuated by the sounds of William crunching loudly on his first gingersnap.

"Maybe we should call the police," I said quietly.

"Already done that," Beth said. "Called them yesterday afternoon when Ben still hadn't come home, or been at work, or answered any of my calls, or been at any of the places I thought he might be."

Mel leaned forward. "What did the police say, Bee?"

"They took some details and told me to call back in twenty-four hours if he still hadn't turned up."

"Have you called them back?"

She nodded, tucking a strand of dark hair behind her ear. "Couple of hours ago. They told me I could go in and give a statement if I wanted to, so I went into Kilburn Police Station. I've just come from there. It's all so surreal, Mel: policemen and procedures, filling in forms and giving statements. Just hope Ben isn't too cross when he finds out."

"What did the police say?"

"Nothing much, really. It was a young chap, a constable. He said most people like Ben turn up sooner rather than later, but that he'd pass my information up the chain tomorrow for one of the detectives to look at."

"Did you tell them about Alex Kolnik?"

She looked a little startled. "How do you know about that?"

"It was in the *Standard*. I was googling him yesterday and found it online."

"I mentioned Alex, yes."

Alex, I thought. Not *Kolnik*, or *him*, or *that man*. She referred to him as *Alex*. It hadn't occurred to me that they might be on first-name terms. But it was one to think about later.

"We could go in and give statements too," I said. "Tell the police what we saw on Thursday night. Would that help, do you think?"

Beth shrugged. "It might."

Mel gave me a sharp look. "He hasn't actually done anything yet, apart from make a mess of his living room."

"Not *yet*," I said. "But he's made threats. What if he comes here when I'm not around? What if it's just you and Wills, and I'm not here to protect you?"

"He wouldn't do that."

"He's out there somewhere with a shotgun, Mel," I said. "We need to do the smart thing. And Beth needs to protect Alice."

"He wouldn't hurt us," Beth said quietly.

"That's what battered wives have been saying since the day marriage was invented," I said.

She glared at me. "Is that what I am now? A battered wife?"

"It doesn't need to be physical abuse to be abuse. Rolling in drunk at midnight, shouting about killing people? I think that qualifies."

Beth gave a tiny nod of acknowledgment. "Perhaps."

Mel said, "You're right, Joe. We should talk to the police. Would you like us to do that, Bee?"

Beth gave another tiny nod. "Would you?"

"Of course," I said. "Is there a number we can call?"

She took a card out of her purse. *Kilburn Police Station, duty desk, nonemergency only.* The words *PC Khan* were written on the back in Beth's smooth, flowing handwriting.

"Can we keep this?"

"Yes, I've got another."

Mel said, "Where's Alice now?"

"Gone to her friend Lily's house. She didn't want to be at home after Thursday night."

"How's she doing?"

"She's frightened and worried for her dad at the same time. Trying not to show it."

"We can cancel babysitting tonight, if you want. It's no big deal."

"No, it's fine. I think she'd probably prefer to be out of the house, to be honest."

"You could both stay over tonight, if you don't want to go home," Mel said.

Beth thought about this for a long moment, then shook her head. "I should be there when he gets back."

"You shouldn't feel like you have to dance to his tune all the time. Maybe once in a while he should find himself wondering where *you* are, instead of the other way around."

"Old habits, you know? Hard to break." She looked at her watch and stood up. "I should go."

Mel stood up too and hugged her, patting her back. "It's going to be OK. You'll see."

"I just want to get back to normal again. It doesn't matter what happened the other night."

"He'll see sense soon enough. But you've got to

ask yourself how long you're going to let it go on for. How many more times."

"I don't know where I am without him," Beth said, eyes downcast. "I don't know what to do on my own."

Mel said nothing in response. They disengaged from their embrace, and we stood as an awkward threesome, me between them, not knowing whether to hug Beth or not. Feeling like a fraud for not telling her the whole truth. We settled for an uncomfortable peck on the cheek, both given and received without much commitment.

Beth checked her phone's screen. Sighed and put it back in her pocket. "What if he isn't just blowing off steam? What if it's more than that?"

"What do you mean, Bee?"

"What if it's another woman?"

Mel smiled, shaking her head. "Ben would never do that."

"How do you know?"

"He just wouldn't, would he? He's not that kind of guy."

15

As soon as Beth left, I did another full circuit of the house to check all the windows were closed. Double-checked the kitchen door and slid both deadbolts across. Mel followed me, saying nothing, William clinging to her like a baby monkey. She had the little vertical line between her eyebrows that appeared when she was stressed or upset, but she seemed to feel safer with me in the room. And right then, I wanted to keep both of them—the two most important people in my world—close by.

"What's going on with Ben?" I said, locking the patio door. "Why is he threatening us all of a sudden?"

She shook her head. "I don't know. No idea. It's crazy."

Eventually, we pulled the curtains in the living room, and I put CBeebies on for William. TV in the daytime was a deviation from the norm, but he seemed to sense that it was better not to question the break in routine, in case I changed my mind. Smart kid. I felt a pang of worry for him as he sat on the rug watching *Chuggington*, a toy car in each hand, oblivious to the mess the adults around him had created.

Should I keep a weapon handy in case Ben turned

up out of the blue? What could I arm myself with if I had ten seconds to grab something? Kitchen knives, a rolling pin, a hammer from the toolbox. Not much, but better than nothing.

From our bedroom window, I surveyed the street, half expecting to see Ben's white Porsche Cayenne careering around the corner and screeching to a halt outside our house, but there was not much going on. A couple of teenagers from a few houses down were doing tricks up and down the curb on their skateboards. Across the street, a woman in her fifties was walking a chubby golden retriever with its tongue hanging out.

Nothing out of the ordinary. No sign of Ben.

This was stupid. I could help to put things right, myself, right now. Rebuild some bridges. I punched Ben's number into my new cell phone, and it rang six times before it went to Ben's terse, no-nonsense voice mail.

"This is Ben Delaney. Leave a message." *Beep*.

I hesitated, hit End and dialed his number again. This time it went to voice mail after one ring.

"This is Ben Delaney. Leave a message." *Beep*.

"Ben, it's Joe. Joe Lynch. I just wanted to speak to you about the other night. I'm sorry—I was out of order. I honestly didn't know what was going on, and I'm sorry about what happened. Give me a call if you want to talk about anything. This is my new cell phone number; I've got a new phone. Anyway, I hope you're OK."

I hit End and looked up to see Mel standing in the doorway.

"Who were you calling?" There was a hint of accusation in her tone.

"Ben."

"Why?"

I shrugged. "Thought it might help if I could talk to him. Clear the air."

"And did it?"

"Got his voice mail. Although I think the second time he was screening my call."

She crossed her arms. "Why would he do that?"

I shrugged again. "Same reason he's not returning his wife's calls, probably. Maybe he's embarrassed now, doesn't know how to come back without looking foolish."

"What were you saying about the other night?"

"Just that if he wanted to talk, this was my new number. It would be nice to be able to give Beth some reassurance that he's OK, to say that one of us has spoken to him."

Mel tilted her head to the side slightly. "You need to be careful with him, Joe."

"Phone call can't hurt, can it?"

"Do you really think calling him is going to help? I don't want him coming around, especially with William here."

"I won't let anything happen to Wills."

Her face fell, and I suddenly realized she was on the verge of tears. I went to her and hugged her tight, her head against my chest.

"It's just so weird, all of this," she said. "It never would have occurred to me that Ben had any violence in him."

I kissed the top of her head. "I'll look after you and Wills. I will never let anything happen to you. Never."

"I know. I'm more worried about what Ben might do to you."

"We should go to the police," I said. "Make a statement, like Beth did."

Mel looked up at me. "About what?"

"About seeing Ben on Thursday, about what he said—he was proper weird with me. We both saw him at that hotel. We need to give that information to the police. Maybe it will help them to find him, sort all this out. Put Beth's mind at rest."

"I'm just not sure that anything I could tell them would help very much."

"We don't know for sure, though, do we? It might be something that we don't think is significant. Something that's relevant to what's going on Ben's life right now, but we don't realize it."

She shrugged. "Like what?"

"That's the point—we don't know what might be important. The police are the professionals. They're the ones who can work out what's relevant and what's not."

William appeared behind her on the landing, looking from me to his mum.

"Are we calling a police car, Daddy?"

"No, matey. Not today."

"Can we call one?"

"No need, Wills. You've already got loads."

"Yes, but they're not big, silly Daddy."

"What are you up to anyway, little man?"

He held out the toy car in his hand, a silver Land Rover. "Can we play airport parking lot?"

I took another look up and down our street. No white Porsche.

No Ben Delaney.

"Of course, Wills. You go and start, and I'll be there in a minute."

He trotted off across the landing.

Mel was silent, staring after our son as he disappeared back downstairs.

"Well?" I said.

"I don't know. It just seems like . . . an overreaction."

"He's not been seen for more than thirty-six hours, Mel."

"London's an easy place to disappear in."

"Is it? But why would he want to?"

"He's always done exactly as he pleases, and screw everyone else." She crossed her arms. "Always."

"I know that, but why now? And why was he so angry on Thursday? He was really wound up, like something was going on. After what Beth said about him taking a gun from the house, I just think we need to do the right thing."

"The right thing?"

"Yes."

"But what if . . ." She trailed off.

"What?" I said gently.

In a small voice, she said, "What if we don't know what the right thing is?"

That made me pause. "What do you mean, love?"

She was about to reply, then looked away.

"Mel?" I said. "Tell me."

She sat down on the bed, shaking her head.

"Mel?" I said again.

"You're always so sure of what the right thing is, aren't you? Good old Joe. How come everything is so black and white for you?"

"We need to help Beth. Help both of them."

"I'm just not sure that us going to the police is the kind of help Ben would want."

"The police are already involved. So are we, whether we like it or not."

"Not involved. Not really."

There was a strange, forced tone in her voice. "What's up, Mel?"

"Nothing. Nothing's up."

"You sure?"

She nodded. I waited, thinking she was going to say something else, but then she seemed to decide against it.

"OK," I said. "Let's give that PC what's-his-name a call. Have you got the card that Beth left?"

She fished the business card out of her sweatshirt pocket.

I took my phone out and dialed the number. The call connected and began to ring in my ear. It rang once. Twice.

Mel stood up abruptly and put a hand on my arm. "Joe. Wait."

"What is it?"

"Hang up," she said.

"Why?"

"Just hang up," she repeated. "Please."

I hit End and cut the call off. "What's the matter?"

"Something I need to tell you first. Before we do this."

"OK." There was a strange tingling feeling at the back of my neck, as if someone had crept up behind me. I turned quickly, but there was no one. Of course there wasn't.

She took a deep breath. "There's something you need to know. Sit down on the bed a minute."

"Are you OK?"

"Yes. Maybe."

I sat down on the bed next to her. "So tell me."

"The thing is . . . I think I might know what's going on with Ben."

16

The silence lay heavily between us.

I trusted my wife absolutely—always had—but she'd never been like this with me before. And her body language was all wrong: tucked in on herself, head down, hands clasped tightly together.

"So what's going on with him, Mel?"

She put her head in her hands and began to cry. I put an arm around her shoulders, pulled her close.

"You can tell me anything, Mel. Anything at all. It's OK, whatever it is. You know that, don't you?"

A tear splashed onto the leg of my jeans. Then another. I let her cry for a minute, rubbing her shoulders, comforting her, the soft, fresh scent of her perfume surrounding us both.

"Just tell me," I said again. "It doesn't matter."

"I made a mistake. A couple of years ago."

A lurching, sinking feeling started in my chest and moved down through my stomach.

"A mistake?"

"I'm so sorry, Joe." The breath caught in her throat. "It was so stupid."

"Try to calm down, Mel. It's OK."

"Can't believe I was so stupid."

"What do you mean, a mistake?"

She reached for a box of tissues on the bedside table, dabbed her eyes and blew her nose. "Do you remember Charlotte and Gary's wedding?"

"The one with the ice sculptures and the free bar?"

"That's the one."

Charlotte was another friend of Mel's from college. She and Gary had gotten married in a posh ceremony in Highgate, followed by a reception at a fancy hotel set in its own parkland estate. William had just turned two. He'd begun to fidget and cry as the bride walked down the aisle, so I'd taken him outside, where we spent the entire ceremony looking at the badges of different cars lined up next to the graveyard. *Audi. Bimmer. Ford. Saydees.*

"What about it?"

"Do you remember the evening?"

I searched my memory. A lot of life was a blur when William had been that age, but this was the first wedding he'd been to, so it was more memorable than most.

"Not much of it. Didn't I take William back to the hotel early for his bedtime? But you didn't get back until after midnight, and you woke us both up falling over the suitcase. Twisted your ankle. You had a massive hangover the next morning."

She nodded but said nothing.

"Something else happened at the reception?"

"Yes," she said very quietly.

"Involving Ben?"

"You took Wills home early because it was past his bedtime. Beth went home because she had her yoga or something in the morning. There were loads of people there that Ben and I didn't know, the DJ played some songs I remembered from college, and Ben asked me if I wanted to dance. Then he got a bottle of champagne, and we sat down and started talking. We had loads in common and talked for ages, about everything. Music, books, films, traveling, work. Future plans." After holding it back for so long, it was coming out in a torrent now as if she couldn't stop. "We drank that bottle, and then Ben got another, and eventually, he said he'd fancied me for ages. Told me he couldn't stop thinking about me, that I was his perfect woman, that he'd had a thing about me since I'd first visited Beth at college, when we were both nineteen."

My stomach lurched again as I guessed what I was about to hear next. A sick, sinking feeling that spread to my arms and legs.

"And?"

"I was flattered."

"Then what?"

She paused, looked away.

"What happened, Mel?" My voice was hoarse.

"And then he leaned in and kissed me."

It was like being sucker-punched in the back of the head. I felt dizzy, disoriented.

"What did you do?" My words seemed to fall over each other.

She shrugged, a tiny movement as if the answer was obvious. "I kissed him back."

"And then what?" Heat was rising to my face.

"He said he was staying in the penthouse and that there was more champagne in his room. And strawberries for breakfast. That kind of brought me to my senses, and I ran out of there as fast as I could, jumped in a cab, and came back to our hotel."

"How long did it last?"

"The conversation?"

"The kissing."

"A minute? A few minutes, maybe."

"Maybe?" I tried to keep my voice level.

"Not very long. I was drunk. I'm so sorry."

I stood up, paced the room once, twice.

A kiss. Just a kiss, two years ago. Nothing else. They were drunk.

It happens. It changes nothing.

"Talk to me, Joe," she said, her voice cracking. "Come and sit down again."

I sat down next to her on the bed again, trying to blink the dizziness away. "Jesus, Mel. This is a bit of a bloody bombshell. What the hell were you thinking?"

"That was it, I wasn't thinking. It was the booze. That's no excuse—"

"No, it isn't."

She paused, seeming to choose her next words with care. "I'm so sorry, Joe."

"Nothing else happened?"

"It was just a kiss, that was all. A stupid, drunken snog."

"Why didn't you tell me about it then, or since?"

"Because I was mortified, couldn't believe what had happened, and worried about how you'd react. By the time I'd started to get over the shame, it seemed like there wasn't any point in telling you because it was over and done with, all in the past. Obviously, I couldn't tell Beth because she's a friend. And anyway, nothing really happened. Not really."

"But you're telling me now."

"Yes."

"Why?"

She sniffed and dabbed her eyes with the tissue

again. "The thing was, after that night, Ben was . . . different."

"With you?"

"Yes. He never let me forget it."

17

Something clicked in my head, like two cogs slotting together. "He wanted more, didn't he?"

She nodded. "He wanted us to be together. Obviously, we'd known each other since college, through Beth, and we'd seen each other at parties, weddings, and christenings in the years after. Stuff like that. Nothing had ever happened. But then after Charlotte and Gary's wedding, he friended me on Facebook and got my email address somehow, then my cell phone number. He wasn't creepy about it, or weird; in fact, he was mostly quite sweet and funny and chatty, at least to begin with. At first, I wasn't too bothered by it, but then he'd want to get closer, make it more than friendship, and the contact would increase—from his side, at least. I tried to keep him at arm's length and got him to back off a few times, then he'd relent and say we could just be friends. Really good friends. But I knew it wouldn't be enough for him, and it would start up again. You know what he's like."

"All or nothing?"

"Exactly. Anyway, eventually he said that one of the reasons he'd moved to London—moved his family, his company, uprooted everything—was to be nearer to me so that we could be together. He said it was our future to be together."

"When did he say that?"

"A few months ago."

"And you never told Beth any of this?"

"How could I? 'By the way, Bee, I snogged your husband by accident, and he's obsessed with me and wants to sleep with me and marry me, and in case it wasn't obvious, he doesn't love you anymore'? I wanted to, but I'd never figured out how I could do it without it being a disaster—for everybody."

"What a scumbag that man is. I never realized."

"Lately, it had gotten to a point, though, where it couldn't carry on. It was starting to make me ill, some of the stuff he was saying—"

"Like what?"

"Like he would do anything if it meant we could be together. Anything. It was kind of like an escalation of what he'd been saying before, and it was starting to worry me."

"What do you think *anything* meant?"

She shrugged. "That he might split with Beth or do something to you."

"Do something? Like what?"

"I don't know. It had just gotten to the point where I thought he was going to do something stupid. So I asked him to meet me on Thursday after work."

"What happened at the hotel?"

She didn't answer.

"Clearly something happened," I said, "otherwise he wouldn't have tried to deck me in the parking lot, gone home drunk, and disappeared with one of his shotguns."

She sniffed again, and when she finally spoke, her

voice was very small. "I told him enough was enough, that it was never going to happen, and if he didn't back off once and for all, I'd tell Beth and tell you everything. I told him I loved you, you were my husband, that we were soul mates and that was never going to change. Ever."

"And he was angry."

"Furious."

"Basically, he's obsessed with you."

"Yes."

"And he hates me as a result."

She nodded but couldn't look at me. " 'A classic underachiever': that's what he says you are."

I remembered the way Ben had talked to me, looked at me at dinner parties and barbecues. We had never been close, more friends of friends, but there had always been the little "jokes" and asides about money and ambition and success—and the unspoken message: *Who has more of all three? Me or you?* He'd never tried very hard to disguise it. It didn't bother me; that sort of thing never had. I'd always assumed he was looking down on me because in his eyes I was just a lowly schoolteacher with a three-bedroom duplex in an OK neighborhood and a ten-year-old car.

But now it seemed there was more to it than that.

Contempt. Jealousy. Hate.

Mel said, "He once asked me what might happen between me and him if you weren't in the picture anymore. As in, whether I'd get together with anyone else."

"And what did you say?"

"That he should stop being stupid. That you were the best, kindest, loveliest man I'd ever met and that I loved you and that was it."

"Did he ever say anything else about me?"

"He used to say, 'There's no one as blind as the person who refuses to see,' or something like that."

The phrase rang a bell.

"He said that to me on Thursday evening too. What did he mean?"

She shrugged, looked away.

"That . . . you could never see it. The way he looked at me, talked to me when we were all together. It didn't seem to register with you, like you couldn't believe anyone would ever do that."

"I'm not blind," I said. "I just happen to trust my wife."

"Are you angry with me, Joe?"

My emotions were all over the place, but there was no anger—at least not for my wife. It had already passed. I just felt sorry for her.

"Come here," I said and folded her in my arms.

She apologized again and hugged me tightly, her breath warm on my ear.

"I didn't want you talking to some policeman without knowing all the background. Can you forgive me?"

I kissed her on the forehead. "Of course. I love you."

"Love you too."

We sat like that for a few minutes, holding each other, Mel clinging to me like she never wanted to let me go. My arms around her, comforting her.

"We should make that call," I said eventually. "Are you going to tell the police all of this?"

"Yes, but you had to hear it from me first." She looked up. "Wait—do we have to tell the police everything?"

"I think we should."

"Oh."

"What is it?"

"The thing I said to Beth about you reversing into Ben's car. If she finds out I lied about it, that I lied to her . . . I don't know what she'll think. I'd be mortified."

I looked at her. She looked tired out from her confession. Small and vulnerable and ashamed of what she'd done. I kissed her eyebrow.

"I'm sure we don't need to go into absolutely every last detail."

The phone number on the business card Beth had passed on connected me to an answering machine at Kilburn Police Station. I left a message and went downstairs to the living room, where William was emptying out his baskets of toy cars one by one. We spent the next hour arranging them in long lines, according to color. Silver was the winner. Silver was always the winner. Each row of cars had a lane in front of it, and William then drove his police cars and fire engines up and down the lanes, responding to imaginary accidents and chasing bad men. The bad men always drove a battered black Renault with only three wheels, for some reason I had never worked out.

As we sat on the rug and William revved his cars up and down, I thought about what Mel had told me this afternoon.

It was just a kiss, that was all. A stupid, drunken kiss.

But was it, though? Was that all? For however many months, years, Ben had courted my wife behind my back—and I had never realized. It felt like discovering your house had a room you'd never even realized was there. A room full of secrets.

My wife is an attractive woman. Men have always been interested in her. Ben took advantage of her in a weak moment. It was a one-off. Now she's admitted to it. We put it behind us. That's all there is to it.

The phone rang somewhere in the kitchen.

"I'll get it!" Mel shouted.

She came in a minute later.

"That was the police officer. He wants us to go in."

18

The reception area at Kilburn Police Station was tired but functional, lots of gray plastic and bolted-down chairs. It smelled strongly of disinfectant and floor polish, but neither could banish the faint smells of sweat and vomit that greeted us as the doors slid open. An old man with Coke-bottle glasses and a cloud of white hair surrounding his head sat alone on the front row of seats, a small shivering dog in his lap. As soon as William and I sat down, the man got up and moved to sit on our row, two seats away.

"Look at that man's dog," my son said in loud voice. "It's *tiny*."

I glanced across. Both dog and man stared back at me with large unblinking eyes.

"Wills," I said, "do you want to play on the iPad?"

He took the gadget from me, unlocked it with the speed of an expert, and began swiping rapidly right and left to slice pieces of electronic fruit tumbling from the top of the screen.

Mel had gone into the interview room first. PC Khan had offered to sit us both down together to save time, but I didn't want William to hear any of it, so we had agreed to go in separately. She came out after half an hour.

"Mummy!" William announced as she reemerged from the security door beside the front desk. He ran over to her and hugged her around the waist as if he hadn't seen her for a year. "I'm bored. Can we get an ice cream?"

"It's too cold for ice cream, William."

"How was it?" I said to her.

She shrugged.

"I just told him . . . you know. Everything."

"You feel OK?"

"Yes. Weirdly, I feel better for it all being out in the open. I'm actually all right."

I followed PC Khan through the steel security door and into a small interview room at the back of the station. He was in his early twenties, slightly built, with calm, intelligent eyes. His uniform was immaculate.

"So, Mr. Lynch, you're a friend of Benjamin Delaney?"

Friend was stretching it somewhat, but I nodded anyway.

He checked his watch and wrote some details at the top of a preprinted form. Careful, neat handwriting, talking as he wrote.

"As you're aware, Mr. Lynch, I've already spoken to Elizabeth Delaney and to your wife about this matter. Mrs. Delaney reported her husband missing yesterday, and obviously she's keen to establish his whereabouts, or at least to confirm that he's safe and well. Can you tell me about the last time you saw him?"

I told him what I could remember about Thursday evening, just the way we had described it to Beth. Mel was right: it felt good to get it all out in the open, like setting a heavy weight down at the end of a journey. The young policeman took notes throughout.

"And that was the last time you saw Mr. Delaney?"

"Yes."

From a file, he produced an identical form with my wife's name at the top.

"Let me make sure I've got these timings right, Joe. Can I call you Joe? Your wife said that she might have been one of the last people to see Mr. Delaney on Thursday evening, at around 5:00 P.M."

Despite what she had told me this afternoon about her drunken kiss with Ben—or maybe, weirdly, *because* of it—the instinct to protect my family, my team, was stronger than ever. Ben had taken advantage of her when she was drunk and on her own, he'd caught her in a weak moment, and even though I knew some of the blame lay with her, I couldn't be angry at her. If I hadn't been too naïve to spot his intentions, if I'd put a shot across his bows sooner, maybe he wouldn't have taken advantage of her. And she wouldn't have been left to fend him off all by herself.

In that respect, it was *I* who had failed *her*. I wouldn't fail her again. What had happened in that parking lot was on me—it was mine to deal with.

"She wasn't the last to see him," I said to the young policeman. "I saw Ben after that, when she'd already driven off. I was the last person to see him in the parking lot."

"After your wife had gone?"

"Yes."

"Do you remember any other drivers arriving or

leaving at that time? Anyone else around who might have seen Mr. Delaney after you?"

"There was a black Range Rover, I think, just arriving as I was about to leave."

"Remember any part of the registration?"

"No, sorry. Can't you check CCTV or something?"

"We may do that further down the line if Mr. Delaney doesn't turn up safe and sound. For now, though, based on the information I've been given today, it appears you were the last person to actually set eyes on him before he went missing."

"I think Beth Delaney saw him later that night."

He consulted another form from the file. "No, she said she heard him at their house but was too frightened to go downstairs."

"He was drunk."

"Apparently so. But roughly 5:00 P.M. was the last direct contact you had with him?"

"Not exactly. He posted on my Facebook account later that evening." I described the Facebook posts as clearly as I could remember them.

"On *your* account?"

"He had my cell phone. I dropped it."

"Right. Got you. Did you leave the posts up?"

"Deleted them. Sorry, was that the wrong thing to do?"

"It's fine," he said. "We can get that stuff back anyway."

He made a note of my Facebook username and was silent for a minute, checking off the other details on the form.

"What happens now?" I said. "With Ben, I mean?"

PC Khan stacked the papers in front of him and stapled them together.

"All the recent paperwork gets passed on to the demand management inspector tomorrow morning, for what we call the daily management meeting. He makes an assessment of the current caseload and decides how resources are going to be allocated each day in our area. We only have a certain number of officers on any given day, obviously."

"So do you think an officer will be allocated to this?"

The constable shrugged, smiled. "That's a bit above my pay grade, I'm afraid. The inspector makes an assessment of the level of potential risk to an individual and allocates resources accordingly. That's how it works with mispers—case-by-case basis, according to the level of risk."

"Mispers?"

"Sorry: missing persons." He smiled again. "Jargon."

"And then what? Is Ben deemed to be high risk, low risk, somewhere in the middle?"

"There are no hard-and-fast rules about it—it's a judgment call by the inspector according to the evidence and the resources he has available. And it depends on the individual. So, for example, if you were talking about a young child, that would almost always get elevated into a high-risk category straight away, for obvious reasons."

"So an adult, a businessman like Ben, he'd probably be lower risk?"

"Like I said, that's a bit above my pay grade."

"And what if he poses a risk to others?"

"How do you mean, sir?"

"Beth said one of his shotguns is missing. He may have taken it with him."

"Mrs. Delaney mentioned that. But in the absence of any other intelligence about her husband and his whereabouts, all I can suggest is that you stay vigilant, and if you have any concerns at all about your family's safety, call us on this number."

He handed me a card and stood up.

"Thanks," I said, taking the card from him.

"Of course, this is all assuming that Mr. Delaney doesn't make contact with his family between now and tomorrow. I can appreciate that you're all worried about him, but the truth is, most people do turn up sooner or later."

"Let's hope so."

We shook hands, and he showed me out.

19

Beth and Ben's daughter, Alice, was due to babysit for us that night. Mel offered to postpone, but Beth insisted it was fine and that Alice was looking forward to it. She was a nice kid, very quiet and polite, supersmart with technology—just like her dad—and sensible beyond her years. In fact, she was more sensible at fourteen than I had been at twenty-one, and she had been our regular babysitter for a while now. William liked her too and wouldn't be frightened if he called out in the night and she appeared at his bedside. We promised Beth that we'd be quick and have her home by ten.

And so we sat in my favorite Chinese restaurant, Mel alternating between Facebook, Instagram, and Twitter on her iPhone, and me trying to pretend this was a normal Saturday evening out—some chat, some wine, nice food, a bit of time for just the two of us. Me talking constantly so that I didn't have to think too much about Mel's Mistake at the Wedding, or the secret she'd kept until today, or Ben bloody Delaney. And because I couldn't have coped with silence between us, not tonight. So I really didn't mind that Mel seemed distracted, agitated, and wasn't listening to my anecdote from the school's Outward Bound week with ninth grade. Her finger scrolled up the news feed, then she would stop, read, move on, type briefly, then go back to the main feed. I was in no hurry to go on Facebook again.

I continued our rather one-sided conversation.

"So it was me and Paul and Martin sharing a room, right? Everybody shares. And on the first night, I wake up at 3:00 A.M., and Martin is snoring like you wouldn't believe. It's like trying to sleep on the hard shoulder of the M25. Unreal. So I start saying to him, 'Martin, Martin, turn over! You're snoring! Turn over!' And what do you think he does?"

I waited, but she didn't respond.

"Absolutely nothing," I continued. "He's oblivious. This goes on for another two hours, until finally he turns over, only by then I'm too wound up to get back to sleep. Next morning, he's up, fresh as a daisy, I feel like death, and do you know what he says to me?"

Again, she didn't respond, absorbed in Facebook. She had stopped scrolling and appeared to be studying something in particular.

"He said, 'Joe, mate, has anyone ever told you that you talk in your sleep?' And I was like, '*I wasn't asleep!*' Paul thought it was hilarious."

I paused, waiting for a reaction. A response. Anything. She continued to scroll up her Facebook news feed, giving no indication that she'd heard a word I'd said.

I wondered, briefly, how we had gotten to this point.

"And then," I said, studying her face, "the top of Martin's head cracked open, and an alien climbed out."

Mel nodded slightly, a piece of Peking duck poised in the chopsticks an inch from her lips as she scrolled up the screen.

"Yeah?"

"And then the alien sang 'Bohemian Rhapsody' in E-flat major."

She smiled and held up her phone to me. "Look at this. It's from Ben—seems like he's all right."

It was a post on Facebook.

Ben Delaney

1 hour ago

Needed to get my head sorted; it's been good to get away. And I've always loved it when everything starts falling into place.

"The truth of the battle is whatever the victor deems it to be . . ."

"That's great," I said. "Beth will be so relieved. You should let her know. And that policeman. Did you look at the comments?"

Mel shook her head, and I selected the comments.

Claire Pridmore

39 minutes ago

Where you been Ben? xx

Sally Ashmore

31 minutes ago

Sounds like you're up to something lol xox

Tom Parish

14 minutes ago

Very cryptic buddy. I'm intrigued, tell me more . . .

I handed the phone back to her. Still smiling, she touched the screen and put it to her ear.

"Bee? It's Mel. Yeah, I'm fine. Alice is fine. Yeah. Have you looked at Facebook this evening? Ben's posted—have a look. Says he just needs to get his head sorted. No. Has he phoned? You OK? That's good. See you in a bit. Probably about ten. You too. Bye."

She put the phone down and looked me in the eye for the first time since the main course had arrived.

"That's a bit of a relief. What were you saying before? About the school trip?"

"I was just . . . oh, nothing. How's Beth doing?"

"Better. Sounds like she's calmer than this afternoon. She's tidied up the mess he made the other night."

"Ben's not come home yet?"

Mel shook her head and went back to Facebook, leaving a comment on Ben's update. I couldn't see upside down what she was typing. Her phone sounded with a text message alert and she read it, smiled, responded.

"Who's that from?"

"Beth, saying thanks."

She went back to Facebook. Most of her Peking duck was still on her plate, cooling and untouched. Mine was two-thirds gone.

"Mel?"

"Yes?" She didn't look up.

"Why don't you put the phone in your handbag for five minutes?"

She looked at me like I'd asked her to shave her head. "Alice might call. If something's wrong with William."

"You'll still hear it ring. And nothing's going to happen to Wills. He's in bed, at home, asleep, front door locked, babysitter on duty."

"I won't hear a text."

"If there's a problem, she'll call."

"All right, Mr. Grumpy." She made a show of putting the phone in her handbag, looking around the restaurant as if seeing it for the first time. Her eyes came back to me.

"What do you want to talk about, then?"

Alice was watching *Time Team* when we got back, archaeologists digging bones out of some ancient burial ground. The novel she'd brought with her was in her lap: *American Psycho* by Bret Easton Ellis.

She stood up and turned the TV off when we walked in, as if she'd been caught doing something she wasn't supposed to be doing.

"Was William all right?" Mel asked.

"Fine. He shouted out once, and when I went in, he was turned around in his bed. Couldn't find his pillows, but he was still asleep. I just turned him back the right way, settled him down, and he went off again."

Mel reached into her handbag for her pocketbook. "You're so good with him. He'd love to have you as his big sister, you know."

Alice smiled shyly and shrugged. "He's no trouble at all."

I said, "Did you have something to eat?"

We always left cookies and chips out for her, but for some reason, she never touched them.

"Wasn't really hungry. Thanks."

Mel took a five and a ten from her pocketbook and handed the notes to her.

I picked up my car keys. "Right, then. I'll run you home."

Mel said, "How many beers have you had?"

"Two. Plus one earlier. Feel all right, though."

"I'll take her. I've only had one glass of pink."

Alice looked embarrassed, like she didn't know where to look. "I could get a taxi," she said in a small voice.

"Of course not. Don't be silly," Mel said.

After they'd left, I checked on William. He was sleeping soundly, so I fetched a bottle of beer from the kitchen and collapsed on the sofa in front of *Match of the Day*. The beer was cold and tasted good on the back of my throat. It had been a crazy forty-eight hours: first I thought my wife was having an affair, then I thought I'd put someone in hospital and might lose my job, my marriage, my liberty.

But instead, here I was on a Saturday night, with a beer on the sofa, and all three were still safely intact. I toasted Gary Lineker and Alan Shearer on the TV.

"Cheers, gents." I took a long pull on the bottle and settled back to watch Man City versus Arsenal.

I woke with a start as the *Match of the Day* theme music played at the end of the program. For a second, I was disoriented and couldn't work out what was going on, then sat up groggily, blinked, kicked over an empty beer bottle, and turned the TV off. The central heating had gone off, and the living room had grown cool while I dozed.

The house was utterly quiet around me as I moved into the hall.

"Mel?" I said softly.

No answer. The hall clock said it was a few minutes to midnight.

Mel's car was still not back on the drive. But there was a text message on my phone, from an hour ago.

Dropped Alice OK. Beth having a bit of a meltdown again. Going to stay for a cuppa, see you in a bit. x

I texted back a short reply, opened the fridge, and contemplated another beer. Decided against it. Contemplated the pile of essays waiting to be marked on the kitchen counter. Decided against that too. Did a final check of all the doors and windows, then climbed the stairs slowly, my legs heavy. William was sleeping on his back, his duvet kicked down the bed and both arms flung over his head like a surrendering soldier. I tucked him in and kissed him on the forehead, closing his bedroom door as quietly as I could. He was a light sleeper.

My last thought as I put my head on the pillow was about all the ways someone might be able to break into our house. *Maybe I should double-check again*, I told myself. *Should have checked it twice. What if Ben comes around the back? Did I take the key out of the door? Should have taken the key out.*

And then sleep took me.

SUNDAY

20

The Stratford was half-pub and half-split-level soft-play area with slides, ball pools, and crash mats, red-faced parents trying to follow their offspring across rope bridges, squeezing through obstacles they were too big for, ignoring the smell of sweaty socks and disinfectant. William loved it. I had spent twenty minutes in there with him as he charged around, but now we'd come out and I nursed a pint of Guinness as we waited for our food to arrive. He was busy with a box of crayons, coloring the sky orange on his paper place mat. Mel had posted about lunch at the pub on Facebook, and her phone pinged periodically with comments from friends.

Our friends Adam and Kate had the table next to ours. Their twin five-year-old girls, Phoebe and Sophie, had both come today as the same character from *Frozen*—in blue-and-white sparkly dresses and tiaras. Right now, though, their table was empty. Adam was in the soft-play jungle with their girls—his pint of lager abandoned, untouched on its coaster—and Kate was outside making a phone call.

There wasn't a good way to introduce the subject, so I just came out with it.

"You know, Thursday night," I said to Mel, lowering my voice, "when you met Ben?"

"Yes." She was looking at the puddings on the menu. "What about it?"

"I just felt really stupid about it. I shouldn't even have been there. It was really weird, seeing you and Ben. And then when you denied it later, denied meeting him, it felt like . . ."

"Like what?"

Just say it.

"Like the worst day of my life. Like everything good was suddenly coming to an end, everything good about my life."

"Because you thought we were having some kind of secret rendezvous?"

"Talk about jumping to conclusions . . . I added two and two together and made seventeen."

She tucked a stray strand of hair behind her ear, blushing. "I'll allow it, considering what happened at that wedding reception."

"That wasn't really your fault. Could've happened to anyone."

"Daddy?" William said.

"Hang on, Wills."

She wouldn't look at me.

"Not you," she said. "You wouldn't have done something like that."

"Daddy?" William said again. He was staring out of the pub window.

"What's up, big man?"

"Look. That man's smoking."

Out in the parking lot was a hugely bearded homeless man sitting on the low wall, surrounded by plastic bags full of his possessions, puffing hungrily on the nub of a cigarette burned almost down to the filter.

"Yes, he is, Wills."

"Smoking makes you die, doesn't it?"

"That's right."

"Look," he said, his nose almost against the glass. "He'll be dead in a minute."

Mel and I exchanged a smile. Our son dealt in absolutes, in the here and now. He lived in the moment. Smoking was bad and it killed you—which meant it killed you right away.

"Well, you'd best keep an eye on him then, matey." I turned back to Mel, talking quietly. "Who knows how any of us would react in that situation? Lots of booze. Everybody loved-up at a wedding reception. It's not your fault. Sometimes this stuff happens."

"It was just so stupid."

"It was." I smiled. "He's too short for you, for a start."

"I know. Ridiculous."

"*Much* too short."

She smiled back, and my chest buzzed with a rush of love.

"Rich, though."

"Still too short."

She put her hand over mine on the table. "Can you really forgive me, Joe?"

"Pick up the tab for lunch and I'll think about it."

"Deal. You're just having the cheap starter, right? No main, no pudding, no booze?"

"Actually, I went for the rib eye steak and the Bollinger. You don't mind, do you?"

"Just this once I'll let it go. Just this once, mind."

Kate returned to the table next to us and sat down. "Bolly, is it?" she said brightly. "Count me in."

"Mel's buying," I said, giving her a grin.

William turned away from the window. "That man's still not dead yet," he said solemnly.

I squeezed Mel's hand. "You OK?" I said to her quietly.

"I'll be fine."

"You look tired. Is it work?"

"Work. Life. You know." She shrugged. "Everything."

Our meals arrived—Caesar salad for Mel, chicken nuggets for William, steak-and-ale pie for me—and attention turned to the food.

William studied his plate. "Don't like peas."

"Just leave them, Wills. Eat the rest."

"Don't like peas."

"Just push them to the side." He stared sadly at his mother, pointing at his plate with a small index finger. "Peas are touching chips."

She picked up his plate and scooped the peas onto mine. "Look. Daddy will have them."

She put his plate back and began cutting his chicken nuggets up, each one twice so that he couldn't choke. She was a good mother, and William was a great kid. Becoming a father had been the best thing that had ever happened to me. I'd always thought we should have another baby, but for some reason it had never happened for us.

William picked up the biggest chip and bit it in half. "Can we go back to soft play after?" he said, chewing.

I contemplated my half-drunk pint of Guinness. "Sure."

Mel said, "It's my turn. I'll go."

Adam returned from the soft-play area, a sheen of sweat on his face, his daughters pulling him along, one hand each. He slumped down in his chair and blew out a breath.

"I do *love* a nice relaxing Sunday at the pub," he said with a smile. "Putting my feet up with a couple of pints and the papers, watching a bit of footie, taking it easy. Recharging the old batteries before the start of the working week."

I'd known Adam since college, and we'd been best mates ever since. He had joined the civil service fast track straight after graduating and now had a sensitive and fairly secretive job somewhere within government that he only discussed in the most general terms. Kate was a teacher, the deputy head of one of the local feeder primary schools for Haddon Park.

"Nah," I said to him. "You'd be bored with just sitting and reading the papers now."

"I guarantee you, Joseph, I wouldn't be bored."

"And besides, chasing the girls around soft-play areas is the only exercise you get."

He wiped the sweat from his forehead with a sleeve. "Not true. I ran for a bus the other week."

"Did you catch it?"

"Irrelevant."

I smiled and picked up my cutlery. "That's a no, then."

The steak-and-ale pie smelled good, beefy and rich. William was continuing to feed chips into his mouth one by one. He would eat all of them first, then all the nuggets. Never a mixture. He was going through a phase of tackling the things on his plate one food type at a time. He was very particular about it. I turned back to Mel.

"How's your salad?"

"Good, thanks. Could do with a bit less salad and a bit more Caesar, but on the whole—"

She stopped, her gaze rising over my shoulder like she had seen someone she recognized behind me. Her eyes widened a little. Then the recognition changed to something else.

Fear.

My back was to the door, so I couldn't see immediately who'd come in. But my first thought was: *Ben. He came looking for Mel. And now he's found her.*

Protect Mel. Protect William.

I turned and looked to see who it was, pushing my chair sideways to shield my son.

Surely Ben wouldn't do something in such a public place. Not in a pub full of people. There must be fifty witnesses in here.

But it wasn't Ben.

It was Beth. Dressed all in black, dark hair tied back, her mouth a hard, flat line. Red-rimmed eyes shifting from left to right and back again as she searched every face in the pub.

She looked the opposite of serene; she looked *furious*. There was something metallic in her hand.

Protect them both.

She saw us, marched straight over, and slammed a cell phone down on the table.

Spoke in a voice that was loud enough for everyone in the pub to hear.

"You fucking *bitch*!"

21

Her words went off like a bomb inside the busy pub.

I had never heard Beth say *fuck* before. I'd never heard her swear before, or even raise her voice. She was the kind of woman who flinched when her husband dropped the F-bomb in polite conversation. For a second, I couldn't process it, any of it, and I sat there staring up at her as she leaned over the table at my wife, hate in her eyes. *Something is happening. Something bad.* In the space of a second, a kind of sound vacuum had grown around the four of us. Around Beth. She had sucked all the other sound out of the pub with a single word.

And it seemed like now she'd started, she couldn't stop. "Fucking whore! How could you?" Her cut-glass Home Counties accent only increased the impact of her words. The anger was coming off her in waves.

Every other conversation in the pub had ceased; all eyes were on us. Phoebe and Sophie stared at Beth, open-mouthed.

Mel had shrunk back in her seat, trying to get as far away as possible. She looked terrified. William's mouth was turned down, and I knew he was about to cry.

Don't swear in front of my boy.

I stood up, my chair scraping loudly in the silence. Adam stood up too. If Beth had been a man, I would've asked her to step outside for what she'd just said about my wife. But as it was, I didn't quite know how to respond.

"Beth—" I said.

"Shut up!" she snarled at me. She jabbed a finger at Mel. "Tell me again what you told me yesterday." Her normally calm, quiet voice was high and brittle and horribly loud in the silent pub.

Mel looked blank. "What?" she said in a small voice.

"Tell me again! Tell me my husband isn't the type to have an affair!"

"He's not . . . that kind of man."

"Really?"

"What do you—?"

"Then presumably you can explain these pictures." She picked up the cell phone she'd slammed down on the table—a Samsung with a big screen—and hit the keypad. A picture appeared on the screen. She showed it to Mel, and I peered around to see who or what it was. There was a lot of flesh. It looked like a topless picture of a woman. I peered closer.

It was a topless picture of my wife.

It looked like she was standing in our kitchen, taking a selfie. Leaning forward and giving a coy little smile to the camera, one arm under her breasts.

For a moment, my brain struggled to process it. *That's my wife. But she's naked. I've never seen that picture before.* I had a cold, acid feeling in my stomach. Helplessness.

There will be an explanation for this. A reasonable explanation.

The pub manager, a skinny guy in his twenties, appeared behind Beth and tapped her on the shoulder. He looked terrified.

"Excuse me, madam. I'm afraid I'll have to ask you—"

She turned on him. "Take your bloody hands off me!"

The manager recoiled as if he'd been punched. Beth turned back to Mel.

"Well?" she said, her voice hard. "This is one of Ben's phones. So explain why there's a pornographic picture of you on it. Go on. Explain it."

Mel put a hand over her mouth and looked like she was about to cry.

I said, "Let's go outside, Beth. We don't need to do this here."

"No, we should do this right here. Because this is not the only picture. Do you want to guess how many others there are on this phone?"

"It's not me," Mel said, her voice cracking.

"Ha! You can't lie your way out of this." Beth turned to me.

"Joe. Why don't you guess how many naked pictures of your wife there are on my husband's phone?"

I opened my mouth. Closed it again. There wasn't really a right answer to that question.

Beth said, "Let me tell you: 139. There are 139 obscene pictures of your Melissa on my husband's phone, sent over the last four months."

"That can't be right," I mumbled.

"Oh, it's right. Trust me. I've counted them. Every single one. Not to mention 281 text messages from the last month alone. Sent from her phone to his. And 195 messages sent back from his phone. Shall I read out one of Mel's?"

Mel shook her head, but it was a hopeless gesture. A tear rolled down her cheek.

"This is from two weeks ago. 'Baby,' " Beth started, her pale cheeks starting to flush red. " 'Miss you soooo much. Want to do last night again SOOON!!! When Boring Beth away next?? xxx.' "

Behind me, I heard Phoebe starting to cry with a high-pitched sob. Within a second, Sophie had joined her.

"Boring Beth, am I? All your fake sympathy and your help and your story about meeting Ben for work— it was all disgusting bloody *lies*. What did I do to deserve this from you? Tell me, what did I do?"

Mel said something, but it was too quiet to hear.

"What?" Beth barked at her.

"I'm sorry." Mel sniffed.

"Of course you are. Sorry you got caught."

"So sorry, Bee."

"If you're really sorry, you'll tell me where Ben is."

"Beth, I don't know." Her breath caught in another sob. "I swear."

"Lying bitch!"

She made to reach for Mel. I put a hand on her shoulder.

"That's *enough*," I said.

"Get your hands off me!"

The pub manager reappeared with a chef from the kitchen. They flanked Beth, took hold of an arm each, and marched her out of the pub.

Mel had her head in her hands, trembling with sobs. Kate had one tearful daughter in her lap, the other clutched to her side.

William, seeing his mother in distress, was crying

too. I crouched next to him and used a napkin to dry his tears.

"It's OK, matey. She's gone now. Shh, it's all right."

"Don't like Alice's mummy," he said, sniffling.

"She's gone now. It's OK."

A low murmur of conversation started up around us as the other customers started to discuss what they'd just seen, like it was some reality show on TV.

Adam turned to me, his face pale.

"What the hell, Joe?" His voice was low and hard. "What's going on?"

"I'll talk to her," I said. "Back in a minute."

With fifty pairs of eyes on me, I followed Beth out of the pub. The manager was standing by the front door, presumably to ensure that she didn't try to come back in.

Beth was in the parking lot, leaning on the hood of her Mercedes Estate. She stared at me as I approached, and I could see that she was crying now, tears on her cheeks, her chest rising and falling with sobs as all the emotion drained out of her.

"What the hell just happened?" I said.

Beth tried to answer, but all that came out were sobs.

"Sh-sh-she *stole* him." Her voice was back to its usual tone and volume, almost as if the strain of her anger had exhausted her.

"Show me the phone," I said. "Show me the pictures."

She handed me the cell phone, and I scrolled through the gallery. There was a folder called "M xxx" comprised entirely of selfies of my wife in various states of undress. Sitting in our bath, lying on a bed, leaning over an armchair in the sitting room. Most of them completely nude, all smiling at the camera, reclining, beckoning, winking, pouting, a secret just for the two of them.

To have and to hold, from this day forward.

Scrolling through picture after picture, I felt like I was out of my own body, floating above myself, watching all this happen to someone else. To someone else's life. Like a spectator at someone else's car crash of a marriage. But I wasn't a spectator. It was my marriage. My life.

Today was the worst day of my thirty-four years, bar none.

For richer for poorer, in sickness and in health.

It felt surreal to see a woman pose like that and realize that she was my wife, in my house, putting on a show for another man. Not for me. For another woman's husband. Pictures that were supposed to stay a secret.

To love and to cherish, till death us do part.

I was the world's biggest sucker. "Has Ben got more than one cell?"

"He has two iPhones—one for work and one for personal use. He normally keeps both with him." She held up the Samsung. "But I never saw this one before this morning."

"Where did you find it?"

"I was looking for something that might help me find him. Something, anything, that gave me a clue about where he'd gone. I'd looked in all the obvious places yesterday, so this morning I went into his study. He doesn't normally let me go in there, says it's his man cave. It was in one of his desk drawers; I'd never seen it before, so I switched it on. There was a list of passwords on a Post-it note taped to the underside of the drawer." She wiped her eyes with a fresh tissue. "I found the text messages first."

"If it makes you feel any better, she had me fooled as well—100 percent. And I'm married to her."

"Even last night, when she dropped Alice home from babysitting, she was all friendly and lovely and reassuring about Ben. About how he would be home soon." She shook her head. "Can't believe I didn't see it sooner."

Something else occurred to me.

"Last night, how long did Mel stay with you?"

"What?" Beth looked confused.

"When she dropped Alice back after babysitting, how long did she stay at your house? She told me she stayed for cups of tea and a nightcap and another long chat about Ben."

"No, she just brought Alice to the door, we had a few words on the doorstep, but she said she had to get back because William was running a temperature."

Another lie. William had been fine last night.

"She didn't stay?"

"No. Why?"

"She didn't get home till after midnight. She was out more than two hours, maybe more. I went to bed before she came back, so it might have been longer. But there's at least a couple of missing hours there."

Beth looked at me, and I could see the same desolation I felt reflected back at me in her eyes. All the fight had gone out of her.

"You think they met up?" she said in a quiet voice.

"Where else could she have been?"

"But that means—"

"Ben must be fairly close by."

22

We drove home in stony silence, my knuckles white on the steering wheel. I felt sick with anger and couldn't bear to look at Mel, let alone talk to her. She sat and sniffed and dabbed at her eyes with a balled-up tissue, occasionally sneaking a glance at me to see if I would meet her eye. William sat tearful and subdued in the back. What I hated most of all was that he had been a witness to Beth's revelation in the pub. He sat silently in his car seat, eyes lowered, the corners of his little mouth turned down in an expression that just about broke my heart all over again.

I should have felt vindicated, justified. My instinct on Thursday evening had been spot-on, after all. But the vindication was hollow. I would have been much happier to be wrong, to have never seen those pictures of Mel meant for another man. *Here's your marriage certificate, a decade of your life. Now light the match, watch it flame.*

None of us had eaten more than a few mouthfuls of lunch at the pub before we'd made a quick exit, so Mel made William spaghetti hoops on toast and sat him down in the living room in front of a DVD. When she returned to the kitchen, she had her head down, arms crossed, and wouldn't look at me.

"Bedroom," I said, and she followed me.

We went upstairs, and I shut the door behind her so that William wouldn't hear anything. I moved away, to the window, so I wasn't anywhere near her. I had so many things I wanted to ask her, say to her, shout at her, my head was fit to burst.

Anger. Disbelief. Heartbreak. Just sheer, wrenching heartbreak.

"So is it true?" They were the first words I'd been able to say to her since our lunch had been interrupted an hour ago. I fought to keep my voice level, to stop it cracking.

She looked at me, eyes wide and full of tears, pleading, remorseful, and I almost stopped right there. Almost went to her and folded her in my arms like I always did when she was upset. Almost, but not quite. She was standing by the full-length mirror, and I realized with a jolt of recognition that she had taken some of the naked pictures right there in the same spot, in front of that mirror. In our bedroom. The pictures sent to Ben.

I stood my ground by the window. "Is it true?" I repeated.

She nodded but wouldn't look at me.

"You slept with him?"

Hesitation, then she nodded again. I felt dizzy, unsteady on my feet.

Everything you know is a lie.

There was a stranger in my house, and I was married to her.

It was impossible to imagine my life without Mel,

life as a single man again. That wasn't me. It wasn't my life. I turned my back on her and stared out of the window, a lump in my throat.

Sunday afternoon. The leaves starting to fall. A couple pushing a toddler in a stroller. Teenage boys cycling side by side up the middle of the road.

How did we go so wrong? It was like finding a trapdoor under the rug in your living room, and you lift it up and there's a whole other world down there right beneath your feet, hidden wheels and cogs and gears all moving, shifting your life one way or another without you even realizing it.

I let the silence stretch out, waiting until the dizziness passed.

Took a deep breath.

Save the weakness for later. At this moment, I need to stay strong, and clear, and focused.

"What happens now?" she said finally in a small voice.

"Now? I'm going to ask you some questions." I reached under our bed and pulled out two empty suitcases that were stored there. I laid them on the bed, unzipped them both, and flipped them open.

She hesitated, looking at me nervously. "OK."

"And if you lie a single time, I'll put you out on the street with whatever you can fit in these suitcases." My heart wasn't in it, but I pressed on, hoping she wouldn't call my bluff. "And good luck seeing your son again, because I'll go for full custody and fight you every inch of the way, and you'll lose."

She sniffled and swallowed a sob. She looked beaten.

"So you're saying that maybe—" Her breath caught in another sob. "We might be OK again? The two of us?"

I closed my eyes, trying to imagine anything worse than my family being shattered into pieces. Nothing could compete.

"Do you want us to be OK again?" I said.

"Yes." She covered her face with her hands. "Of course."

"No more lies."

"No lies," she repeated. And so she told me.

23

It had started five months earlier, in the spring, at a barbecue in the Delaneys' extensive garden. I remembered the way she talked to him, smiling and laughing at his jokes as I tried to think of things to talk to Beth about. How Mel looked at him, ready to laugh, eager to please. That was where it all began.

Ben had texted her to say thank-you for bringing a particularly good bottle of red to the barbecue, and it just went on from there. She gave him some helpful advice on employment law, he sent a bottle of Château Mouton Rothschild '99 to her office as a thank-you. Ben joined the tennis club and started having lessons so he could see her more often. Then they bumped into each other at a corporate awards ceremony on Park Lane where both were guests at different tables. *I thought it was kind of like fate, us meeting like that*, she said. *It seemed like fate brought us together.* They shared a bottle of champagne, and another, stayed till the end of the night and ended up sharing a taxi. Then sharing the bed in Ben's hotel room—the Presidential Suite (of course). That was the first time they'd spent the night together. June, four months ago. *It just happened*, she said. *It wasn't planned out or deliberate. I was flattered*, she said. *He paid attention to me, he was confident and funny, he had his big house and these fancy cars and his own company, and he was still interested in* me.

"Christ, Mel, I'm interested in you too!" I said. "Because you're my *wife*! We're *married*!"

She dissolved into a fresh bout of tears at that, and I began pacing the room, waiting for her to calm down enough so that she could carry on.

"I was bored," she said finally in a shaky voice. "The same routine, every day. Work, commute, home, bed. This was exciting, different. He was exciting. I know it's no excuse."

"So you slept with him *because you were bored*?" I said.

"No. Well, a bit. Not just that. He looked at me the way men used to look at me."

"Men still *do* look at you that way, Mel."

"They don't, not really."

"Yes, they do. I'm one of them."

"It's not the same."

"You were bored with me, then."

"No," she said unconvincingly.

"But this is our marriage, our family, our home," I said. "This is life; this is how it is. Life is not a roller coaster all the time. Sometimes you have to just get on with it and look forward to the next good thing."

"Is that true, though?" She looked up at me. "Sometimes I would wake up in the morning and try to think what I was looking forward to about the day. And there were days, weeks sometimes, when I couldn't think of anything. Nothing at all."

I looked down at her and wondered at the size of

the void that had grown between us. Whether it could ever be bridged.

"Some days are like that," I said. "You just have to get through them, keep going, and get past them. Some days you just have to be satisfied that nothing bad happened. There are big days and small days, and big days are not always good. But sooner or later you get past them as well."

"That's what my mum thought too."

That brought me up short. Mel's mum, Pamela, had suffered a psychologically abusive marriage for twenty years, but she had stuck it out, month after month, year after year, all the while planning to leave her husband as soon as her daughter reached eighteen and went to college. On the day Mel got her A-level results and a place at the University of Nottingham, her mum was diagnosed with an aggressive form of breast cancer. She had died barely four months later, never fulfilling her dream of escape.

"Your mum was . . . that was a tragedy. I can't imagine what that was like for you. She was so, so unlucky, but she's not you, Mel."

"She waited for her life to get better, she planned for it, but it never did. She ran out of time."

After the funeral, Mel had found a notebook among her mum's possessions—lists of all the things that Pamela had planned to do, all the places she would go, once she freed herself from the domineering husband who hated flying, foreigners, and "funny" food. But that freedom never came. For years afterward, Mel said she cried whenever she looked at that notebook. She had only ever shown it to me once; as far as I knew, she still kept it somewhere.

I said, "We can be better. *I* can be better. Things do get better sooner or later, for most people."

She shook her head. "That's you. It's not me."

"What does that mean?"

"Nothing."

"Come on, what does it mean?"

She looked at me for a moment, then dropped her eyes to the floor. "How long have you been teaching, Joe? Twelve, thirteen years?"

"Thirteen years, including my PGCE year."

"Three different schools?"

"Yes. You know that."

"And you're still only deputy head of department. Of a department of four teachers."

"So?" My neck felt hot.

"So I know teachers our age who are assistant heads. Kate's a deputy head. Some are even heads already. People who've really gone for it, put themselves forward and made the most of their opportunities."

Trying to keep the anger out of my voice, I said, "And you think I haven't done that?"

She shrugged. "I don't know."

"It sounds like you do."

In a small voice, she said, "Do you think you have, Joe? Honestly? Or have you just been treading water for most of your career? Just let yourself get carried by the current, nice and steady, until you've gotten into a bit of a rut?"

I could feel my cheeks flushing, heat rushing to my face. "A *rut*?"

"Ever since you stopped playing hockey. Since your injury. You just seemed to give up trying, and settle for being . . ."

"What?"

She looked away from me.

"Settle for being what?" I said again.

"Average."

I rounded on her, speaking through gritted teeth. "Don't you put this on me. Don't you *dare*. This was your decision, and no one else's. It was *your* decision to go to bed with another man, *your* decision to break our marriage vows. Don't you *dare* say it's my fault."

I hated her saying that. Mainly because I'd caught myself thinking it too in the last few years but thought I was the only one who could see it. And I was the only one who was qualified to have an opinion on it.

She looked as if she was starting to regret going down this route. "I'm sorry, Joe. I didn't mean that. I didn't mean to say that. It's my fault. I'm just lashing out in every direction because I know what I did was . . . inexcusable."

I rubbed my temple with shaking fingers, waiting for the anger to subside. This wasn't getting us anywhere. What was done was done. I sat down on the windowsill.

"You should have at least told me," I said after a minute. "Talked to me about how you felt, rather than looking for answers in someone else's bed."

"I know. I'm sorry. I'm so, so sorry. The truth is . . ."

"What? What's the truth?"

She covered her face with her hands as if finally, fully ashamed of what she was about to say.

"The truth is, ever since William was little, I've felt so useless with him, like I don't know what I'm supposed to do half the time. Don't know what's expected of me or what a good mother does. More and more, it's like you don't even really need me, you two boys. You've got this bond that I can't even get close to."

"It's not a competition, Mel. You're his mother. Every boy needs his mother."

"But it seems like sometimes you two would be better off without me. And I hate myself for thinking that."

"That's not true. And even if it were, it's no excuse for what you did."

"I didn't go looking for it. Things just happened." She started crying again.

I was so upset that I could barely see straight. *Things just happened.* The bedroom felt alien to me and too small for the two of us. But the more I thought about it, the more it made sense. There had been the team "meetings" that ran on well into the evening. Phone calls at home, quickly ended when I turned my key in the front door. And the email, her Hotmail account, how she always minimized it or switched screens in a hurry when I got close.

She said the naked pictures she sent him had started off as a joke between them when she had taken a picture of him in the hotel room after their first night together as he stood naked at the sink, brushing his teeth. She had texted it to him, just for laughs. He had insisted that she send one of herself as well so they were even. And then it had just become a running joke that he would expect his daily selfie of her.

"What about the story you told me yesterday, about kissing him at that wedding? Was that all bullshit too? Or did it actually happen?"

"It happened. And he wouldn't leave it alone, like I told you. He wanted more, but I kept him at bay for a long time. He wouldn't get the message. He kept

going, and going, and going. It was an obsession for
him. And then in July, we met again at that awards
do on Park Lane, and my resistance was worn down,
and . . . I already told you what happened that night."

I felt like I was standing in someone else's clothes,
in someone else's house, living someone else's life.
This wasn't *me*. It wasn't *us*.

Think.

"So the meeting on Thursday at the hotel, that
wasn't you telling him to stop stalking you and pester-
ing you. And it wasn't about work either."

"No."

"The story you told me and Beth yesterday, about
some programmer at his firm stealing code, that was
all lies?"

"That was made up for her benefit. I couldn't exactly tell her the truth, could I?"

"So you had sex with him at that hotel?"

She shook her head.

"I asked you a question," I said. "Did you have sex
with him on Thursday afternoon?"

"No."

"I don't believe you. What *were* you doing there?"

"Talking."

"About what?"

"About us. He told me he was in love with me like
he'd never loved anyone before. That he'd do anything
for me, anything I wanted—leave Beth, leave Alice.
Sell the company. Sell the house. Move away. Leave
everything behind so we could be together."

Her words were like spikes of ice between my ribs,
each one sharper than the last. But I had to keep going,
had to get it all out in the open.

"Have you had sex with him in our house?"

"Yes," she said, almost inaudibly.

"In our bed?"

She nodded.

Our marital bed. It had been our present to ourselves when we moved in. The first time we'd had a decent-sized bedroom big enough for a king-size bed. As far as I knew, it was where William had been conceived.

As far as I knew.

"Have there been others, before him?"

She looked up at that. "No!" Very definite.

"You sure about that?"

"That's not fair, Joe."

"Fair?" I laughed, but there was no humor in it. "You'd be in a better position to talk about being fair if you hadn't just admitted to sleeping with another guy behind my back."

She stared at the floor. "There's no one else."

I turned to a framed picture of William on the dresser. A chubby-cheeked toddler in dungarees and a bib, laughing at the camera with a big piece of birthday cake clutched in his small hand. *His mother's eyes.* A horrible, sickening thought lodged like a splinter in my brain. I couldn't get rid of it, couldn't push it away.

Should think about getting a DNA test. They're cheap nowadays. And easy. Just send two samples away in the mail, and a few weeks later, you'll know, one way or the other.

One way. Or the other.

The thought of it made me want to curl up in a corner and cover my head. I couldn't deal with that, on top of everything else. A DNA test would provide information that I could never unknow. Once that genie was out there, it would never go back in the bottle. So

I would have to decide what I would do with that knowledge if it confirmed this new fear. Because if I wasn't going to act on it, what was the point of finding out in the first place?

No.

William was *my* son. Nothing could take that away from me.

My boy. Today, tomorrow, forever.

"I suppose I'll have to take your word for it, for what that's worth."

"Joe, I've been such an idiot. Can you forgive me?"

It wasn't a question that could be answered. Not in that moment.

"So many lies, Mel. So many."

"I know. I'm so, so sorry. Once I'd started, I just couldn't stop, like I was in a car with no brakes."

"Tell me about last night, after you dropped Alice home from babysitting."

She sighed, wiped her eyes again. "I drove back."

"You were gone for the best part of two hours. Where did you go?" I indicated the open cases on the bed. "And remember what I said about the suitcases."

"I . . ."

"You what?"

"Ben had left me some messages. I called him back and talked to him for a bit."

"And?"

"He's staying at a hotel near Brent Cross."

"The Premier Inn from Thursday evening? Did you go and see him?"

She shook her head. "We just talked."

"What about?"

"Listen, I know it probably doesn't make any difference now, and there's no reason for you to believe me." She looked me in the eye for the first time since we'd gotten home. "But I want you to know something."

"Go on."

"It was over between us."

"What do you mean?"

"I met Ben on Thursday evening to end it. For good."

24

"Bullshit," I said, the word hot in my throat.

"It's true."

"I told you, no more lies."

"I swear to you, on my life." She plucked a tissue from a box on the nightstand and blew her nose. A stray thought popped into my head. *I used to love the way she blew her nose.* I would tease her about it, that she was dainty like a duchess. Like she didn't want to wake the baby, even before there was a baby. I used to love everything about her. Now the thought just gave me a painful feeling in my chest, for all the things that had been lost between us. Maybe forever.

"That's why Ben was so angry when you were talking to him?"

"Yes."

"Why did you want to break it off?" I said, my voice quiet now.

"I'd been trying to finish it for weeks. I'd already tried two or three times before, but he never got the message. He said we were meant to be together, that we should do what we felt was right and forget anything else. And he'd keep right on texting and emailing me, not leaving it alone, not taking no for an answer."

"So basically you got bored with him too?"

Her face crumpled, and I regretted asking the question.

"The guilt got too much," she said. "It was like gorging yourself on chocolate cake, and you know you shouldn't but you just can't stop. Sooner or later you realize that you have to quit because it's no way to live your life. It's fantastic for an hour, or a day, or a week, but you can't sustain it for a lifetime. Deep down I knew it, even right at the beginning when we first got together. And I couldn't bear the thought of what it would do to Beth, or the thought of explaining it to William."

"And me?"

"Or explaining it to you." She raised her hands. "Either of you, but you most of all."

"So what happened on Thursday?"

"I agreed to meet him, not at his house but a neutral venue instead. A hotel."

"And did he get the message this time?"

"Oh yes. I'm pretty sure he got the message."

A cold feeling crawled down my spine. "Why? What was different this time?"

"I . . . told him some things. Made some things up, about you and me. I said you'd gotten suspicious about us, you'd found my phone bill, and you were asking all kinds of questions."

I remembered Ben's hostility on Thursday evening. His anger.

Mel added, "And I said that you'd threatened me."

"*What?*"

"That you'd threatened to hurt me, beat me up, if I was ever unfaithful."

Her words landed like a punch to the kidneys.

"*Jesus*, Mel, I would never hurt you. Never. I'd jump off a cliff before I did that."

"I told Ben we had to end it, because I was afraid of what you might do."

"Dread to think how *that* little bombshell went down."

"He . . . wasn't happy."

I paused to digest this new information. Things were starting to fall into place.

"That's why he got drunk on Thursday night. Because you told him you were calling the whole thing off."

In a small voice she said, "I think so, yes."

"And that's why he went off with one of his guns?"

"You've got to understand, I had to have something to stop it dead, right there, something that would shock Ben into staying away for good."

"So you told him some lies about me being an abusive husband."

"I made up a story."

"But Ben still wanted to carry it on?" I didn't want to name it, refer to it as *an affair*. It made it seem more real, more serious, more final somehow.

My wife nodded. "He's been bored with Beth for years. Whatever spark they had, it went out a long time ago—that's what he said. He told me that if she hadn't gotten pregnant at college, they would probably have split up within a few months. But then Alice came along, and he felt like he had to do the decent thing. So they got married instead, and she gave up her degree to have Alice and look after her. She was going to go back to finish her degree, but it never happened for one reason or another."

It wasn't something that Beth had ever spoken to

me about, but I knew from what Mel had told me previously that they were married young. Beth had dropped out of her degree program in the final year. I couldn't remember what she'd studied, something arty. It was before I'd met Mel, but I had seen the wedding photos once: they looked like a couple of teenagers, Beth in a loose-fitting cream dress to disguise her bump, Ben with a crew cut and glasses, looking like an awkward kid who had borrowed his dad's suit to go to the prom. They were the first people either of us knew to get married, the first to have a baby by a long way. Alice was fourteen now, a smart and focused teenager who had a maturity that belied her age. Beth sometimes joked that she was a daddy's girl, but in the best possible way—she and Ben had a closeness, an understanding, that was clear to see when they were together. Most of our peers from school and college—all in our midthirties—either had young children in nursery or primary school or had not even gotten started on babies yet.

I remembered something from the wedding photos. "You were her bridesmaid, weren't you?"

Mel nodded, head bowed. "Maid of honor."

The irony of that seemed particularly black in the circumstances.

"Did you fancy him, even back then?"

"No, of course not."

"Why, *of course not*?"

"I just didn't. It was fifteen years ago."

"Because he didn't have four cars and a six-bedroom house in Hampstead?" It was a cheap shot, but I couldn't resist it.

"It wasn't that."

"What was it, then?"

"Don't do this to me, Joe. I can't cope with it. If you want me to go, I'll go, but don't torture me."

"What about Beth?"

She looked up suddenly.

"Oh my God, you're not going to tell her all this, are you? All the details of what we did?"

"I don't know yet. I don't think so. But you're going to tell Ben again. Tell him you're done, that it's over. For good."

She dabbed at her eyes with a tissue. "Now?"

"Now."

She blew her nose again, then took her cell phone from her pocket and tapped the touchscreen.

"No," I said. "Show me."

"Pardon?"

"Show me." I gestured to her phone. "The number."

She terminated the call, started again with the phone held out in front of her so that I could see. I watched as she selected "Ben cell" from her address book and called the number. She put the phone to her ear again.

"No," I said. "Put it on speakerphone."

She touched the screen again, and the tinny metallic ringing filled the bedroom as the call went through. I watched Mel's face as it rang. She seemed drained, exhausted. But also relieved, as if she were glad to have finally gotten all of it off her chest.

The call connected, and she sat up a little straighter on the bed, holding her head up a little higher. In the stillness of our bedroom, I heard a male voice answer.

"Hello?"

It was him.

25

"Ben?" Mel said, her voice tight.

There was a pause.

"Yeah?" He sounded instantly impatient or angry. Or both. I moved a little closer so I could hear better.

"It's Melissa."

Melissa, not Mel. She was Melissa to him, then.

A pause on the other end of the line. One beat, two. I thought I heard an intake of breath.

"What do you want?"

"Ben, I've got Joe with me. He's here with me now. I've told him everything. And I've told him it's over between you and me; it can't carry on. Like I said the other night—"

There was a click from the other end of the line, and her phone beeped.

"Ben?" Mel said, leaning a bit nearer to the cell phone. She checked the display. "He hung up," she said, a flicker of sadness in her voice.

"Try him again."

She redialed, and it rang just once before going to voice mail.

This time she hung up before dialing again. It rang six times before the voice mail message started.

"This is Ben Delaney. Leave a message."

Mel looked at me, as if to ask the question.

"Go on," I said.

"Ben," she started, hesitating over her words, "I just need you to know that . . . I can't see you anymore. Like I told you. Beth knows. She came to the Stratford today and caused a hell of a scene. She's in a bad way. I'm worried about her."

A bit late for that, I thought darkly.

"Anyway," Mel continued, "Joe knows everything. I've told him all of it. Please don't call me again, just . . . send me a text so I know you've gotten this message." She hesitated for a moment. "Goodbye, Ben."

She looked up at me, and I nodded. She ended the call, and silence filled our bedroom.

I looked back at her, wondering how we had come to this. Wondering if I'd ever really known her at all. She couldn't look me in the eye. Eventually I turned and looked out the window again, out onto the street.

"Do you think he'll come here?" I said. "To the house?"

"Honestly? I have no idea. He's a bit unpredictable when he's angry or upset. I really don't know what he'll do."

"Well, if you see him before I do, you call the police. OK? No messing about. And I'll do the same."

There was shouting coming from downstairs, muffled through the bedroom door.

"Daddy! Daddy!"

I took the stairs two at a time and found William on the back of the sofa doing a headstand, propped against the wall with his feet halfway to the ceiling. His face was flushed red. The sofa itself was covered with dozens of cars.

"Daddy! Look! I'm going upside down!"

In spite of everything, I smiled, glad of the distraction. Today had turned into the worst day of my life—worse than when my parents split up or the day I wrecked my sporting career—but my son still had the ability to make me smile with his four-year-old craziness.

"That's good, Wills. Now why don't you come down for a minute and get back to normal."

"I *am* normal."

"The normal way up, I mean. So you don't get dizzy."

"Don't feel dizzy."

"Come on, matey. You're very red in the face."

I picked him up carefully and put him back on the sofa, right side up. He sat for a minute and got his breath back, his cheeks still flushed.

"Do you want to play a game?" I said. Anything to take my mind off Mel and what I was supposed to do next.

"What game?"

"Footie in the garden?"

He thought for a moment. "Is everyone cross with Mummy?"

"What do you mean, Wills?"

"Alice's mummy is cross with her. You're cross with her."

"No, I'm not, Wills."

"You shouted at her."

"You heard that?"

He nodded solemnly. "You were *mean* to her."

"I did shout. I was just a little bit upset."

"What about?"

"It's gone now. It's nothing."

He rolled a car across the sofa. "Why were you mean to her?"

"It's grown-up stuff, Wills. We were both a bit mean to each other, but we're OK now."

He began lining the cars up on one of the sofa cushions. "Are you sad, Daddy?"

The question stopped me in my tracks. I swallowed painfully, tears springing to my eyes, and I turned away so that William wouldn't see.

What a godawful mess we have made, your mother and me.

"No, matey. I'm fine." I gestured toward the back garden, wiping my eyes quickly. "Do you want to play football, then?"

We went outside into the late-afternoon drizzle, a net at each end of the garden, kicking his sponge ball until it was sodden and heavy with water. Before long, William's jeans were streaked with mud and wet grass, and his coat was slick with rain. But it didn't seem to bother him as he ran around and kicked and rolled over on the ground, calling for penalties.

I let the tears come then, glad of the rain to disguise them.

Mel came out in a raincoat and stood by the back door, the hood pulled over her head. We looked at each other, and for a moment, I thought she was going to come and talk to me. She took a step toward me, faltered when she saw the look on my face.

I turned away. I didn't want to talk.

She sat down on the swing seat instead and stared straight ahead, fresh tears on her cheeks. She felt like a stranger, like someone else's wife. It was as if I were standing outside someone else's house in a different street, a different city, where I didn't belong and never had. For the first time in years, I didn't know what the future held—only that it held less hope than when I'd woken up this morning.

Mel had only ever talked about being unfaithful once. Truth or dare at the blurry tail end of a house party, before we were even engaged. A game of "stand up if you've ever." The game played by drunken adults who had played spin the bottle when they were teenagers. As in, "Stand up if you've ever . . . kissed a girl," aimed at the girls.

"Stand up if you've ever had sex at work."

"Stand up if you've ever been unfaithful." That last one had gotten her on her feet, swaying slightly and grinning a charmingly plastered grin in the middle of the room. She'd admitted to a single infidelity. But insisted it didn't count, because it happened when she was still at school when she was fifteen years old. I had asked her later, in the taxi home, but she'd just smiled and kissed me and said it was a long time ago. I'd forgotten about it. Until now.

William was winning our football game 9–8 when my cell phone buzzed in my pocket.

I dug the phone out of my jeans and held a hand up to stop play. He ran straight past me and scored into the empty net.

"Ten!" he shouted, a smear of mud on his chin. "I'm first to ten! I win!"

"Good game," I said.

"First to fifteen?" he said hopefully, blinking up at me.

Shielding my phone from the rain, I looked at the screen. It showed the text message icon in the notifications bar. I clicked on it, checking over my shoulder to see if Mel had noticed. She was still sitting on the swing seat, looking at our son, a desolately sad look on her face.

The message was from Ben.

> You want to know the truth big fella? Let's
> meet. There's something I need to show you.
> 3:25 P.M. Ben cell

Raindrops spotted the phone's screen, distorting the words.

Let's meet.

26

I kept my distance from Mel for the rest of the day. Seeing her, hearing her voice, gave me a pain in my chest like there was a boulder pressing on my rib cage. I didn't know what to say to her, what was supposed to happen next. We were in uncharted territory: my marriage was a shipwreck, and I had been washed up on some strange shore where I didn't speak the language. There was anger too, but mostly a plunging sadness, a sense that much had been lost between us that might never be regained.

Mel put William in the bath after we came in from football and then made his tea. I shut myself in the study with a bottle of red wine and thought further about the invitation from Ben.

There's something I need to show you.

But what? And why now? Not to apologize, surely. That was not his style at all.

It could be a trap. Maybe he was going to finish what he'd started on Thursday, with a shotgun to even the odds. Mel had been taken away from him, and he couldn't deal with it. He thought I had threatened to hurt her if she didn't end their relationship; God alone knew what kind of man he thought I was. Perhaps he thought he had to protect Mel from me, teach me a lesson. I had learned things about Ben in the last forty-eight hours that I would never have suspected, and I had to be ready for him if he turned violent again.

It still begged the question: What did he have that he *needed to show me*?

I booted up the PC and refilled my glass as the computer whirred into life.

Ben had texted a map of the meeting place: a close-up picture of a page from a London A–Z, lots of green space, the A4140 going through the middle of it, Kingsbury HA9, Barn Hill, Fryent Country Park.

Bridge in the park near the open-air theater.
10 A.M. tomorrow.

Fryent Country Park wasn't too far away. A few miles northwest, near the bottom of the M1, but still in London. Ben did his triathlon training there, something about being able to run and run without bumping into anyone you knew when you were red-faced and pouring sweat like you were going to have a heart attack. I guessed he knew it pretty well. The satellite image on Google Earth showed an open-air stage by a lake in the southern part of the park. It looked fairly isolated on the map, plenty of trees and no houses nearby. It was an interesting choice. If he had wanted to meet in public, with lots of witnesses and bystanders, he could have chosen one of a thousand other places. But instead he had chosen a big country park with plenty of trees and uneven ground where—at 10:00 A.M. on a Monday morning—we might not see another soul.

The cell phone buzzed in my hand. Another text.

Come alone.
5:31 P.M. Ben cell

I stared at his latest message for a moment before
returning to the Google Earth image. *Come alone.* It
hadn't occurred to me to do anything else, but I
would need to take precautions. Get there early and
check the place out. *Tell Mel where I was going too?* I
couldn't bring myself to confide in her, not yet. She
had kept the truth from me for months, and it was better that she didn't know her ex-lover was asking to
meet. No one at school could know either, because
meeting him on a Monday morning meant taking a
sick day from work. Nor could Adam, because I knew
he'd advise me against the meeting, but it was something that I had to do. *Should I take a weapon, in case
Ben lost it?* Bad idea. Really bad.

There was a much better option.

I found the business card with PC Khan's name on
it and dialed the number. It went through to a duty
sergeant, and I explained who I was, asking that a
message to be passed on to the demand management
inspector as soon as possible in the morning, telling
them where and when Ben had asked to meet. I
asked—if it were possible—for an officer to meet me
at the entrance to the country park so they could see
Ben for themselves. See that he wasn't missing anymore. Put an end to this charade.

The printer clicked and hummed as it printed a
map of the park. Paths, tracks, a lake, a parking lot, a
road running through the middle of it all. I drank the
last of the red wine and just sat there in the chair for a
few minutes, wondering whether meeting Ben at the
park might turn out to be a mistake. Or my best chance

to close things out, draw a line under what had happened, and start putting my family back together. There was only one way to find out. In any case, there were some things I wanted to say to him: to look him in the eye and tell him that Mel was mine and I was hers, and nothing would ever change that. To tell him she was human, she'd made a mistake, and now we would put it behind us and start again. Part of me— maybe a big part—also thought briefly about hurting him, punishing him for what he'd tried to do to my family. He had forfeited his right to a fair fight.

I didn't notice the webcam until I was about to shut the computer down. The red light glowed next to its tiny digital eye, looking back at me from its perch on top of the monitor. The camera's red light only lit up when it was in use. When there was someone at the other end, the webcam's view displayed on their computer screen.

Someone was watching me. No, not *someone*. It wasn't a coincidence—there was only one person that it could be.

Ben.

MONDAY

27

Mel left for work at 7:10 A.M., as usual. We had not spoken last night or this morning. As soon as she shut the front door behind her, I rang school, leaving a message for the head of year to tell him I was sick in bed with food poisoning and would not be able to make it in today.

Waiting in line with William in the school playground, I turned and caught one of the mums staring at me with a mixture of pity and curiosity. Her face rang a bell somehow, but she quickly looked away, saying something to the woman next to her. Then I realized why: she had been two tables away from us in the Stratford Arms yesterday and had witnessed the confrontation with Beth.

Get used to this. People will find out, that's just the way life works. So be it. I could handle that.

The rendezvous wasn't due to happen until ten and there were still only three other cars in the small parking area at Fryent Country Park by the time I pulled in, just after nine. One of them was a white Aston Martin DB9, registration W1NB1G.

Damn. He beat me to it.

I parked at the end of the row and sat for a moment,

peering at his car, looking for movement behind the tinted glass. My cell chimed with a text message.

> I'm so sorry, Joe. Please forgive me. Love you
> xxx
> 9:03 A.M. Mel cell

Reading the words gave me a painful ache in my chest again. I put the phone back in my pocket without replying and waited another minute to see if Ben was still in his car. It would be better to do it here in the parking lot near the road, whatever it was he wanted to show me. This was nearer to an escape route, nearer to houses and people and *witnesses*, rather than some tucked-away part of the park. And I wanted, suddenly, to get it over with.

There was no movement from the Aston Martin. I got out of my car and walked over to where Ben was parked, trying not to walk too fast or too casually, just calm and controlled and taking everything in my stride. I peered into the sports car's window. A large Costa coffee was in the cup holder, and there was a pile of clothes on the back seat. Almost like he'd emptied them out of a bag to make space for something else. To make space for what?

One of his guns is gone.

I stared at the pile of clothes for a long moment, then switched on the GPS on my phone, checked the map, and set off up a long, winding track that led over a small rise and into a stand of trees. It was a crisp October morning, and the birds were making plenty of noise high in the branches, but I saw no one as I tramped up the path, keeping my eyes peeled and my hands out of my pockets, ready to react if necessary.

The trees thinned out on one side, then disappeared, and a small lake took their place. Low autumn sunlight slanted through the trees at my back.

Footsteps behind me. A young woman in a Lycra running top and shorts, jogging with headphones on. She passed by and on up the path without meeting my eye.

The stones on the path clicked beneath my feet, and the open-air theater came into view across the lake. It looked out of place, a gray concrete amphitheater in this oasis of green trees and blue water. My pulse was picking up. *Show yourself, then.* I thought about what I would say to Ben. What do you say to a man who's been sleeping with your wife? Maybe he still thought Mel would come back to him?

He wouldn't leave here with any doubts on that score.

The path circled almost all the way around one side of the lake, the bridge coming closer and closer. There didn't seem to be anyone around, but that didn't mean there was no one there. Trees and bushes stood close to each end, and the open-air theater itself looked like it offered places to hide.

My phone buzzed in my pocket, and I snatched it out. A text from Ben.

Are you alone?
9:14 A.M. Ben cell

There was no one about except an old woman walking a dog beside the lake, maybe a hundred meters from me. I studied her for a minute. She gave no indication of even being aware I was there.

I hit Reply.

Yes
9:15 A.M. Me

I walked up onto the bridge, feeling exposed as I got to the center. It had a shallow incline and a waist-high stone parapet. On a different day, it would be nice to come here with William. A different day, a different month, a different year maybe.

Turning 360 degrees, I tried to get my bearings. It was a fair way from the parking lot, which was invisible on the far side of the trees. Apart from the jogger and the dog walker, I had seen no one. I leaned on the bridge's stone parapet and looked out across the lake, stirred into small choppy waves by a fresh autumn breeze from the north. The sky was starting to cloud over, and what had been a clear, sunny October day was now threatening to turn darker. My eyes came to rest for a second time on the open-air stage on the other side of the bridge, its walls and angles seeming to offer a natural hiding place.

I walked down off the bridge and tramped through the long grass to the series of concrete semicircles that formed the theater seating, each deeper than the next, until I was in a depression in front of the stage. The theater building itself, a two-story wooden façade on a one-story base, was locked and shuttered for the off-season. The amphitheater looked tired and sad and windswept, as if it had been abandoned to the elements now that winter was on its way.

There was no one around. I went back to the middle of the bridge, checked my watch, sent another message.

I'm here
9:18 A.M. Me

I had barely put the phone back in my pocket when the reply came back:

So am I.
9:18 A.M. Ben cell

I spun around, the phone still in my hand, to look behind me.

The path was empty. The open-air theater still abandoned for the winter. No signs of life. I searched the tree line across the lake from left to right, trying to spot him as my heart thumped harder in my chest.

He has a gun, remember.

Suddenly—now that it was really happening—it occurred to me that coming here on my own, to a half-deserted city park, was maybe not such a good idea. The meeting time I'd given to the police was still more than half an hour away.

Maybe they'll be early.

Maybe not.

Maybe they won't come at all.

I checked over my shoulder again and then went back to studying the tree line, scanning right to left this time, looking for any movement or shape or color that would give him away.

That was when I saw him.

28

Ben was on the far side of the lake, maybe fifty or sixty meters away, just standing there. Wearing the same jacket he'd worn on Thursday night: the Louis Vuitton, the one Mel had told me cost more than £1,000. He had on a black baseball cap and was carrying a long blue canvas sports bag that looked slack and half-empty, but weighted down in the middle. As if it held something long, thin, and heavy.

I stared at him for a long moment, trying to make sure it was him, waiting for him to make a move, give a signal, show some sign that he had seen me on the bridge and recognized me. But he just stood there, absolutely still, staring back across the choppy water of the lake. It was the first time I had seen him since Thursday evening, and I was trying to work out what I was feeling, through the surge of emotion.

Anger at his betrayal. Sadness at all the lying. Determination that this would be the end of it.

The rough stone of the bridge parapet was coarse beneath my fingers. It was clear now why he had chosen the bridge for our meeting: not because it gave a perfect all-around view of the surrounding heath but because anyone standing on it was elevated, exposed, raised ten or twelve feet above everything else. Because if you were standing on the bridge, it would be very obvious if you were alone or not.

And still he stood there. Him on one side of the lake, me on the other. He put a hand in his pocket and put a cell phone to his ear. He spoke, listened briefly, spoke again, then put the phone away. He raised a hand in a wave, then turned and walked away up the path.

Now what—follow him? Why not? I wasn't going to let him just walk away after bringing me all the way out here to this place.

I walked down the bridge's incline to follow him, keeping my eyes on him all the while. He had a big head start on me and was walking quickly, not looking back. He reached the fork in the path and took the left-hand side, quickly disappearing from view behind the screen of trees that led back to the entrance. I broke into a jog, my footsteps loud on the path. *Can't let him get away.* I cut across the grass to gain on him a little more, but the path looped away behind the trees, and he was still out of sight.

I reached the fork and stopped. There was no sign of him. *Shit.* Running farther, retracing my steps from earlier, the path curving in a big semicircle around to the left as it went back to the parking lot. Ben was still nowhere to be seen. I stopped, panting with the exertion, looking around. How had he gotten away from me so fast? He'd had a head start, but even still . . . I looked around, cold October air scouring my lungs. There was no wind; the trees were completely still. A high-pitched whistle of birdsong far off in the distance.

I was completely alone. Or was I?

Maybe he hadn't run off at all. Maybe he was hiding here, nearby. Watching me. Stalking me. Laughing to himself. There was lots of cover, dense bushes, and trees standing close together, lots of places to conceal yourself. I looked around quickly, with a powerful sense that I was being watched. Listened hard, my ears straining for the tiniest sound that would give him away.

Off the path, a flash of bright blue stood out against the autumn undergrowth. Ben's sports bag. The one he'd just been carrying. It was only a few feet off the path in a small clearing. A quick calculation told me that straight through the trees here would bring me out into the parking lot.

He had taken a shortcut to get there before me.

Moving branches aside, I left the path and headed into the undergrowth. Twigs scratched and snagged at my coat and jeans. Ducking my head, I pushed on and through, the bushes closing up behind me and hiding me almost completely from the path. The bushes were heavy and wet, streaking my clothes with water. A low branch scratched my cheek. Another stabbed the back of my hand.

The blue sports bag was slack and unzipped. I nudged it with the toe of my shoe, feeling it yield under the pressure. I picked it up. Empty.

So he took the gun out?

I stopped for a second, an icicle of realization sliding into my stomach.

Ben's here, with a gun. Full of hate and anger and jealousy.

He's led you here, got you where he wants you.

There's no one else around. No witnesses.

You idiot.

He had played me to perfection.

Shit.

The bushes and trees were thick around me. Lots more places to hide. No fast way out. Where the hell were the police? I'd asked them to meet me here, given them the time and place.

Maybe they weren't coming.

Crouching down, I listened to the sounds of the woodland. The drip of moisture from overnight rain. The wingbeats of a bird high overhead. Faint sounds of rustling in the fallen leaves. Expecting at any moment that Ben would step around the trunk of a tree and level his shotgun at me.

Can't stay here.

My sense of direction had never been brilliant, but it seemed that a route directly away from the path and slightly to the left would be the quickest way back to my car and safety.

I stood up and ran.

Pushing back the undergrowth, branches cracking as I plowed through, head down, ignoring the scrapes from protruding branches, ducking and weaving between tree trunks, a thick carpet of leaves beneath my feet. Hearing my own breathing loud and labored in my ears. Imagining Ben appearing in front of me. Or maybe I wouldn't see him. Maybe I'd just feel the impact of a shotgun blast.

Where is he?

I kept on running, my legs getting heavier. Stumbled into a dip and almost fell, barking my knuckles on a tree stump as I struggled to stay upright.

Just get back to the car. Get the hell out of here and don't make the same mistake again. Worry about the rest later.

I burst through the last line of bushes and out into the parking lot, breathing hard, streaked with rainwater and dirt, shoes caked in mud, tree-branch scratches on my hands and face. Clutching the blue sports bag in my hand.

But I was too late. Ben's white Aston Martin was gone.

29

There was no sign of Ben anywhere. The only people in the parking lot were a middle-aged man and a younger woman getting out of a nondescript sedan, him in a dark jacket and tie and her in a charcoal-gray trouser suit. I studied them as I got my breath back, the blue sports bag loose in my hand, panting hard from my run through the trees. The woman was slim and attractive in an uncomplicated way, with dark brown hair tied back in a ponytail. The man was a good ten years older than she was, maybe forty, with a day's worth of stubble on his face and his tie at half-mast even though it was not yet 9:30 A.M. He wore a hangdog, almost apologetic expression, like he'd seen a lot of life and didn't care for most of it.

"Joseph Lynch?" he said, walking over to me.

"Yes?"

"My name's Detective Chief Inspector Marcus Naylor, Metropolitan Police." He indicated the woman next to him. "This is Detective Sergeant Rachel Redford."

We all shook hands, and I gestured back toward the way I'd come.

"You missed him. You literally *just* missed him."

"Who?"

"Ben Delaney. He was here. Just left. Must have been right before you arrived."

Naylor looked at his watch.

"Didn't get the message from morning briefing until half past eight, and we came straight here," he said in his flat South London accent. "Thought we might be early. You said ten o'clock?"

"He was early. So was I."

"Ah. Shame."

He seemed to notice the bedraggled state of my clothes for the first time.

"Are you all right?" he said.

I was still trying to get my breath back. Hadn't realized how out of shape I was.

"Fine. Just a bit out of condition."

"You were running."

"Wanted to catch Ben before he left. And then . . ." I suddenly realized how foolish it sounded, but I had started the sentence now and had to finish it.

"And then?" Naylor repeated, raising an eyebrow.

"Then I thought he might have been, sort of . . . lying in wait for me, so I legged it back here to get to my car."

Naylor put his hands in his pockets, regarding me with a quizzical expression.

"*Lying in wait* for you? Why do you think he would do that?"

"It's a long story."

"So I've heard. But you didn't actually talk to him?"

I shook my head. "Saw him, but not close enough to talk. He was texting me."

"You sure you're all right?" Naylor said again, indicating my right hand. "You're bleeding."

"It's fine; it's nothing." A line of blood trickled between my knuckles where I had caught it on a tree branch. The knuckles were barked red raw from where I had lost my balance and almost fallen over, the hand stiffening up already.

"What's in the bag?" Naylor said, indicating the blue sports bag in my other hand.

I'd almost forgotten I was holding it.

"Oh, this? Nothing. It's Ben's. He dropped it back there."

"Are you sure it's his?"

"He was carrying it earlier. I think it might have had one of his shotguns in it."

"What makes you say that?"

"It looked like he had something in it just now. Something long and heavy."

"But he left the bag behind?"

"I found it in the bushes back there." I held it out to him. "Here, take a look."

Naylor didn't take his hands out of his pockets. "Rachel, would you mind?"

His colleague was already around the back of their sedan, opening the trunk. Returning with a large, clear Ziploc plastic bag. She opened it and held it out to me so I could drop the sports bag into it.

As she sealed the bag, I realized she had put on white rubber gloves.

Naylor said, "Thanks, Mr. Lynch. So we just missed him, did we?"

"By a couple of minutes at most. He left in a white sports car with a personalized plate."

"Didn't see one." He turned to his colleague. "Did you, Rachel?"

"Nope," she said, writing something on the Ziploc bag in black marker. It was the first word I'd heard her utter.

"Since we appear to have missed the boat here," Naylor said, "would you have some time to talk to us now?"

"Sure."

"At the station?"

"No problem."

Naylor opened the back door of their sedan. "Great. Shall we?"

"Can I follow you in my car?"

"Probably easier if you ride with us. It's an absolute bugger to park near the station anyway, especially on a weekday. Rachel can drop you back here to your car after we're done, if you like." I studied him for a moment, trying to read him, to work out what he was thinking. His left ear was cauliflowered like a rugby player's and he had a small white scar curling below his lip. His eyes were a very pale, icy blue and gave nothing back. Before this weekend, I had never in my life spoken to a policeman for longer than required to ask directions. Now I'd met three in as many days.

Assuming they are *actually police.*

"This is going to sound a bit weird," I said, "but aren't you supposed to show me your ID or something?"

Naylor looked pained, as if I'd offended him. "Do you not believe that I'm a police officer, Mr. Lynch?"

"No. I mean, yes; it's not that. It's just that I'm not really sure what to believe, these last few days."

A trio of geese flapped noisily overhead, squawking to each other. Naylor kept his eyes on me.

"Really?" He produced a black wallet ID from his jacket pocket. I looked briefly at the picture on his warrant card—name, rank, collar number—alongside the crest of the Metropolitan Police before he snapped it shut again. "Bad weekend?"

"Bad doesn't really cover it, to be honest."

I got in the back seat and DS Redford pulled the Ford smoothly around in a semicircle, back out to the exit onto the main road.

"Sorry to hear that," Naylor said to me over his shoulder.

"I had sort of assumed that young officer I met on Saturday would be the one who came out this morning. Didn't realize they'd send a detective chief inspector."

"Things have moved on a bit since Saturday."

"How do you mean?"

"Let's talk at the station."

We passed the rest of the journey in silence.

30

For the second time in three days, I found myself in the reception area of Kilburn Police Station. There were a couple of tramps sitting half-asleep on the back row of seats and a bored-looking custody sergeant behind the counter who nodded at Naylor as we came in. Redford punched buttons next to a heavy security door, and it opened into a bare corridor with three doors on each side. The last door on the left bore the black plastic nameplate "Int Room 3." Inside were four chairs and a table. Redford gestured for me to take a seat.

"Tea or coffee?" she said. She had a clear, kind tone to her voice, which made me instantly warm to her. I couldn't tell what her accent was, but it wasn't London. Something northern.

"Tea, please. Milk, no sugar."

She nodded and disappeared, closing the door behind her.

Before this weekend, I had never been inside a police station except for a bike-coding day they'd held at Harrow Road last year. It was a thoroughly depressing place, as was this one. The interview room was a case in point. Bare walls, four nondescript plastic chairs, and a plastic-topped table that was pockmarked with cigarette burns. I guessed the table had been there long before the smoking ban.

There were no missed calls or messages on my phone. I wondered again what had happened with Ben at the country park. *Maybe he'd clocked the detectives before I had and panicked?* Not smart to get caught by the police with a shotgun in a gym bag. I typed a new message to Ben.

Why did you leave the park earlier?
10:33 A.M. Me

The door opened again, and DC Redford came in with a steaming cup of tea in a Styrofoam cup. She set the cup down in front of me, and I sat up straighter, assuming we were about to start.

"Is your colleague joining us?" I asked her.

"He's just sorting a couple of things out," she said. "Back in a minute."

She disappeared back into the corridor, closing the door behind her. I looked at my watch. Monday morning at 10:34 A.M. should mean a tenth grade class on *Of Mice and Men*, but instead I was here in a dingy police station waiting to be interviewed about Ben bloody Delaney. I stood up and went to the barred window. Beyond the police station parking lot there was a railway siding with tracks butted up next to each other, a dozen steel lines crossing my view in parallel from left to right. Gray high-rise blocks looming up behind. Drops of rain spattered the window.

My phone remained obstinately silent. I typed another text to Ben.

What the hell was this morning all about
anyway? If you've got something to say to me,
just say it.
10:35 A.M. Me

The door opened again, and Naylor came in with
Redford behind him. They took the two seats opposite
me, both holding white mugs of tea. Naylor's mug had
the words *Property of the BOSS* in large red letters on
its side. Redford had a brown cardboard folder and a
notepad under her arm.

Naylor's chair scraped loudly on the floor as he
pulled it into the table.

"Sorry about the delay," he said. "Let's get started,
shall we?"

He took a small digital Dictaphone out of his
pocket and set it on the desk between us, a red light
blinking on-off-on-off.

"You don't mind if I use this, do you? Saves me
making notes."

"Of course."

"Great," he said, clasping his hands on the table in
front of him. "So: Benjamin Delaney. As you know,
his wife reported him missing on Friday, and we're
trying to establish his whereabouts, so thanks for
coming in on Saturday to talk to PC Khan and also
giving us the heads-up about this morning—much ap-
preciated. I've read through your statement and those
made by your wife and Mrs. Delaney, and I've got a
few questions."

"No problem."

"Mr. Delaney's a friend of yours, correct?"

"He was."

"Past tense?"

"He's not a friend anymore, no."

"But he was?"

"Our wives went to school together. I'd met him at weddings, christenings, things like that over the years. But I've only gotten to know him more this past year, since he moved to London."

"More of an acquaintance, then."

I shrugged. "Through Mel."

"How often do you see him and his wife?"

"Maybe once every six weeks, couple of months, when Mel and Beth organize a get-together—dinner, barbecue, or whatever."

"You go to the pub with Mr. Delaney sometimes?"

"No."

"Never?"

"We don't have a hell of a lot in common, to be honest."

That brought me up short. *Except we do now. We definitely have something in common.*

"You mean you don't have the same interests."

"He tried to get me to join his poker night a few months back. Mel wanted me to join in, make an effort to get to know him a bit better."

"Mr. Delaney likes his poker, does he?"

I shrugged. "He's good at it. He knows when to push his luck and when to fold. He's very good at reading people, and he's got more money than the rest of the players put together. So, yes, he likes his poker."

"How about you?"

"I only went once. It wasn't really my thing."

"You lost money?"

"A bit. I'm not very good at bluffing."

"So what is your thing, then?"

"My wife and I have a four-year-old son, William.

He just started last month at Saint Hilda's Primary. He gets a lot of my time. And sports—I used to play hockey at county level until I got injured. Now it's squash once a week with my friend Adam, five-a-side football sometimes. And I'm an English teacher at Haddon Park Academy."

"So you're not friends anymore because of this thing he had for your wife?"

"You've read Mel's statement from Saturday?"

"I've read all of them."

From the brown manila file DS Redford produced printed forms that looked familiar from my first visit to this police station.

"Well," I said, "it turns out there was a bit more to it than that."

He studied me across the table. "In my experience, Mr. Lynch, there usually is."

31

I shifted uncomfortably in my seat.

"The truth is, since that weird run-in with Ben on Thursday night, some things have happened and . . . I've found out some other things that I didn't know before."

"Such as?" Naylor said.

It wasn't something I wanted to say out loud in front of strangers: saying it made it real, official somehow, while it still felt very much to me like it was in the realm of the unreal. It would mean the story of Mel's betrayal would be recorded on tape, maybe forever. The red light on Naylor's Dictaphone blinked on-off-on-off.

"What did you find out, Joe?" Naylor repeated, sitting forward in his chair.

My hands were shaking. I clasped them in my lap. "He and Mel. They were . . . involved."

Naylor waited for a few seconds before he spoke again. "Involved in what way?"

"An affair. He pursued her for ages, and she finally gave in a few months ago. It's been going on since the summer."

"And you discovered this on Thursday evening?"

"No. Well, kind of. It was yesterday that I found out, but Thursday was the first sign I had that something strange was going on. That's where it started."

"Tell me how it happened."

I gestured to the forms that Redford had produced from her brown manila file.

"It's in there, in my statement. Most of it anyway."

"Tell me in your own words."

And so I told him. From Thursday night until today, how it had all gone down—including Beth Delaney's revelation in the pub yesterday and her husband being on the loose with one of his shotguns. Naylor listened to the whole sorry tale, nodding from time to time, his face impassive as Redford made notes alongside the form I recognized from Saturday, the statement I'd made to PC Khan. I told them everything as quickly as possible, trying to get it over with, and when the story was finished he gave me a moment before continuing.

"What we do with a missing persons case like this, Joe, is try to establish a timeline of a person's movements and activities. We take the timeline as far as we can and see where it stops. Along with other information, that gives us a framework of facts to work with. These are the notes taken by PC Khan when he interviewed you and Mrs. Lynch on Saturday afternoon." He turned pages in his folder, found the one he was looking for. "So before this morning at the country park, Thursday was definitely the last time you saw Ben?"

"Yes."

"And how *exactly* did you part company? On friendly terms?"

"No."

"Explain."

"I reversed into his car. He wasn't best pleased."

Naylor tapped the page in front of him with a pencil. "Interesting."

"I'm not proud of it."

"Interesting, in that your wife said there was a bit more to it than that."

A swooping, lurching sensation in my stomach.

Shit. The story we told Beth on Saturday.

"Oh?" was all I could manage.

"She told PC Khan that there was an argument. That Mr. Delaney ended up on the deck."

"Erm. Yeah." I could feel my face getting hot. "That's what happened. I had to leave in a hurry to get my son's inhaler because he was having an asthma attack. And when I went back to the hotel soon after, Ben had left."

"You had a fight."

"He hit me. I pushed him. It wasn't really a fight."

"Why didn't you tell PC Khan that, Joe?"

I felt like I was ten years old again, standing in the headmaster's office. At the same time, I was annoyed that Mel couldn't have just stuck to the story we'd agreed.

"I'm sorry. I should have. But Ben's wife came over on Saturday and was asking about him, so Mel gave her the story about the car to cover my back, and then I said the same thing to your colleague so Beth wouldn't find out she'd lied."

"I see," Naylor said.

"All that's by the by now, of course, after what happened yesterday." I held my hands up. "I'm sorry. It was stupid. *Stupid.*"

"So she lied to Beth Delaney, and then you lied to a police officer."

"She was trying to protect me. It was a spur-of-the-moment thing. Beth was upset, she was crying, I was going to tell her the truth, but then Mel jumped in with this story about me reversing into his Porsche. I thought she'd say the same to the policeman. All we were trying to do was help find Ben."

"You thought she'd lie to the police for you?"

I could feel the sweat beneath my shirt. "No, that's not what happened. She told the truth."

"Or maybe both of you are lying."

"I'm sorry. It was dumb. I'm a terrible liar, as you can probably tell."

Naylor nodded. "Lying well is a lot harder than most people think. Things gets complicated, people lose track. 'A liar should have a good memory,' so they say. Most people don't, not for this kind of thing."

"So what are you saying? That you don't believe me?"

"I'm saying nothing—we're just trying to track a man down. A prominent, successful, well-off businessman who seems to have disappeared. Do you know where he might be?"

"No idea. But he hasn't disappeared."

Naylor frowned and cocked his head to one side slightly. "Hasn't he?"

"I told you, I saw him this morning."

"Is that another lie?"

"No. I swear."

"Are you sure?"

"Absolutely. Mel spoke to him on the phone yesterday, and he's been texting me."

Naylor made another note on his pad.

"You can see why we're concerned, though, right? We're not talking about a drunk, or an addict, or a person with mental health issues, or a serial runaway. We're talking about a highly successful businessman who might have trampled people, turned people over, on his way up the ladder."

"There's no 'might have' about it. Ben does exactly what he wants, and screw everyone else. He's destroyed people. Have you heard of Alex Kolnik?"

"We're talking to him this afternoon."

"I doubt he'll have many nice things to say about Ben."

"We'll see." He drank from his *Property of the BOSS* mug and then held a finger up as if he'd just remembered something.

"What was this meeting at the country park all about, by the way?"

"Ben texted last night and said he wanted to talk to me, in private."

"About what?"

"He didn't say. Just that it was important. Presumably it was about Mel."

"And he couldn't just call you up?"

"He wanted to do it face-to-face."

There was a muffled knock on the door of the interview room, and Naylor called for the visitor to come in. A young officer leaned in, apologized for interrupting, and handed Naylor a folder with the words *Forensic Support Unit* in thick black letters on its front cover.

"From the FSU, boss. Just came in."

"Much obliged, James."

Naylor opened the file so I couldn't see the contents. He scanned the two sheets briefly, grunted with something that was either satisfaction or disappointment—I couldn't tell which—and passed it over to Redford.

"You said you saw his car at the country park this morning?"

"His Aston Martin was in the parking lot. Did you see it?"

Naylor shook his head. "Nope. Was Mr. Delaney in the vehicle at the time?"

"No. He got there before I did."

Naylor's icy-blue eyes regarded me, studied me. "On the subject of cars, though, we have found something else. In circumstances that cause us concern."

"What?"

"You asked me earlier why it wasn't PC Khan who came out to meet you at the country park this morning."

I nodded, and he continued.

"A Porsche SUV registered to Mr. Delaney was found on Friday, three days ago, in an alleyway next to some lock-up garages. This is about half a mile from the Premier Inn where you two had your falling out."

"The big white one, the Cheyenne or whatever it's called?"

"Cayenne. That's the one."

"And?" I prompted.

"Someone had tried to burn it out. But they didn't do a very good job."

32

"We cross-reference every vehicle-related fire against the national database of stolen vehicles and persons of interest," Naylor continued. "Of course, it's entirely possible that Mr. Delaney's car was stolen by joyriders in a completely unrelated incident and then torched to destroy evidence. Happens every day somewhere in London. It's possible that's what happened with the Porsche—except for a couple of things. First, he hadn't reported his car stolen. And second, because the fire didn't take hold properly, a lot of the car escaped damage. Whoever tried to torch it was very much the amateur arsonist, didn't know what they were doing. So even on a fairly cursory initial examination, we were able to recover forensic evidence from inside the vehicle. Including traces of blood on the front passenger seat."

Naylor let that hang in the air for a minute.

"Blood," I repeated dumbly.

"Traces, yes."

"Do you know whose it is?"

"I'll get to that in a minute. First, a bit of history." He took out another sheet from his folder. "Last year, Mr. Delaney was involved in a minor traffic accident on the M6. No serious injuries—he was lucky—but when his vehicle was being repaired, they found his brakes had been tampered with. Police investigators then found microscopic traces of blood on the damaged brake cables. As part of the investigation," Naylor continued, "they took a DNA sample from Mr. Delaney so they could cross-reference it with the trace evidence and ensure he wasn't the source."

"So did they get him?"

"Who?"

"The guy who did it."

Naylor flipped a page in the green folder that had been handed to him a few minutes before.

"No. A former employee of Mr. Delaney's was charged and went on trial, but he was acquitted. Matthew Goring."

"That name rings a bell." Though I couldn't remember where from.

"*Anyway*, the long and the short of this little piece of history is this: Mr. Delaney's DNA information went into the database. And it turns out that his DNA is a match for the blood we found on the passenger seat of his car yesterday."

"I'm sorry to hear that. But why are you telling me this?"

Naylor shrugged. "Just wondering if you can shed any light on it, that's all."

"But I've told you everything."

Naylor considered this for a moment. "Does it bother you that Ben Delaney's a self-made millionaire and you're a teacher?"

"Not particularly."

"Does it bother you that he has a six-bedroom pile

in Hampstead and a fleet of flashy cars to turn ladies' heads?"

"Honestly? No."

"And what did it feel like," Naylor said, leaning forward, "when you found out he'd been fucking your wife?"

He slid the swear word in quietly, almost gently, like a stiletto between my ribs.

I looked from one detective to the other. "You seriously expect me to answer that?"

"But you were angry, right?"

"Of *course* I was angry."

"You beat him up, didn't you?"

"No."

"You beat the shit out of him in that parking lot. You gave him what he deserved, didn't you, Joe? I would have, in the same position."

"No, that isn't what happened."

"But then you realized you'd gone too far."

I shook my head, unease crawling through my veins like a toxin.

"I didn't even know about the affair then."

"He punched you, and you didn't retaliate?"

"I pushed him. That's all."

"You punched him?"

"No. I never hit him."

"Why not?"

"He's half my size."

That was a stupid thing to say.

"So would you say you're a lot bigger, physically stronger, and more powerful than this man who was shagging your wife and has now gone missing?"

I tried to stay calm, think about what I said next

before it came out of my mouth. "He's not missing, not in the way you're talking about it."

"But you're a lot taller and stronger than he is."

"I suppose so."

"You're a big guy. I bet you hit pretty hard."

"I told you, I didn't hit him."

"But you left him there, on the ground? Weren't you concerned about him?"

"My son was having an asthma attack, a bad one. I thought he was going to die on me. I went back as soon I could to check Ben was OK, but he had already gone."

Naylor frowned, lines bunching together across his forehead. "Gone where, do you think?"

"I don't know. Just gone."

"So he was in a bad way when you left him, then?"

It occurred to me that I had already said too much. Probably way too much. "Am I being arrested?"

Naylor smiled, the frown lines on his forehead disappearing. "Of course not. You can leave whenever you want."

"So I can leave now?"

"Yup."

"I can just get up and walk out if I want to?"

"That's right."

He paused, as if daring me to do just that. Now I knew I was free to leave, it seemed churlish to do it when I had nothing to hide. But I suddenly felt intensely claustrophobic, as if I might be stuck here forever if I didn't get out now.

"And what happens next?"

"We continue to gather evidence. On the back of these blood results"—he indicated the green file— "I'll be requesting additional support to carry out a full proof-of-life inquiry over the next thirty-six hours, starting this morning."

"What's a proof-of-life inquiry?"

"We start from the premise that Mr. Delaney is alive and well, and then try to confirm that using all the different avenues available to us: cell phone data, banking records, social media, utility bill payments, DWP, tax, CCTV, you name it. Everything we can get our hands on, basically, to see if there is evidence that Mr. Delaney is out there somewhere. It's actually very difficult to live nowadays without leaving any trace at all."

"He's already been on Facebook, and text, and on the phone to Mel yesterday."

"Yup," Naylor said, leaning back in his chair. "I've made a note of all of those. We'll be looking at them along with everything else."

"And there might be CCTV at the Premier Inn? So you could see for yourselves what happened on Thursday."

"There's a system there, but it's pretty ancient and more for show than anything else. Four cameras, three of them out of order, the other one covering the reception desk."

"You've checked it already?"

"Yup. The footage is not much use to us, I'm afraid."

I sighed, my shoulders dropping. "So how long does the whole process take?"

"We'll be fast-tracking this one, for reasons I think I've outlined."

It all sounded very formal, very official. Very serious. "Should I have a lawyer?"

"Do you think you need one?"

"I've no idea. This is all new to me. I've never had any real contact with the police before." I spread my hands. "What do you think I should do?"

"Completely up to you. As the senior investigating officer, I'm obliged to advise you of your rights, but I'm not allowed to give you an opinion on legal representation. That sort of thing could end up going against us."

"Against us in general, or against you in particular?"

"Against me." He smiled again, but there was no humor in it. "Stay local, Joe. We'll be in touch."

33

The three-story redbrick police station felt like a presence squatting behind me as I emerged, blinking, back out on Salisbury Road. People walking past me left and right, cars passing on the street, the smells of diesel and dirt and greasy takeout food mingling in the autumn drizzle.

What did I just admit to? Why don't they believe me? What the hell is going on?

The police interview had lasted less than an hour, but it felt like I'd aged five years. It seemed I'd entered a game whose rules I didn't understand, and bet everything on the outcome. My life was juddering from one disaster to the next.

Time to get some legal advice.

I turned down DS Redford's offer to drop me back at Fryent Country Park. I wanted to get away from the police as quickly as possible. I got a black cab instead and drove my car home.

It was strangely quiet in the house in the middle of the day, without William's chatter and questions and car noises. There were times when my son was full-on and bouncing off the walls with energy and I sometimes craved the stillness of a quiet house, but when those rare times came, it felt unnatural.

It didn't feel much like my home without William in it. Or Mel. The thought of my wife threw a shadow across everything.

I took my phone out and texted her.

Why did you tell police Ben and I got physical on Thurs? Thought we were sticking with story we told Beth?
12:26 P.M. Me

The reply came back quickly.

Oh god oh god I'm sorry Joe I forgot honestly are you OK?? I'm so sorry my head's all over the place at the moment, what did they say? Call me? xxx
12:27 P.M. Mel cell

I put the phone down—I didn't feel like talking to her at the moment. A minute later, it rang, vibrating on the countertop. I rejected the call and switched it to silent.

Ben's timeline on Facebook showed nothing new since his post on Saturday evening. It was tempting to direct-message him again and ask him what he was playing at, but the answer to that seemed pretty obvious. I checked my email and phone messages as well. Nothing doing there either, beyond the usual junk.

I found an old envelope on the kitchen counter and wrote down four questions.

1. *Where is Ben?*
2. *What does he want?*
3. *Why did he ask to meet yesterday?*
4. *What "evidence" did he want to show me?*

Next to each question I made notes, writing down possible answers. Arrows looping from one point to the next. Question two was the only one I had a solid answer for: he wanted Mel, that seemed pretty clear. And if he couldn't have her, he wanted to drive us apart.

That is never going to happen, Ben.

The heat of anger was in my chest, threatening to choke me like bile. Anger at Mel. Blended with betrayal and a dash of humiliation for good measure.

I had to get back on the front foot.

I went upstairs to the master bedroom and opened Mel's bedside drawer. It was full but neatly ordered: makeup, jewelry boxes, a couple of books, our three passports in a pile, a point and shoot camera, a stack of receipts clipped together, an Hermès watch that she wore on nights out. Various medicines and creams arrayed at the back, pill bottles and boxes standing upright. I wasn't really sure what I was looking for—maybe to feel like I was back in the know, having spent the last five months walking around blind to her affair. What else went on in her secret life? What was going on in her head?

Most of all, I wanted to find a clue to why she had chosen another man over me.

But there was nothing out of the ordinary. The bottom drawer was stacked with holiday brochures and bank statements. Perhaps an extravagant purchase or strange pattern of spending might spill more of the secrets she'd kept from me. Had Ben given her money? Had she bought him expensive gifts?

Again, there was nothing that looked suspicious on the face of it. No doubt Ben had picked up the tab for everything. He never missed an opportunity to remind everyone how wealthy he was. Probably Mel most of all. I remembered her words from yesterday.

He told me he was in love with me like he'd never loved anyone before. That he'd do anything for me, anything I wanted—leave Beth, leave Alice. Sell the company. Sell the house. Move away. Leave everything behind so we could be together.

Further searching turned up nothing of note in her other drawers and cupboards.

This is pointless. Do something practical, useful. Necessary.

Back in the kitchen, drinking a strong coffee, I hunted for an old copy of the Yellow Pages before remembering that Mel had thrown it out long ago. *Who needs that cluttering the place up when you've got Google?* she'd said. She was right, in a way, but it was still good to have something with pages, something you could hold in your hand. Google was fine, but you couldn't turn down a corner and cross out entries that were no good. Even though I'd charged it yesterday, my phone was almost dead already, so I plugged it in and went upstairs to the PC in the study. The bigger screen was better for web browsing anyway.

The monitor flickered into life as the fan started up inside the base unit. The PC was nearing the end of its useful life and usually took a few minutes to boot up. It beeped and whirred and went through its usual start-up procedures. While I waited, I thought of what Naylor had told me an hour before, the *proof-of-life* inquiries to establish when Ben had last raised his head above the parapet. The computer beeped and displayed some incomprehensible message about BIOS and RAM and memory and various other stuff that I didn't understand.

I hit Enter to get it moving.

The screen went blue, then black. The fan whirred slower, then kicked in again like an old Hoover on its last legs. Down and up. *Typical. This is the moment the PC chooses to finally give up the ghost, in my hour of need. Just what I don't need.* The red light by the webcam came on, but the screen stayed black. Various chugging and whirring noises came from the base unit beneath the desk.

Still nothing on the monitor. A black screen.

"Just give me a break here," I said, talking to the machine.

I was about to switch it off and go back downstairs when a message appeared in the bottom left-hand side of the screen.

White text on black.

*Boot sequence interrupted_*

A blinking cursor instead of a period. Our PC had been getting slower and slower, but I'd never seen that message before.

The words disappeared. A black, blank screen. Black.

Black.

Then two words.

Hello Joe_

34

For a few seconds, I just stared at the words, at the blinking cursor after my name, wondering whether this was part of the computer's recovery sequence. A plunging sensation in the pit of my stomach told me it wasn't.

The greeting disappeared and was replaced by a line of text.

I bet your wondering what the fucks going on?_

I couldn't breathe. I was paralyzed, the breath trapped in my lungs. Again, the text disappeared. Again, it was replaced by another line of text.

Let me explain_
She said she still loves you and cant leave you because your a good man_
The BEST KINDEST man she has ever met_

She was everything to me but she destroyed what we had_ FOR YOU_
You worthless pathetic piece of shit_

The words began to scroll up the screen now, quicker, each line coming so fast I could barely read it before the next appeared.

Think you can beat me? That your better than
me?_Im going to break you_
Your whole fucking life is about being the
GOOD MAN. How about SUSPECTED
MURDERER instead?_

Naylor's words returned to me: a full "proof-of-
life" inquiry.

I hit the Print Screen button three times and was
greeted with a sullen beep. The printer was off. Damn.
Get a picture. I patted my pockets for my cell phone.
Not there. *Shit*. It was charging downstairs. I was torn
between wanting to see the rest of the message and
needing to photograph it as evidence. The message
continued scrolling, lines of text disappearing as new
ones appeared.

Im going to destroy your reputation_ Im going
to destroy your marriage_ Then Im going to
destroy you_
No one will believe you and that will make it all
the sweeter_ This is going to be the best game
yet_
Adios_

I ran downstairs to get my cell phone, grabbed it
off the kitchen countertop charger and all, ran back
upstairs, and crashed back into the study.

Just in time to see the last words on the monitor
disappear.

I hit the Escape key. Back arrow. Return, Back-
space, Delete. All the keys at once.

But it was gone. The webcam light had gone off
too. I guessed Ben had seen everything that he wanted
to see.

The computer beeped happily, and the normal login prompt appeared on the screen, alongside my regular background—a picture of me, William, and Mel.

Ben, you bastard.

The force of my fist slamming onto the desk was enough to make the mouse jump and land upside down with a clatter.

Think.

I got my cell phone out, got the camera ready, and restarted the PC. Same whine as the fan slowed then speeded up again, same beeping and whirring as it went through its booting-up process. This time there was no warning message from Ben. The screen filled with the same family picture and the normal login prompt. I shut it down again, waited for a minute, then turned it back on. It booted up normally.

The threatening message was a one-time deal, it seemed. I called Naylor and explained what had happened.

"Did you get a picture?" he said, his tone skeptical. "Or a printout?"

"Didn't have time. It all happened too fast."

"A screenshot?"

"No, nothing like that."

"Did he sign off with his name?"

"No, but this kind of computer stuff, hacking my PC to send me a message, this is pure 100 percent Ben Delaney. It's him all over; it's what he's good at."

I'm going to break you. Destroy you.

"OK," Naylor said. "We may need to take your computer in at some point, Joe. Have our digital forensic guys look at it."

He asked me to write down the text of the message, as best as I could remember, and email it to him.

Once I'd done that, I called up Google and typed in a new search.

This had gone far enough. It was time to get some legal advice.

35

Peter Larssen was a short, round man in his early forties, with sandy-blond hair and a firm handshake. He gestured toward the hallway and followed me up two flights of wide wooden stairs. His office, at the firm of lawyers that bore his name, was warm and tastefully furnished, one wall entirely covered by bookcases and a large desk by the window. The room smelled of fresh flowers and floor polish.

After dispensing with the pleasantries, he ran through the firm's hourly rates and the terms on which they would represent me. Signing my name at the foot of an agreement, I wondered whether I was being premature in seeking legal advice.

"Better safe than sorry," Larssen said in his crisp Home Counties accent. "So, Joe, tell me what brings you to us today."

He took notes on a yellow pad as I ran through a potted version of the events of the last four days.

"So what can I do about Ben?" I said finally. "To keep him away from my family, away from my wife? Stop him sending threatening messages? And make sure the police don't waste any more time on him?"

"I'm a fan of simple solutions, Joe. Have you tried talking to him?"

"We were going to meet this morning, but it didn't quite happen."

"Let's give it a few more days, see if he calms down. Most people do. Meanwhile, I'll make a few discreet inquiries about him, see what I can find out."

"Is that it?"

"For now. Our more pressing concern is your discussion with the police this morning. Were you cautioned, arrested, or advised of your rights in any way?"

"No. None of that."

"Tell me exactly what you said to DCI Naylor, in as much detail as you can remember."

I shrugged. "I told him everything."

"Define *everything*."

He took more notes and frowned as I described the conversation, wincing visibly at times as if he had indigestion.

"So you admitted to being in the hotel parking lot on Thursday evening?"

"Yes. I *was* there."

"That's for them to prove, not for us to serve up on a platter."

Them and us.

"He asked me a direct question."

"So?"

"I answered it."

He put the pad on the table and capped his fountain pen with a *snap*.

"Mr. Lynch, this process is not about making polite conversation. Normal social niceties don't apply when you're talking to the police. They can ask what they want, but you're not in any way obliged to answer— particularly when it's a devious, underhanded little rat like Detective Chief Inspector Marcus Naylor."

"He didn't seem devious to me," I said quietly.

"That's half the problem with him. By the time you realize what he's up to, your neck's halfway into the noose. You did the right thing, coming to us."

"You've dealt with Naylor before?"

"Enough times to know I wouldn't trust him as far as I could throw him."

"Do you think he might say the same about you?"

Larssen sipped his tea and gave a curious little half smile. "Possibly. But the point is, we're playing big boys' rules now. Forget being a good citizen and re- spect for the boys in blue and answering every loaded question they throw at you. Forget helping the police with their inquiries, having a friendly chat at the sta- tion, all of that. That's for people who want to end up getting convicted. From now on, you don't say any- thing to the police without me being there, not even small talk about the weather or last night's TV. Noth- ing at all. Are you able to do that?"

"Sounds like what a guilty person would do."

"It's what a *smart* person would do. A person who doesn't want to end up in jail."

"But I haven't done anything wrong."

"You're 100 percent sure about that, are you?"

I paused, wondering for the first time whether he believed my story. "I'm not a criminal."

He nodded. "Well, all right, then. The good news is that you hadn't been arrested and told of your rights to legal representation when you talked to them ear- lier. That's right, isn't it?"

"I asked Naylor whether I should have a lawyer, but he said he couldn't advise me."

"Hmm," said Larssen as if this were a highly unsatisfactory answer. "It's more likely that he didn't arrest you because he wanted to get your unguarded reaction."

"Well, it worked."

"But it also means he'll struggle, on legal grounds, to use the answers you gave earlier to implicate you in any crime."

"If we end up in court, you mean?"

"Yes. If we end up in court."

"If that's the good news, what's the bad news?"

"The altercation between you and Mr. Delaney on Thursday is . . . unfortunate."

"That's one way of putting it."

"Do you have any idea how his car came to be dumped and set on fire, or why there was blood found on the seat?"

"No, but I can make a pretty good educated guess."

He nodded, made a note on his pad with the expensive fountain pen. "Let's avoid guesswork, Joe. On the face of it, your wife's relationship with Mr. Delaney is interesting to the police because it puts you and him on something of a collision course. It's motive. You can see that, can't you?"

"Can I ask you a question, Peter?"

"Certainly."

"Do you believe me?"

"If you say you're not guilty, that's all I need to know."

"But do you think I did this? That I hurt Ben?"

"I didn't say that. You seem like a good chap to me, but we have to deal with the situation we face and study it piece by piece. Break it down piece by piece. That's how we win cases, and it's why most of our clients walk out of court with smiles on their faces. Everything else is a distraction."

"You see that Ben's trying to set me up, don't you? I've taken Mel away from him, he's in love with her, and he's mad and egotistical and obsessed to the point that he can't bear to lose her." My hands were fists on the table between us, my heart thumping hard. "He's trying everything to land me in it. Do you see?"

"He certainly sounds like a dangerous individual."

"He's nuts. Crazy. But he won't break my family up. Never."

Larssen handed me a business card with his numbers on it. "We've done what we can for now. To a certain extent, we have to see what the police do next, but the most important thing is that you do not, *under any circumstances*, speak to DCI Naylor again without me being present. Give me a call on the cell phone, and I will be there as quickly as I can. And let me know when Mr. Delaney contacts you next, whether by phone, email, social media, anything at all."

"Everything's just happened so fast, it's a struggle to get my head around it."

"Try not to worry too much. You've not been arrested. That's a long way down the road and will probably never happen in any case. As likely as not, Mr. Delaney will turn up at his house sooner or later, a little bit calmer and hopefully a bit wiser too. And all of this will go away."

It was a comforting thought. A good speech to wrap up our first meeting. But it wasn't long before I found out how very badly wrong he was.

TUESDAY

36

No matter how many times they were told, and how many detentions they got, there were always boys who insisted on keeping their shirts untucked as they walked into school. Who felt like today was the day to push boundaries on the dress code. The only problem was, the boundaries at Haddon Park Academy had no flexibility. Every day, according to the assistant head teacher's unyielding view of discipline, I was required to stop dress code offenders and tell them to report to the sports hall at the end of the day so they could spend an hour in general detention.

The assistant head was like that. There was no compromise in his world. *The rules are all that stand between us and special measures*, was one of his favorite clichés. So every morning, on my walk from my car to the staff room, there would be detention-bait crossing my path. And so it was today. Three pupils, in ninth grade and therefore old enough to know better, strolled toward me as I got out of my car. All three with untucked shirts flapping in the wind. I duly told them to report to general detention at 2:45 P.M. Most days they would simply accept defeat and report as instructed to take their punishment, but today, instead of shuffling away in the direction of their form rooms, they stayed where they were, right in front of me. I looked at the tallest boy, who was six feet plus with a shock of blond hair standing up off his head. There was a smirk on his face, something in his eyes that said he knew something I didn't.

"You all right, sir?"

"Yes, fine. Thanks for your concern. Now you'd better get moving if you don't want to be late for registration."

He stayed standing in front of me, with the annoying teenage grin still plastered to his face.

"Just asking how you're doing, sir."

"Never better. Now tuck your shirts in. You know the rules."

You little smart-ass, I added in my head.

All three of them sniggered as if my answer was hilarious. Some other boys drifted past, and the three of them joined onto the larger group, tucking their shirts in as they went.

There was a strange atmosphere in the staff room. Subdued, as if someone had died. Or maybe it was because so much had happened to me since Friday that the staff room felt foreign—like it belonged to my nice, comfortable old life, not the dark and dented new one.

I turned my mug right side up and dropped a teabag into it. Flicked the kettle on.

"Anyone else want a brew?" I said.

I looked around at my colleagues in the room. Some standing, some sitting, some holding exercise books, or sheets of paper, or just a cup of tea.

All eyes were on me.

"What?" I said to the room in general.

Jenny Lucas, who taught French and German, caught my eye and spoke in a quiet voice.

"Joe, Darth Draper wants to see you."

For all our mockery, Carl Draper was assistant head in charge of pastoral and disciplinary issues, and I couldn't remember ever being called into his office before in the nine years I'd worked here. *Maybe he's heard about me and Mel and wants to offer me some time off to sort my head out.*

Unlikely.

More likely was that someone had spotted me out and about yesterday, when I was supposed to be off sick, and he was going to give me a dressing-down for it. Draper was the head teacher's hatchet man, who gave out reprimands on the head teacher's behalf.

At that moment, I could not have been less bothered about getting on his bad side.

"What does he want to see me about?" I said.

"He didn't say. He came in here first thing looking for you, then put his head around the door a second time just now. Seems keen to have a word before first period."

"Right." I flicked the kettle off.

"Are you OK?" Jenny said.

"Yes. Why does everyone keep asking me if I'm OK?"

She gave me a sad little smile as if she didn't believe me. "Just asking, that's all."

"I'm fine."

Draper's office was on the executive corridor, which was home to the head teacher and his senior management team.

Draper was both younger and more senior than I was. Since hitting my midthirties, there seemed to be an increasing number of people who fell into this category, in all walks of life.

He glanced at me as I walked in, indicated a chair in front of his desk with a quick nod. He was a short man with sandy, slicked-back hair and a smile that never reached his eyes.

"Joe. Hi. Have a seat."

"I was told you were looking for me, Carl."

"Yup. Won't be a second." He continued typing, eyes on his monitor.

I sat down in one of the high-backed chairs in front of his desk. The wall behind him was covered with framed certificates, sporting awards, and newspaper clippings in which his grinning face was the common feature. Shaking hands with local councilors, standing next to trophy-laden captains of the school's numerous sports teams, giving the thumbs-up with successful eleventh grade pupils on GCSE results day. And grinning, always grinning.

He finished typing, clicked on his mouse a couple of times, then leaned forward in his chair. He clasped his hands together on the desk in front of him.

"So. Feeling better, Joe?"

"Yes, much. Thanks."

"Good. That's good. Migraine, was it?"

"Food poisoning."

"Ah. The old Delhi belly. Nasty. You're OK now, though?"

"Yes. I'm OK."

This is ridiculous. Here I am, my marriage on the critical list, getting pulled in by the police, and I've got to justify one day off sick. Hasn't he got better things to do with his time?

"Spent most of yesterday laid up, did you?"

"Most of it."

"At home?"

"Yes."

"You didn't go out at all?"

So someone did spot me out of the house. I could bluff him, say they were mistaken, or I could just admit it.

The latter seemed a better option.

"Felt a bit better in the afternoon. Went to pick my son up from school."

He nodded slowly, fixing me with what he probably thought was a penetrating stare. "And how old is your son now?"

"He just turned four in the summer. He's in reception at Saint Hilda's."

"It's a good school. Good record."

"He seems to enjoy it."

Draper leaned back in his chair, hands clasped in his lap. "Joe, do you know about my role at our school?"

"You cover pastoral issues, disciplinary, staff development . . . other things."

"Other things. Yes. Do you know why I've asked to see you today?"

"No, not really."

"You know I also deal with the PR side of things? The reputation of the school?"

In fact, I didn't. I knew he did next to no actual teaching of real live pupils.

"Of course. Reputation is important."

"You know the importance the *head* attaches to reputation, don't you, Joe? Reputation is linked to parental choice, getting the right parents is linked to pupil achievement, which in turn is linked to the school's reputation." He made a circling gesture in the air with his index finger. "It's a virtuous circle."

"Sure."

"Or a vicious circle, depending on your point of view."

"Right."

"Reputation is really important to him, Joe. I mean *super* important."

"I understand. But I don't see how me being off sick can affect the school's reputation. I think on the whole my sickness record is good."

"Are you a fan of social media, Joe?"

"A fan? I use it like everyone else, I suppose."

"Do you go on Facebook much, for example?"

"I'm on it from time to time, yes. Not that often."

He nodded. "Biggest social network in the world, you know. More than 1.2 billion users, which equates to every fifth person on the planet. Amazing stat, isn't it? Have you looked at it recently?"

"Yesterday morning I had a quick look, I think."

The stuff Ben had posted on my Facebook account was too cryptic, too obscure, to mean much to anyone else. Draper couldn't be referring to that. Could he?

"Have you been on Facebook this morning?"

"Don't really have time to look at it in the mornings."

"Last night?"

"No."

"Because, as I said, the head is a big believer in the power of reputation, of leading by example. The importance of staff setting the very highest example for our young people to follow."

"Of course."

"Which is why I wanted to see you this morning."

"I'm sorry, Carl, I'm not sure what you're talking about."

He had two widescreen monitors side by side on his desk, and he turned one toward me.

"I'm talking about this, Joe." He indicated the screen. "Recognize anyone?"

Facebook. A picture of me.

A picture of me being escorted into a police station by two detectives.

37

The picture showed me walking into Kilburn Police Station on Salisbury Road, flanked by Naylor and Redford. My face was etched with worry. DS Redford had one hand touching my elbow and was indicating the way with her other hand. I didn't even remember her doing it at the time, but now, looking at the picture, it added a whole new perspective: as if I were being escorted into the station against my will.

Something was not right with the picture.

There. It was subtle. You had to look twice to be sure. Handcuffs.

Leaning forward, I squinted at the screen.

I was handcuffed to DS Redford. My left wrist, her right.

Someone had Photoshopped the image to add handcuffs where there had been none in reality. They had done a good job of it too. They even looked real to me, and I knew they were fake. It was skillful, subtle work. And damning.

Jesus Christ.

Next to it, a picture of me standing outside the station after the interview, on the pavement, looking shell-shocked, stunned, as if I didn't know where I

was or what day it was. The pictures looked like they
had been taken from across the street. Each picture
had a date and time stamp on the bottom right-hand
corner, showing they had been taken an hour and ten
minutes apart, yesterday morning.

I looked at the text.

Ollie Fulton shared **David Bramley**'s photo—
13 hours ago Gotcha! Look who's been arrested
Joe Lynch! Looks like a few months/years/
decades off work might be needed from **Haddon
Park Academy** Lol #IFoughtTheLaw ;-)

It had eighty-nine likes and forty-one comments.

It was the Facebook account of someone I didn't
know. Ollie Fulton. One of Draper's friends, presumably.

"Who's David Bramley?" I said, trying to keep my
voice level.

"These pictures," Draper continued, ignoring my
question, "were shared on Facebook a number of times
yesterday afternoon. They were then shared by half a
dozen of our students, and, well, it pretty much went
viral at that point. On a school-wide scale, at least."

Now I understood the behavior of the smirking
boy with the untucked shirt: he'd seen the picture of
me going into the police station, handcuffed. Probably
everyone in school had seen it. Circulated and shared
on social media like so much celebrity tittle-tattle.

"Viral, as in it spread like smallpox," I said, trying
to keep the nerves out of my voice.

"Well, you know, pretty much every student in school has a Facebook account. Even though they're supposed to be thirteen to qualify, there's no actual check to verify that. They're all on it, and their parents too, which makes this place one massive connected network of three thousand–plus people. You know what Facebook's like: most of the things they're posting and sharing are cat videos, selfies, and shots of what they're having for tea. Pretty dull. So a picture of a teacher at their school getting arrested is bound to get a lot of interest and spread pretty fast. Which is exactly what happened."

"I wasn't arrested," I said, my jaw tight.

"You're handcuffed," he replied, pointing to the screen.

"No, that's been Photoshopped onto the picture."

"Really?" He sounded skeptical.

"Yes. It's been added digitally to the picture after it was taken."

He leaned in to look at the picture again. "Looks real enough to me."

"That's the point of Photoshop. To make it look real."

"You know what I mean, though. Arrested or interviewed or helping the police with their inquiries, or whatever words they use. The distinction gets lost in translation almost immediately. All those people on Facebook see is a teacher from their school getting pulled in by the cops, wearing handcuffs, and given a grilling."

"It wasn't a grilling. It was a conversation."

"Doesn't really matter, does it, Joe? People will make their own assumptions."

David Bramley—whom I'd never heard of—had

tagged Haddon Park in the picture, so it would have appeared on the school's Facebook page, for pupils and parents to see. As well as the countless other Facebook accounts it had been shared on since yesterday afternoon. And commented on. And liked.

"Why haven't you untagged the school in his caption? You could at least stop it from appearing on the Haddon Park account if you did that."

"It's next on my list for today, Joe. After seeing you."

"Who's Ollie Fulton anyway?" I managed to say.

"One of my Facebook friends, used to work with his father. What were you talking to the police about, Joe?"

"A friend of mine's missing. Ben Delaney. They thought I might be able to help find him."

"They took you to the police station for that?"

"It's where they work," I said.

"How long did they hold you for?"

"They didn't *hold* me. I wasn't arrested. They asked for my help, that's all."

"Help with their inquiries?"

"Yes."

"And you told them what?"

"That I didn't know where he was, but he wasn't missing."

Draper pulled a face like I'd said something stupid. "I'm not sure that makes sense, Joe."

"What I mean is, I saw him yesterday morning, so he isn't missing. He's been in touch with me. He's just messing everyone around."

"Presumably the police would take a pretty dim view of that."

"They're not the only ones. His wife's tearing her hair out."

"So how long were you in the police station for?" he continued.

"Not sure exactly. An hour, maybe."

"And then they just let you go?"

"I told you, I wasn't arrested; I was just answering some questions, trying to help them track him down."

"Something doesn't add up, Joe."

Tell me about it, I thought.

"I'm as much in the dark as everyone else," I said.

Draper looked thoughtful for a moment, rubbing his chin. "This Delaney person, does he have any children?"

"A daughter, Alice. She's fourteen."

"That's it. Alice." He tapped his computer keyboard. "Here we go. I knew the surname rang a bell—she's in tenth grade. Something of a star pupil, by the looks of it. Predictions A-star, A-star, A-star across the board."

"She's a bright kid."

He sat back in his chair again, lacing his fingers together over his small potbelly.

"So is there anything else I should know, Joe? Anything else you want to tell me?"

"About what?"

"About this . . . situation we find ourselves in."

I briefly considered telling him about Ben and Mel's affair but quickly dismissed the idea. It would be another stick to beat me with, another way to humiliate me. And it was none of his damn business anyway.

"No, I don't think so."

"Sure?"

"Yes."

"Anything else that the police were talking to you about? That might be related to Mr. Delaney's disappearing act?"

I got the uncomfortable feeling that he knew more

than he was letting on. Or maybe he was just fishing. It was impossible to tell with him.

"It was just what I told you. They're looking for Ben, talking to all his friends. Trying to establish his movements in the last few days. His wife's out of her mind with worry."

"Poor woman," Draper said without much conviction.

"Just so we're clear on this point, Carl—for the record—the police are not accusing *me* of anything. They didn't arrest me, I'm not involved, I didn't *do* anything. People need to know that."

"Understood."

"Good. As long as that's clear."

"To a large degree, it's not actually important *what* they pulled you in for. What *is* important is that we can't afford for the school's reputation to be besmirched. I also understand from the deputy head that two detectives were here yesterday afternoon. Came here, Joe, to the school. To ask about you. Seems awfully involved just for a missing person, doesn't it?"

"They're being methodical."

"You know how the head feels about having police on-site. It's the sort of visit that makes the rumor mill grind that little bit faster."

Naylor. So much for his assurance that he'd be discreet.

"Sorry about that," I said through gritted teeth. "I'd no idea they were going to come here."

"So, in light of all this"—he gestured at the computer monitor—"I've talked to the head this morning. He's really rather exercised about the whole thing."

He let it hang there for a minute, seeming to relish the moment.

"And?" I said finally.

"And as of now, you're suspended from teaching duties until further notice."

I wasn't sure I'd heard him correctly. "You're suspending me?"

"That's right. Effective immediately."

"On the basis of a picture on Facebook?"

"On the basis of you being embroiled in a police investigation."

"Embroiled? What does that mean?"

"You're part of a police investigation. The school has to be seen to have acted responsibly if this leaks to the media. Which, as we both know, is pretty much inevitable in this day and age."

What he was saying finally registered with me. "You're actually serious, aren't you?"

"Deadly serious. There will also be an internal investigation overseen by the chair of governors, as per school regs."

"Whatever happened to being innocent until proven guilty?"

"This is not a court of law, Joe." He spread his hands wide as if indicating the world around us. "This is the court of public opinion, which is much more fickle and likely to judge by appearances."

"A kangaroo court, you mean."

"It's reality. It's how the world is, how people are."

"The rule of the mob, more like."

"The decision has been taken."

"You can't do this."

"I'm doing it. With the head's full sanction."

I felt the blood pounding in my head, and I swallowed hard on a dry throat. "This is crazy. It's not fair. It's wrong."

"Don't worry, you've got enough years of service here, so you'll be on full pay. At least for the time being."

"The pay's not the point. People will assume there's no smoke without fire." I was suddenly furious at the unfairness of it all, shaking with anger. "It's my *reputation* we're talking about here."

"No." He pointed a stubby index finger at me. "It's the *school's* reputation we're talking about. And as we both know, no teacher here is bigger than the school. No one is more important than the school. You seem to have forgotten that."

I shook my head. "I haven't forgotten anything. I haven't forgotten the nine years of good service I've given this place."

"Every so often we have to take one for the team, my friend. Today just happens to be your turn."

I thought for a moment how satisfying it would be to lean over his desk, grab the front of his shirt, and pound my fist into his smug, self-satisfied face. See if he'd like to "take one for the team." I looked away from him and put my clenched fists on my knees, trying to get my emotions back in check.

"How long am I suspended for?"

"Until this has run its course. Until your business with the police is resolved."

"I haven't *got* any business with the police! They just wanted to talk to me!"

Draper sat back in his chair. "Shouting at me won't help your cause."

I took a couple of deep breaths, feeling my heart thumping against my rib cage.

"How do you expect me to react? This is complete bullshit."

"Using inappropriate language won't help you either."

"Right. Whatever. I've got to talk to my union rep."

"Of course. Have him call Jane and we'll get an appointment in the diary."

"Are we finished?"

"I think so." He gave me a thin smile. "For now, at least."

I stood up and headed for the door.

"Oh, and by the way, Joe?"

"What?"

"Would you do something for me?"

"Do I have a choice?"

He had already returned his attention to the computer monitor on his desk. "Stay off school property while you're suspended. There's a good chap."

I slammed his office door on the way out.

38

It seemed as if everyone in school was staring at me as I walked, head down, back to my car. Registration was over, and a thousand kids were heading to their first lesson of the day, in pairs and threes, in groups, in packs, and I found myself right in the middle of them. Every pupil I passed gave me a look of recognition. Before, I had just been a member of the teaching staff, known to some, semi-anonymous to the rest. Now I was *that teacher who got arrested on Facebook*, and it seemed everyone knew me. My progress through the crowd of navy blazers was accompanied by whispered conversations and pictures snapped as I passed by.

How long will it take before this is forgotten? Weeks? Months?

Never?

Back in my car, I synced my cell phone to my Facebook account and found the picture of me being led into Kilburn Police Station. I couldn't delete it—or the copies that had been made by others who had shared it—but by untagging myself I could at least reduce its visibility just a little. It wasn't much, but it was better than nothing.

A thought came to me. I clicked on David Bramley's account and checked through his profile. His avatar picture was Hulk's snarling face from the latest *Avengers* movie. No information about school, or hometown, or relationship status. He had eleven friends, a few of whom I recognized, and had set up his account this year. He had only ever posted once: the picture of me being led into the police station. There was almost nothing that looked genuine about the account, but I needed to know who my enemies were—even though I had a pretty good idea who "David Bramley" would turn out to be. I sent him a friend request.

I drove home and sat in the kitchen, talking on the phone to my union representative. It turned out there wasn't much that could be done, in the short term, about being suspended. An appeal would take several weeks before the process even got going, for appointments to be made, meetings to be had, second opinions to be given on whether my suspension was legitimate in the circumstances. If there was no further action taken on the suspension, it would be expunged from my record and would not count against me. But that was the best I could hope for.

For the time being at least, I was suspended, and that was that. It felt weird to be sitting at home on a Tuesday morning during term time, the house quiet, watching the clock tick by. First period, second period. It was just after 10:00 A.M. and I should have been discussing *The Coral Island* with the children of 7D. Instead I was sitting at the breakfast bar in my kitchen, drinking tea, wondering how everything had gotten messed up so badly.

A few days ago, my life had been pretty good. I just hadn't realized it. *You don't know what you've got till it's gone*. It was a cliché for a good reason: because it was true. Now I had to put my family back together again, and it seemed that meeting Ben might not be a bad place to start. Not only to tell him to stay away from Mel—and ensure he got the message loud and clear—but to get a picture of him. Give the picture to the police, get them off my back.

My phone buzzed twice on the kitchen table: two notifications. David Bramley had accepted my friend request, and then messaged me straight away.

How's work, big fella?

I stared at the message. Could he be so brazen about it? Wondering how he had found out so fast about my suspension, I hit *Reply*.

Who is this?

The reply was almost instant.

Who do you think?

There was only one person it could be. *Ben, you bastard*.

You're enjoying this, aren't you?

The reply was a single emoticon.

☺

He had been two steps ahead of me since the beginning, and it seemed he still was. It was time to end this. He had made his point, had his fun with me. Now it was time to get on with our lives: him with his wife, and me with mine. Frankly if I never saw him again after that, it would be just fine with me.

I typed another message.

Let's meet up. Properly this time.

The reply was just three letters.

Lol

The anger came again then, the blood pounding in my ears. He *was* enjoying tormenting me, dropping me in it with the police and with school. He was doing what he said he'd do—ruining my life—and laughing at me while I squirmed on the hook.

The phone rang in my hand before I could send another reply.

A cell phone number I didn't recognize. "Hello?"

"Joe, it's Peter Larssen. Can you talk?"

"Sure."

"I was going to leave a message. Didn't think you'd be free before lunch."

I told him about the Facebook picture and my suspension from school.

"Surely that's harassment?" I said. "We can do something about it legally, right?"

"We could look into that, yes. Take a screenshot of the post and email it to me."

"It's proof that he's hounding me, trying to sabotage my career."

"Hmm." Larssen didn't sound convinced. "The truth is, Joe, things have been moving rather fast on the police side. That was actually why I was calling."

"What do you mean?"

"Things may be more serious than we previously thought."

My stomach lurched. "More serious?"

"They're starting to focus on the theory that something bad may have happened to Ben Delaney."

I sat down in a kitchen chair. "That's exactly what he wants them to think. But I thought the police were finding proof that he was alive? Proof-of-life investigation, Naylor said?"

"They're looking, but if they can't find proof—and soon—they'll start to go down different avenues. Like an accident, or the possibility that foul play might be involved."

"Foul play," I repeated. It was a phrase from the TV news, from newspapers, but not one that was supposed to feature in your day-to-day life. "Involving me?"

"Possibly."

"But that's crazy! He's harassing me on social media, he's posting things trying to get me in trouble, trying to drive a wedge between me and Mel. I saw him yesterday. We spoke to him on the phone the day before that. I was talking to him literally a minute before you called."

"You spoke to him?"

"On Messenger."

"Ah. From his account?"

"No, he's using a fake account under the name David Bramley. The point is, he's taking potshots at me, so he's obviously alive and well and hiding away somewhere."

"Why would he have disappeared?"

"He hasn't disappeared; he just doesn't want to go

back to his wife. He wants mine instead. That's why we need to find him, put a stop to this."

Larssen paused for a moment, his voice slow and measured. "You could have posted those updates yourself."

"That's insane."

"You could be posting as Ben, or David Bramley, or whatever his name is. Harassing yourself, in effect. Stranger things have been known."

My chest felt tight, as if there were something pressing down on it. "You don't really believe that, do you?"

"Of course not. But Naylor might. It doesn't help that Ben's not been seen for several days."

"*I've* seen him."

"You don't count, Joe."

"What, so I'm a suspect?"

"That's one of their lines of inquiry."

I thought for a moment, trying to take all of it in. This had to stop.

"What are you doing in the next hour?" I said.

"My diary's clear until 1:30 P.M."

"Good. Meet me at Kilburn Police Station in twenty minutes."

39

"I'm being set up," I said.

Naylor looked at me across the pockmarked table, frowning slightly.

"Explain," he said.

And so I did. About the Facebook post, my suspension at work, my conversations on Messenger with David Bramley. About his message on my computer at home and his obsession with Mel.

"He already hacked my Facebook account on Thursday night, like I told you yesterday. He's hacked my home PC, he's basically trying to wreck my career, and he's taunting me on social media using a pseudonym. I just want all of it to stop now. Enough's enough."

We were back in interview room 3 at the station, Larssen by my side. Naylor had given me the standard police caution at the start of our conversation, and now he scrolled up the exchange of messages between me and Bramley, studying a few longer than others, before handing the phone back to me.

"Well?" I said.

The detective shrugged. "You could have sent those messages yourself."

"What possible reason would I have to do that?"

"To put a different slant on things."

"I don't understand."

"So it looks like you're the victim, not him."

"The victim of what?"

"A smear campaign. Or whatever it is you claim Mr. Delaney is doing." He crossed his arms. "We'll run down this Bramley account on Facebook anyway. That should tell us one way or another."

"There's no way I could have taken that picture, and anyway why would I post something that would get me in trouble at work? With handcuffs Photoshopped onto a picture so it looks like I got arrested?"

"I don't know, Joe. Why would you do that?"

"You must be able to see that Ben is behind this, surely? The spurned lover? He's trying to break me down, get me out of the picture so he can have Mel for himself. He has to *win* at everything; that's just who he is. Whatever the cost." I leaned forward, fists on the table. "He's trying to destroy my family."

Larssen put a hand on my arm. "Calm down, Joe."

Naylor sat back in his chair. "My problem with all of this, Joe, is that you're the only one who's allegedly *seen* Mr. Delaney. Corresponded with him. Spoken to him."

"Mel was there too when we spoke to him. She can back that up."

"OK, we'll talk to your wife again. But it's all coming through *you*, Joe. Do you see? Everything seems to revolve around you. Why is that?"

"Because Ben is a very clever guy. Smarter than I am. Smarter than most."

"That may well be true. But the proof-of-life investigation has come back with absolutely zero for the last twenty-four hours, and unless that changes soon and we get a sniff that he's safe and well, we'll have to start working on the basis that he might not be."

"Proof? What about Beth Delaney? She was there when her husband came home on Thursday night, hours after I supposedly beat him up in that hotel parking lot."

Naylor shook his head. "She didn't see him. She *heard* someone moving about in her house. Through a closed door, a floor below her. She *heard* someone."

"What about the texts he sent me? The post on Facebook? The meeting at the country park? Surely that's all proof?"

Naylor looked from me to DS Redford by his side and back to me again.

"I wasn't planning on doing this just yet, but since you're here, we might as well." He opened a black ring binder in front of him on the table and flipped a few sheets until he found what he was looking for.

"So you *have* found something?" I said.

"Yes and no."

"What does that mean?"

Larssen shifted uncomfortably in his seat next to me. "My client would certainly appreciate it if you can give us a heads-up, Marcus."

"Sure, OK. So the texts first. We pulled the records from your network provider and from Ben's. You received three texts from Ben Delaney's cell phone on Sunday evening, two on Monday morning. Correct?"

"Yes. The first ones arranging the meeting, then when we were at the country park in the morning."

"When we interrogate cell phone records, we can establish which cell phone mast your phone was 'talking to' at any point during a call. Which means we can work out with a high degree of accuracy where you were—or at least where your phone was—when a call was made or a text was sent."

"I was at home on Sunday evening and at Fryent Country Park on Monday morning. So that's what my phone records will tell you. Or they should do."

"Here's the thing, Joe." He turned another page in his file, ran his finger down a column of figures. "When you sent those texts on Sunday, the records show they went via a cell phone mast at the end of your road. It's the nearest transmitter to your house."

"Well . . . that's right, isn't it?"

"The texts sent from Ben Delaney's phone went via the same mast."

I looked from one detective to the other. "I'm confused. What does that mean?"

Naylor frowned as if he were having to explain something very simple to someone very slow.

"Rachel, can you elaborate for Mr. Lynch?"

DS Redford took up the explanation. "Both phones—yours *and* his—were within the narrowly defined range of the same phone mast when those texts were sent and received. It means both phones were very close to each other."

"How close?" Larssen said.

"*Very* close," Redford replied.

Naylor said, "As if the same person was holding both phones, for example."

"Or if he was right outside my house! What the hell?"

Redford held a hand up, cutting me off. "I'm not finished," she said, her soft northern vowels a counterpoint to the hard knot of fear growing in my stomach. "On Monday morning, we get the exact same thing happening, the same pattern, in a different location. Again, both handsets within the very narrow range of the same cell phone tower."

"But he *was* near to me, maybe fifty or sixty meters away."

"Witnessed by you and no one else," Naylor said quietly.

"So what are you saying, that I sent those messages from Ben's cell phone? Why would I do that?"

Larssen put a hand on my arm. "Joe, take it easy." He turned to the detectives. "There was a Facebook post on Saturday evening. Mr. Delaney said he was fine and that he'd been away to think about things."

Naylor flipped to another page in his black ring binder. "OK. The Facebook post next."

Something in the way he said it made the knot of fear in my guts grow heavier, but I said nothing.

"Facebook always take bloody ages to turn over location data, so we don't have much on that front yet. What we do have is a quick and dirty forensic authorship analysis, done by academics at Goldsmiths of the Facebook post and those text messages. They can do an initial analysis in a matter of hours, and they're always eager to help."

He snapped the ring binder open and removed two sheets, laying them side by side on the table in front of me. The page on the right was a screenshot of Ben's message from Saturday:

Needed to get my head sorted; it's been good to get away. And I've always loved it when everything starts falling into place.
"The truth of the battle is whatever the victor deems it to be . . ."

The page on the left contained multiple screen-shots of previous Facebook status updates.

"These are all Ben's as well, are they?"

Naylor nodded. "They're all from his account. So our pointy-headed friends at Goldsmiths did a comparison of grammar and punctuation in Saturday's Facebook post to his previous stuff. Here's an example: their analysis showed Mr. Delaney had never used a semicolon or a period in a Facebook update—until Saturday, when he posted to say he was all right."

"OK." I scanned the printouts on the desk, hoping to find something to prove the detective wrong. But there was nothing.

"The language analysis shows that he's not a big fan of punctuation on social media. Never has been. Until this Saturday just past, when he seems to have had something of a grammar revelation and he's used a semicolon, an apostrophe, and two full stops in the same post. The text messages also include discrepancies in the use of apostrophes, capital letters, and the spelling of certain common words where he's previously used textspeak abbreviations, but this time types them out in full."

Larssen's face was impassive, his unblinking eyes on the detectives.

"And what preliminary conclusions have your college people drawn?" he said calmly.

"Their considered opinion is that Saturday's Face-book post"—Naylor tapped a thick index finger on the right-hand page—"is very unlikely to have been written by the same person who wrote these previous posts. Likewise, these five text messages were very unlikely to have been written by the person who was previously sending texts from this number. In other words, not Ben Delaney."

"Well, that doesn't make sense," I said.

"How about you, Joe? You're a history teacher, right?"

"English."

"Bet you could teach Mr. Delaney a thing or two about grammar and punctuation, couldn't you?"

I said nothing, not wanting to dignify his tacit accusation with a response.

"Spelling and full stops, apostrophes and semicolons," Naylor said. "You must know all the rules back to front and inside out."

"Ben could have written them that way deliberately, to throw you off the scent."

It didn't sound convincing, even to me.

Naylor said, "Some sort of criminal mastermind, is he?"

"He's a very, very clever guy. I wouldn't underestimate him."

"Proof of life, Joe. That's what we're about right now. That's the name of the game. And I'll be honest with you: this latest stuff is giving me real cause for concern."

"What about the message that appeared on my computer at home yesterday? He blames me for everything."

"No one saw that apart from you. Ditto your 'close encounter' with Mr. Delaney at the country park yesterday morning. You're the only witness. How's your hand, by the way? Your knuckles all right?"

He indicated the dark bruises and scabbed-over scratches across my right knuckles, where I had stumbled in the woods.

"Fine." I put my hands in my lap. My mouth was dry, and my head was starting to ache. I wanted more than anything to be out of this room, out of here, away from this place.

"Is there anything else, Joe? Anything else you want to tell us?"

Larssen was about to speak, but I cut him off.

"I've told you everything."

"Like I said, Joe, the name of the game is proof of life. But it might not be for very much longer."

I stared at him across the table, my jaw rigid.

"You want proof? I'll get it for you. I'll get it myself."

40

I sat in my car, sweating and shaking, in a side street behind the police station. The plan had been to convince Naylor that I was being framed, and that had blown up in my face in spectacular fashion. Larssen had told me to go home, stay home, and take it easy—but that was easier said than done when your life was disintegrating before your eyes.

I looked again at my last exchange with David Bramley on Messenger.

Let's meet up. Properly this time

And his response:

Lol

But you wouldn't be laughing if I were standing in front of you right now, mate.
He might be shouting, or arguing, or maybe even telling me how much he loved my wife and how I was to blame for everything—but I was pretty damn certain he wouldn't be *laughing out loud*.

Standing in front of him was exactly where I needed to be. Face-to-face. No social media, no gadgets, no emails, no direct messages, no screens, no internet. No bullshit. Just two guys having a conversation. An actual, real conversation.

He had been close on Sunday evening—close enough to my house to fool Naylor with the phone data. And again on Monday, at the park—watching me, stalking me, coming close then disappearing like a shadow. Because he knew the police would interrogate the phone logs, and he knew what they would show. There had been no one else there by the lake. No one but Ben.

I turned the ignition and sat for a moment, listening to the purr of the engine. Turned it off again. I couldn't go home, not yet.

Proof of life.

The clues were there; I just had to find them.

I got my cell phone out. Ben had 389 friends on Facebook, and we had a couple of dozen in common, but most of his were not familiar to me. So I sent friend requests to the twenty or so people who regularly left comments in Ben's feed. Some would ignore me, but others who were less discerning—who just wanted to boost their virtual popularity—would accept, and then I could start going through their profiles too, looking for that one nugget of information that would help me put an end to Ben's campaign. Mel commented quite regularly on his Facebook posts, but nothing that aroused suspicion. A scroll down her timeline yielded pictures of William, selfies of Mel, pictures of the two of them together.

A picture from March—more than six months ago—made me stop and scroll back. A flash of recognition. Mel had shared a link to a gallery of pictures posted to celebrate twenty years since her GCSEs, entitled: "Good times at Claremont Comprehensive." The title image was from some sort of drama production, a lineup of teenagers in medieval dress, swords, and gowns to go with their nineties haircuts. Four men—or, rather, sixteen-year-old boys—and four young women, arm in arm, full of smiles, receiving the applause of the audience at the end of a show.

The picture was familiar, but not from March. Much more recently. It was one of the pictures that Beth and Ben had on the wall of their living room. And there Beth was, in the center of the shot, beaming at the audience and looking like it was the best day of her life. She looked so happy, with her long hair, huge smile, cheeks flushed with the buzz of a great performance. She looked ready to take on the world. A smiling sixteen-year-old Mel was there too, at the other end of the row. Both girls looked like innocents, untroubled and unguarded, with no idea of the loathing and jealousy and destruction that one of them would unleash on the other with her infidelity twenty years later, or how many lives would be ruined. How friendship would turn to hate.

My chest ached with the feeling of something lost.

I stared at the picture until I couldn't stand it anymore, then scrolled down to the comments just to get it off the screen.

Jo Knightley

March 29

Great days xxx

Martin Coffey

March 29

Had forgotten about this! How young do u look **Beth Delaney**?

Ian Howard

March 29

Love this. Remember when **Charlotte Lowe** cracked up on stage when she was supposed to be dying? x

Charlotte Lowe

March 29

Least I didn't forget my lines **Ian Howard**! ☺

Claire Grimble

March 29

Nice hair **Mark Ruddington** xx

Mark Ruddington

March 29

The after-show party sticks in my memory for some reason, **Melissa Lynch** ;-)

And so it went on, more than fifty comments and eighty likes on that post alone. The cryptic comment about the after-show party was intriguing. Mel had not responded to it, which was a bit weird—she'd shared the link to the pictures but not responded to a comment directed at her. The guy who'd posted the gallery in the first place—Mark Ruddington—was not a name that was familiar.

I tapped on his profile picture to take a closer look at him, then double-tapped on the school picture to zoom in on the smiling group of young actors. I was 95 percent sure that the black-clad teenager with his arm around Mel was Mark Ruddington. There was a certain facial similarity between him and Ben. Both dark-haired, both about the same height, same build. I remembered again the drunken game of "stand up if you've ever" and Mel's single infidelity—which she'd said was at school and therefore didn't count.

Perhaps Mark Ruddington had been that first time she had been unfaithful. She had never told me who at the time—she had just pulled me close and given me a drunken kiss—but the more I thought about it, the more there seemed to be a kind of weird logic to it, a parallel. That she had cheated twice in her life, twenty years apart, with men who bore an uncanny resemblance to each other. First this Mark Ruddington guy, then Ben. Maybe that was just the type she went for, when she got bored.

The after-show party sticks in my memory for some reason, Melissa Lynch ;-)

Mark Ruddington was married and living in Enfield. He had an open Facebook profile, so I spent ten minutes stalking through everything he'd posted this year. It seemed more important than ever to find out about my wife, to find out who she *really* was. To know about the experiences that had made her, the teenage infidelity that she had admitted to under the influence of house party tequila. It seemed that lots of people knew her better than I did. I sent him a friend request. Maybe a chat on Messenger would get a bit more out of him.

Staring at the phone's small screen was making my eyes ache—an hour had passed with no sign of Ben. It was time to try something else.

The Delaneys' home phone rang six times then went to voice mail, Ben's brief-and-to-the-point message carrying just the faintest trace of his Sunderland accent. A while ago he'd explained to me the difference between Sunderland and Newcastle accents, but I still couldn't really tell them apart. The second time it went to voice mail again. I hung up without leaving a message. It occurred to me that I could do better than calling Beth up for a chat. I was a teacher with no one to teach, no homework to mark, no lesson plans to prepare.

Thirty-five minutes later, I was parking on a wide, tree-lined street in Hampstead, a slow-curving avenue of high walls and immaculate driveways. It looked exactly like what it was: a street full of multimillionaires. Immediately opposite me was an imposing Edwardian house that had been tastefully extended several times. Like its widely spaced neighbors, it was elevated slightly from the street at the end of a sloping driveway so that its considerable size was exaggerated even further to the casual passerby.

Ben's house.

He probably wouldn't be very pleased with me visiting his wife, alone and unannounced, in the middle of the day. Just dropping in out of the blue, asking a few probing questions about our mutually cheating spouses. He wouldn't be pleased at all. In fact, knowing Ben, he'd probably be mightily pissed off.

Good, I thought. Let him be on the back foot for once. See how he likes it.

41

Ben's house sat at the end of a gently sloping gravel driveway, bordered by immaculate shrubs and fruit trees. An ornate ivory-painted birdhouse stood on a tall pole halfway up the drive. There were two cars: Beth's silver Mercedes Estate, and another of Ben's cars, a white convertible Audi TT. All his cars were white. The house itself was huge, a three-story Edwardian family home built when six kids was the norm and servants lived on the top floor. Additions over the last century had included a tennis court, game room, and a conservatory big enough to seat twenty. As was the way of things, even as family sizes had grown smaller the house grew bigger still: the Delaneys—who had just one child—had owned it barely a year and were already busy with plans to extend it further.

Watching from the street, I saw the front door open. Beth emerged, slowly, holding something in both hands out in front of her—an upturned pint glass, facedown on a postcard. She knelt by the flowerbed beneath the bay window, lifted the pint glass, and tapped the postcard gently. *A spider.* She knelt for a moment longer, then stood up and went back inside the house.

Gravel crunched beneath my feet as I walked up the driveway. The doorbell chimed with old-fashioned tones, echoing in the rooms beyond. I waited and was about to press it again when Beth opened the front door, her weary look quickly turning to surprise when she saw me on the doorstep. She looked beautiful—she pretty much always looked beautiful—but she wore no makeup to disguise the paleness of her face. She never wore makeup. Like she never did bright colors—always calm shades, soft tones.

Beth Delaney had always believed in the fundamental goodness of people. But her expression suggested she'd just discovered a different truth, and it had tilted her world on its axis. I felt hugely sorry for her.

"Oh," she said in a small voice. "It's you."

"Can I come in, Beth?"

She hesitated, looking past me down the drive. "What do you want?"

"To talk."

"About?"

"Ben."

She pushed the door almost shut, and I heard the rattle and click of metal sliding into place. When the door reopened again, a thick brass chain stretched across the gap.

It wasn't surprise on her face—it was fear.

"Why did you come here?" she said. "To our house?"

"I thought it would be easier to talk face-to-face, rather than on the phone."

"The police were here again this morning," she said. "Asking about Ben and *that woman*."

"You mean Mel?"

"She lied about you and Ben falling out on Thursday evening."

"She lied about a lot of things."

"The police said you had a fight with Ben. You hurt him."

"He's trying to set me up, Beth."

And maybe he's not working alone, I thought.

She frowned and stared hard at me. "What do you mean? How?"

"He's trying to get me in trouble with the police. At work. At home."

"Why would he do that?"

"Because of him and Mel. Listen—I've seen him. I've seen your husband."

Her face was suddenly brighter, her eyes wider, and it was clear how hard Ben's disappearing act had hit her. He was the head of the household, the millionaire entrepreneur alpha male, and I guess she had grown used to living in his shadow. Without him she was lost.

"Really? Honestly? Is he OK?"

"I didn't talk to him, but yes, he seemed OK."

She pursed her lips as if she were about to cry. "And he's all right?"

"He seemed all right."

"Thank God." She put a hand over her mouth and stifled a sob. "Thank God. I've been so worried."

"Can I come in, Beth? We could talk more inside."

She stared at me for a moment longer, then pushed the heavy front door shut. I heard the door chain being taken off, and she opened it again, still looking unsure whether I was safe to be around. The home phone was clutched in her other hand, and I realized with a jolt that she must have been ready to call the police.

The Delaneys' living room was huge, handsomely furnished in cream and white, and dominated by a sixty-inch plasma TV on the far wall. The large dining table was piled high with paperwork, files, and ring binders. Bay windows looked out onto the extensive back garden, workers camped in the middle of the lawn with their excavators and tarpaulins, digging out the open-air pool and summerhouse that were Ben's latest projects. One entire side of the room was dominated by framed pictures of family scenes—weddings, christenings, birthday parties—and groups of friends arm in arm. The shot from the school play was there too, the one on Mel's Facebook timeline, a row of smiling teenagers dressed to play Shakespeare.

Beth gestured for me to sit down on the corner sofa at the far end of the room. She took a seat at the dining table, at least a dozen feet between us, nearer the door.

"It's a bit of a mess. I wasn't expecting visitors."

I gestured to the files and folders on the dining table. "What is all that?"

"On Saturday, I had this mad idea that Ben going off might be to do with his company, somehow. Maybe there was a problem and he hadn't told me. So I was trying to find something, any kind of small clue about what's going on. And then Sunday happened, and I just haven't felt like clearing up since."

"I don't think it's about his company, Beth. I think it's about his obsession with Mel. It's about destroying a rival. It's about winning."

She winced visibly. "He always has to win."

I told her the whole story about Ben and Mel's relationship. His obsession with her. About the message that had appeared on my computer and Ben's mission to beat me by whatever means—fair or foul. I left out the part about my latest suspicion: that Mel wasn't necessarily on my side either. I didn't even want to say it out loud. Not yet.

"He's been in contact with me today, on Messenger."

"Really?" She looked hopeful at this. "What has he said? Can I see the messages?"

I handed my phone to her, and she scrolled through the messages, the look of hope slowly leaving her face.

"Who's David Bramley?"

"Ben's set up a fake account so he can taunt me. They're his initials, but reversed, do you see? DB instead of BD. Just close enough for me to know who it is."

"He doesn't mention me or Alice."

"No."

She handed the phone back. "He's not asked you about me?"

"No."

"Tell me about when you saw him. How did he look?"

She listened as I described our near meeting at the country park. She asked again quietly, hopefully, whether Ben had looked OK. Then there was silence for a moment between us, each caught in the very personal pain of betrayal.

"I wish I'd never found those damned pictures on his phone. Never found out about all the lies. Given the chance to turn the clock back to Sunday morning, I would just put that cell phone back in his desk drawer, turn the key, and never open it again."

"But you did see the photos."

"Yes. I did."

"And so here we are."

She looked as if she might cry. "Yes." It came out as a whisper.

"Look, it's done now," I said, surprised at how Sunday's anger had deserted her. "Neither of us can put the genie back in the bottle. Maybe it's better that way, better for everyone to move on."

"I just wish he'd call me. Wherever he is."

Something came back to me from the story in the *Standard*. "What about Alex Kolnik?"

"What about him?"

"Ben drove him out of business a few months ago. Big guy, maybe six foot four, ponytail, goatee beard, trench coat. Brain the size of a planet, apparently, but looks like something out of *Sons of Anarchy*. His nickname is Kalashnikov because of his initials—AK. Have you seen him recently?"

"There was a chap like that, came to the house the other week. Him and a couple of others."

"What happened?"

"Ben answered the door, and they talked for a bit; it got heated, there was shouting and swearing. Alex was threatening all kinds of things. Ben ended up getting one of his shotguns to make him leave, then slammed the door in his face. Alex reversed his Range Rover into my rosebushes when he left, spun his wheels so they went everywhere. Made a real mess."

Something about the story made a connection in my head, but it was just out of reach. Just beyond my sight line.

"Did you tell the police about it?"

She sighed. "Of course. But I don't want to cause any trouble; all I want to know is that Ben's OK. He doesn't have to come home straight away, as long as I hear from him."

It would have been too cruel to say, but I couldn't

stop thinking it: *Ben's not coming home, because he's in love with another woman.*

She put her head in her hands and began to cry. Her body shook with sobs, short breathless gasps mingling with the tears.

"Beth?" I said as gently as I could manage.

"I just want him back," she managed through the sobs.

I waited for the crying to subside. After a minute, she took a deep breath and plucked a tissue from her sleeve.

I said, "That phone you found, with the pictures of Mel on it—where exactly did you find it?"

"In his study." She wiped her eyes and stood up. "I'll show you."

42

Ben's study was large and deep-carpeted, with a pair of iMac computers side by side on the huge oak desk. There was also a fridge, a leather sofa, and an antique Space Invaders arcade game that I recognized from the pubs of my youth. Against one wall were three floor-to-ceiling filing cabinets, all open, half-filled with black ring binders. Against the other wall were a dozen or so framed photographs of family, friends—and Ben.

"It was in the top drawer of his desk," Beth said, pointing.

"Unlocked?"

"No, but I knew where the spare key was."

"You've looked for other stuff, I take it?"

She nodded. "I went through everything I could find. His computers are password-protected, but I made a start on his paper files, hence the mess downstairs. Although to be honest, I can't make head nor tail of most of it. And then I was looking through more of his things and I found that phone with the naked pictures of Mel on it, and of course Sunday happened, and . . ."

"Yeah. Sunday."

"Not sure what came over me. I was just so . . . angry. It was like I was going to explode." Her voice cracked as she fought to hold the tears back. "This whole thing is so unfair. After everything I sacrificed for him, he just . . . leaves."

"I'm sorry too, Beth."

She nodded, biting her bottom lip.

"You know what? I'm having a drink," she said. "Do you want one?"

"Tea would be good, thanks."

"A proper drink, I mean."

It was half past one in the afternoon. Ordinarily, Beth was the kind of woman who could make a single white wine spritzer last all night.

"Tea's fine."

"Well, I'm having one."

She turned and headed back downstairs.

I walked a circle around Ben's desk, not sure what I was looking for. It was neat and ordered: a pair of fountain pens, a printer, and work trays alongside the two computers. Front and center was a short samurai dagger mounted on a rack with an inlaid brass plaque on the base that read: *"The truth of the battle is whatever the victor deems it to be"—Sun Tzu*. Alongside it, a block of black marble with military insignia I didn't recognize, and the words: *Two is one, one is none*. I had no idea what that meant.

I listened for any sound on the stairs, heard nothing, and quickly opened the top drawer of the desk. More pens, paper, a box of business cards, half a dozen silver memory sticks with stickers on them bearing handwritten notes—*phone convs 2017*, *phone convs 2016*, and so on. A stack of multicolored Post-it notes with something written on the top sheet. I tore off the top few sheets and took a closer look, realizing it wasn't ink but the indentation of something that had been written before. I held it up to the light. Looked like one word and a question mark, but it was difficult to make out. The wastebin under his desk revealed the original square yellow note, scrunched up into a tight ball. I unfolded it. Four letters and a question mark.

STEB?

What was STEB? Or where—was it a place? I had no idea.

I shoved the note in a pocket and resumed my search of the desk drawer: a handful of credit cards in a clear plastic wallet, a stack of books about business, and a bottle of aftershave. A box of condoms, the cellophane wrapper open. I shut the drawer and moved away from the desk.

The pictures on the wall seemed to be mostly of Ben's family when he was younger: mum, dad, Ben, and a younger girl I assumed was his sister. One showed them tanned and relaxed in a beachside restaurant, deep-blue sea behind them. Another of them arm in arm at Disneyland, all four of them grinning at the camera with the towers of the Magic Kingdom rising behind them. In another family shot, they were in Sydney with the opera house as a backdrop. A school picture—larger than all the rest—showed Ben, big fringe and glasses and "Prefect" badge on his lapel, accepting a framed certificate from a teacher at his school in front of an ancient-looking stone building. The teacher wore a black gown like something out of *Goodbye, Mr. Chips.*

None of the pictures rang true.

Ben had always maintained he was a tough

comprehensive-school kid through and through. It was part of his backstory, part of his northern-lad-taking-on-southern-softies persona. But it seemed that this—along with much else that I had learned in the last few days—was another fiction. The truth was private school and prefect badges and expensive holidays all over the world.

Beth returned to the study holding a glass of red wine and a china cup and saucer. She handed me the cup of tea and planted herself on the leather sofa, raising the glass.

"Cheers," she said without a trace of mirth. "To marriage."

I took a sip of the tea and pointed to the pictures on the wall. "Is this Ben? I thought he went to the local public school?"

"God, no," she said. "His parents sent him private from the age of five. His father was the MD of a big shipping company. Loaded."

"But he always said . . . you know, about being the poor kid from the wrong side of the tracks. He said he was the son of a shipyard *worker*, not that his dad was the boss."

She shrugged. "That's Ben. It's just his way. You stop noticing it after a while."

The fact that he had made stuff up about his working-class upbringing didn't actually surprise me: it was becoming apparent that he was one of the biggest bullshitters I had ever met. It was disconcerting to be confronted with it face-to-face, but it also fitted with what I had learned since the weekend.

The truth of the battle is whatever the victor deems it to be.

That pretty much summed him up. Truth was changeable to Ben, malleable, to be shaped in whatever way he wanted. So he could get what he wanted.

I pointed to a picture of Alice at the end of the row of frames. "How's Alice doing, by the way?"

"She's fine."

"How much have you told her?"

"I never need to tell her much, as far as her dad's concerned. She picks up most of it on her own. She's actually better than I am now at picking up on his moods and his little jokes. They copy each other's little phrases and habits, you know. The slang and the textspeak and abbreviations." She smiled, but it faded quickly. "Sometimes it's scary how alike they are—Alice is very much her father's daughter. I've just told her that her dad's gone away for a few days."

"She must be missing him," I said.

She paused, the glass frozen inches from her lips, her eyes fixed on mine.

"I can assure you that Alice is quite innocent in all of this," she said slowly, carefully, her gaze steady. "Alice has nothing to do with it. Any of it."

"Of course. Absolutely. I didn't mean to suggest anything else."

It would only strike me later, when I mulled over the conversation that evening, what a strange phrase this was. A strange response to a question that had not even been asked. *I can assure you that Alice is quite innocent in all of this.* As if blame should be apportioned in one way or another. *Alice is quite innocent.*

"You know what, Beth?" I said. "We're the victims here: you and me. We're the ones who have been let down, lied to, cheated."

She took another sip of wine and nodded eventually.

"But there must have been signs that it was coming," she said quietly. "I should have been a better wife, made him happy, made him content so he didn't need anyone else. So he didn't cheat on me with my best friend."

"It's not your fault. Don't punish yourself."

"It's just that he did his thing—and we live very well off it, thank you very much—and I did mine. I looked after Alice and took care of the house and the building projects, I had my hobbies, the gym and my community theater and my work for the PTA. I kept myself busy, and I thought everything was hunky-dory."

"That's what I thought about me and Mcl too."

"I just want him back. Nothing else matters."

It occurred to me that not once had she said—not once—that she would kick Ben out. Not once had she suggested she would get the locks changed, cut up his favorite suits, put one of his cars on eBay with a reserve price of a penny. She had not said she would talk to a lawyer or think about starting divorce proceedings. He had betrayed her, broken his marriage vows to her, humiliated her, but since her fury on Sunday, all the fight seemed to have gone out of her.

Of course, I had not done any of those things either—but hers seemed an abject surrender, and it made me immensely sorry for her.

I had never really been close to Beth before, never seen her as someone separate from her husband. She had always been in his shadow, always the calm perfection by his side. But now, at her lowest ebb, I saw her for what she really was: a kind, decent, forgiving woman who had never asked for much and had certainly not asked for this.

She was hurting, and lonely.

"You'll have Ben back, then? Back here?"

She nodded. She had very clear, green eyes, I noticed for the first time. She was an attractive woman—beautiful, intelligent, kind—but there was much more to her than that. There was a vulnerability about her, an openness, a lack of cynicism, that was very appealing. I wanted to protect her, make sure she wasn't hurt again.

"I'm going to find him, Beth. And I'm going to send him back to you."

A flicker of hope crossed her face, then it was gone. It was heartbreaking to watch.

"What if he doesn't want to come back?"

"What he wants or doesn't want is irrelevant now. He's not going to have a choice."

As she showed me out, I remembered why the mention of Alex Kolnik's visit to her house had fired a connection in my brain. *The parking lot of the Premier Inn, Thursday night. A black Range Rover came down the ramp just as I was leaving.*

"One other thing, Beth. The Range Rover that Kolnik came to your house in. What color was it?"

She thought for a moment. "Black. Jet black."

I pondered this last piece of information as I walked back down her driveway. *If Kolnik had finally caught up with him, maybe that was why Ben was lying low? Had their dispute boiled over into violence?*

Was Kolnik involved too?

43

As soon as I stepped through the front door of my house, something felt wrong. At first, I thought it was just because it was weird to be coming home at 2:00 P.M.: last period on a Tuesday was 8C, currently reading *The Boy in the Striped Pyjamas*. I liked 8C. They were a good bunch.

But then my skin registered a breeze coming through the house from the kitchen. I stopped, listened, and eased the front door shut very, very slowly. Taking care not to let the lock click into place.

Someone had been here. Maybe they were *still* here. And then only one thought. Only one possible culprit. *Ben.*

I stood still again, listening for any sound. The house was quiet. *Weapon?* There were a couple of umbrellas in a stand by the front door, a paperweight on the dresser, a vase on the windowsill. None of them great, especially if he was armed with a shotgun. I grabbed the paperweight, a snow globe of New York City, and crept through into the kitchen. Stopped again by the sink, listened, heard nothing. An artery in my neck pulsed hard, and I swallowed against the sensation, putting down the snow globe and picking up the rolling pin from the drying rack. The smooth wood had a decent heft to it. I moved through into the conservatory.

The back door stood slightly ajar. Its top half had nine square glass panels—the one nearest the handle was smashed. Jagged pieces of glass were scattered on the floor, the key nowhere to be seen.

I looked around trying to see what had been stolen.

A pair of speakers was still on the end table, a pot half-full of coins on the windowsill. Nothing seemed to be out of place in the kitchen either. The family iPad was still there. Then the living room, where the TV and DVD player were still in their proper places. I went upstairs. Mel's PC was in the study, untouched, and nothing else looked like it had been disturbed. In the bedroom drawers, and Mel's jewelry box, everything seemed to be in its proper place. There was no mess anywhere.

I stood on the landing, trying to work it out. What was Ben looking for? Perhaps he'd been disturbed. Perhaps he had still been here until a few minutes ago and had bolted when he heard my car. Or perhaps he hadn't gone at all.

Perhaps he was still in the house.

Gripping the rolling pin tighter, my heart thumping, I stood very still and listened for any noise, any creak of the floorboards that might give him away. Silence. Behind the silence, in the distance, the everpresent dull hum of traffic on the North Circular. My house suddenly spooked me. *Ben.* Just in case he was hiding, I went from room to room, quickly pulling open wardrobes, looking under beds and behind doors. A full sweep of the upstairs, followed by the same in every downstairs room.

There was no one. I finally began to relax and went back into the kitchen to return the rolling pin. That was when I saw it on the kitchen counter, next to the kettle.

A shotgun cartridge.

It was pink, standing upright, with a brass base and lettering up the side. *Eley Hi-Power #00 Large Game.* It was thick and heavy, and I wondered suddenly what it would feel like to be on the receiving end of the lead shot inside.

I didn't own a shotgun and only knew one person who did.

There was a note underneath the cartridge, letterhead from Ben's company, Zero One Zero. He had once told me what his company name meant, something arcane and techie to do with programming language or binary code or something similar. I couldn't remember exactly. On the paper were just five words, written with a thick black marker.

STAY AWAY FROM MY WIFE.

I stared at the paper for a minute, my pulse thrumming in my ears. Until now this had felt like some stupid game where I didn't quite get the rules, but for the first time, I was genuinely worried, frightened. What if William had been here? What if Ben came back tonight, in the middle of the night? What do you do if you wake up and a man is standing over you with a shotgun? It didn't bear thinking about. But the fact was that he was out there, armed and dangerous, and able to break into my house.

I called the police and reported the break-in. The operator spent five minutes going through my personal details, then asked me to describe what I thought had been stolen.

"Nothing's been taken. At least not that I've found so far."

"There are no items missing from the property?" she said, a skeptical tone in her voice.

"Don't think so. But he left a shotgun cartridge."

"Beg your pardon, sir?"

"A shotgun cartridge and a note, a warning, were left in my kitchen."

Her tone changed. She gave me a crime number and said an officer would come over this afternoon to collect the evidence, telling me not to touch anything that might have fingerprints on it. I hung up and stood in the middle of my kitchen, unable to take my eyes off the white sheet of paper with five black words scrawled across it.

STAY AWAY FROM MY WIFE.

I was too worried to really appreciate it, but the irony was so thick you could cut it with a knife. This man, who was breaking up my family and had tried to take my wife away from me, was warning me off further contact with *his* wife. It sounds naïve, but it was only then—at that moment—that I realized what a sick bastard he really was. He actually meant all of this. I thought of Beth and what she'd told me earlier. Ben must have driven by his house this afternoon, seen my car outside, and it had spooked him. Was this payback for getting closer to finding him?

Mel would be here in a couple of hours. I thought about calling her but decided against it—better to tell her face-to-face. Instead I found the spare key for the back door, nudged it shut with the toe of my shoe, and locked it again—taking care not to put my fingerprints on anything else.

The phone still in my hand, I added a new message to the conversation with David Bramley.

Stay away from my house, Ben.

The reply came back within a minute.

STAY AWAY FROM MY WIFE

I shook my head in disbelief. *Irony klaxon going off here.* Another message followed almost instantly.

You shd get better security on your back door
BTW big fella never know who might b waiting
4 you one of these days

I typed a reply, deleted it. Took a breath and typed it again—without the swear words this time.

You come to my house again, you'll be leaving feetfirst. That's a promise.

As before, his reply came back quickly.

Wd love to see your face today bet its an absolute picture!!!

I slammed my fist on the kitchen table, making cups and plates jump. *Calm down.*

A minute, two minutes, five minutes. Nothing more. It looked as if he might have gone offline. *I wonder if he's with Mel right now?*

No, that's a stupid idea.
Is it?

There was the familiar dull ache in my chest that I got when I thought about my wife now. Like I wanted to shout until my throat was raw. Wanted to be with her, wrap my arms around her, and hold her close, tell her she was forgiven. Tell her we could start again. Maybe all those things at the same time.

I texted her. Told her that I would be able to pick William up from after-school club today. Then made a cup of tea to calm my nerves and had drunk most of it before she replied.

OK. Love you. xxx
3:23 P.M. Mel cell

Staring at that text, feeling the lump in my throat, I knew that despite nine years of marriage, I really had no idea whether she meant it or not.

I grabbed my car keys and headed back out.

44

William was embroiled in a complicated game of toy cars with his friend Lucas at after-school club, the two of them lining up all the cars they could find around the edge of the room until it stretched around in a long line, bumper to bumper. I signed him out in the carers' register and fetched his coat and book bag, watched him for a minute while the two of them finished creating their miniature traffic jam. There was something wonderful about the simplicity of my son's routine, his games, the patterns of his life. For a few moments, watching him, I was able to forget the madness of the last few days.

But then it all came crashing in again, Naylor's words ringing in my ears, and it felt like everything was spinning away from me once more. Things were happening too fast. My family, my life, my world—everything that mattered—was about to go over a cliff.

It was up to me to stop us falling.

Back home in the kitchen, I put gloves on to move the note and shotgun cartridge that Ben had left, dropping them into a Ziploc bag. Maybe the police would be able to find fingerprints. With my phone in one hand

and a spatula in the other as I made William's dinner,
I looked again at the last message Ben had sent.

> Wd love to see your face today bet its an
> absolute picture!!!

He was trolling me, deliberately provoking me to
get an online slanging match going. In the last five
years, it seemed, the world had suddenly filled with
trolls. Full of bravado when they were anonymous
behind a screen, but would no doubt shit their pants at
the thought of saying anything face-to-face. *How
about it, Ben? You going to show your face? Or just
keep on trolling me until I'm charged with murder?*

I stared at his message.

Bet your face is an absolute picture. Your face.

That was it. A picture.

All I needed was one picture of him, walking
around, large as life, and this would be over. He had
taken covert pictures of me at Kilburn Police Station—
all I had to do was return the favor. But I needed
something that was tempting enough to draw him out,
make him break cover and come out into the open.

He wouldn't break cover for me. But he might for
Mel.

If she gave him the right motivation. If she pre-
tended she wanted to get back with him. It might work.

She picked up on the second ring.

"Mel? Can you get home early tonight? I've got a
plan."

I watched Mel as she sent him the text, telling him she
was sorry for breaking it off, she couldn't live without

him, and she was desperate to see him again. *Kingsway, one hour, the usual place.* A shopping center not far from our house. She signed off with three kisses.

"Where's the usual place?" I asked, my voice low.

"Starbucks."

"That's where you used to meet?"

She looked down and away from me. "One of the places."

"There were other places, were there?"

She nodded but said nothing, and we both lapsed into a loaded silence. The only things I could think of to say would make me sound wounded and resentful, so I clamped my teeth together and said nothing.

We waited for five minutes, ten. William came into the kitchen rubbing his eyes and asking for his bath. Mel picked him up and moved to take him upstairs.

I held out my hand to her. "Give me your phone."

"Why?"

"Need to be sure that you don't warn him."

She looked like she'd just been slapped. "I would never . . . Don't you trust me?"

"I don't know who to trust anymore. But trust is earned, and we have to start from scratch on that score."

She nodded, eyes down, and handed me the phone.

"Daddy's got all the phones," William said, his chin on Mel's shoulder.

I followed them upstairs and stood in the bathroom doorway as Mel ran our son's bath, tested the temperature, helped him get undressed, checked the temperature again, and helped him up onto the plastic step and into the water. She sat on the little stool and played with him in a way she'd done when he was a toddler, filling cups and saucers with foamy water and talking with William as he chattered away happily, asking if she wanted tea or coffee or beer or soup or hot chocolate. Each drink had a different price. Watching them play together brought a lump to my throat.

I hit Adam's number in my phone. I had not spoken to him since the debacle at the pub on Sunday—out of shame at what he'd seen—but now I needed his help.

He seemed to have other ideas.

"I, er . . . can't look after William tonight, mate," he said, his voice hesitant.

"Just for an hour?"

"Got to take the girls to their ballet lesson."

I checked my watch. "At this time of night?"

"Sorry, mate."

"Please? I wouldn't ask unless it was important."

His voice dropped, as if someone were listening in. "What's going on with you, Joe? Kate said you got arrested for beating some guy up. She saw it on Facebook."

"I wasn't arrested. It's bullshit."

"Really?" A note of disbelief in his voice.

"Yes, really. I wasn't arrested."

He made a *hmm* noise on the line as if he were considering my answer, and for a moment, I didn't know what to say. I couldn't believe he wasn't instantly on my side.

"Adam, you do believe me, right?"

"Kate heard you got suspended from school as well."

"That's bullshit too. A smear campaign. Listen, mate, I really need your help. William won't be any trouble."

He hesitated. "Sorry, Joe, I just can't. Give me a call at the weekend. We'll go for a pint or something, yeah? Gotta go."

He hung up.

The other phone beeped in my left hand as Ben texted a reply to Mel's invitation.

Knew you'd change your mind beautiful girl ☺
8 P.M.? xxx
6:29 P.M. Ben cell

I checked my watch. Eight o'clock was feasible. "Mel," I said. "He said yes."

She stood up and dried her hands as I showed her the message.

"Tell him yes," I said. "Say it in the way you would have done while you were . . . together. You know what I mean."

She nodded, blushing, and typed a reply.

Will b there. Can't wait 2 see you again
Mr. D xxx
6:30 P.M. Me

Staring at the string of messages, it felt like I had stumbled into a private conversation between two strangers and was intruding on their intimacy. It made me feel hollowed out all over again. *Focus.* One decent picture of Ben was all I needed to clear my name and keep my family intact. For the first time in days, I felt like I was in control for once, guiding events rather than being bounced from one situation into the next.

Ben had taken the bait.

I've got you now, finally. This ends tonight.

"Get changed. Put some makeup on. Get ready like you're going out on a date."

Mel's cheeks were red with embarrassment. "A date?"

"As if you were meeting him again." Even saying the words, my throat was tight.

"What about William? It's his bedtime."

My parents lived near Bath so they were out of the question for short-notice babysitting. The truth was, there were very few people we could drop William with, out of the blue, on a weeknight, without arranging it well in advance.

"Adam couldn't do it. You said Emma and Peter are away for the week. We're out of options."

"So what are we going to do?"

"We'll go together. The three of us."

45

I thought back to my promise to Beth and rang her as we were on our way to the mall. Her husband was about to reappear—she deserved to be in the loop.

The Delaneys' home number rang six times before a young voice answered.

"Hello?"

"Hi, Alice. It's Joe Lynch. Is your mum home? I need to speak to her."

"Why?"

"Need to tell her something."

"Did you talk to her earlier?"

"Yes. I just need another quick word now, OK?"

There was a silence before she answered, more quietly now. "I don't think she can speak to you."

"What?" I wasn't sure I'd heard her correctly. "What do you mean?"

"She's been . . . acting really weird since I got home from school. And I think she's taken some tablets."

"What tablets?"

"Valium. Supposed to be for when she goes on

plane trips. She's crashed out on the sofa, and I found the packet next to her."

"Can I talk to her?" I said.

"I tried earlier, but she was totally out of it, not making any sense."

From my jacket pocket came a tinkling wind chime sound—a text message on Mel's cell phone.

> We still on for 8, beautiful girl? xxx
> 7:12 P.M. Ben cell

I shook my head at the incongruity of receiving a text from Ben, meant for *my* cheating wife, while I was trying to speak to *his* cheated-on wife.

I handed the cell phone to Mel.

"Send him a reply as if everything's fine."

She took her phone from me and did as she was told, showing me the message for my approval before hitting Send.

> Of course! Can't wait Mr. D ☺ xxx
> 7:13 P.M. Me

"Joe?" Alice's voice sounded small and very far away. "Are you still there?"

"I'm here," I said into my phone. "Listen—just ask your mum to give me a call when she's feeling better."

I hung up as Mel's cell phone chimed in my pocket again.

> Not going to stand me up again like last time
> are you? xxx
> 7:14 P.M. Ben cell

I stared at the message, confused. *Last time?* What last time?

We split up at the mall, Mel taking up position in the front of a Starbucks on the ground floor of the main atrium, William and I taking the escalator up to a second-floor balcony where metal tables and chairs were arranged outside a mostly empty Costa Coffee. My heart was starting to thump in my chest. I was actually excited, elated almost, about the prospect of bringing Ben's runaway train to a halt. I was leaving nothing to chance: I had my Nikon, plus zoom lens, to make sure I got him in focus. Three good pictures should do it. *Bang bang bang.* Press the shutter and just keep pressing it. Christ, *one* good picture would do it. One good shot of his face.

7:49 P.M. I put the camera's viewfinder to my eye.

From my vantage point on the second floor, I could see Mel on the ground floor about sixty feet away, sitting at a table in front of Starbucks, sipping a skinny cappuccino. There was a copy of *Metro* that someone had left behind spread out in front of her. It was odd seeing her with a newspaper—she didn't read them, not even free ones. She'd choose *Heat*, *Closer*, or *Hello!* every time.

William sat cross-legged on the floor behind me with his cars, oblivious to everything. I turned away from him, back to the balcony, and put the camera's viewfinder to my eye again. A slim figure all in black—black jeans, black jacket, black baseball cap—crossed my field of view. I adjusted the lens but not quite quickly enough as the figure disappeared from sight beneath the first-floor balcony just as they came into focus. I waited for the figure to reappear. Ten seconds, twenty, keeping the camera pointed at the same spot.

A minute went by, and the figure in black still didn't reappear. The world seemed to go quiet around me. Mel still sat alone at Starbucks, cup cradled in both hands. Her instructions were that she was not, *under any circumstances*, to look up at the balcony. One glance up here, at me with my camera, and Ben would be gone.

Mel's phone buzzed in my pocket, and I lowered the Nikon. A picture message. An image filled the cell phone's small screen.

It was a picture of William playing with his cars on a blue-and-white tiled floor. Quite close, maybe twenty feet from the camera. In the background of the shot, I could see a tall figure in a blue jacket hunched over a table, camera poised as if ready to take a shot.

I looked down. It was *this* tiled floor. The tall figure in the picture was me. The message read:

Whatever you do Joe keep 1 eye on little
William. If he was to wander off I doubt you'd
ever find him again
7:56 P.M. Ben cell

My stomach lurched, a flutter of panic.
William—
My coffee went flying across the table as I turned.
His toy cars were there on the floor. His little rucksack.
William, no, not that—
My son was there too.
Lying flat out on the floor, rolling a car in each hand.
He's OK.

I stood up quickly to see if the picture-taker was still there, but saw only two elderly ladies, a cleaner mopping the floor, and a lanky teenager talking on a cell phone. No one who looked like Ben.

The phone buzzed in my hand as another message dropped in. This time it was a picture of Mel, sitting in Starbucks, pretending to read *Metro*.

You must think I'm a fucking idiot.
Mel + newspaper = epic fail
7:57 P.M. Ben cell

The picture was taken from the same side of the mall where I was, but directly below me. Two floors down.
Ben's here.
In the same building as I was, thirty feet of concrete and steel and fresh air separating us.

This was my chance. It was now or never.

I stood up, grabbed my son, and *ran*, slamming through the double doors and hitting the escalator at a run, taking the steps down two at a time as the Nikon bounced against my chest.

"My cars!" William cried, reaching out with both hands as he tried to squirm out of my grip.

"We'll go back for them," I said breathlessly.

We hit the first floor, and I turned and leaped onto the next escalator down to the ground floor, running down it full pelt, William bumping against my hip, his arms tight around me, clinging on. I jumped the last two steps, skidded, turned, and sprinted out into middle of the main atrium—where Ben would have been when he took the last picture.

A frowning security guard looked over at the commotion, arms crossed.

Mel looked alarmed to see me. "What's happened? Are you OK?"

"He was here," I panted. "Did you see him?"

She shook her head. "No. I don't think so."

"Christ. Well, he certainly saw you. And me."

"Where? When?"

"Just now, not more than a minute ago. He was right here. He took your picture. You sure you didn't see him?"

"I didn't recognize anyone. I'm sorry, Joe."

"Damn! Thought we had him."

The frustration was bitter in my mouth. Ben had just played me to perfection. *Again.*

"Damn," William repeated, imitating me. "Damn damn damn. Can we get my cars now?"

Mel's phone buzzed in my pocket again.

Game, set and match big fella ☺
7:59 P.M. Ben cell

I sat in the passenger seat of Mel's VW on the way home. I wanted to drive, but Mel took one look at me, the frustration coming off me in waves, and refused point-blank to let me drive in that state with our child in the back.

Think. There were two possibilities, as far as I could tell. It was possible that he had seen me first and realized it was a setup. Either that or he had been warned in advance.

And there was only one person who could have warned him.

46

William was sluggish with drowsiness, wanting to be helped with everything. I took his coat off and knelt to help him with his shoes, all the while watching my wife out of the corner of my eye, waiting until she had taken her jacket off and put her handbag down on the hall table.

"Could you put Wills to bed tonight?" I said. "I need a drink."

She nodded and leaned down to him, arms outstretched. "Of course. Come on, little chimp."

"Do you want a drink?"

"Go on, then, if you're having one."

William allowed himself to be picked up, clinging to Mel like a limpet, head on her shoulder straight away. Quarter to nine was a late night for him. Mel turned and headed slowly up the stairs, William mumbling into her neck something about having a story.

"You're too tired for a story, William."

Our son made a noise like he didn't agree but was too tired to argue.

I walked through into the kitchen noisily and

deliberately. Took my shoes off and tiptoed back into the hall, in time to see Mel reach the top of the staircase and turn right onto the landing, out of sight.

For a second, I almost changed my mind. I didn't want to find evidence that my wife might still be lying to me, but at the same time, I had to know. To find out if my instincts could be right about what had happened tonight. To be right about *something*, for once. It had to be better than the feeling of slowly going mad, inch by paranoid inch.

It is better to know than not know.

Mel's lightweight black jacket had four pockets. A packet of chewing gum, some tissues, a lip balm, but nothing that was the right size for a cell phone. I draped it back over the banister and unzipped her handbag, my pulse starting to throb as if I were shoplifting and about to get caught. The handbag was soft brown leather, expensive, smooth to the touch. My son and my wife were talking in low voices in his bedroom. He would be trying to convince her that he was too tired to clean his teeth, but I prayed that she would stick to the rules on that subject, tonight of all nights. It would buy me another minute or two while he brushed. The bag was full of pockets and zips and flaps, and I went through them as fast as I dared, pulling out and putting back three lipsticks, another lip balm, her purse, a makeup compact, a folding mirror, a small packet of sanitary pads, her keys, a key ring–sized flashlight, a rape alarm, a hairbrush and assorted hair bands, three pens, half a packet of mints, her small diary. Standard twenty-first-century woman's handbag.

No good. I checked the outside zip pocket. More of the same.

Nothing hidden. No phone.

And yet, there *was* something. Extra weight that should not have been there, a solid shape that didn't correspond with any of the contents I'd found. Using both hands, I pressed the leather sides of the bag together. There it was again. A shape: small, flat, about the size of a packet of playing cards, but thinner. I checked the bag again, trying to trace the location of the shape from the inside. My fingers traced the bottom seam of the bag.

There was a slit in the lining about six inches long, hidden by the folded leather seam. Straight and deliberate, a cut rather than a rip.

I reached in, feeling the sweat under my shirt.

There was a brush of carpet as William's bedroom door opened, and I hurriedly put the handbag back on the hall table, stepping back into the shadows of the living room. I could just see their feet crossing the landing as Mel shepherded William in front of her to the bathroom. A *click-clack* as the bathroom light cord was pulled, a slab of light spilling out onto the landing. I hesitated—just for a second—feeling my heart thudding in my chest. My wife had already betrayed me, I knew that, but she had asked for my forgiveness. She had lied, and I had found her out. So what was this?

It is better to know.

I stepped back out into the hall and went back into her handbag, reaching up and through the lining until my fingers touched smooth, hard plastic. I grabbed it and pulled it out.

It was a compact Samsung cell phone—black, no case, new-looking.

Mel had owned an iPhone for as long as Apple had made them, she wouldn't use anything else.

I had never seen this Samsung before.

It only had one button that I could see. The phone's lock screen came to life, a keypad and prompt asking me for a four-digit pin.

Four digits. What would she use? Presumably I had three chances to get it right before the phone locked me out.

Her birthday? September 15. *0915.*

The digits of the keypad shook. No good. The sound of Mel's voice reached me from upstairs, calm but firm, her *you-will-clean-your-teeth* voice. It would be maybe sixty seconds before they were done in the bathroom.

When was Ben's birthday? I didn't know. Shit. Sometime in January.

What else would she use? We used our house number as the parental lock on the TV to make sure William didn't stumble across *Game of Thrones.*

4343.

The keypad numbers shook again. Wrong. A bead of cold sweat traced a line down my rib cage.

Last chance before the phone locked. I tried the only other combination I could think of: William's birthday.

0614.

The phone unlocked to reveal a screen full of apps. *His birthday. Of course.*

I was in.

Work fast.

It was on silent mode, which made sense. I hit the text messages icon.

The screen showed: *Empty*.

She must delete as she goes along, I thought. *Smart*.

I heard the toilet flush from the bathroom upstairs. *Concentrate*. Call history: see what calls had been made and received from this handset in the last few days.

The screen showed: *Empty*.

No calls in memory. No texts either. *I found this bloody phone, figured out the passcode—this can't be a bust. It can't be.* There had to be something, somehow, that I could learn from it. This must have been the phone she used to take pictures of herself, the naked selfies she had sent to Ben. It would have been too risky with her iPhone—William played regularly on both our cell phones, and half the apps we'd downloaded were games to keep him occupied in the supermarket or the car or sitting on the bus. He seemed to have an instinctive knowledge for navigating the average cell phone, and the risk of him accidentally finding a compromising picture was too high.

No. She would have used another phone to keep Ben happy.

This phone.

I hit the app marked Album on the home screen. For the third time, the screen showed: *Empty*.

So: no texts, no calls, no pictures. Almost as if it had been wiped. But I knew that was not actually very easy to do, unless you selected Factory Reset and literally went back to square one. Like an old phone she'd given me when William dropped mine in the paddling pool last year—she thought everything had been deleted, but there were still some random selfies that he had taken, saved in an automatic backup file.

It gave me an idea. I found the File Manager app, opened it. A screen full of options. Going more or less at random, I selected Internal Storage and scrolled down the list.

Alarms Android Demovideo Downloads Edited

Then:

File Backup

That was it. I selected it and saw a couple of file types I didn't recognize, and one that I did: a JPEG file. A picture. I clicked on it.

An image of Mel, topless, filled the screen.

It was a shot of her leaning forward with a coy little smile on her face, one arm under her breasts. I had seen the picture before, last Sunday. In the Stratford Arms, when Beth had stormed in and confronted us both with the evidence of my wife's infidelity. For a moment, I stood staring at the screen. It felt different, seeing it in my own home, a few yards from where the picture had been taken. The shock of novelty, the pure visceral shock of seeing a picture that should never have been taken, had knocked me sideways when I first saw it. But now the shock was blunted, replaced with a kind of grim fascination in knowing that it had been taken in my own house, right under my nose. Without quite knowing why, I selected Options, Messaging, then Text Message. Punched in my number with shaking fingers.

Ben had the picture. I would have it too. She was my wife, after all. Perhaps there was something I could learn from the picture, something that would help me find him.

Message sent

I deleted it from the list of sent items, my own phone bleeping in my pocket as the picture message dropped in.

William spat out toothpaste loudly—*blat*—in the bathroom. There were eight numbers in the address book: three cell phones, five landlines. No names, just initials. It hadn't occurred to me that I might want to write something down, make a note of phone numbers I had never seen before. I had not thought past the idea of finding out whether she had a second cell phone or not. I patted my jacket pockets for a pen and something, anything, to write on. Nothing. Looked around the living room. We tended to keep pens and pencils out of reach after William had gone through a stage a few years ago of drawing pictures on the walls.

Shit shit shit. No time.

Come on, think. Cell phones were designed to make pen and paper obsolete.

I stood there, a phone in each hand, my breathing hard and ragged, staring around for something to write with. *Think.*

The sound of water running reached me from the bathroom. William was still cleaning his teeth. He didn't like doing it. Said he wanted his teeth to fall out quickly so the tooth fairy would come sooner, and she would give him pound coins that he could buy more cars with.

Why do you always think of useless crap at times like these?

Something clicked in the back of my mind at the thought of the word *tooth*.

That was it. Bluetooth.

The bathroom light *click-clacked* again as Mel switched it off.

In her phone settings, I switched the Bluetooth function on, doing the same on mine. Now the two devices would talk to each other as long as they were within six feet or so.

Just Mel's feet crossing the landing. She was carrying him.

I set Mel's phone to find other handsets within range, and two showed up: my Sony and Mel's iPhone, which was still in my jacket pocket. I selected the option to sync with my Sony and went back to the address book, selected all the numbers, and pressed Send. A blue bar started to progress across the screen from left to right.

1 of 8 sent.

"Night night, Big W." Mel's voice from William's room.

2 of 8 sent.

I checked my phone to make sure it was receiving. It showed two new numbers.

3 of 8 sent.

A click from upstairs as Mel pulled William's bed-room door shut.

She turned the landing light off.

Out of time.

4 of 8 sent.

Mel's feet reappeared at the top of the stairs and began to descend.

47

I shoved the two phones into the back pockets of my jeans as Mel reappeared.

"He wants a Daddy kiss." She looked at me, at my empty hands. "Are you not having a drink, then?"

"I was just about to get—"

"Mummy! Mummy!" William's voice, shouting from his bedroom.

"Not quite as tired as I thought he was," Mel said.

"Mummy!" His voice was high and frightened.

"Coming!" Mel shouted back. To me, she said, "I'll have a G&T, if you're pouring."

She headed back up the stairs to his bedroom. "Surely it's Daddy's turn."

When she was back upstairs, I took the two phones out of my back pockets. A crumpled Post-it note was stuck to my phone, "STEB?" scrawled on it in Ben's looping handwriting. I peeled the note off and shoved it back in my pocket.

The display on the Samsung said:

8 of 8 sent, transfer complete.

I slipped the Samsung back into the secret pocket of her handbag, pushing it up through the cut in the lining and trying to position the bag as it had been on the hall table. Almost too late, I remembered the Bluetooth function was still enabled, retrieved the phone again, and switched it off before replacing it in the handbag's lining.

Mel returned a moment later.

"What was Wills shouting for?" I asked, trying to keep my voice level.

"Said there was a noise outside his window and he thought it might have been a policeman trying to get in." She stopped, studied me. "Are you OK, darling?"

I shrugged. "Still a bit freaked out by Ben being there tonight."

"You look a bit peaky."

"Can't believe how close we got." I studied her, looking for a reaction. "You sure you didn't see him?"

She picked up her handbag and headed for the kitchen. "Yes, I'm sure." Her words came out too quickly.

"Was William all right just now?"

"Just a bit scared."

I followed her into the kitchen, busying myself with gin, lemon, and a sharp knife. "He normally shouts for me when he's scared."

"It's because I tucked him in, that's all."

"He's barely said a word to me today." A sudden thought hit me like a punch to my heart. "It's as if he's frightened of me."

She handed me a tumbler from the cupboard. "He's not frightened. He's worried."

"Worried about what?" I dropped ice into the tumbler, topped up the gin with tonic water, and handed it to her. She half filled a glass with red wine and handed it to me.

"He's worried that his daddy's going to prison."

I nodded slowly, a lump in my throat. I hated what this was doing to our son. Hated that he was caught in the middle.

"How about you? Are you worried?"

"Not about that. But I am worried about the toll this is taking on you."

"I'm all right," I said, taking a large sip of cabernet sauvignon. The wine was strong and heavy and dark, a deep, deep red that seemed to absorb the light in the glass. It matched my mood.

"Are you, Joe? I'm not even sure you realize the effect all this is having. You just keep plowing on, keep going, keep going, without thinking about what this is doing to you."

"You know me. Good old reliable Joe."

"Seriously, you look exhausted." She took a sip of her drink. "I'm going to take this up. Are you coming?"

"In a bit. Just going to watch a bit of TV first." *And try to work out why you have a second cell phone I've never seen before.*

"Don't be too long."

I went into the living room and sipped my wine, listening to the creak of the stairs as she went up, the click of a light switch, the toilet flushing, a tap running, the buzz of an electric toothbrush, soft steps across the landing. A few more minutes and she would be settled in bed.

Good.

I stood quietly, switched the TV on low, and went out into the hallway.

48

There were three cell phone numbers among the eight I had copied from Mel's phone to mine. That seemed to make sense: Beth had told me that Ben had three cell phones. An iPhone for work, another for personal use, and his third phone—the one she had brandished in the pub, full of naked pictures of Mel. All the landlines were central London numbers, but only one looked familiar. Calling them would have to wait until tomorrow when Mel had gone to work.

Instead I topped up my glass and opened the picture message from Mel's secret cell phone. She was holding the phone out with her right hand, left arm cupped under her breasts, hair falling forward around her smiling face. She looked so happy, so smiley, so *good*. She'd always looked good, clothes on or off. The first time I'd seen her naked it had taken my breath away. Now, more than a decade later, the effect was the same—but this time, it was like a punch under the heart, knocking the wind out of me.

Holding the phone closer, I double-tapped the screen to enlarge the background, zooming in on a cupboard and bulletin board over Mel's left shoulder. The picture wasn't taken in the bedroom, I realized abruptly. It struck me as a bit weird that the picture wasn't taken in the bedroom but in the kitchen where I was sitting right now. Maybe Ben demanded variety. To *me* it was weird anyway, and there was something else odd about it. Something I couldn't quite put my finger on. Her expression? No. She looked pleased as punch. What she was wearing? Not very much, apart from dark blue jeans. When did she have her hair styled that way? Recently? I couldn't be sure. I tapped the More Info option to find out when the image had been taken, but the date and time fields were blank.

Move on. Think.

I turned to a fresh page of the pad and wrote out the numbers Bluetoothed from Mel's secret cell phone onto mine. Eight numbers that were a part of Ben's secret life, and one of them almost certainly belonged to him. Eight numbers he didn't know I had—which meant they might help me find him. Which meant they might be the key to clearing my name and making a fresh start.

The first cell phone number was not listed with a name, just the letter *A*. I opened the house address book, flipped to *D*, and compared them to the numbers against Ben's name. No matches. I checked again, digit by digit, but none of them tallied with the numbers listed as Ben's work cell phone or his personal phone. That was a surprise. Or was it? I guessed it made sense if Ben had a secret phone too.

There *was* a match for one of the landlines. *BH* corresponded to Ben's home number, which was definitely unlisted. Another one I recognized straight away—*JW*—was the number for main reception at my school. *JW* seemed to mean "Joe, Work." So she could check up on my whereabouts, perhaps. A third landline number, designated *H*, produced a string of results on Google: top of the list was the Days Inn, Ealing, just off the A40. A small, three-star hotel about five miles from our house.

So *H* stood for *Hotel*. Presumably another place she met Ben when they could grab a few hours together. I wondered how many of the times she'd been away from home "on business" when she might actually have been just a few miles west of here, sharing a bed with Ben Delaney.

Concentrate.

A landline designated with the letter *W* looked vaguely familiar, but I couldn't remember from where. The only results on Google were a random matching string of numbers for a car rental firm in Boston, Massachusetts. No joy there. I drew another blank with a landline listed as *BW*.

The next search yielded a curious result. I deleted the number in the Google search box and typed it in again more carefully, assuming it was a mistake. But no: the second search gave exactly the same result. I clicked on the first link.

VIP Escort Services. Male and female escorts available, complete discretion assured. Highly reputable service—thousands of satisfied customers. Choose from our range of escorts and call now . . .

Below a paragraph of introductory text, the rest of the home page was taken up with inviting pictures of pretty women and well-groomed men in various states of undress. *Anya, 24. Matty, 31, Billie, 28.* I sat back in the chair. In a week of horrible surprises, here was another: Mel had the number for an escort agency stored in her secret phone. From what I could work out, clicking around the site, it was like an online brothel—you hired someone for an hour or two, or dinner, or all night, and met them for sex. At your own house or a hotel.

VIP Escort Services is a social companionship escort agency dedicated to providing the very best in personal dating, to delight clients of all ages, persuasions, and backgrounds.

I stood up, paced the kitchen for a minute. Put the kettle on and thought about what Mel had said to me on Sunday, when she had confessed to the affair. *I was bored. The same routine, every day. Work, commute, home, bed. It was exciting, different.* There seemed to be three possibilities: either Mel had played the field before she met Ben, or she was still playing the field behind his back, or they liked to get a third party involved every now and again. For some reason, the third possibility seemed the most likely.

So they'd gotten someone else involved. A threesome. Man? Woman? That would depend on Ben's tastes.

This wasn't helping. *Move on.*

The other landline numbers produced no results on Google, which meant they were either ex-directory or were internal company numbers that—for whatever reason—did not appear on any public web page, anywhere. But it would be easy enough to find out what they were.

Deleting the iPad's search history, I tucked the list of numbers into my wallet.

I had some calls to make tomorrow.

WEDNESDAY

49

I woke at 5:00 A.M. and couldn't get back to sleep. My mind was churning, exploring every possibility as I watched a sliver of predawn sky fade from ink black to slate gray. After an hour, I got up and made coffee, pacing the kitchen, doing chores, checking Facebook, checking the local TV news on the early bulletin to see if there was anything about Ben. I found the Post-it note I'd taken from Ben's study and googled "STEB" on my phone to see what the acronym might stand for.

Security Tamper-Evident Bags used for duty-free goods at airports.

The *State Tax Equalization Board* of Pennsylvania.

Standard Test and Evaluation Bottle for use in experiments.

None of them seemed to make much sense or offer much help in the hunt for Ben Delaney. I made another cup of coffee and sipped it, watching through the kitchen window as a fat pigeon balanced precariously on the fence next door. The bird wobbled, shifted its weight, and flew off again.

There was an email waiting for me in my Hotmail account.

Just a subject line and a link. No text. No sign-off. The sender's address was unknown to me.

To: Joe_Lynch79@hotmail.com
From: bret911@gmail.com
Cc:
Subject: You next
http://www.bbc.co.uk/news/uk-england
-lincolnshire-17767192

The link opened a new window in the iPad's browser. It was a BBC online news story from May 2010, with the headline: JANINE COOPER MURDER: FORMER LOVER FOUND GUILTY.

A middle-aged man's face, emotionless as a tombstone, stared out from the screen.

Andrew Blaisdale has been found guilty of the murder of missing Lincolnshire woman Janine Cooper.

The body of the 34-year-old beauty therapist, who disappeared in February 2008, has never been located despite extensive police searches in Market Rasen and the surrounding countryside. Prosecutors believed that Blaisdale, 39, buried his former lover in a shallow grave in a remote part of north Lincolnshire.

A jury at Lincoln Crown Court reached a majority verdict after almost two days of deliberation. Blaisdale will be sentenced on June 21. He had denied killing Ms. Cooper and attempting to pervert the course of justice, but detectives were able to use cell phone data that revealed his movements on the day of the murder.

I read to the bottom of the story, a numbness in my stomach as each new detail added another parallel to my own situation.

A missing persons inquiry that became a murder case. A married man having an affair. And it seemed the victim was attacked in an underground parking lot. Electronic footprints left behind that led to the conviction.

There was no text in the body of the email, but the meaning of it was clear: *The police don't need a body to get you sent down.*

Ben. His latest taunt.

"Daddy?"

I jumped, startled, at the small voice behind me. My son stood in the doorway in his *Thomas the Tank Engine* pajamas, his hair sticking up in all directions.

"Is it schooltime?"

"Not yet, Wills. Did I wake you up?"

He yawned and shook his head. "Daddy?"

"Yes, Wills?" I pulled out a chair for him at the kitchen table next to me.

"Erm." He yawned again and seemed to forget what it was he was going to say.

"What is it, matey?"

"Do you love Mummy?"

Out of the mouths of babes, indeed. "Yes," I said automatically. "Of course. More than anything."

"More than me?"

"Except you, big man."

"And does Mummy love you?"

"Yes," I said, pouring him a glass of apple juice.

He thought for a moment, rolling a toy car along the kitchen table. "What happens if one of you doesn't anymore?"

"Doesn't what, matey?"

"Love the other one."

I wondered what he'd seen, or overheard, or picked up from the adults around him. He was a smart boy and picked up lots of things, without necessarily letting on at the time. Often he'd ask about things right out of the blue, days or weeks after he'd first heard them.

"Well," I said slowly, a painful lump in my throat, "then they both have to be really nice and kind to the other one, and remember how they got married because they were in love, and try really, really hard until they love each other again."

"So are you going to be nice and kind to Mummy?"

A new thought struck me. In all this mess that had been created, I'd thought Beth and I were the biggest victims, with the most to lose. But that wasn't true; William would be the biggest victim, if things weren't put right. He was not even five years old and stood to lose more than all of us.

"Yes, Wills. I'm going to try as hard as I can to be nice and kind."

He picked another of the cars scattered around under the kitchen table and rolled it absently back and forth, back and forth.

"Can I have Golden Nuggets for breakfast?" he asked.

If Mel realized that I'd discovered the secret cell phone in her handbag, she gave no sign of it. She got ready for work as usual, kissed me, and asked me twice if I was all right or whether she should take a personal day and stay home with me.

"I'm worried about you, Joe."

"It's fine. I'll be all right. You go. I can do the school drop-off."

"Are you sure?"

"Sure."

I took our son to school, stood with him as he lined up with his class, and watched him trot happily into his classroom. His teacher, Mrs. Ashmore, gave me a smile. I smiled back.

Then I drove home and hacked my wife's email account.

I had a suspicion that all of Mel's passwords were the same, and I guessed right on the third attempt: *WilliamLuke4*.

An egg timer appeared on-screen, then it went blank for a moment.

Bingo.

Her in-box appeared.

I scanned the list of emails. Forbidden territory. A strange, voyeuristic feeling like you get when looking over someone's shoulder on the Tube, reading their Kindle. In the last few months, I had caught glimpses of Mel's in-box, but only for a second or two before she minimized the screen or shut her laptop or dragged another tab over the top of it to hide its contents. The reason for that secrecy was no longer a mystery.

There were only eighteen messages in the in-box, so I checked each of them one by one and then went through the subfolders looking for anything that looked like it might relate to Ben. But it was all routine. Nothing, as far as I could tell, from Ben. Next I went through the sent items, slowly at first, checking the sender, subject line, and first line of every message that she had sent from her Gmail account in the last three months.

Nothing. Maybe there was nothing to find? She

had obviously been good at covering her tracks while the fling with Ben was going on, but now she had promised the affair was over. It made sense. That was why she had deleted everything.

Or *almost* everything.

There were seventy-two emails in her deleted items—she was ruthless with her in-box and never liked to have more than she could see on the screen at one time. *Delegate, deal with, diary, or delete*, that was her mantra with both work and personal email accounts. Most of the deleted emails were from the last few days. Special offers, circulars, marketing stuff, companies trying to sell product.

There was a liquid feeling in my stomach as I saw a message from an account named BD007@yahoo .com.

Received Monday evening, two days ago. The subject line was blank.

BD: Ben Delaney.

I clicked on it, a painful lump in my throat.

I need you. Don't let him do this. You know we are meant to be together. Please let's just talk one more time. Need to see an old mate at home on Thurs but then back. 10 A.M. Sat, usual place? Begging you, beautiful girl.
Will dream of you tonight, like every night. B xxx

I read it once, then again, then a third time, feeling a vein pounding in my forehead.

On the pad beside me, I wrote: *Meeting: 10 o'clock Saturday. B+M.* And underlined twice: *Where?* At 10:00 A.M. on Saturdays, I was at the swimming pool with William for his regular weekend lesson—we would be out of the house between 9:30 and 11:00 A.M. *Maybe he was coming right here to our house, then. Maybe I'll arrange a playdate for William and make a surprise appearance at home.*

There was no maybe about it. I would be there; it was just a case of finding out *where.*

I checked the sent items again but could find no response to this plea from Ben. Either she had deleted her reply, or she had not replied at all and simply deleted his email.

A brief hope flared in my chest. *Maybe she didn't reply, because it's finished between them?*

I stared at the screen.

Do you really believe that?

No. That was just wishful thinking, plain and simple. They were planning to meet, which begged the question: What else were they planning?

I forwarded the email to my Hotmail account—copying in Peter Larssen with the short message *"From Ben—can we discuss?"*—then deleted it from her sent items so she wouldn't know what I'd done.

The message was interesting for another reason.

Need to see an old mate at home on Thurs.

Home. It was the only mention that I could find of Ben saying he was going somewhere, a definite indication of where he might be found. But where was home for Ben? His home in Hampstead, where his wife was slowly falling to pieces in his absence?

Or home as in where he came from, where he was born?

50

At 10:00 A.M., I called Larssen to fill him in on our close encounter at the mall and the text exchanges between Mel and Ben. He listened, asked a few questions, and said he would inquire about CCTV footage.

"The email you just forwarded to me," he said. "Where did you find it?"

"In Mel's Gmail account."

"With her knowledge and permission?"

I paused. "No. She doesn't know."

"Hmm. Any indication that she replied to this message?"

"Not that I could find."

"OK." He paused as if he were writing something. "I was about to call you, actually."

"About?"

"Good news and bad news."

"Well, that's better than just plain bad news, I suppose. What's the good news?"

"It isn't really good news, to be honest."

"Great." A feeling of dread rose from my stomach.

"They found your cell phone. The one you lost on Thursday night."

"And the bad news?"

"They found it at Fryent Country Park."

"Where? How?"

"It was in a patch of woodland, half-hidden in a pile of leaves. In the area they've been searching."

"But . . . that doesn't make sense."

"The police are tearing the woods up now, looking for a body. Using ground-penetrating radar, scent dogs, the full house of forensics. They also have divers in the lake, looking for weapons and anything else that might have ended up in there. They're treating it as their secondary crime scene."

I sat down slowly at the kitchen table. "Say that again."

He repeated it, word for word. It felt like I was floating above myself, disembodied; as if this conversation was happening to someone else and I was just a spectator.

"How can they be sure it's my phone?"

"The IMEI number is registered to you. Plus, your fingerprints, numbers, photos, and various other bits and pieces. It's your phone, Joe. There's no doubt about that."

My mind was racing. A million possibilities, but only one that made sense. "Somebody planted it there."

"Somebody?"

"Ben. Ben planted it there. It's part of his plan to set me up. Convince the police that he's been done in."

"Right," Larssen said, stretching the syllable to breaking point.

"He convinces the police, they finish the job of wrecking my life."

Larssen sighed audibly. "Joe, you need to keep your mind focused on this. Just this, nothing else." He couldn't keep the exasperation out of his voice. "Forget about other theories, other ideas. That's not your job. And the fact that you're persisting with it is making my job harder."

"I'm persisting with it because it's the truth."

"Your cell phone has just been linked to a potential crime scene, and you don't seem to have an explanation. I expect DCI Naylor is feeling pretty pleased with himself at this moment."

"All I can tell you for certain is that phone didn't end up there because of anything I did. That's the truth."

"Of course," he said in a tone that sounded like it was reserved for guilty clients. "It's a rather unfortunate truth, though, isn't it?"

When Larssen hung up, I called Beth at home to fill her in on what had happened at the mall. Alice picked up again, and I was momentarily thrown by the sound of her voice.

"Is your mum there?" I asked.

"She's asleep."

"Is she OK today?"

"She's not, like, come down from her room yet this morning."

"How come you're not at school, Alice?"

There was silence for a moment at the other end of the line.

"Felt a bit like, sick, this morning." She said it without any conviction, and I was almost certain that she was lying. "And mum needed looking after."

"I need a favor from you."

More silence.

Then: "What favor?"

"Your granny's address in Sunderland. Do you have an address book handy?"

"Why?"

"It's just something I need to know."

"Why can't you tell me?"

"It's . . . delicate."

"Don't treat me like I'm just a kid."

But you are *a kid*, I thought. Instead, I said, "OK. I think your dad might be heading up there. Tomorrow."

"Why would he do that?" She sounded surprised at the suggestion.

"Not sure yet, but I've got a hunch that's where he's going."

"A hunch?"

"An educated guess."

"I don't think he'd go there."

"Really? What makes you say that?"

She paused before answering. "He's, like, always telling me how bad it is, how rough Sunderland is compared to where we live now. I speak to Gran more often than he does."

"I'm sure your gran will want him found too. Want to hear that he's safe."

"S'pose so."

"Is there anything else you can think of that might help me find your dad? Anything at all?"

"No," she said, her voice flat. "Don't think so."

"Everything will be better," I said, "once we know your dad's OK. That's all I want."

She didn't reply.

"Alice, are you there?" I said.

"It's what I want too," she said in a small voice.

"So help me. To find him."

There was a muffled click on the other end of the line, as if she had closed a door.

"Are you going to sort everything out? Find my dad and bring him back?"

"Alice, I'm going to do everything I possibly can to bring him back. I promise."

"I miss him," she said quietly.

Then she gave me the address.

51

I couldn't call from an identifiable cell phone or from our home phone—it had to be from a number Ben couldn't link to me. A number that was anonymous. There were still a couple of phone booths on the High Street. Most of them had been swept away by the popularity of cell phones, but a few remained. One of the two was out of order. I went into the other one, looked around to see if anyone was watching, and dialed the first landline number, designated in Mel's phone as *BW*. The phone booth was grimy and cigarette-burned and stank of stale piss, but I didn't mind too much; in a strange sort of way, it was almost reassuring to find that some things hadn't changed since my youth. The number rang three times before a female voice picked up.

"Hello, CEO's office. How can I help you?"

"Oh, sorry, think I might have the wrong number. Who have I called?"

"Zero One Zero Limited, sir. Can I help you?"

I hung up. Ben's company.

The next number in the list was marked *W*. Mel's secretary, Gavin, picked up after one ring.

W was her work number, her direct line. I never

used it, preferring to call her on the cell when she was in the office. But it seemed a bit weird that it was on this list—why would you have your work number on an illicit cell phone? I hung up without a word. Stared at the phone for a second, then redialed. Gavin answered again, giving the exact same greeting.

"Hi," I said, trying to raise my voice half an octave. "Could you put me through to Melissa Lynch, please?"

"Who's calling?"

I looked across the street. A Burger King. "Mr. King."

"Will she know what it's concerning?"

"Yes, I'm sure she will."

He put me on hold and came back half a minute later.

"I'm afraid Mrs. Lynch is out seeing clients this morning, Mr. King. She should be back about 3:00 P.M. Can I take a message?"

I hung up. It struck me again how little I knew about her day-to-day work, her movements, and who she was with at any given time. And in that context, the work number also made sense—because it would allow her to coordinate absences from the office, make excuses, call in with a bogus appointment here and a fictitious client conference there when she had an opportunity to spend time with Ben. Pieces of the puzzle were starting to fit together: this was how you used new technology to conceal the oldest of sins.

It wasn't warm in the booth, but sweat was already making my shirt stick to my back. The next number rang three times before a young female voice answered. Home Counties accent, confident, posh.

"Good afternoon, Pollard and Clarke. How may I help you?"

"Hi. Sorry, who have I called?"

"Pollard and Clarke, sir. How can I help?"

"Oh. What exactly do you do?"

"We offer a range of legal services, sir. What's your particular requirement?"

For the third time in five minutes, I hung up. A Google search on my cell phone told me Pollard and Clarke was a law firm based in Holland Park, just around the corner from Mel's office.

They specialized in family law and divorce.

I felt winded, like I'd been punched in the stomach. Mel had been unfaithful, she had deceived me—but to have lawyers involved gave a ring of finality to it. I leaned against the side of the booth, my head on the glass, a hard pain in my chest. How was I going to tell William what was going on? How was it possible for a four-year-old to understand that his parents might split up?

I turned back to the list of numbers, the blood pumping in my ears.

The cell phones were next, the first of them designated with the letter *A*. Presumably this was her main method for contacting Ben—and the way she had warned him about my plan in the mall last night. I put another coin into the pay phone, but my fingers hesitated over the keypad. If he picked up, what would I say? What should I say? Or was it better to say nothing?

It is better to know than not know. I dialed the number and waited, my hand on the receiver, slippery with sweat. It rang once, twice. Six times. Then went to voice mail, an automated female voice asking me to leave a message. I hung up. Dialed it again. Six rings and then voice mail again. What should I say? *Hi, Ben. This is Joe. You tried to wreck my marriage, you bastard—let's meet up to discuss*? I hung up again and was about to hit redial when I stopped myself. A couple of random calls might be OK, but a third from the same number might arouse Ben's suspicion. I put the phone back in its cradle and checked my list of numbers again. Lover, hotel, work, husband's work, and so on. They performed a very specific function: enabling Mel to run her double life, to carry on the affair, while keeping it contained and airtight from the rest of her life. Keeping the two separate and distinct so they could not overlap, so they always ran in parallel and never converged. Except they *had* converged, the moment our four-year-old son spotted her car in traffic last Thursday night.

The pay phone rang, tinny and loud in the enclosed booth.

Then a second time.

For a few seconds, I was completely frozen.

What?

It rang a third time, the digital display showing the last cell phone number I had called.

But the last number was—

Ben was calling me back.

52

I picked up the phone before it could ring again and held it silently to my ear, listening as hard as I could. Background noises. The sound of someone breathing. Faint traffic noise, wind blowing, a siren, distant and almost inaudible. He was taking the call outside, in the open air, maybe in the street or in a parking lot. We were connected at either end of this electronic silence, but separated in every other way possible. We might be a thousand miles away from each other. Or a few meters away.

He could be watching me right now.

"Hello?" I said quietly, pitching my voice low.

The silence stretched out further. Five seconds. Ten. I was about to speak again, but held back. *Don't show your hand.*

A click, and the line went dead. Instantly, I regretted my silence.

"Don't hang up," I said to the dial tone. "You bastard, don't hang up!"

I smashed the phone back into its cradle. In the distance, a siren sounded, and I had a sudden irrational sense that I'd heard it moments before, down the phone line. It felt like we were close, in the same neighborhood. As if Ben was nearby.

So close.

The sound of teenagers sniggering reached me from outside the booth, one of the lanky youths impatiently tapping a pound coin on the glass. I ignored him and rang the number straight back, using the last coins I had. This time it rang six times and went to a computerized voice asking me to leave a message. Instinct told me not to. I hung up.

There was still one number left on the list. It was the most puzzling of all: the escort agency. But all my coins were used up. My wallet was empty. There was an ATM down the street, but then the lanky teenager would claim this one remaining phone booth. And I couldn't stop now.

Screw it. I took my cell phone out and dialed the last number, with only the germ of an idea of what I might say. It rang four times and went to voice mail, a woman's voice, husky and deep. *Hello, you're through to VIP Escort Services. You're just one chat away from the most sensational night of your life. Leave your number and we promise to call you right back.*

I hung up, not wanting to leave my name on their answering machine.

The last number I dialed wasn't on the list and hadn't been on the secret phone in Mel's handbag, but that didn't matter—I'd known it by heart for years. I knew it better than my own.

I sat on a bench in Regent's Park, hands in my pockets against the cold, watching the joggers as they circled the lake. The water was gray and choppy with the autumn wind, a cluster of tired-looking rowboats tied up and covered for winter next to the café.

It was here, in a rowboat on a scorching July day, that I had asked Mel to marry me. Pulled the oars in, mustered my courage, and gone down on one knee with the ring. She had been so surprised that she stood up and nearly tipped us both into the water, but I had held on to her and steadied her, sat her down, watched as she pushed the ring onto her finger, smiling, laughing with delight, the small diamond flashing in the sunlight.

Ten years ago.

I stood up as she approached, watching her walk quickly up the path, hands deep in the pockets of her long winter coat. Her face was pale and drawn. She looked exhausted.

We hugged awkwardly.

"You OK?" she breathed.

"Fine. Thanks for skipping your meeting."

"It's fine. I sent Andrea instead." Her office was only a five-minute walk away from Regent's Park. "What's going on? What did you want to talk about?"

"Let's sit down for a minute."

We sat, and she put her handbag down between us, the wonderful soft scent of her perfume surrounding us both.

"What is it?" There was a wariness in her voice, a reticence, as if she were getting ready to apologize again but didn't yet know what for. "Is it Ben? Has he called you?"

"No. Not exactly."

"You've seen him?"

"I *called* him. I've spent half an hour this morning making phone calls."

"To Ben? What did he say?"

"Nothing."

She looked confused.

"OK. I don't . . . Should I know what you're talking about, Joe? Who have you been phoning?"

In answer, I picked up her handbag, unzipped it, and reached inside. Under normal circumstances, she would have slapped my hand playfully away, told me off for being nosy. But not today. Today she just looked sad and defeated, and too guilt-ridden to try to stop me. So I rummaged through the contents, feeling for the cut in the inner lining.

I couldn't feel the secret phone.

It was gone. She'd taken it out, moved it. She was going to deny it.

No. My hand closed around something flat and solid. It *was* there.

I fished it out and put it on the bench between us, saying nothing. Mel looked at the little cell phone, and her shoulders slumped. She couldn't meet my eyes.

"Oh, Joe. Darling. No. That isn't . . ." She shook her head, trailing off.

"Just one question, Mel."

"OK." Her voice was barely a whisper.

"And remember what I said on Sunday about packing those two suitcases with your stuff if I think you're lying."

She bit her wobbling bottom lip. Nodded once.

"No lies," I said.

"No lies," she repeated.

"Are you still in contact with Ben? Is it still going on, even now? Is this the phone you're using to call him on?"

"No," she said.

"Look at me."

She did, the first tears starting from her beautiful brown eyes. "It was," she said, her voice catching on a sob. "While I was seeing him, but not anymore. I forgot it was there in my bag. Should have taken it out, smashed it, thrown it away. *Stupid*."

"Is that the truth?"

"Yes."

"Do you promise?"

"I promise."

"Do you swear on your life?"

"Yes."

"On our son's life?"

"*Yes, yes, yes.*" Not even a half second of hesitation. "Please, Joe. I swear. It was only while we were . . . while it was going on. Ben bought it for me when we first started seeing each other. If you've ever believed anything I've said to you, believe this: it's finished between me and him. Finished. I'm so sorry that it ever started."

"So you haven't used the phone since the weekend?"

"No."

"Why didn't you tell me about it on Sunday?"

She shrugged, sniffing. "I don't know, I thought . . . I'd told you everything. Everything important. I was going to draw a line under my mistake, a line under everything, and I just forgot it was in there with all the other crap I have in my handbag." She looked thoughtful for a moment. "How did you even find it?"

"Checked your bag last night when we got back. I was angry, confused, couldn't believe we'd been so close to Ben and still missed him."

"You thought I warned him off."

"Yes, I did, actually."

"Oh, Joe, I promise you, swear to you, I didn't warn him." She paused, desperation in her eyes. "You do believe me, don't you?"

I looked at her for a long moment, trying to decide whether I was ready for my marriage to be over. Ready to lose my wife, my best friend.

It felt as if we had already crossed that line. That I had already lost her.

I ignored her question.

"I want you to call him again."

53

She looked startled, dabbing at her eyes with a tissue.

"You want me to call Ben? Now?"

"Now." I handed her the phone.

"I'm not even sure it'll have any charge left. It's been off for quite a few days."

"Give it a try."

She turned it on and put in her passcode, the one I'd guessed last night. The screen came to life, showing the battery was at 18 percent. She selected the address book, picked Ben's cell phone number, her finger hovering over the green Call icon.

"Are you sure?" she said.

I nodded. "And put it on speakerphone."

She hit Call and selected the speaker option.

Two rings, then it was picked up. I thought I could hear the same faint background noises, traffic noises, steady breathing, that I had heard in the phone booth an hour ago.

Mel looked at me, eyebrows raised in a question. I nodded again.

"Ben?" she said into the phone. "Are you there?"

No answer. But a rustling noise, a click.

"Ben? Talk to me. Please."

Another click, and the line went dead. Mel breathed out a big sigh.

"Try again," I said.

Six rings this time. No pickup. It clicked into voice mail, the automated *Stepford Wives* voice asking us to leave a message. Mel left a brief one asking Ben to call her back and hung up.

"What now?" she said.

I slipped the little Samsung phone into my jacket pocket. "I'm going to keep this for the time being."

"OK. Maybe you should give it to the police or something? It might help them to find Ben."

"Good idea."

"I'm sorry, Joe. So sorry."

I gestured toward the lake, a painful lump in my throat.

"Remember when I took you out on that rowboat, ten years ago?"

"Of course," she said in a soft voice.

"You nearly tipped us both into the water."

"I didn't mean to."

"Thought you were going to jump out and swim for it before I could—"

"Joe." She said it abruptly, cutting me off. Her face was paler than ever.

"Yes?"

She looked away from me, and I thought she was going to cry again. "Oh, God," she whispered. "Oh, God."

"What is it, Mel?"

She shook her head and said nothing.

"Mel," I said again. "What is it?"

She paused for the longest time, gathering herself, gathering her strength. Seeming to come to a decision.

Finally, she said, "I need to tell you something."

"OK."

"Something important."

"OK," I said again, the now familiar feeling of creeping dread worming its way into my stomach.

She closed her eyes. Swallowed. Took another deep breath. "Joe, I should have said this before, right back at the beginning. I wish I had."

My cell phone chimed loudly. A text.

Call me ASAP re: police
1:29 P.M. Peter Larssen

"Who's that?" Mel asked.

"The lawyer. Something about the police. It can wait."

"No, you should call him. Go on."

"Really?"

"Of course."

I dialed his number and got the busy signal. Hung up, tried again. Same result. Put the phone back in my pocket.

"Sorry. I interrupted you."

She looked away from me. A moment ago, it seemed she was about to open up, but now the shutters had come down, and her face seemed closed somehow.

"It doesn't matter now."

"You said it was important."

She stared out over the gray water of the lake, not looking at me. "Joe, do you think I'm like my mum?"

"You have her eyes."

"Sometimes I think however much we try to avoid walking the same path as our parents, we always end up repeating their mistakes. One way or another."

"You're not your mum. We all have to find our own way in life."

She stood up, wrapping her coat more tightly around her.

"I should be getting back to the office."

I stood too, and she moved as if to hug me again, then thought better of it and settled for a peck on the cheek.

"See you later," I said, more out of habit than anything else.

She nodded and turned away. I watched as she walked quickly back up the path, until it curved away behind a stand of trees and she was out of sight.

54

William and I went to the candy store on the way home from school. Buying him candy usually cheered me up. Then the park for a quick go around the swings, slides, and climbing frames. While my son played, I called Adam's number. I needed to talk to a friend, someone who knew me. Someone who had stuck up for me in the past. He was a smart guy, and I needed his take on everything that was going on.

His cell phone rang three times and went to voice mail. Second time it rang only once before Adam's recorded voice kicked in. I left a message asking him to call me.

William and I made our weekly visit to the library next, where I had been trying—without success so far—to get him interested in books other than those he was reading at school. We went along the shelf on the ages five-to-seven bookcase, me pulling books half-out and testing the titles on him.

"*The Tiger Who Came to Tea*?"

"Got."

"*One Hundred and One Fairy Tales*?"

"No."

"*Mr. Grumpy*?"

"Had that one at school."

"Well, what *would* you like?" I asked.

"'*Spicable Me*."

"That's a film, matey."

"Can we get the film, then?"

"They don't do films here, just books."

That wasn't entirely true, but I knew he'd get more out of one good book than ten DVDs.

"Why?"

"It's a library."

He frowned as if this was a ridiculous answer. "Lucas has '*Spicable Me*."

I was about to tell him why a good book was better than *Despicable Me* any day, when my phone rang in my pocket, vibrating against my thigh. A library assistant gave me a stern look as I took my phone out and checked the display, thinking it would be Adam calling me back. But it wasn't.

"Joe?" It was Mel, tension in her voice.

We had not spoken since lunchtime at Regent's Park, but now she sounded stressed again.

"Hi," I said quietly. "You OK?"

"The police are here. They want to talk to you."

I suddenly remembered Larssen's text from earlier. *Shit*. I'd forgotten to call him back again.

"Where are you?"

"At home."

I put my hand out to William. Obediently, he put his small hand in mine, and we walked quickly out of the library, past a sign on the wall that said, "Cellphone–Free Zone."

"They took their time," I said. "I called them yesterday."

"You called them?"

"Yes. To report the break-in."

"What are you talking about?"

"We had a break-in yesterday, someone came into the house. Not someone: Ben."

"What? Why didn't you tell me?" She sounded frightened.

"I was going to tell you, when the time was right. But I didn't want to freak you out."

"Well, I'm pretty fucking close to freaking out now, Joe! The house is full of police!"

Her voice was edged with panic, close to hysteria.

"OK, OK," I said. "Try to calm down. How many police are there?"

"A lot. A dozen, maybe more. They're going through everything."

I didn't like the sound of that at all. "Looking for what?"

"They won't tell me. They're taking things away."

"What things?"

"*Our* things."

"All right, I'm leaving now. Be home in ten minutes."

William climbed up into his car seat in the back of my Hyundai.

"Can I eat my Haribos, Daddy?" he said, holding the packet up.

"No. Yes. Just have half, OK?"

"How many's half?"

"Just don't eat them all, Wills."

We pulled out onto the High Street, a numbness in my chest.

I felt like I was going to be blindsided again.

Not this time. This time I'll be ready.

I slotted the cell phone into its hands-free cradle

and rang Peter Larssen, leaving a message to call me urgently.

Mel had not been exaggerating about the police—they were all over the place. Milling about in the front garden in white coveralls, a couple of them examining Mel's car, a steady stream going in and out of the open front door like worker ants. A flatbed was parked at the curb ramp laid down to the street ready for a car to be taken away. William was wide-eyed as I unstrapped him from the car seat. He took it all in, mouth slightly open.

I held out my hand, but he didn't move.

"Police," he said quietly. "Police are here."

"Come on, Wills. Let's go inside."

"Why are police at my house?"

"They're looking after Mummy," I said.

He still wouldn't get out of his seat. "Who are the white men?"

I didn't know who he meant for a moment, then he gestured toward one of the scene-of-crime officers in white coveralls.

"They're police too, matey. Come on."

I lifted him out of the car seat and set him down on the pavement. As we walked up the drive to my front door, a scene-of-crime woman emerged wearing full protective gear, including gloves, face mask, and plastic overshoes, as if she were coming out of a serial killer's house. She had something under her arm, wrapped in a clear plastic Ziploc bag.

My laptop.

I held both hands up to stop her, and she moved to walk around me.

"Hold on," I said. "That's my laptop. What are you doing?"

The white-suited policewoman gestured over her shoulder with her thumb. I followed where she was pointing and saw DCI Naylor in the hallway of my house, white plastic overshoes on. He had his arms crossed and was talking to another scene-of-crime officer.

"Boss's orders," said the policewoman carrying my laptop. "You'd better talk to him." She walked away from me down the garden path, toward a parked police van that said *Scientific Support Unit* on it in large blue letters. William clutched my hand tightly.

A uniformed officer by my front door stepped in front of me and put a hand up as I approached.

"Sorry, sir. That's far enough."

"What?"

"You can't go inside."

"I live here."

The officer scrutinized me for a moment. "Name?"

"Joe Lynch."

"The owner of the property?"

"Yes. Now could you let me in, please?"

He hesitated, then moved out of my way.

55

I stepped inside, William still clutching my hand. Yesterday I had stood here in the silence, knowing that someone else had been there without my permission. I had that same feeling again—but now the house was filled with noise, muffled conversations, footsteps, strangers, smells that didn't belong here. My home had become public property.

A white-suited officer came down the stairs, carrying the base unit of our PC wrapped in plastic.

"'Scuse me," he said as he came past. Another officer followed after him, carrying a load of clothes in a clear plastic sack. I could see my work shirts, socks, William's red school jumpers and gray trousers: the contents of our washing basket.

"Who's that man?" William said in a loud stage whisper.

"He's a policeman too. Come on, let's find Mummy."

The kitchen was also a hive of activity, crowded with forensic people brushing and scouring, swabbing and taking samples. One of them was removing both the wastebin and the recycling bin, putting them into clear evidence bags.

Mel looked upset, a smear of mascara around her

eyes. She was still dressed smartly for work—she'd not even taken her jacket off—and threw her arms around me like she'd not seen me for a year. She folded into me and held on tightly, head against my chest, like a lost child. There was still something about that embrace—the way our bodies fitted perfectly together like two pieces of a jigsaw puzzle—that felt so right, despite what had happened between us. Painfully, achingly right.

"Are you OK?" I said quietly into her hair. "Are you all right?"

She nodded but said nothing. When she couldn't speak—when she didn't trust her voice—she was really, *really* upset.

"What's going on?"

She shook her head. *Don't know.*

William held his hands up to her, and we separated so she could pick him up, balancing him on her hip. His gaze switched back and forth between his mother's tears and the strange men in our kitchen, as if he couldn't decide which was the more worrying.

I turned to DCI Naylor.

"What's happening? Why are all these people here?"

"We're executing a search-and-seizure order, Mr. Lynch."

"I can see that, but why? We were broken into yesterday and I reported it, but this seems like a bit of an overreaction."

"We're not here because of a break-in."

"So why are you here?"

"Benjamin Delaney."

"Ben sent you here?"

"In a manner of speaking, yes."

"You know he's playing you, don't you? He's sitting

in a bar somewhere, laughing at how easy it is to hoodwink the police."

Naylor stared at me, unblinking. "Fresh evidence has come to light since our chat yesterday."

"Evidence of what?"

"We'll get to that. All in good time."

There was a silence between us for a moment as I waited for him to expand on this. But he didn't elaborate.

"That's it? That's all you're going to say?"

"Not quite."

DS Redford appeared at his side, as if summoned by a secret signal.

"Well?" I said.

Naylor's next words hit me like a cinder block.

"Joseph Lynch, I'm arresting you on suspicion of murder."

56

Murder.

For a moment, I couldn't breathe out, the air trapped in my chest, hot and heavy, as I thought about the word Naylor had used. The oldest and gravest sin. The worst thing that one human being could do to another.

Two days ago, it had been about a missing person. Now it was a murder investigation.

The bustle and noise of police activity and of Naylor reading me my rights receded as I scrambled to think what had changed since yesterday, since they had told me they were simply trying to get a missing man back to his family. And in parallel, at the corner of my mind—right on the edge—another thought was putting down dark and twisted roots.

What would it be like in prison?

What would it be like to spend twenty years behind a wall?

To be absent when my son sat his GCSEs, passed his driving test, graduated from college?

But that wasn't going to happen. Because I was innocent. This was all some giant mistake, Ben wasn't even—

"Mr. Lynch?"

It was Naylor. I blinked, stared at him.

"Mr. Lynch," he said again. "Do you understand what I just said to you?"

I nodded dumbly.

He held out a white-gloved hand. "I'm going to need your car keys."

The room came back into focus. Mel looked stricken. She wouldn't let go of my hand, clutching it to her stomach as if she could keep me in the house by the sheer force of her desperation.

Naylor took the car keys from me and passed them to DS Redford.

There was an audience in the street as I was led out to a police car. Bystanders, spectators, neighbors. A woman across the street, standing in her open front doorway, talking on the phone as she looked at the scene unfolding in front of my house. We babysat her kids sometimes. The softly spoken widower who lived opposite, half-hidden by lace curtains in his front window as he peered out on all the police activity. I fed his three cats when he went to visit his grandchildren up north.

Despite my protests, Naylor insisted on handcuffing me.

A teenage boy on the pavement opposite filmed the whole thing on his cell phone. He was in tenth grade at Haddon Park, and I wondered how long it would be before his video appeared on Facebook. *They wouldn't use handcuffs if he wasn't guilty as sin.*

Redford stayed with me, a silent presence, as I was booked in with the custody sergeant at Kilburn Police Station and told to empty my pockets. It all went into a clear plastic bag: two cell phones—both mine and the secret phone that I'd found in Mel's handbag—wallet, keys, a ballpoint pen, and loose change, before I signed at the bottom of a form and it was sealed for storage in a custody locker behind the counter.

The custody sergeant slid two more forms across the desk. The first was basic information about my name, address, and any medical conditions. The second form requested consent for the police to take fingerprints and DNA samples from me. I had done nothing wrong, and yet . . . there was something about this that felt like crossing another line. In the system, forever, my unique set of numbers stored in a computer, waiting for the day when I stepped out of line. It felt like giving up a small piece of freedom.

Being arrested was starting to feel very real indeed.

I signed the form, and the sergeant fingerprinted me, carefully and methodically. He led me into a side room where another officer took a sample of DNA, a swab in my cheek for saliva. Left cheek, right cheek, sealed tight inside a labeled tube, job done. Then another one: identical procedure, identical routine.

"Why do you need to do it twice?" I asked the policeman, a young officer who looked barely old enough to drive.

"One's the control sample, one's the secondary," he said. "We test them both to make sure they're consistent with each other before we put them into the database. It's like a backup."

"In case of mistakes?"

He shook his head. "It's about our procedures being watertight. A match is a match: DNA doesn't lie." He glanced up at me. "Unlike people."

Redford swiped us through the reinforced door that led into the back of the station, showing me into a small interview room, smaller and shabbier than the one I'd been in yesterday. She disappeared. There was no offer of tea or coffee this time.

Forty minutes passed.

Redford was the first to return, a laptop under her arm, her face as blank and expressionless as marble. She was followed by Peter Larssen, who sat down next to me in a cloud of aftershave. Naylor was last to arrive, his tie pulled down below an open top button, folder in hand, hangdog expression firmly in place.

Larssen asked for five minutes alone with me before we got started. The two detectives left us, and I told him about my discovery of Mel's secret phone— her link to Ben during their affair—and that I had surrendered it with my own phone at the front desk.

"Naylor should have his people look at it," I said. "Maybe it will help to track Ben down."

"They're going to want your wife's normal cell phone as well."

"OK. Why?"

"The texts from Ben last night, when you were setting up the meeting between him and Mel at the shopping mall. There could be something in the phone records that they can use."

He made a note to that effect on his pad, then capped his fountain pen and spoke quickly and quietly, laying out the rules of engagement: he would deal with questions; I was not to comment or respond unless he indicated it was OK to do so—and then only with short, factual responses that related directly to the question. There were to be *no* exceptions to this rule. I was to remain calm and courteous, not let them rattle me, and not introduce new theories about Ben's whereabouts. *That's their job, not yours*, he said with some force. Above all, I was to say *nothing* about my relationship with Ben, Beth, or my wife.

His rules seemed clear enough.

"I don't get it, though."

"Don't get what?" he said.

"How they've gotten to this stage already. What evidence can they possibly have to justify arresting me?"

"We're about to find out, Joe."

Naylor and Redford came back into the interview room and sat opposite us. There were butterflies in my stomach, but it felt good to have Larssen riding shotgun beside me. Redford pushed a button on the Dictaphone.

"Interview with Joseph Michael Lynch commenced at 5:51 P.M., October 11." She turned her dark brown eyes on me. "Please state your full name, date of birth, and current address for the recording."

She went through various formalities and the names of the other three people present in the interview room. Naylor reminded me again that I was under caution and that anything I said could be given in evidence, but it might harm my defense if I failed to mention something now that was used later in court. He gave me his *we're-all-friends-here* smile.

"So, Mr. Lynch," he said. "You know why you're here, correct?"

Larssen said, "My client is here because you arrested him."

"Of course," Naylor said. "I'm merely asking about Joe's knowledge of the bigger picture."

"Please fill us in, Detective," Larssen said.

Naylor ran through the spiel he had given me on

Monday morning, about the missing persons report being filed on Ben Delaney and the proof-of-life inquiries they had been carrying out over the last forty-eight hours. Since yesterday, new evidence had come to light, he said, which had altered their focus on the case.

"As I mentioned, this is not being treated as a missing persons inquiry anymore."

He let it hang in the air for a moment, waiting for either me or Larssen to bite. Neither of us did.

"It's now being treated as a no-body murder inquiry."

That word again. Hearing it once, in front of my wife and child, had been bad enough. But to hear it again inside a police station, with my DNA sample on the way to a lab, was a whole lot worse.

One word. Two syllables. Enough weight to send you to the bottom of the ocean.

Murder.

"On the basis of what new evidence?" Larssen said.

"We'll get to that in a moment. Suffice it to say we now have enough to elevate the status of the investigation."

I looked from him to Larssen and back again.

"A 'no-body murder' sounds like a contradiction in terms," I said.

Larssen frowned at me but said nothing.

"Not really," Naylor said. "We have very grave concerns for Mr. Delaney's safety. We have a steadily increasing amount of evidence that foul play is involved, even without the discovery of a body."

"There's no body to find," I said. "Because no one's died."

"Our evidence suggests otherwise."

I shook my head, and Larssen shot me a look that said, *Let me handle this*.

"It's not common, Joe," he said. "But it does happen. Makes the police's job much more difficult."

"That depends on what else we've found," Naylor replied.

"Can you give us an idea of what that is?"

"You know that I don't have to disclose it at this stage, Peter."

"I realize that, absolutely."

"But I'm going to all the same, in the interests of keeping you fully and properly informed. Three further items of evidential value that have developed over the last twenty-four hours."

"Thank you, Detective Chief Inspector. We appreciate it."

Naylor opened a folder he'd brought in with him. "Remember on Monday, Joe, when I told you about the blood found in Mr. Delaney's car and how we were able to match it to his record in the database from a case last year?"

"The guy he fired from his company."

"That's the one. Blood traces recovered from the underground parking lot of the Premier Inn, near Brent Cross, have also been matched to Mr. Delaney."

In my mind's eye, I saw the blood dripping from Ben's ear onto the concrete.

"We found a second blood trace at the scene," Naylor added. "Not matched to Ben Delaney. We're still working on tying that sample to a suspect."

Larssen wrote something else on his pad and circled it. "Sure. What else?" he said in a tone that suggested he thought the DNA match was nothing to worry about.

I couldn't believe how calm he was.

"DNA at the scene is number one," Naylor said. "Number two was also found at the scene."

He produced a clear plastic evidence bag from his folder and laid it on the table.

57

There was something thin and black inside the evidence bag. Circular. The right size to fit around a wrist. A leather bracelet. *My* bracelet. The one that Mel had given to me on our third wedding anniversary. I'd lost it in the scuffle with Ben on Thursday night.

"Evidence item four-four-one-nine-six-slash-A is shown to the suspect," Naylor said. "This item, a bracelet, was recovered from the scene, and it also has traces of Mr. Delaney's blood on it. Do you recognize the bracelet?"

"My client has no comment," Larssen said without looking up from his pad.

"Sure?" Naylor asked me.

I said nothing.

"I was rather hoping that Mr. Lynch *would* recognize it. Because he posted a message on Facebook about losing it on Thursday night."

"That was Ben," I said.

"When he supposedly hacked your account?"

"Yes. I lost my phone; he must have picked it up."

"Where?"

Larssen shot me a look and said, "No comment."

"Is that why you deleted the message later?"

I said nothing.

"It's an obvious thing, but we can often learn more from the messages a person thinks they've deleted than from the ones they leave up. In fact, you deleted two Facebook messages you posted on Thursday night."

"I didn't—"

"My client has no comment," Larssen interrupted.

"Of course, nothing's ever *really* deleted, you know," Naylor said. "From anywhere. There's always an electronic footprint. A record on a computer server somewhere in the world. Imagine that. Every message you ever sent, every website you ever visited, every picture you upload, every post on social media. *Everything*. The amount of information people are putting out into the public domain about themselves today . . . it's unprecedented in human history. It's all out there, all that data about you, stored forever. It's just a case of knowing where to look." He paused for a moment. "And our technical people are very good at knowing where to look. It's a gold mine, as far as law enforcement goes."

"The thing about a gold mine," Larssen said, "is you generally just end up with lots of worthless rock to show for your trouble."

"But when you uncover a nugget of gold, it makes it all worthwhile. And it's the nuggets that we're looking for. Which leads me on to our third evidence strand. Mr. Lynch's cell phone."

"My client's already indicated that he lost his phone," Larssen said.

"Convenient," Naylor replied.

"Happens to thousands of people, every day of the week."

Naylor said, "Do you know what metadata is, Joe?"

I shook my head.

"Literally speaking, it means 'data about data,'" he continued, turning to another sheet of paper in his file. "Information generated as you use technology. In the case of your average smartphone, metadata will give you a list of numbers, coordinates, dates, and times."

"OK," I said slowly.

"We've gathered your phone's metadata from Thursday night, which has allowed us to plot all your movements over the course of the day and into the evening. It shows you at or near the Premier Inn for thirty-three minutes last Thursday, between 5:01 P.M. and 5:34 P.M."

"No comment," Larssen said again, for what felt like the fiftieth time today.

"You went in first at 5:01 P.M. You claim that you left and then went back a short while later, staying for just a few minutes. That's pretty weird behavior, don't you think?"

"I already told you about this on Monday. Check my home phone records—I called the hotel from the landline when I got home—"

"Joe," Larssen said, a warning tone in his voice.

"It looks like there was a call from your house phone to the hotel. But there's no way to prove who made the call, the receptionist doesn't remember it, and there's no recording of the conversation. So it doesn't really move things any further forward. It doesn't help us. Or you. Why'd you go back? Because you realized you'd left your phone there and you knew it would incriminate you?"

Larssen said, "No comment."

"Maybe you returned to the scene to look for your missing bracelet as well, knowing that it would link you directly to the crime? With Mr. Delaney's body already in the trunk of your car?"

I shook my head once, a small movement. I couldn't stop myself.

"Is that a no?"

"No comment," Larssen said again.

"Either way, you needed to sort out the situation you were in. Clean up the mess." He traced his finger down a column of figures on a sheet in his file. "So at 5:34 P.M., you're on the move again, northwest, and then you stop again for twenty-four minutes. At this point, you switched your phone off—bit late by this point, considering the data trail it's already left. You see, Joe, when a cell phone is switched off, it records the phone mast it was last communicating with so it can find it again quickly when you switch it back on. The nearest to your phone when it was switched off on Thursday night was a mast on the roof of the Kingsbury Leisure Center. Which is right next to Fryent Country Park."

He paused and turned another page. I remembered my first meeting with Naylor at the park, two days ago—him getting out of his car as I emerged from the undergrowth, muddy, out of breath, with bloodied knuckles and an empty sports bag that belonged to Ben.

Naylor said, "Why *did* you switch your phone off on Thursday night, Joe?"

"I didn't switch it off. I lost it at the Premier Inn."

"During your fight with Mr. Delaney?"

Larssen gave another "no comment" response.

Naylor said, "The metadata from your phone records show that you left the North Circular at Neasden and headed northwest on the A4140, taking you to the country park."

"My phone may have done it, but I didn't. I went straight home to deal with William's asthma attack, then back to the hotel. Then back home again, where I opened a beer and put my son in the bath."

"You went back to the country park on Monday morning. Why?"

I looked over at my lawyer, and he gave me a brief nod. "Ben invited me there to meet him. He said he had something to show me. I told you this two days ago."

"Are you sure you weren't looking for something else?" he added. "Something you left behind? Or maybe you were finishing the job of concealment that you'd started on Thursday night?"

"My client has no comment."

"Did you kill your wife's lover and bury his body in that park?"

"My client has no comment."

"How did you kill him? With your fists?"

"My client has no comment."

"He slept with your wife. Did you beat him unconscious and then just keep on hitting him?"

"My client has no comment."

"Or did you kick him to death? Did it feel good?"

"This is ridiculous," I said finally.

"Joe!" Larssen said sharply, giving me a stern look.

Naylor said, "Ridiculous in what way?"

"My client has no comment," Larssen said again.

Naylor sat back in his chair, a pained look on his face.

"That's a lot of *no comment* for someone who's not done anything wrong."

DS Redford took over the questioning.

She said, "Is it not the case that you found out Ben Delaney was having an intimate relationship with your wife? You killed him in a jealous rage. Maybe you didn't mean to kill him. Maybe you just meant to teach him a lesson. But you saw red and gave him a proper hiding, and before you knew it, he was bleeding and dying on the concrete in front of you. So you thought, *What the hell do I do now?* and you concealed his body and took his phone, and you've been trying to cover your tracks by posting various Facebook updates and sending text messages supposedly from—"

"This is *bullshit*!" I said more forcefully than I had intended. "And it's exactly what Ben wants you to think. How can it be a murder when no one's died? I've seen him, heard him on the phone, talked to him on social media. This is ridiculous."

"Joe—" Larssen began.

Redford said, "Would you say you lose your temper quite easily, Joe?"

"My client has no comment," Larssen said, his tone that of the disappointed parent of a child misbehaving in public. He turned in his chair to face me and said, "Do you remember our discussion a few minutes ago, in this room, Joe?"

"Yes, I remember."

"Certain advice that I gave you?"

"Yes."

"It would be in your interests to proceed on that basis. Agreed?" His expression said, *Calm down and keep your mouth shut.*

"OK," I said.

Naylor put his hands behind his head and swiveled slightly in his chair.

He said, "You'd be amazed how common it is, you know."

"What?"

"Suspects going back to the scene of wrongdoing. Like a dog returning to its own vomit. People just can't help themselves, a lot of the time, even though they know it might draw suspicion. Sometimes they just can't leave it alone. Sometimes it's about showing the police how clever they are."

"I told you: Ben asked me to meet him at that park."

"So you said. We'll know soon enough either way—we've got a full evidence recovery team at the park tonight, checking sites of interest."

A shiver of fear went through me, like a razor blade sawing up and down my spine.

Larssen said, "Of interest in what way?"

"There are some interesting areas of woodland at the country park. Isolated spots. Quite private even though they're not too far from the road. There are a couple of spots in particular that we're taking a closer look at."

"Why?"

"Because they show signs of recently disturbed earth."

58

Larssen spoke slowly, as if he wanted to make sure there was no room for confusion.

"Could you be more specific about what you mean when you say 'disturbed earth'?"

"Potential burial locations."

The room suddenly seemed airless, claustrophobic, and I had a powerful feeling of wanting to be somewhere—anywhere—else in the world at that moment.

Larssen said, "Burial of what?"

"Burial as in shallow grave. Of human remains."

"With all due respect, Detective, that seems incredibly presumptuous at this stage of the investigation."

"Does it? We've got the cell phone data taking us there after our last known sighting of the victim. We've got the relationship between Mrs. Lynch and Mr. Delaney, blood on the seat of his burned-out car, we've got your client returning to the country park on Monday. We've got a six-foot patch of recently turned earth in the woods there, very near to the spot where your client emerged from the woods on Monday morning—muddy and out of breath. We have your client's phone found at this secondary crime scene at the country park. And this afternoon the forensic team found a cigarette lighter at the scene with Mr. Delaney's DNA on it. Believe me, there's nothing presumptuous about it." He let this sink in for a moment before asking his next question. "Tell me again, Joe. What words would you use to describe your encounter with Mr. Delaney last Thursday?"

Larssen said, "No comment."

"When you left the parking lot on Thursday evening, he was unconscious, correct?"

"No comment."

"Describe to me again what you did in the following two hours."

Larssen gave me a small nod, so I ran through my movements as briefly as possible. The drive home, William's asthma inhaler, the return to the parking lot. Home again, a bath for my son, dinner, washing-up, TV, bed.

Naylor addressed his next point directly at Larssen, opposite him at the small table.

"Despite appearances to the contrary, I'm not giving you all this case-relevant material because I'm a warm-and-fluffy human being and I want to be your best friend, Peter. I'm telling you so that your client is absolutely clear about the weight of evidence we already have in the bag. So we can perhaps shorten this whole process and save a lot of time, legwork, and heartache for the victim's family. Bearing in mind we're only just getting started on forensic searches of your client's car, his computer, and his house."

"We appreciate your candor," Larssen said.

"In the light of the new evidence, is there anything else that you'd like to tell us?"

"A minute alone with my client?"

"Of course."

Redford picked up the Dictaphone and said, "Interview suspended at 7:26 P.M."

She hit a button on the machine and followed Naylor out of the room.

Larssen half turned in his chair and looked at me with an intensity I hadn't seen before. "Well, Joe?"

"Well, what?"

"They've been rather busy, haven't they?"

"Busy chasing the wrong man."

"But they seem to have put together a fair amount of evidence in a short time."

I looked at him for a sign that he believed me. A sign that he was on my side, that he would fight my corner. That kind of person seemed to be in short supply just now.

"I've never been in this situation before. Never even been arrested before. How bad does it look?"

"Hmm. Well, that would depend."

"On what?"

"On how honest you want me to be at this point."

I swallowed hard, my throat dry. "Just give me your professional opinion."

"Well, they've got the evidence from the cell phone data, DNA evidence, physical evidence. They've got motive, in the affair between him and your wife. Opportunity, in your meeting at the hotel that night. A possible shallow grave site. It's a rather . . . unfortunate collection."

"It's bloody unfortunate, considering I didn't do it."

"Do what, exactly?"

"Kill him."

He paused for a moment before asking his next question. "You're quite sure about that?"

My stomach dropped, and I stared at him for a moment. It felt like I'd just discovered my best friend—who was supposed to be watching my back—didn't actually care either way what happened.

"Yes. Certain."

"Do you ever play cards, Joe?"

"Played poker with Ben a few months back. I was pretty terrible at it."

"Well, this is the point in the game when it's time to put your cards on the table."

"OK," I said slowly.

"The truth."

"OK."

"Can anyone else corroborate your movements last Thursday night?"

I shrugged. "Only William."

"What about your wife?"

"She came back from tennis a bit before sevenish, I think."

He checked his notes. "And that was . . . an hour and three-quarters after your confrontation with Ben."

"Give or take, yes."

"Enough time for you to drive to Fryent Country Park, dump a body, and drive home again."

"With a four-year-old in tow? In Friday-night traffic? Without being seen?"

"It's Naylor's primary theory at the moment."

"It's bonkers."

"Of course. But we also need to be ready for forensic results from property seized today from your house. How often had Ben been in your house, or your car, in the last three months? We can look at using any recent visits to counter forensic evidence they might find."

"Pretty sure he's never been in my car, but he's

been to the house a half dozen times." I thought about the geography of his affair. "Of course, there are the other times when he might have been there, with Mel."

"Of course." Larssen nodded sympathetically.

"Surely they can't go ahead with a murder charge if they haven't got a body?"

"It's unusual, but it does happen occasionally if the rest of the evidence is strong enough. There used to be something called the 'no body, no murder' rule. But things have changed since then, and you do see a few cases where the police proceed without a body and still get a conviction."

"Like the Blaisdale case. The email from Ben."

"That would be one example, yes."

"What did Naylor say about the Facebook posts?" I said, unable to keep the exasperation out of my voice. "The David Bramley account? Can't he see that's proof Ben's still alive, for fuck's sake?"

Larssen shrugged, unmoved by my frustration. "There's no proof that Ben sent them. Anyone could have sent them. So their evidential value is limited."

"Can't they trace the IP address they were sent from? Trace the account in some way?"

"Usually they can, if the person is using an existing cell phone account, or a desktop PC, or accessing Facebook via the app on their phone—which is the way most people do it. That will leave a trace that they can pick up. But according to DS Redford, the Bramley Facebook posts and the Messenger texts you received were sent by someone using a pay-as-you-go phone, via a web browser rather than the app."

"And what does that mean?"

"It means there is no trace. You've got multiple layers of disguise: not only is the Facebook account an empty shell, but you're also not generating metadata via the app. And in any case, you've got nothing to link the IP address to apart from a pay-as-you-go phone, which apparently hasn't been used for any other calls or texts and hasn't been topped up using a credit or debit card. It's one of the few ways of evading this type of check. It basically gives the police a bit of a dead end."

I shook my head. "Who the hell *knows* this stuff?"

"Someone who's very smart indeed. Someone who lives and breathes technology and knows exactly what they're doing."

"He lives and breathes it, all right. Ben's very much alive. You see that, don't you?"

Larssen capped the end of his pen and put it down on the pad. He sat back in his chair. "You realize, Joe, that if they *had* found a body, they would have charged you already? Naylor certainly wouldn't be so keen to lay out all his new evidence."

"So why did he?"

"Because he wants you to be overwhelmed by it all and admit that you did it. In the absence of a body, he's looking for the next best thing: a confession."

"Well, they're not getting that from me, so what's our plan of attack?"

"Attack?"

"What do we do next?"

"Short term, we see this out tonight. When they come back in here, they'll start with the questioning all over again, right from the beginning." He checked his watch. "After that, we try to get bail and get you back home to your family tonight. Then it's just a case of seeing what they come up with, staying calm, and keeping our powder dry."

"What else?" I said.

He looked at me, cool and level, his face absolutely without expression. "Pray the police don't find anything at that country park."

59

Mel gave me a large whiskey when I finally got home just before 11:00 P.M. We sat at the kitchen table like mismatched strangers on an awkward first date, and I gave answers to her questions about Naylor and Ben, about evidence and accusations, pictures on Facebook, and cell phone data. About what might happen next. It was beyond weird not being able to trust my wife, my supposed soul mate. While I wanted to confide in someone other than my lawyer, my instincts told me not to trust her. So I kept my answers short and basic.

She decided I was in shock.

"Poor Joe. You poor thing. You're exhausted, aren't you? What a day. What a horrible day."

She patted my hand, soft fingertips against my skin, the floral scent of her perfume stirring all kinds of wonderful memories. Her touch felt so good, *so right*, that my guard almost crumbled right there. I wanted more than anything to hug her, bury my head in her shoulder, tell her she was forgiven. Tell her I wanted more than anything for life to go back to how it was before Thursday night. Tell her everything.

But the barb of betrayal was buried deep, and it

made my heart ache with sadness whenever I looked at her.

"It's going to be OK," she said quietly.

"It's not looking great at the moment."

"The police can't do anything to you. You haven't done anything to Ben."

"They seemed pretty gung-ho today."

"Sooner or later they'll see."

I took a large swallow of whiskey, enjoying the burn as it went down.

"Ben just has to break cover once. Just once, long enough for the police to realize that he's still very much alive and kicking. And then I can get my life back."

Her face crumpled as if she might cry. "I don't know how I could have been so stupid, Joe. Can you forgive me?"

I still loved the *idea* of us, but maybe that was all it was now. An idea. My emotions were all over the place, and any thoughts of forgiveness now seemed a long, long way away. Maybe further than I could reach.

"Mel—"

She put her index finger to my lips. "Actually, you don't have to tell me. Take your time. I don't deserve to know either way, not until you want to tell me." She put her small hand over mine. "I'm going to bed. Are you coming?"

I looked at her then, my wife, my beautiful wife, my heart aching harder than ever. "I'll be up in a bit."

I poured myself another whiskey and sat at the kitchen table a while longer, thinking how fast everything in my life had gotten fucked up. Six days. That's all it had been. Six terrible days.

By the time I went to bed, Mel was already asleep,

and I dozed for an hour or so, dreaming about Ben chasing me through an underground parking lot, blood running down the side of his face, jumping out at me, running me down in his big white Porsche. Then I was awake again, staring into the darkness, looking at the cracks of street light filtering through the blinds and listening to Mel's slow, rhythmic breathing beside me. Larssen had told me that if the police did end up charging me with murder, it was highly likely that I would be remanded in custody rather than being bailed.

So if I'm charged tomorrow, this might be my last night in my own bed for months. Or years. The last night at home. As soon as that thought had taken root, sleep was out of the question. I lay there wondering what Ben would come up with next, what Naylor would throw at me.

Eventually I got up and went downstairs to the kitchen, the clock on the wall glowing red digits. Six minutes past three in the morning. The house was a mess, and in the deep shadows, it looked like a burglary or some kind of domestic disaster had struck the family home. The police had taken clothes, computers, tools from the cellar and spades from the shed, shoes, bags of rubbish from both inside the house and from the wastebin outside. There was stuff strewn everywhere in the aftermath of the police search. I realized absently that I'd forgotten to ask about the shotgun cartridge and the note Ben had left. Presumably they'd been scooped up with everything else. My car was gone. My laptop, iPad, and desktop PC were gone. My cell phone was gone.

They might as well have sent me back in time to 1900.

THURSDAY

60

William kept his distance from me the next morning. He looked at me warily, the way he looked at barky dogs and homeless people at the Tube station. I knew that—for him—the world was a very black-and white place. You were either a goodie or a baddie. And goodies didn't get handcuffed and taken away by the police.

I fetched him his cereal and sat with him at the dining table while he ate it, and I drank a strong coffee. Normally he would talk to me, ask me all kinds of questions or tell me about random four-year-old things, like which one of the Angry Birds was his favorite, or how many times he'd peed the day before, or whether Citroëns were better than Fords. But today he ate in silence. He seemed wary of even catching my eye. It broke my heart to see him like that, frightened of talking to me. As soon as he had finished his Cheerios, he shuffled off his chair and carried the bowl into the kitchen without even being asked.

He talked to his mother in the kitchen as she helped him on with his shoes and coat. I loved the sound of his voice; there was none of the sarcasm or smart-aleck sass of half the kids at Haddon Park. No condescension, no deceit. Just straight up.

"Are you taking me to school today, Mummy?"

"Yes, Wills."

"Why?"

"Because Daddy's not got his car."

"Why?"

"The police wanted to borrow it for a few days."

He thought about this for a moment. I suspected he would know it was another parental lie: he was a smart little guy.

"Why?"

"They sometimes do that when they need an extra car."

I said, "It's a Mummy car day today, matey."

Mel came over and gave me a tentative peck on the cheek, more for William's benefit than mine, I thought. She had her working-day armor back on: crisp white blouse, killer heels, and perfectly applied makeup that accentuated her beauty.

"You sure you're OK with me going to work today? I've got a personal day to take—I could stay home and we could have a day together, just the two of us."

"Go on. It's fine."

She searched my face. "Really?" She picked up her briefcase. "Listen, I've got meetings this morning, but how about I take a half-day's leave this afternoon? I'll be back in time to pick William up from school so he doesn't have to go to after-school club, and then we can have an early tea together. What do you think?"

"OK."

"Great. So what are you going to do this morning?"

"Sort things out," I said. "Did the police take your work iPad?"

"No."

"Can I borrow it?"

She hesitated. "I've got meetings and things . . ."

"Just for today? You've got your work iPhone for emails, right?"

"I suppose." She shrugged and took the iPad out of her briefcase.

"Thanks," I said. I kissed William and watched them walk down the drive to her car, my son's small high voice cutting through the crisp autumn air.

"Mummy?"

"Yes?"

"Is Daddy going to prison?" Straight up, no deceit.

"No, of course not, William."

"Are you sure?"

"Yes, I'm sure."

"But if he does go to prison, do we have to go with him?"

"No, William. And Daddy's not going to prison, so you don't have to worry about that."

"Jacob P. says Daddy's a bad man."

William climbed up into his car seat in the back of Mel's VW Golf, and her response was lost to me as she bent to strap him in. I stood on the doorstep for a long moment, arms crossed, watching Mel's VW pull away. Then staring at the space by the curb where her car had been. *Jacob P. says Daddy's a bad man.* So the stories were spreading at William's school as well. The old-fashioned rumor mill plus Facebook was a deadly combination.

It felt like a disadvantage to be without a cell phone

at a time like this. Mel had dug out one of her old handsets from a drawer—a two-year-old iPhone, unused since she had upgraded—and lent it to me while I waited for mine to be returned by the police. I walked around the corner to High Street and paid in cash for a new SIM card from Carphone Warehouse. I put it into the iPhone before leaving the shop and felt like I was back in the twenty-first century, instead of some time traveler from the 1970s.

Sitting on a bench, I texted my new number to Mel, Larssen, Beth, and a few others, downloaded a few apps, and got the hang of the phone's menus and navigation. I rang the number for VIP Escort Services again hoping the call would be answered this time, but it went to voice mail again. I hung up without leaving a message—again—and checked the phone's memory. Mel said it had been wiped completely, and she was almost right—the only thing I could find were a dozen funny selfies that William had taken, stashed away in a backup file. I smiled at the blurry series of pictures of our son in his pajamas, who seemed to have snapped them without her knowing. He'd also taken three pictures of his breakfast cereal, one of a spoon, and five of his big toe. But everything else that indicated this phone had once belonged to someone else—numbers, texts, videos, music—Mel seemed to have deleted when she upgraded.

I synced my Hotmail to the new phone and found a second email from bret911.

No text, just a picture attachment. It was a photograph of a letter, just the top half. Formal letterhead addressed to Ben at his home address, from a company I had never heard of. Smith & Rivers.

Dear Mr. Delaney,
Further to our phone conversation today we
are pleased to be able to represent you in the
matter discussed. Smith & Rivers offers
the very best in professional advice and
support—our terms are attached. We would
seek to meet at your earliest convenience in
order to establish the full details of your wife's
unreasonable behavior as grounds to proceed
in this matter. With allegations as serious as
you have made—

The crop of the picture cut the rest of the letter off.
The subject line of this email was the same as the last
one.

You next.

The date on the letter was last Monday, October 2.
Nine days ago.

You next. Meaning what?

I forwarded the email to Larssen and sent a three-
word message in reply to bret911.

Who are you?

According to Google, Smith & Rivers was a legal
firm in Hammersmith, near Ben's office. They specialized in family law. *To establish the full details of
your wife's unreasonable behavior as grounds to proceed in this matter.* So Ben was happy to destroy the
reputation of his child's mother, just to win. To get
what he wanted. *Scorched earth*: that was the way he
operated. Beth should be told what was coming down
the tracks at her—it was only fair.

I texted her, asking if she could meet this afternoon.

Think. Perhaps the previous email, the one about the Blaisdale murder, had not been from Ben. Maybe it wasn't a taunt.

You next.

Maybe it was a warning.

There was no reply from bret911, so I rang Larssen.

"It's important that you don't do anything else that could be construed in a negative light by the police, Joe. Do you understand?"

"Such as?"

"Such as rushing around hither and thither trying to find Ben, asking people about him, trying to solve the police's case all on your own. You need to keep a low profile. Don't give them any more sticks to beat you with."

"But if we find him, then there's no case left to solve."

"Well, yes. I suppose." He didn't sound convinced.

"Have you thought any more about the email I got with that link to the court case in Lincolnshire?"

"The Blaisdale murder? That could have come from anyone who has your email address, Joe. Somebody mischief-making."

"Today's message wasn't. Have you looked at your emails just now? Ben was taking legal advice from a family law firm."

Larssen said he would take a closer look at the letter and hung up. There was a notification for me on Facebook. Another user had accepted me into his electronic circle of friends, although he'd never met me. Mark Ruddington was Mel's school friend, who had posted the "twenty years ago" gallery of pictures of their school play. He had also been her boyfriend—

one of the first, I assumed—and had posted a cryptic message in the conversation below that gallery. I wondered if he knew more about my wife than I did.

I opened up Messenger and typed a quick message to him.

> Hi, Mark, nice to *meet* you. I know this sounds weird, but could you give me a call? It's about Mel. I think you two were friends at school. Thanks—hope you can help, Joe Lynch.

I added my cell phone number and pressed Send.

He seemed to be on Facebook frequently: most recently last night, a sweaty selfie saying he'd run 6.2 miles and the name of the app he used to record time and distance. The day before that was a picture of his kids—three small boys—all wearing Superman outfits, and so it went on. Once again, I was reminded that looking at a stranger's Facebook timeline gave a warped view of that person's life.

I decided to ignore Larssen's advice—showing the police Ben was alive would mean I'd get my life back too, so I texted and emailed Adam again, in case he'd seen or heard anything, or had any ideas on what else I should do. Either way, I could really do with talking to my friend again, to get his view on things. He'd been behaving strangely these last few days—almost as if he was keeping me at arm's length.

Almost as if he was worried the contagion of my problems would infect his own marriage.

61

My car was gone, taken away by the police. The only alternative was Mel's old moped, propped in the corner of the garage for a year or so, gathering dust since her short-lived attempt to avoid the Underground on her daily commute. It turned out that riding into central London every day had proved just too hazardous, even for my daredevil wife. I found her old helmet on a shelf and set off, taking it slowly.

Fifteen minutes later, I sat down next to Beth on a bench at Golders Hill Park, halfway between my house and hers. We watched a small boy, perhaps three or four years old, clamber up the steps of the slide and sit down at the top. He didn't move for a moment, then shuffled forward on his bottom once, twice, three times, until gravity took him and he slid slowly to the bottom, a look of intense concentration on his face.

"I can hardly remember when Alice was that age," Beth said, wrapped up in a cream cashmere overcoat against the October chill. "It's all a bit of a blur when they're young, isn't it? Up in the morning, breakfast, school run, play, story time, bedtime. Sometimes I wish I'd stopped to appreciate her a bit more when she was small, but at the time you don't realize it. You just think it will last forever."

"We all do what we have to do. Alice is a good kid. You should be proud of her."

"Oh, I am proud. More than I can put into words. I just wish sometimes I could turn the clock back to when she was little. Things seemed so much less complicated then."

We both watched as the small boy ran around to the steps at the foot of the slide and began climbing again.

"How are you holding up, Beth?" I said.

She shrugged. "Oh, you know. Not terribly well, if I'm honest."

She listened in silence as I told her about the lawyer's letter, then about my close encounter with Ben at Kingsway Mall, and my previous night's interview with the police. There was uncertainty in her eyes. Not fear—I think we were past that—but maybe she was still trying to decide whether I could be completely trusted.

"The police seem to be focusing a lot of their energies on you," she said.

"Your husband's got them dancing to his tune."

"It seems impossible to think that he could carry this on for so long."

"He's only ever really cared about himself, though, hasn't he?"

"That's not true," she said, her voice quiet. "Not always. He was very sweet when we first met, when Alice was born."

"The last few years, though?"

She didn't answer. Instead, she looked away from me and started to cry, helpless tears rolling down her cheeks. She was utterly unguarded about it, and I thought about how far she had fallen and how fast.

"It's going to be OK, Beth," I said. "We'll figure it out. Together."

She produced a wadded tissue from her sleeve and wiped away her tears.

"It's stupid," she sniffed. "My spirituality has always taught me that everything turns out OK in the end, that things work their way back to a kind of equilibrium. Yin and yang. But I don't know if that's true anymore. I think sometimes things go wrong and they just stay wrong, and there's nothing we can do to change it."

"I don't believe that, Beth."

She gave a sad little laugh. "That's a bit like saying you don't believe in gravity, Joe—it doesn't change the fact that it exists."

"You know, we could be a team, me and you."

"A team?"

"We need to work together to stop this. To bring Ben to his senses."

"Makes it sound like it's us versus him."

"Well, Beth, I hate to be brutal about this, but that's the way it is now."

"Does it have to be? Can't it just be about bringing him back? Not even back to me—I mean, it doesn't have to be. Bringing him back so that Alice knows he's OK, nothing more. There doesn't have to be anything else. Just that."

"That's what I want too."

"Ben will be so angry if he finds out."

"We have a better chance if we work together."

She seemed to think for a moment, searching my face. Struggling toward a decision.

"OK," she said finally in a small voice. "But just until he comes back."

"Deal," I said.

We shook hands quickly, awkwardly, her soft hand in mine for just a second before she withdrew it. She seemed to hesitate again, as if mulling something over.

"If we're a team, then you should probably know about this. It arrived today."

She put a hand in the pocket of her overcoat and took out an envelope that had been torn open. It was addressed to Ben.

"What is it?" I said.

"Have a look. I've been opening all his mail, hoping I might find something. Anything."

At first I thought it was a credit card. There was a letter with something the size of a credit card attached to it, like you get from the bank. But when I opened the envelope, it was a platinum membership card, from somewhere called the Mirage Casino.

Dear Mr. Delaney,
Thank you for your email of October 4. We are delighted to welcome you back to the exclusive membership of our Platinum Members' Lounge at the Mirage . . .

"The Mirage was his favorite casino in Sunderland," she said as I read. "He used to go there a few years ago to see his old friends from home."

"And he emailed them to renew his membership last week." The day before the parking lot.

The letter listed some of the exclusive benefits of

platinum membership. Something about the name of the place rang a bell, but I couldn't remember why.

Beth added, "I don't really know why I brought it with me. It just seemed really weird—I couldn't understand why he would have renewed his membership there with everything else that's going on. Feels like indulging in a bit of hometown nostalgia should be bottom of his priority list at the moment."

There was a second sheet promoting an upcoming poker game called the "Las Vegas Platinum Tournament": the buy-in was £1,000 per player, and the minimum guaranteed first prize was £35,000. The sheet showed an attractive young blond dealer in a low-cut top, leaning over a poker table where stacked bundles of ten-pound notes were piled up. She was flanked on either side by hard-eyed bouncers in tuxedos, protecting the money.

Beth said, "Surely he's not going back home to play poker at a time like this?"

"Your husband's a very good player. Calm, sharp, great instincts. He reads people brilliantly." *Including me.* I looked at the picture for a long moment before handing the letter back to her. "But no, I don't think he's gone back to play poker."

"What do you mean?"

I took out my wallet and unfolded the Post-it note from Ben's study.

STEB?

Only it wasn't one word. Now that I looked at it again, more closely, the space between the third and fourth letters was slightly larger than the rest.

STE B?

Not one word. A first name and an initial. A person.

The world froze for a second as I made the connection.

Two is one, one is none.

It had been in an old story in Ben's hometown local newspaper. I took out my phone and googled "Sunderland Echo Ben Delaney." The news story was the fourth search result. I clicked on it and studied the picture.

There he was: Steven Beecham. Or *STE B* for short.

"This guy"—I tapped the picture of the larger bouncer in the picture, Celtic tattoos climbing up his neck—"is called Steven Beecham. Ben knew him from when he went back to the Mirage Casino in Sunderland to play in his old hometown. Beecham was charged with GBH a few years ago—he was paid to beat some guy half to death with an iron bar—but got off on a technicality. Ben's name came up in court because Beecham had his number in his phone, and Ben admitted to a reporter that he knew him."

Beth looked confused. "So he *is* going to play poker?"

"You know that piece of black marble he's got on the desk in his study?"

"Vaguely."

"Its inscription says, 'Two is one, one is none.' I googled it after I saw it on his desk: it's a saying they have in the U.S. Special Forces. It means having just one plan is not enough; it's as good as having no plan at all."

370 T. M. LOGAN

"I'm sorry, Joe. I don't follow."

"I think Steven Beecham is Ben's backup plan. In case plan A—to frame me—doesn't work out. He's going to Sunderland to make Beecham an offer: to teach me a lesson I'll never forget."

Knees, ankles, and elbows, all shattered with an iron bar. That was what Beecham had been accused of.

"Ben wouldn't do that," she said quietly.

"No, *Ben* wouldn't. He'd pay someone else to do it for him."

She shook her head in disbelief. "I don't believe it," she said.

"I know he's going back home, and I know when." I pointed to the letter. "Now I know why."

"This is getting worse and worse with every day."

"Has Ben had any other interesting mail?"

"Not particularly." She took a bundle of envelopes from her handbag held together with an elastic band. She pulled the band off and began to leaf through them. "Do you want to see them?"

I held a hand up, not wanting to intrude any more than I already had. She put the envelopes back in her handbag, and we sat in silence for a moment, Beth sniffing gently and dabbing at her eyes with a tissue. The playground wasn't busy. Six kids and five adults. Four women, one man, none of whom looked the thug-for-hire type. A man walking a dog near the parking lot.

"There's something else, actually," I said.

"Yes?"

"What else can you remember about Alex Kolnik's visit to your house last week?"

She seemed thrown by the abrupt change of tack. "Who?"

"Alex Kolnik. The man who worked for Ben, then

set up on his own and went bust. He came to your house with a couple of his mates last week. Did you remember anything else about him?"

"No, not much. They weren't there very long. They talked to Ben on the doorstep for a minute or so, there was some shouting, then they were gone."

"What did Ben say about it?"

"That if they effing came back again, he'd effing shoot them."

"And what about their car?"

She shrugged. "A Range Rover."

"With tinted windows?"

She looked at me, frowning. "Dark windows, yes. How did you know that?"

I felt a buzz like electric current snapping through my veins. "Beth, don't turn around when I tell you this, OK?"

"Tell me what?"

"There's a black Range Rover with tinted windows in the parking lot right now."

62

She started to turn in her seat, and I put a hand on her arm to stop her.

"Beth?"

She stopped, turned back to look at me, fear slackening her face.

"What now?" she breathed.

"They pulled in a few minutes ago. Let's not spook them, OK?"

"OK," she said, her eyes wide. Her hands were clenched into tight fists on her knees. "Can you see the driver?"

I squinted over her shoulder, not moving my head. I assumed they were watching through a camera or binoculars. The Range Rover was parked at a diagonal to us, almost sideways, perhaps thirty meters away. It sat like a huge black beetle on the asphalt, solid and unmoving.

"The glass is too dark."

She stared rigidly forward, unwilling to chance a look to her right toward the Range Rover. "What do we do now?"

"Let's just wait a minute. I don't think they'll stay."

"Why not?"

"They're looking for Ben. Maybe they think you arranged to meet him here. When he doesn't show up, they'll leave."

Beth said nothing.

I said, "Ben's not *going* to show up, is he?"

"Who knows? What if . . ." she started, before the words caught in her throat.

"What?"

"What if they've given up on Ben? What if they're not looking for him anymore, if they're looking for me instead?"

"I won't let anything happen to you."

She covered her mouth with her hand. "I'm frightened, Joe."

"It'll be OK," I said, my hand on her arm. "I'm not going anywhere."

"What if they come to the house again? If Alice is there?"

"I'll follow you home, if it comes to that."

"But what about tomorrow?" she said, her voice rising. "And the next day, and the day after that? What then? Who's going to look after us then?"

"Beth, listen to me. I'm not going to let them hurt you, OK? We're in a public place here. They're not going to do anything."

"I can't take this," she whispered, her voice cracking. "Not on my own. Not without Ben."

There was a sudden flare of anger in my chest. Anger at these men, at their intimidation of a decent woman whose only fault was her choice of husband. Anger at Ben, architect of the insanity that surrounded me at every turn. Beth was frightened. I was frightened.

I was tired of being frightened.

Get proof. Something you can show to Naylor.

I found a pen in my jacket and wrote the registration on the back of my hand. Holding my phone low in my lap I took three pictures of the car, trying to get it in good sharp focus, then switched to video.

The Range Rover backed out smoothly and drove away.

Beth asked me to follow her home, and so I did, parking the moped at the bottom of her drive and walking her to the front door of the big house on Devonshire Avenue. There was no further sign of the black Range Rover, but she was still pretty shaken up.

"You sure you're going to be OK?" I asked as she stood in the doorway.

"Yes. Thank you, Joe."

"Call me if you think of anything else, OK? Or if Alex Kolnik turns up here again."

"I will. We're a team, aren't we?"

"Yes, we are."

She gave a flicker of a smile. "I'm glad."

"Me too."

"Goodbye, Joe."

She pushed the big door slowly shut, and I heard two locks click home, followed by the metallic slide of a door chain being slotted into place.

I didn't want to go home again to my empty, messed-up house. Not yet. I was restless and wanted to keep moving. So instead I emailed the images of the Range Rover to Larssen—with a message asking if the police could run the registration plate through their computers—and rode the moped to Edgware Road.

The cell phone rang as I was taking off my helmet. It was Larssen, on speakerphone. It sounded like he was driving.

"Joe, where are you?" There was an urgent tone to his voice.

"Cricklewood, I've been—"

"I was on my way to your house, but can I meet you where you are instead?"

"OK. What's up?"

"There's a wine bar on Cricklewood Broadway called the Monkey Tree. Do you know it?"

"It's just down the road from here. What's going on, Peter?"

"I'll tell you when we meet. Should be there in ten."

The Monkey Tree was smart and bright and had lots of mirrors on the walls. Not really my kind of place—I preferred a good honest pub with decent beer on draft and logs crackling in the fireplace. I ordered a black coffee and sat at a corner table, with one eye on the door. The local lunchtime news was on a large plasma TV high up in the corner of the bar.

A police search at Fryent Country Park was the top story. There was footage of the search shot from some distance away—presumably the police were preventing the media from getting too close—showing two white police tents set up in the woods near the lake, and maybe half a dozen white-suited forensic officers at the scene, carrying boxes, crouching, digging, photographing, pointing, like so many worker ants around the nest. I knew it was happening but felt a jolt of recognition all the same: the lake, the open-air theater, the bridge. I had been there three days ago to meet Ben. There was a hollow feeling in my stomach, a feeling of impending doom, like something very bad was just around the corner and I had no choice but to keep pressing on until it hit me right between the eyes.

The TV was muted, but the subtitles appeared at the bottom of the screen.

Police are tonight searching a park in northwest London as part of a murder investigation, the subtitles said. *Forensics teams have been at the scene, at Fryent Country Park in Kingsbury, for more than twenty-four hours as they look for evidence following a tip-off from a member of the public.*

Larssen came in, breathing heavily, his cheeks red. He saw me, hurried over, and sat down. While he got his breath back and extracted his iPad from his briefcase, I told him what I'd been doing and detailed my latest discoveries. He cut me off.

"We don't have much time," he said, "so I'll be as quick as I can."

63

"Two developments," Larssen said. "The police took various possessions of yours from your house earlier this week, correct?"

"Yes, loads of our stuff."

"Your last cell phone as well?"

I nodded and took a drink of black coffee. It was strong and hot, an instant caffeine hit on an empty stomach. The caffeine would give me a headache—it always did when I was wound up—but it was the only way to fight the exhaustion of too many nights with too little sleep.

"Only had that one four days. It was almost brand new."

"The Met's forensic data people have been looking at it."

"Forensic data?"

"The team that analyzes phone and computer evidence, the digital footprint a suspect leaves behind. Ten years ago, they were focused on child abuse cases, pedophiles, white-collar crime, that kind of thing. But they're now routinely used in every investigation of serious crime, cell phone data being so ubiquitous."

I tried to remember who I might have called or

texted on my phone. Ben. Mel. Our home number. A few others maybe. Nothing too suspicious.

"OK," I said.

"It seems the forensic data chaps are particularly interested in some internet searches they found on your phone."

A stab of concern in my stomach.

"What searches? I only got it on Saturday, and they took it away last night. Don't remember using the browser once."

"So you never did a Google search on the legal difference between murder and manslaughter?"

"No."

"The definition in law of a crime of passion and how a sentence might be reduced for that?"

"No."

"How much blood or saliva is needed to make a DNA comparison? The location of the nearest landfill sites to your house?"

I shook my head, incredulous. "They found all these on my phone?"

"So it seems."

"I didn't do those searches. There was no reason for me to do them."

"Someone did."

Mel?

But she didn't know the passcode to unlock my phone. She'd never asked, and I'd never told her. In any case, I'd only had the bloody thing for a few days. The alternative? It had been hacked, by someone who knew computers inside out, someone who lived and breathed computers, someone who knew all the tricks and could bypass the usual security.

Someone like Ben.

"What about the message that appeared on my home PC on Monday—the threat from Ben? Have they found it?"

Larssen shrugged. "Indications are it's a Trojan virus that was either downloaded intentionally, sent in an email, or installed at source. They can't tell which yet, but it's recent. There were other viruses on your machine that would have given a remote user the ability to take it over and use it as a 'slave' device. It's not that uncommon."

"Can they trace it back to Ben?"

"Unlikely. They actually think it's more likely you put it on there yourself, to reinforce your story of being the victim."

I shook my head in disbelief. Outside on the street, a bus rolled up, stopped, disgorged a dozen passengers onto Cricklewood Broadway, and moved off again. People shopping, taking a late lunch, meeting friends, going for a swift half at the pub. Living their lives, quite happily, as mine disintegrated at increasing speed.

Larssen said, "Who else has had access to your phone in the last four days?"

"No one. I don't know. My wife, I suppose, but she doesn't know my passcode."

"Perhaps she guessed it," he said, picking up his coffee.

It was a fair point. *You hacked her phone. Why couldn't she have done the same to you?*

"What does it mean that they found these searches?"

He took a sip of his latte. "It's another piece of the puzzle as far as Naylor is concerned. Circumstantial, but telling all the same, in the eyes of a jury."

"A jury?"

"Yes."

"As in court, trial, prosecution?"

"Yes, Joe. We need to start being prepared for that."

"A few days ago, you were saying it would probably fizzle out long before it came to this."

"A few days ago, the police didn't have the evidence they have now. They weren't digging holes in the park looking for a body."

"Christ." I rubbed my face with my hands. "What a mess."

For a moment, neither of us spoke, and I could hear the muted sounds of traffic in the street outside. I was hungry and exhausted and suddenly wanted all of this to be over.

Larssen said gently, almost apologetically, "That's not all, Joe."

"What do you mean?"

"I'm afraid . . . that's not the worst of it."

My coffee cup was still half-full, but I couldn't face it. I was starting to feel sick.

"Go on," I said, trying to keep my voice even.

"When they took your cell phone, they took away your car too?"

"That's right."

He lowered his voice still further, making me lean closer so I could hear him.

"Their forensics people have been doing various tests as part of the investigation, as you can probably imagine." He paused, checking over his shoulder to ensure there was no one coming out of the toilets behind him. "And I have it on very good authority, from a highly reliable source, that they have found blood and hair in the trunk of your car."

"Blood?" I repeated.

"From two different individuals. Small amounts."

I shivered involuntarily. *Someone walking over my grave.* "It's possible I cut myself taking things to the dump, something like that."

Larssen stirred his latte, put the spoon delicately back on the saucer, and leaned in a little closer. The noise of the wine bar seemed to recede, everything else sliding into the background apart from me and my lawyer opposite. A fluttering in my stomach. Fear.

Larssen said, "One sample's been matched to you. The other one to Ben Delaney."

64

For a moment, I couldn't speak and just stared at his face, a numb feeling spreading out from my chest into my arms and legs.

"Do you understand what I'm saying to you, Joe? Both blood and hair samples have been DNA-matched to Ben Delaney."

"Ben."

"Yes. In the trunk of your car."

"How much blood?"

"Enough to make a match. They don't need much—microscopic traces are enough."

"It's not possible."

"Why not?"

"He's never been in my car, for one thing."

Larssen shook his head. "You're missing the point, Joe. This is not him traveling as a passenger or as the driver. They found blood *in the trunk*."

I stared at him, blinking fast. My caffeine headache was getting worse, a rigid band of pain across my temple.

"How do you know all this?" I said. "Who's your source?"

"Don't ask."

"I'm asking. It's pretty bloody important at this stage."

He considered for a moment. "The source is my wife."

"How does she—"

"I told you—don't ask. The point is, we need to be prepared, Joe. We need to look at your options here. We should look at the smartest thing for you to do in this situation."

"I don't like the sound of that."

"From a legal perspective—based on my twenty years' experience in criminal law—the smart thing to do is for me and you to go down to Kilburn Police Station today, this afternoon. Tell Naylor you're coming in voluntarily, you're keen to cooperate, because you have nothing to hide. Take the initiative away from them."

"Are you serious?"

"We should be prepared for charges, and this is your best option in light of that. It's my professional advice to you."

I was struggling to get the words out in the right order.

"I don't . . . I don't . . . understand. Charges. What . . . what does that mean?"

"For the police to charge you, within the next twenty-four hours. We need to prepare for that. They have enough—more than enough—to arrest you again, and I would expect that to happen very soon."

I opened my mouth, closed it again. Words seemed inadequate—everything was happening too fast.

"It's not true."

Larssen put a hand on my arm. "Joe, you need to go home, talk to your wife, tell her what's going to happen. And your son. Give them a little bit of time to prepare for it. There will be nothing worse for them than having this happen out of the blue."

"You think it'll be today?"

"There's not really any reason for Naylor to hang about now."

"He'll want to be sure, though?"

Larssen drained the last of his coffee. "Oh, I think he's well past that stage."

65

As I rode the moped home, I tried to think of what to say to my wife. How to phrase the fact that I was about to be charged with murder.

Listen, Mel, I have to tell you something.

I'm not capable of committing this crime. You know it's crazy, what they're accusing me of.

But we have to agree on what we're going to say to William.

I don't want him to be frightened, or sad, or worried. We just need to—

There were two police cars outside my house. People walking up my driveway.

DCI Naylor was one of them.

I braked sharply and pulled over to the side of the road, a couple of car lengths short of my house. Naylor had come in force today: as well as Redford, he had brought two tall uniformed officers in high-vis jackets, bulky with gear, flanking the detectives on either side. Maybe to discourage me from doing something stupid.

The front door opened, and Mel stood there, looking from Naylor to the uniformed officers and back again, as if she couldn't understand what they were doing there. As if it were all some huge mistake.

William appeared at her side, half hiding behind her leg, peering up at the police on the doorstep.

Naylor was talking to Mel. She shook her head, giving short replies. Her eyes came to rest on me, sitting on her moped across the street. She knew I was using it, knew I was using her helmet too. Naylor would not recognize me with the helmet on, but she would. She stopped, did a little double take, and then shifted her position so that William couldn't see me. I half expected her to point her finger, call out, give me away—but instead she went back to talking with Naylor as if she had not seen me at all.

A bead of cold sweat rolled slowly down my side. It was one of those moments where you either surrender or you push all your remaining chips into the middle of the table and see what the last card brings.

I revved the moped back into life and sped away.

There was a small retail park about a mile from my house, with a Sainsbury's and a few other chain stores. At the end of the row was a Frankie & Benny's. I went in, bought a bottle of Beck's, and sat in a booth at the back of the bar. Rested my head back against the wood paneling and closed my eyes.

My whole life had been spent as a law-abiding, tax-paying member of the public. I played by the rules. Except that Ben was playing by a different set of rules entirely: the rules of the jungle, red in tooth and claw, the rules of *hooray-for-me-and-fuck-you*.

The rules that said, *It's not enough for me to win— everyone else has to lose.* And right now he was winning hands down.

I needed backup. Advice. Help. I rang Adam.

"Yup."

"It's me, mate. It's Joe. Can you talk?"

"Not really."

"Just for a minute? I really need your advice."

"Not a great time right now."

"I'm in deep shit, Adam, I need—"

His voice turned low and hard, as if he were hunched over the phone to prevent anyone eavesdropping.

"You need to stop calling me on this number, OK? Get yourself some legal help, and stop calling me at work, all right? I can't be talking to you. You're the subject of an active police investigation, and my boss will have my balls for cocktail olives if he knows we've even been speaking."

With every word, my heart sank further into my stomach. I felt like a climber dangling at the end of a rope, hanging over the abyss.

And my friend was about to cut the rope.

"Adam, please," I pleaded, trying without success to keep a note of desperation out of my voice. "I need your help. Now more than ever."

There was a click as he hung up. I stared at the phone for a moment, thinking how fast fifteen years of friendship had evaporated. I took a long pull on the Beck's, then another, the lager icy against the back of my throat.

Almost immediately the phone started ringing, Larssen's number showing on the screen. I rejected the call; I had to get things straight in my head before I talked to him again.

Going back to my house was not an option. And in any case, there was only one place that I could think of to go—one place that might hold some answers. I had to follow Ben, find him before the police found me. What had he said in his email to Mel?

Need to see an old mate at home.

He had just renewed membership at his favorite casino, in his hometown. It couldn't be a coincidence. I did a quick Google search and checked my watch. It was tight, but just about possible if I didn't hang about. The cell phone beeped as I took another long pull on the Beck's—a new message as Larssen spoke to the answering machine. The phone's battery was showing about 50 percent, and I had a moment of unease about doing what I had to do with a dead phone battery, cut off from everything—it was the one thing I had left to rely on. I went into the Sainsbury's next door and bought an Apple charger, then withdrew £200 from the cashpoint outside, my maximum daily amount. The cell phone rang again, a withheld number.

"Hello?"

A woman's voice. Husky. "Hello there. This is Lorna. You called me earlier."

Lorna. It didn't ring a bell. "I did?"

"This morning. Lorna from VIP—you were too shy to leave a message."

"Oh. Yes, of course." The escort agency. "Thanks for . . . calling back."

"So what sort of thing are you looking for, sir? What's your fantasy?"

Think. VIP provided "male and female companions" for dates, nights out, and consensual sex. The truth was, I had no idea how it was relevant to Mel's affair with Ben—but it must be relevant *somehow*; otherwise, she wouldn't have tried to conceal it.

"I'm . . . I'm looking for a repeat booking, actually. My wife and I used your company recently and were very satisfied with the evening. I was hoping to book in another visit. Same again."

"Surname?"

I told her.

"Sorry. We've had no booking under that name."

What name would she use?

Of course. Her maiden name.

"She would have booked it under the surname Bailey."

A pause.

"Ah. Yes. Here we go." The sound of keys clicking on a keyboard. "Are you sure you want the repeat booking? I could text you a little selection, in case you'd like to meet one of our other escorts."

I checked my watch again. Time was getting short.

"Listen, Lorna, sorry, but can I call you back a bit later? I've got to be somewhere."

"Sure, darlin'. I'll send you links to a few pages on our site, see what you think she might like."

"Including the original booking?"

"Of course."

"Great. Sounds good."

"Oh, our boys and girls are always good," she said, the practiced patter of an experienced madam. "Very, very good."

I swung my leg back over the moped and headed for King's Cross. I pushed it as fast as it would go, went through three red lights and up on the pavement a couple of times to save time getting through traffic-clogged junctions. It was ten past five by the time I was buying a single ticket for the 17:18 to Sunderland—paying in cash—and then I ran all the way from the ticket office across the concourse, through the barriers and down the platform, jumping aboard the train just before the guard slammed the last of the doors shut.

I was headed north. In search of answers.

66

North London slid past outside the train window. Tunnels of Victorian brick and graffitied concrete, a dual carriageway winding overhead. Old terraced houses pushed up too close to the tracks, grimy and tired, sagging with age. Ben was out there somewhere, hiding, laughing, congratulating himself on how clever he was for outsmarting everyone. Waiting for his moment. But how long would he wait before he came back? His endgame was all about Mel, about driving a wedge between us and exploiting that weakness to prize our marriage apart. Wrecking my reputation was a part of that, throwing enough mud so that some would stick, so that I would always be tainted with guilt. Because eventually he would—at a time of his own choosing. I was sure of it. He would be back, sooner or later, to show who had won. Who was the best. And to the victor, the spoils.

I felt totally alone, cut adrift from everything normal, carried along on a powerful current.

My phone was plugged in and charging. It buzzed with a notification, making a rattling sound on the table in front of me.

Where are you? Worried sick. Police just left.
Call me. xxx
5:25 P.M. Mel cell

I stared at the text for a minute, typed a reply,
thought about it for a moment, then deleted it. Typed
another reply. Deleted it again. As I contemplated a
third, the phone started ringing in my hand, the tone
loud and intrusive in the half-empty carriage.

Larssen's cell phone number showed on the display.

"Joe?"

"Yeah, it's me."

"Are you all right?"

"Fine."

The train sounded its two-tone horn as it built up
some speed, and Larssen was silent for a moment.

"Where are you?" he said slowly.

"On a train."

He gave a little sigh of disappointment. "A train to
where, exactly?"

I told him, feeling his disapproval coming through
the phone line like white noise.

"And when are you planning to return from this
jaunt?" His tone was acidic.

"As soon as I find Ben."

"And that means what? Days? Weeks?"

"Not long. A day or two."

"The longer you leave it, the longer you are not
available for interview, the harder my job becomes.
And that means it becomes harder for me to represent
you effectively."

"I know all that, and I'm sorry. But did you call me

up to tell me off again, or was there something else that you need to tell me about?"

"You asked me to call."

"Did I?"

"Yesterday you asked me about a car registration number. A Range Rover you saw at the park."

A surge of adrenaline made me sit up straight. "Did you trace the owner?"

"Remember what I said to you earlier, about information I'm not supposed to have access to?"

Please let it be good news, just for once. Just for a change.

"Yes?"

"This falls into the same category, so don't ask where it comes from."

"OK, I understand. But did you find the driver of the Range Rover?"

"Yes and no."

"What does that mean?"

"The vehicle is owned by a company, not a person."

"Like a shell company?"

"No. Enterprise Rent-A-Car."

"You're saying it's a rental?"

"So it would seem. Although it's conceivable the plates had been switched."

"Can you find out who it's rented by?"

"A PNC check—that's the Police National Computer—only provides ownership information. We're not going to get client detail like that without a proper police investigation of the rental records."

"Do you think Naylor could be persuaded?"

"On the basis of a random sighting in a parking lot? Not a hope in hell."

"It wasn't random. They were clearly following Beth, looking for her husband."

"Still, there's not a hope of persuading Naylor without something more concrete."

"There's something going on with this Alex Kolnik guy. He's been to Ben's house. He's harassing Ben's wife. That's his car, and he's up to something, I'm just not sure what yet. Have you asked Naylor about him?"

"Sure. Can do." He didn't sound enthusiastic.

"And can your source get the info about who's rented this car?"

"No. And I'm not going to tell you the reasons why, so don't go there."

I sat back again, deflated. "The Range Rover is basically a bust, then."

"It seems so."

"You know Naylor turned up at my house earlier?" I said. "And his partner and two in uniform."

"I did warn you the time was coming, today or tomorrow. There's no running away from this, Joe. You've got to stand and face it head-on. Deal with it."

"I'm not running away."

"You're doing the exact opposite of what I advised earlier today when we met at the wine bar. Go in voluntarily, show willing, take the initiative away from the police."

"Spend the next six months on remand for a crime that hasn't even happened?"

"That's a very pessimistic view."

"Or realistic, maybe. I'm sorry, Peter, but this is something I have to do."

For a moment he said nothing, and I thought the

connection had been lost. I pressed the phone to my ear.

"You keep saying that, Joe, but you're forgetting what *I'm* trying to do for *you*."

"They haven't found it yet, have they?"

"Found what?"

"A body. All that police manpower at the country park, all that expertise and technology, all the sniffer dogs, all the digging, ground-penetrating radar, and whatever else they've got, all that time and effort in such a small area. And still they've come up empty-handed. You know why that is?"

More silence.

"You still there?" I said.

"I'm starting to suspect that we no longer have an understanding, Joe."

I didn't like the sound of that. "My understanding is that I'm paying you for legal advice."

"Yes. But unless you get off that train at the next stop and come right back to London, I'm going to have to reconsider our arrangement."

"What does that mean?"

"It means I will have to consider whether the best interests of both parties are served by our continuing involvement." His words were intermittent now, the line breaking up as the train moved through tunnels and cuttings bordered with concrete.

"Or if it would . . . for all concerned . . . our con-tractual relationship was terminated at this . . . you find an alternative—"

The line went silent. Larssen's voice was gone, cut off by another tunnel. It didn't matter: his message had been clear enough. I put the phone on the table in front of me. The train was gathering speed as it threw off the shackles of the capital, climbing out of a cutting and onto an embankment overlooking a dual carriageway. The red brake lights of hundreds of cars matched our pace, snaking into the distance, heading north. The cell phone vibrated with a new call. Larssen again. I rejected the call, put the phone on silent, and put it in my pocket.

It was four hours to Sunderland. Night was creeping in, casting my reflection in the window. There were dark shadows under my eyes, two days' worth of stubble on my cheeks. I looked tired, frightened, hunted. Like a man who had already been tried and found guilty.

My wife had cheated on me. Her ex-lover was trying to set me up for murder. My best friend had turned his back on me, and my lawyer was about to drop me like a condemned man.

From here on in, I was on my own.

67

The Mirage Casino was dark and busy. A pair of bouncers turned their unsmiling faces on me as I walked in, but neither of them looked like Steven Beecham, and they almost immediately shifted their attention to a loud group of lads coming in behind me. I hadn't been in a casino since Adam's stag trip to Las Vegas five years previously, and while the city of sin had very little in common with Sunderland, all casinos had certain things in common: plenty of booze, no clocks, no windows, good-looking dealers, and happy drunks who thought they were on a winning streak. The blackjack area was toward the back, past the roulette tables and slots and small-stakes poker. It looked like a poker tournament was on, a couple of dozen players hunched around four tables, colorful chips stacked up in front of them.

Aside from poker, blackjack was Ben's other favorite casino game because it was the nearest you could get to being even odds with the house. A player with a sharp brain and a good memory could do well at it. Ben had both. Tonight, my instincts told me that if he was here, he would be playing whichever game allowed him to stake the most. I couldn't see him from the bar—it was too dark, too crowded—so I bought a beer and took a slow walk around the blackjack tables. Five players, ten-pound minimum bet. Much too small-time for Ben. The tables farther back were twenty and forty pounds per deal, still too much like small change for a guy who thought nothing of spending three grand on a Savile Row suit.

I did a slow, careful check of the poker tables. Not there either. My eyes were drawn to another bouncer at the back of the room, standing in front of heavy black curtains, black double doors beyond. A small bronze plaque on the wall said, "Executive Lounge."

That would be where the high rollers would be. Free drinks, attentive service, the prettiest dealers, somewhere a little bit separate from the hoi polloi. I strolled over as if I were a regular. The bouncer here was a few inches shorter than I was, but broader and heavier, solid with muscle, the shoulders of his dinner jacket strained taut. He had very short blond hair and eyes like chips of blue ice.

I moved to step past him, and he put a big hand on my chest like a policeman stopping traffic.

"The executive lounge is members only, sir."

"I am a member."

He gave me a little smile. "No. You're not." His broad Sunderland accent was calm and quiet and all the more menacing for it.

"Listen, I just need to go in there for a minute. I'm looking for my friend Ben. A group of us were out earlier and we got separated. We were going to meet up here."

The bouncer appeared utterly unmoved.

"It's his birthday," I added.

"Members only," he said again.

"I just need half a minute. That's all. Just to check he got here OK."

The bouncer's head swiveled an inch toward me. "You tried calling him?"

"He's got it switched off."

"Bad luck, that."

The bouncer moved aside to let a miniskirted waitress through carrying a tray with a bottle of Moët champagne and four glasses. I watched her disappear behind the curtain, perfect poise on four-inch heels.

As the double doors closed behind her, I heard a laugh like Ben's from the other side, a barking half shout, loud with alcohol and alpha-male self-confidence.

A week ago, I would have been angry that Ben was sitting in there on the other side of the curtain, drinking champagne and gambling and laughing while my freedom hung by a thread thanks to him. But in the last day or two, I had started to become used to it. I *expected* it. Expected things to happen that would underline the fact that life wasn't fair. The point was to stop whining and acknowledge it, embrace it, take advantage of it.

Law of the jungle, baby.

I was starting to think like Ben.

"How do I become a member?" I said to the bouncer. His nose had been broken at least once, and I wondered what had happened to the man who'd done it.

He pointed a thick index finger toward the exit. "Front desk."

"Then I can play at a table in there?"

"Yeah."

"Great." I turned to go.

"But registration takes twenty-four hours."

I turned back. "Sorry?"

"It takes twenty-four hours for your registration to be processed. Then you can play."

"You're kidding."

"Company policy."

"But I have money to spend and the tables out here are no good—stakes too low."

"Twenty-four hours," he repeated.

"Well, that is a real shame."

The bouncer regarded me for a moment, ice-chip eyes unblinking. "Who's your friend?"

"What?"

"Your friend inside. What's his name?"

"Ben Delaney."

His expression gave nothing away, but I could see the name meant something to him.

"Is he in there?" I said.

"Are you a copper?" An edge of suspicion in his voice.

"No, just a friend from London. But I'm worried about him."

"I'm sure your friend'll be out sooner or later, sir."

"What time do you close?"

"Four A.M."

Crap. That was almost four hours.

I went to the front desk but had the same answer from the duty supervisor, a lad in his early twenties with floppy blond hair and an adolescent beard. He put a form on the counter in front of me, with a pen.

"There you go, sir. Takes twenty-four hours to process."

Through a glass panel in the door behind him, an older man in a suit was talking on the phone in a small office, one hand on his hip.

"Can you give me a temporary pass for the executive lounge for tonight?"

"Sorry, we don't do that."

"Could I speak to the manager, then?" I pointed at the man in the back office. "Would you be able to fetch him for me?"

The lad looked past me, over my shoulder, as if hoping there would be a less annoying customer for him to speak to instead of me. Finally, he accepted that I wasn't going to go away.

"Hold on just a minute, sir."

He turned and disappeared through the door into the back office.

My options were running out. They weren't going to make an exception to the rule. And if I couldn't go in, Ben would have to come out.

There was a small red box on the wall behind the front desk.

White text on a black background: "Break Glass— Press Here."

Law of the jungle.

The supervisor had his back to me in the back office. He was still talking to the manager, jerking a thumb over his shoulder in my direction. A few people were milling about in the foyer, a couple walking in, a group of young women leaving to go on somewhere else, loud with booze and laughter.

I leaned forward over the front counter and smashed the glass of the fire alarm.

68

The alarm erupted instantly, a piercing two-tone sound that was so loud it set my teeth on edge. I ducked away from the desk and out of sight just as the supervisor came rushing through from the back office.

I didn't think he'd seen me. But it didn't matter. This wouldn't take long.

The house lights came on.

Pushing my way through the tide of people coming out, I selected the camera on my phone and got ready to snatch a picture. Looking out for Ben to come toward me in the surge of punters heading for the front exit. Imagining the moment, surely only a few seconds away now, when we would be face-to-face again. I would grab him with one hand, snap a picture with the other. The look on his face would be priceless. And then it would be my turn to post a picture on Facebook—right after I'd sent it to the police, my lawyer, and his wife.

"Everybody out," the bouncers were saying loudly and without much enthusiasm, waving people toward the front door.

On the main gambling floor, two side fire exits had opened up onto the parking lot, cold midnight air rolling in. *Shit.* I'd assumed everyone would go out of the front door. Wincing against the harsh whine of the fire alarm and taking their drinks with them, tonight's gamblers shuffled toward the fire exits as I moved to stand in the small shadows that remained by the blackjack tables. My eyes were fixed on the exit to the executive lounge. A couple of middle-aged dark-haired men emerged through the doors, pulling on leather jackets. They spoke loudly to each other over the wail of the alarm. A Slavic language I didn't recognize, maybe Russian. One gave a cigarette to the other and put another cigarette in his own mouth, and they headed for the fire exit.

I waited by the door of the executive lounge, ready to snap a picture of Ben when he came through. The blue-eyed bouncer reappeared, looking at me like I wasn't right in the head. He took me firmly by the elbow, walking me out of the fire exit and into the parking lot.

"Everybody out, sir," he said loudly above the noise of the fire alarm.

The cold October air was like a slap in the face after the casino's warmth. It was obvious that I'd not been quick enough: Ben must have gone out through one of the side exits before I'd gotten back through the crowd of people near the front desk.

There must have been a couple of hundred people in the parking lot, lit up in the glare of security lights, and Ben was somewhere among them. I started walking slowly through the assembled group, scanning left and right, phone at the ready to take a picture. He was here somewhere. I had worked my way from one side of the group to the other and was about to work my way in deeper when I saw the blue-eyed bouncer staring at me, brows knitted into a deep frown. By his side, the supervisor from the front desk was talking to him, close in his ear, pointing at me. I turned away and pushed into the crowd again.

That was when I saw him. Twenty-five feet away, his back to me. Dark hair, five feet eight, smart jacket. Smoking a cigarette, as usual.

I barged someone out of the way and pushed through a group of people, eyes fixed on the back of Ben's head. Abruptly, the fire alarm ceased, leaving a deafening quiet broken by a little cheer from the shivering crowd of gamblers assembled in the parking lot. They started to move toward the doors, obscuring my view. I shouldered someone else out of my path. Almost there. He was definitely the right build, right height, right hair.

The bastard started walking quickly away from me, without even looking around. I held my cell phone up above the crowd and pressed the shutter to take a picture. So close—

A strong hand on my shoulder pulled me abruptly backward, and I stumbled, just about managing to keep my balance. The iron grip belonged to a hugely muscular bouncer with a flat-top haircut and Celtic tattoos up the side of his neck. *Steven Beecham*, I thought but didn't say. *It's him.* Another hand—the blue-eyed bouncer I'd spoken to earlier—grabbed my other arm, and together they marched me backward, stumbling, almost falling, into the alley at the side of the casino. A few in the crowd watched with interest as I was marched off, but most were more interested in getting back inside, back into the warmth of the bar and the tables and the action.

As soon as we were far enough up the alley to be

out of sight of the other customers, Blue Eyes spun me around and punched me in the face before I could get a word out. I had never been hit so hard. It was like getting belted with a cricket bat.

My head spun with the punch, and my mouth was flooded with the warm salty taste of blood. I staggered backward but stayed on my feet.

"Fuck off back to London," the blue-eyed bouncer said.

Beecham stood next to him, his huge hands balling into fists.

I shook my head, trying to clear it. A back tooth felt loose. I spat blood.

"You know what happens," Beecham said, "when you pull the fucking fire alarm and all the customers end up in the parking lot?"

"Listen, guys, I'm just trying to find my—"

"The customers stop spending money. And the boss gets upset."

"And then *this* happens."

"I'm looking for Ben D—"

Then it was Beecham's turn to hit me, and everything went black.

69

Pain.

Awake.

Not in bed. Not indoors, even. Outside. Dark.

Hard pavement. Wet.

A bright throbbing pain in my jaw and the side of my head.

My cheek pressed against rough gravel.

I blinked, winced, sat up with a groan. Fought back a feeling of nausea. Put a hand to my face and it came away sticky with blood. I was in an alleyway at the side of the casino, big trash cans lined up side by side against the wall. The mingling smells of piss and fresh rain and rotting food, the October cold keen as a blade. My ribs were raw with pain. Evidently the casino bouncers had given me a bit of a kicking into the bargain, after knocking me out. How long had I been unconscious? Ten minutes? An hour? It was hard to figure out.

Brushing the gravel off my face, I got gingerly to my feet, the world still spinning. Walked unsteadily out of the alleyway and saw that the crowds in the parking lot had gone. The casino doors were shut, faint sounds of music coming from inside. For a moment I thought about trying to get back into the casino, but one look through the front windows into the foyer told me that wasn't going to work. The blue-eyed bouncer was there, staring at me. He saw me looking and shook his head slowly, definitively. *Not tonight, mate.*

My cell phone. I had taken a picture of Ben in the parking lot, just before the bouncers grabbed me. *Maybe this is it.* A little buzz of excitement pushing through the pain in my head. I called up the image gallery and found a dark, blurry shot of heads and up-turned faces, half smears of color, not enough light for a clear picture. Ben's head turned to the left. I double-tapped on the screen to zoom in on his face, studying the hairline, the jaw, the shape of his nose. *Could it be?* Looking closer, I frowned. It was hard to tell because of the quality of the image, but the harder I stared at it, the less sure I was that it was him. I held it closer, my hope disappearing.

The guy in my picture had a beard. It wasn't Ben after all.

I stabbed the screen to delete the picture, swearing loudly enough to startle two girls skittering past in the tiniest of miniskirts.

The street was deserted. No taxis. I googled nearby hotels, picked a Travelodge that was nearest according to the GPS, and started walking in that direction, back toward the city center. Going to the police would waste time—and in any case, they'd probably think I'd gotten what I deserved. There was also the possi-bility that Naylor had put out a warrant for my arrest. Too risky. A group of teenage lads was coming toward me, a loose gang walking up the middle of the street, all in T-shirts despite the cold and eating french fries out of white polystyrene trays. Heckling one another in voices loud with beer and bravado. One of them saw the fresh marks on my face and gave me a knowing grin. I looked away and moved on past, hands jammed in my pockets, through the dark streets of this unfamiliar city. A siren, the noise piercing like a stiletto. Blue flashing lights reflecting off the glass front of an office building made me duck into an alleyway, between two shops closed and shuttered for the night. I stumbled forward into the shadows and crouched behind a dumpster, listening to the rise and fall of the siren getting nearer. It seemed to stop, then started again, then flashed past on the street and was gone. I waited for a minute in case more police were coming. Then another minute.

I felt more alone than ever. Adrift in a strange city, I knew no one and belonged nowhere. I certainly didn't belong here. My aim had been to find Ben, but I'd found a beating instead.

I checked into the hotel, ignoring the stares of the night receptionist when he saw the state of my face, and locked the door of my room behind me. In the tiny bathroom, I splashed cold water on my face over and over again, the cuts and grazes stinging, the water running pink with blood from a gash above my eye. The man in the mirror looked like a victim. Cut, bruised, and bloodied, eyes shadowed dark with exhaustion. A long way from home.

I stared at my reflection for a moment.

Then straightened up, took a deep breath that filled my chest.

Chin up. Shoulders back.

Beaten up, maybe. But not beaten. Not yet. I still had a couple of cards left to play.

FRIDAY

70

I slept badly and woke early with a pounding head-ache, my face sore and my ribs stiff. I'd left the cell phone on overnight in case any important calls came in, and its chirrups and bleeps had kept me in the shallow waters of sleep for most of the night, unable to fall all the way into a deep, uninterrupted slumber. My limbs felt heavy. After a bleary check of the phone for texts or emails—nothing significant in the precious few hours I had been asleep—I stood under a scalding hot shower for ten minutes, head down, eyes closed, feeling the water beating hard against the back of my neck. I tried to remember what I'd been dreaming about. It felt like something important, something relevant, hovering just out of my reach. Some fact or connection that had eluded me for too long. But it was a blur, and the more I willed it to snap into focus, the further it drifted away.

By the time I was dressed, it was still only 7:20, too early for what I had planned, so I sat on the bed and scrolled through my Facebook feed on the cell phone. Three new notifications. A colleague's birth-day and a belated comment in response to the picture

of William I had posted last Thursday. At least someone hadn't noticed I was now a pariah.

My last notification was the most interesting.

It was a response on Messenger from Mark Ruddington, one of Mel's friends on Facebook who'd
accepted my friend request a couple of days ago. I
had asked him to get in touch with me after seeing
the post about their schooldays together. And now
he had.

> Hey there Joe, nice to *meet* you. Yes can give
> you a call—what do you want to talk about?

I typed another message:

> We're having a party for our 10th wedding anniver-
> sary and I'm gathering stories from her school-
> days. I didn't know her back then so thought you
> might be able to fill me in.

He replied almost straight away.

> No probs. School run now but can call you a bit
> later this morning?

An hour later, I sat silently in the back of a taxi,
watching street after street of terraced houses slide
by, working-class neighborhoods clustered near to the
docks. The air was cold under a sharp blue sky, people
walking to work, standing at bus stops smoking or
staring at their phones, teenagers slouching to school.
Lines of cars bunching up in the morning rush hour.

My cell phone rang in my hand, *Mel cell* on the
display.

"Joe, are you OK? Where are you?"

It occurred to me that these two questions always went hand in hand when she tried to reach me. *And why do you think she always asks the second question?*

"I'm all right," I said quietly.

"I'm worried about you, Joe. When are you coming home? William keeps asking what's happening and why you weren't here this morning to take him to school."

"What did you say to him?"

"That you were visiting a friend."

Despite everything, I almost laughed. "Yeah. A friend."

"What did he say?"

"Who?"

"Ben. Did he say where he's been the last few days?"

"I didn't get a chance to ask."

"Oh," she said, trying hard to keep the disappointment out of her voice. "But you saw him?"

"Listen, I'm busy right now. I have to go."

"Are you sure you're OK, Joe? Your voice sounds a bit strange."

"Just tired," I said. This last week I had become a stranger to myself.

"Is there anything I can do to help?"

"Look after our boy."

"Of course. You would tell me if there was anything else, wouldn't you?"

The taxi turned a corner and pulled to a stop by the side of the road.

"Got to go."

"I love you, Joe. When will you—"

I hit End, cutting her off.

The taxi had stopped on a broad, well-kept street of smart Victorian houses. I paid the driver and got out, checking up and down the street. No police. No Ben. It was 8:51 A.M.—just getting to a time when I could reasonably knock on the door of a complete stranger.

The garden of number 33 was immaculate: neatly cut lawn, trimmed edges, shrubs pruned back away from the path. A spotless cream Mercedes A-Class sat on the driveway, latest license plate. Just a few months old. The front curtains were open, upstairs and down. I rang the doorbell and stood back from the door. She was a widow who had lived alone since Ben's dad died of a heart attack a couple of years ago, and I didn't want to freak her out before we'd had a chance to talk.

A figure approached down the hallway, outline blurred through the frosted glass, accompanied by the yelping and yapping of small dogs. For one mad moment I wondered whether it might be Ben walking down the hall toward me. Or maybe I'd walk in and find him sitting on the sofa in his pajamas, munching a piece of toast, watching Jeremy Kyle with eight days of beard on his face. After all, what better place was there to lie low than in your mum's spare room, 250 miles from London? Maybe he'd been here all week, monitoring everything via social media.

The door opened, and a thick security chain snapped taut.

71

A woman looked at me through the gap.

Not Ben.

She was in her midfifties, younger than I'd expected, trim and tanned and dressed in white jeans and a long gray woolen cardigan belted at the waist. She had the same oval face shape as Ben, the same eyes, deep dark brown—eyes that narrowed now at the arrival of a stranger on her doorstep. There was a scramble of growling and jumping at her feet as two Jack Russell terriers tried to get through the two-inch gap allowed by the door chain.

She looked up at me without saying anything—studying me like a headmistress awaiting an explanation.

"Mrs. Delaney?" I said.

"Yes."

"I'm a friend of your son's. A friend of Ben's, from London."

Her expression changed immediately, lines of worry appearing on her brow. "What is it? Have you heard from him?"

"I was going to ask you the same question."

She shook her head. "The police say he's a missing person."

"Could I come in and talk to you for a minute, Mrs. Delaney?"

"No, I don't think so."

Maybe the idea that Ben's been hiding out here isn't so crazy.

"Just for a moment?" I said, keeping eye contact.

"Who *are* you?" Her soft Sunderland accent was tight with tension.

I was about to tell her my real name, but instinct told me not to. A colleague's name came to mind.

"My name's Sam King. One of Ben's poker friends from London."

She studied me for a moment, her eyes on my face. I realized she was looking at the bruises from last night's beating. The dogs continued to paw at the door, half whining, half growling, one trying to climb over the other as their blunt claws clicked and scraped down the doorframe.

I added, "I was wondering whether you'd—"

"Maisy! Billy!" Mrs. Delaney spoke sharply to the two terriers, ignoring me. "Go to your bed. Go on now!"

The two dogs whimpered but trotted off obediently down the hall, tails down, claws clicking on the wooden parquet flooring. She returned her gaze to me, more inquisitive now.

"How did you get my address?"

"Beth gave it to me."

"My daughter-in-law?"

"Yes."

"Why?"

"I've been worried about Ben," I said. "We all are.

Trying to find out whether he's OK. I'm at a conference in Sunderland this weekend, and I've been going to a few of his favorite places to see if anyone's seen him."

Her eyes narrowed.

"You've come all the way from London to do that?"

"I was here anyway, thought I'd try to help. Have you heard from him recently?"

"Not this week. But I told everything to the policeman who came around on Tuesday."

"Is he here?"

"Of course not. Why would he be here?"

There was the tension in her voice again. Her anxiety was palpable—but was it the despair of having lost her son, or the strain of lying to protect him?

"Has he been here at all this week?" I said.

She ignored the question, indicating my bruises with a slender index finger.

"What happened to your face?"

"Last night I was at a casino in town looking for Ben. The bouncers took exception to me asking questions."

"Clearly. What do you know about my son?"

"Could we talk inside for a couple of minutes?"

She crossed her arms, and her voice took on a harder edge. "I'm not sure you realize quite how odd it is, Mr. King, you just turning up here out of the blue—no phone call, no warning. Just arriving on my doorstep asking about my Benjamin."

"I know. I'm sorry. Everything was a bit rushed, there was no time to call a—"

"It's not normal behavior."

"This is not a normal situation."

Her eyes narrowed. "I've no idea who you are. You could be anyone."

"I'm a friend of Ben's."

"So you say. How do I know it wasn't Ben that gave you those bruises?"

That's uncomfortably close to the truth. I held my hands up.

"Listen, Mrs. Delaney, I just want to make sure that your son's all right. He's a great guy and I know he'd do the same for me if I went AWOL. That's all."

She peered at me then, a little less certain. "Do you think he's in some kind of trouble?"

"He's been out of contact, which is unlike him. He's not answering his phone, and . . ."

"And?"

I checked up and down the street again, in case anyone else was in earshot. "He and Beth are having some . . . issues."

"So the police said, but I don't believe it. Not my Ben."

"It's true. I wish it wasn't."

She stared at me, sizing me up, concern for her own safety tempered by fear for her son. She seemed torn between the prospect of letting a complete stranger into her house and the worry for her boy and his situation. I wondered whether she would be guided by her head or her heart.

Finally, her concern as a mother won out. She called the dogs back to her side and unhooked the door chain.

"Why don't you come in for a minute?" Her voice softened a little. "Since you've come all this way."

72

Mrs. Delaney showed me into the immaculate living room while she busied herself in the kitchen making a fresh pot of coffee. The wall and mantelpiece were decorated with pictures of the Delaney family. Holidays in Sydney, Rio, Florida, and Egypt among them. Many of the pictures I recognized from Ben's own study back in Hampstead.

Mrs. Delaney appeared again, both dogs trotting alongside her. She handed me a coffee in a bone china cup and saw the picture I was looking at, teenaged Ben with his prefect badge.

"That was the year our Ben got the school prize," she said. "Such a clever boy."

I sipped my coffee. It was good, smooth and strong, an expensive blend.

"His school looks a bit posher than mine."

"Top three in the northeast."

"Your daughter-in-law said he didn't go to the local comp."

"Brayfield? God no, pet. I'd rather have home-schooled him than sent him there. Terrible place, full of all the wrong sort. And it's even worse now than it was when Benjamin was a lad."

She gestured toward an armchair at the end of the living room and asked me to sit down. I liked her, liked the fact that she had listened to me, let me into her house, given me the benefit of the doubt when most people would have slammed the door in my face. She seemed genuine, and the worry on her face was clear to see.

"My name's Ruth, by the way."

"Thanks for letting me in." I sank back into the deep leather armchair. "Can't believe that Ben's been out of touch for this long. You must be worried sick."

"I've barely slept. A few hours a night."

"When did you last hear from him?"

"He was never the best at staying in touch, to be honest. Normally every other weekend, sometimes every third weekend depending on what he had going on at work. He was so busy with his business, he wasn't in touch the weekend just gone."

"I think he came up here from London last night," I added. "I thought he might have dropped in to see you."

"Benjamin's not been to visit me since the summer," she said slowly.

My cell phone rang. The display showed a cell phone number that the phone didn't recognize. Probably junk. I rejected the call.

"Sorry about that."

"Tell me more about the . . . *woman* they say he's involved with," she said. "A friend's wife, the policeman told me?"

"Don't really know her that well," I lied. "Apparently, they'd been having a fling for a few months, but she wanted to break it off."

"Probably realized she couldn't get her hands on

his money. Trollops like that are always after something."

I felt myself stiffen involuntarily. "I'm not sure that's quite how it happened."

"Really?" she said slowly, her tone changing. "So how *do* you think it happened?"

"From what I heard, it was more of a mutual—"

A flickering in the glass-framed pictures on the mantelpiece caught my eye. Pulses of reflected light.

Flashing lights. Flashing *blue* lights.

There was a police patrol car outside the house, blue lights revolving. As I watched, both doors flew open and a pair of uniformed officers jumped out.

And now Ruth Delaney was on her feet, a kitchen knife in her hand—the blade up and pointed toward me.

"You're *him*, aren't you?"

"Who?"

"Her husband! The husband of the woman who threw herself at Benjamin. I knew it the moment I saw you."

"You called the police." I couldn't quite believe it.

"They warned me about you!" Her voice was suddenly as hard as stone.

I stood up quickly, adrenaline jolting me upright. The police officers were across the road, one of them talking into his radio.

"What? What do you mean?"

"The police said you might come here. And I should call them if you did. And now you're going to stay right here and tell them the truth about what you did to my boy!"

The sound of boots crunching quickly up the gravel drive to the front door. I moved toward the hallway. I had only seconds.

"Mrs. Delaney, I had nothing to do with—"

"Don't come near me!" She jabbed the knife in my direction, and the dogs picked up her fear instantly, their hackles raised, mouths drawn back in a snarl to show rows of teeth.

I held my hands out as I edged past her. "I'm not going to hurt you."

One of the Jack Russells leaped forward and locked onto my ankle with a growl. I stumbled backward into the hall, dragging the dog with me, its teeth like a line of needles in my flesh. There was a hammering on the front door and shouts from the two police officers, dark shapes through the glass.

Got to get out of here.

The dog continued snarling and biting down, and I half dragged it down the hallway with me as I headed for the kitchen, feeling its hot breath on my skin, blood in my shoe. Finally, I shook it loose, turned, and ran as Ruth Delaney started screaming.

"This is your bitch wife's fault! God help you if you've hurt Benjamin, you bastard! I'll kill you myself, I swear it!"

I turned right into a conservatory, sent a wicker side table flying, and burst through the open French doors, sprinting the length of her garden without looking back. I could still hear wild barking and screaming as I smashed through a trellis panel and dived headlong over the wall into her neighbor's garden.

I kicked through a panel in the next fence and kept going.

73

There were seven splinters in the heel of my right palm from the variety of fences I had vaulted, climbed up, and heaved myself over as I ran from the police. Four of the tiny wooden shards came out, but the other three were lodged too deep, and the more I tried to wheedle them out, the deeper they went. *The harder you push, the more you struggle, the deeper the barb is buried.*

I had pushed too hard, and now it was me that was about to be buried.

With the hood of my sweatshirt pulled over my head, I sat on a bench at Sunderland train station, near the end of the platform. As far away from other people as I could get. I had dodged a slack-looking young policeman on the way in and was keeping an eye on him as he checked slowly up and down the platforms. Looking for someone.

My right arm ached from where I had jumped a wall and landed badly. The wound from the dog bite on my left ankle had bled down into my shoe, four distinct punctures on each side of my leg, and was now a low throbbing ache stiffening the joint and making it painful to walk on. I flexed my ankle, rotating it, teeth gritted against the pain. It had never been great since metal pins were put in it more than ten years ago, after one drunken night that had wrecked my sporting career.

I dialed Larssen's number, and he picked up after the first ring.

"Joe, your phone's been off. What have you been doing?"

I touched the bruise by my eye socket. "This and that."

"Are you OK? You sound terrible."

"I've been worse. Can't remember when, but hey-ho."

"Where are you?"

"Waiting for a train."

"You're coming back to London?"

"Yes."

"Good. We need to talk about your options."

I tensed, anticipating another sucker punch, unsure how it was possible to make things any worse at this point. "Options?"

"As in what we do next. Your best course of action at this point."

I took a deep breath, let it out slowly. Turned my head slightly so I could track the progress of the young police officer. He'd moved to the next platform over and was talking to a fluorescent-jacketed member of the station staff.

"So what do you think I should do? What's your advice?"

"Well, Joe, the police have your admission that you were at the scene of the incident, backed up with forensic evidence, they've found your cell phone at the supposed burial location, plus Mr. Delaney's blood in

the trunk of your car. They also have suspicious internet searches on your cell phone and metadata that
looks like you were sending messages using his phone
to mislead the police. They have forensic authorship
analysis indicating that he was not the author of messages posted. And underlying it all, of course, is the
fact that your wife was sexually involved with Ben
Delaney."

He said nothing for a moment, letting the news
sink in. All I could think of was Ben's grinning face.

Game, set, and match, big fella.

The bright steel railway tracks were only a few feet
in front of me. I sat forward on the bench and stared at
them. How much pain would there be if you got hit by
an intercity doing a hundred miles an hour? Probably
nothing at all, or maybe just for a second. It would be
too fast. One second you'd be there—living, breathing, thinking. A functioning member of the human
race. The next second scattered, extinguished, destroyed. Gone.

Larssen said, "Joe, are you still there?"

"I'm fucked, aren't I?"

He paused before answering. "We need to sit down
and talk about this properly, Joe. Face-to-face. No
more phone calls, no more getting on trains and
running around the country. That's my advice."

"Are you still representing me?"

He hesitated again, more electronic silence hanging between us. "If we start doing things my way."

"Does that include walking into a police station
and giving myself up?"

"You make it sound like you've been on some kind
of crime spree."

"Just asking the question."

"The advice I gave you yesterday still stands, yes."

The phone was hot against my ear.

"So this is it, then."

"How do you mean?"

"Police, a murder charge, bail if I'm really lucky."

"Nothing's certain at this stage. But we need to start being smart about all this."

"Do you think I'll get bail?"

Once again, he avoided my question. "Are you on your way back to London?"

"Due back in about three and a half hours."

I agreed to get a taxi from King's Cross and go straight to his office as soon as my train got in—no detours, no visits, no unscheduled stops—for 3:00 P.M. He and I would prepare and discuss strategy for an hour, and he would send one of the firm's young associates to my house to pick up a suit for me to change into. Then he would drive me to Kilburn Police Station, and I would give myself up to DCI Naylor before the end of the day. Except Larssen didn't call it "giving myself up"; he called it "making myself available for further questioning."

It was 10:55 A.M. A week and a day ago, at this very moment, I had been standing in front of a tenth grade class discussing *Of Mice and Men*. Eight days ago.

I promised Larssen I would be there at 3:00 P.M.

74

In the rearmost car on the train home, as far from other passengers as possible, I sat in a corner seat with the hood pulled over my head. I had nothing to do. Nothing to read, no one to talk to. Nothing to think about apart from police stations and DNA evidence and what I would say to my son. My cell phone, on the train table in front of me, was my only companion. And however much I tried to look out of the window as eastern England rolled by, my eyes were drawn back to the rectangle of black plastic time and again. It was my only connection to my family. My only weapon in the fight.

Except this weapon—or rather its predecessors—had already burned me twice. The first by its discovery in a suspicious place. Then by a suspicious internet search history stored in the memory of its replacement. Maybe this expensive piece of highly engineered electronics was ready to betray me for a third time. What else could it be hiding?

I opened up Google and went through the search history from the last couple of days. How did you even hack into that? The searches all looked familiar in any case: train timetables, maps, the lawyer's number from

Mel's secret cell phone, searches on Sunderland and casinos in the city center. No surprises there.

What else could it be? All the text messages looked familiar. I put the cell phone on the train table in front of me, turning it over so it was facedown. The camera lens looked at me, reminding me of the webcam on our home PC, how it had been watching me on Sunday night.

Maybe it's not what I'm doing, but what the phone's doing.

The train was pulling out of Newark Northgate station. Maybe halfway home. We picked up speed and soon the outskirts of the market town were left behind, replaced with flat countryside plowed brown for the coming winter.

I turned the phone face up again.

How are you going to betray me next time, you little bastard?

A dozen or so apps were in the memory, most of which were familiar.

Except one. An app called SysAdminTrack, the only one that had been downloaded. Its icon was a pair of crossed wrenches encircled by an old-fashioned cog. I opened the app, and the icon enlarged to fill the cell phone's small screen, a short menu appearing on the left-hand side. Just four items in the menu: About, Version, Upgrade, and Permissions. The first three yielded almost nothing, but the Permissions tab was more revealing. When I tapped it, a drop-down list appeared, detailing what the app could use on the phone. It had permission to access and use both front and rear cameras for stills and video, plus the microphone for audio, GPS location, internet browser, text messages, emails, apps, and internal storage. In other words, permission to access pretty much everything on my phone—for no obvious reason.

A string of results came up for it on Google, a Wikipedia entry at the top:

> SysAdminTrack is a piece of software developed by hackers to demonstrate the weaknesses of cell phone operating systems and their vulnerabilities to potential intrusion. The app opens up the phone's functions to a third-party cell phone user. That user can then operate the phone's functionality from a remote location, including access to the cameras and microphone, which can be activated without any of the standard visual cues.
>
> The app has been banned in a number of countries because of fears over privacy and the potential for users to unwittingly reveal personal information, pictures, and video to third parties.

I felt a shock of realization, as if I had grabbed hold of an electrified fence. If it could record audio, and if this app was installed on my previous phones as well, it could have recorded every conversation I'd had—with my lawyer, with the police, everyone I'd come into contact with. My cell phone was always there. And if it could access texts and emails remotely as well, it could have sent that audio to a third party.

A lot of ifs. But who could have done it?

Ben. It was him to an absolute T. A way of using technology to get what he wanted and proving how clever he was into the bargain.

The File Manager showed one audio file, just four-teen seconds long.

Two voices, one of them mine.

"You know, we could be a team, me and you."

"A team?"

"We need to work together to stop this. To bring Ben to his senses."

"Makes it sound like it's us versus him."

"Well, Beth, I hate to be brutal about this, but that's the way it—"

And then it cut out. Almost as if it had been a test. Or a mistake.

I remembered the conversation: it had been at the park with Beth yesterday morning. Ben had been eavesdropping on us the whole time. The recording meant he knew Beth and I were working together. He knew I'd ignored his various warnings to stay away from her.

It also meant Beth was in even more danger from him.

I deleted the SysAdminTrack app and sat back in my seat. The bruises on my face had started a slow, constant throb, a steady pain that flared higher whenever I touched a fingertip to my jaw or eye socket. I stared out of the window for a few minutes before remembering the call I'd rejected earlier, at Ruth Delaney's house, before she'd gone crazy with the knife. The number was stored in Received Calls, probably an automated message on how to make a payment protection insurance claim. My finger hovered over the Delete option.

I called it instead.

A male voice answered. "Hi, Joe. How are you doing?"

"Uh, OK, thanks. Who's this?"

"Mark. Mark Ruddington." From the background

noise, it sounded like he was driving. "You messaged me on Facebook, remember?"

"Oh, sorry. Of course. Thanks for getting back to me."

"So you're Melissa's other half?"

"Yes."

"Cool, cool. How's she doing? She all right?"

"She's good, thanks."

"Cool. This is so weird, you know? She was like my first proper girlfriend at school. And now here you are, her husband, messaging me on the Book of Face twenty years later, and it's like, *wow*, you know? One of those connections you never expect to make."

I had a feeling this might go on for some time before it got to the point.

"So I was writing this speech for our tenth wedding anniversary party," I said, "and I thought I'd try to get some funny stories from her schooldays. You mentioned something in a Facebook post a while back that sounded interesting. About a production of *Macbeth* in your GCSE year?"

"Oh. That." The tone of his voice changed. "The after-show party?" He paused, and I thought I heard him take a deep breath. "Melissa hasn't told you about that, then?"

"I don't know. I don't think so."

"It's not really a funny story," he said, his voice suddenly serious. "At least it wasn't at the time."

"Why not?"

He paused again. "Are you sure you want to know? Don't think it'll work very well in a party speech."

"I'm just gathering everything I can find, Mark,

then I'm going to use the best bits and edit out the rest. Any embarrassing stuff I'll just leave out."

"You'll probably want to leave this out."

"No problem. It's just useful to know, for background."

"Just for background?"

"Sure."

"OK, then. It's your party." And then he told me.

75

The pull of London was strong, like a gravitational force that was impossible to resist. It was the center of everything. My family. My home. My fate. Exhaustion caught up to me, and I dozed for twenty minutes as we neared the capital, strange half dreams flickering behind my eyelids. Images and faces. Just fragments. William in his school uniform. Beth passed out on her couch. Ben snarling, sneering in my face, fist raised. Mel in our kitchen, topless, one arm under her breasts, smiling for a selfie—

I jerked awake as the train rattled over points coming into King's Cross, my whole body jumping like I'd touched a live wire. An elderly man across the carriage looked away nervously. *Mel. A picture in our kitchen. A topless selfie for the other man in her life.*

Suddenly I knew why the picture had bothered me.

The iPhone vibrated in my hand: a text from a number I didn't recognize.

Hi Joe, here's your repeat booking www
.vipescortservices/33605 or you and your wife
might like to meet www.vipescortservices
/33699 or www.vipescortservices/33681.

Let me know. We have someone for everyone
☺ Lorna xx
2:08 P.M.

Lorna from VIP Escort Services. I had spoken to her after finding the number in Mel's secret cell phone. I clicked on the first link and waited as the phone switched to the internet browser. It seemed to take an age for the page to load.

The train slowed and finally pulled to a halt. Still the screen was blank, the loading icon whirring at the top of the screen. I waited a moment, expecting it to appear, then got off the train and started walking up the platform among a stream of passengers, head down, keeping one eye on the phone as I headed for the ticket barrier. Fumbling in my pocket for my ticket, I passed through the barrier and onto the main concourse, the latticework atrium arching high overhead. Still a blank screen on my phone. It was early afternoon on Friday, before the main commuter rush hour, but the station was already busy with workers getting off early and visitors arriving for the weekend.

The page finally loaded: a head-and-shoulders picture of the escort that Mel had booked previously with VIP. The repeat booking.

I stared at the picture. Stopped walking.

The guy behind me walked straight into me, muttering an apology as he carried on past. I stood staring, blinking fast, my mouth slightly open, the concourse alive with movement around me. I scrolled down to the name and description, scrolled back up to stare at the picture again. I could feel a vein pulsing hard in my temple, the noise and bustle of King's Cross station retreating until it felt like I was standing alone in a bubble of silence.

A single horrible thought crawled out from somewhere dark. It was so twisted I didn't want to look at it head-on, didn't want to shine a light on it for too long in case it became real. In case it refused to crawl back to the dark place in my head that it had come from. *What do you know? What do you actually know for sure? What does everything add up to?* The thought wouldn't go away.

But it couldn't be. Could it?

I had been wrong about so much these last eight days, it was time to find out if I had finally gotten something right.

It was time for answers. Time for the truth.

Time to lay it all out for Larssen and Naylor, piece by piece, and let them decide.

The phone chimed as another text message dropped in. A picture of a black Range Rover with tinted windows on the driveway of Beth's house. The shot had been taken from an upstairs window, by the look of it. Beneath it were just three words:

Please help us

My phone didn't recognize the sender's number. Not Beth—I had her number stored. So who could it be from?

Alice.

It had to be. Kolnik had gone back to their house, making threats, looking for revenge, and she was frightened. She was the innocent caught in the middle of all this.

Larssen and Naylor would have to wait. I fired back a quick reply.

On my way. Call the police
2:13 P.M. Me

I switched out of the browser and texted Larssen:

Can we push our meeting back to 4 p.m.?
2:14 P.M. Me

His reply was almost instant:

OK. Why?
2:15 P.M. Peter L

Somewhere I need to go first
2:15 P.M. Me

I shoved the phone in my pocket and ran for the taxi stand.

76

The black Range Rover was parked at an angle at the top of Ben's drive, blocking Beth's Mercedes in. I approached it at a run, put my hands up to the tinted glass to peer in. Empty. I went to the front door, ringing the bell and hammering on the door, calling Alice's name, but there was no answer. I crossed over onto the lawn and looked through the window into the living room, then walked around the right side of the house, through the gate to the garden, and around the back. The builders weren't working today, the new summerhouse still little more than foundations. Treading softly, I walked to the big windows onto the sunroom to see if I could see anything from there. A doorway into the living room gave me the same view from the other side. I moved on.

The door to the conservatory stood slightly ajar, a panel of glass shattered and lying in pieces on the thick carpet.

Shit. Maybe I was already too late.

I pushed the door open more fully and stepped inside. Listened. Heard nothing.

"Alice?" I said in a loud voice. "Beth? Are you there?"

No answer. I walked farther into the room, moving quietly. "Alice?"

Nothing. The house was silent.

I took out my cell phone and called the unrecognized number. No answer. Strained to hear a ringtone somewhere in the house.

There was a thud upstairs. I froze. They *were* here. Another one. *Thud.*

A female voice. Indistinct.

I took a step toward the hallway and hesitated. Another thud, louder this time.

Whatever was happening upstairs, it didn't sound good. Somebody was in trouble. I went quietly into the hall, across to the staircase, craning my head up to the first-floor landing.

The female voice came again, high and frightened, the words still muffled.

I moved quickly up the stairs, trying to be as quiet as I could. A crash and the sound of breaking glass. A scream.

Beth?

The main landing had five doors, all of them open. I opted for the second flight of stairs instead, taking them two at a time. Her voice came again, clearer now.

"Please! I promise I didn't tell him anything! Don't hurt me!"

The master bedroom at the end of the hallway. The door was closed.

"*Please, no!*"

A huge booming gunshot, muffled through the door but still horribly loud in the enclosed space.

I ran the length of the hallway and charged into the door with my shoulder. Wood splintered from the frame, and then I was standing in the open doorway of the master bedroom, breathing hard, adrenaline coursing through me, everything else forgotten.

There was a body sprawled on the floor by the side of the bed.

Oh no. I was too late.

77

A woman, my brain registered. She was lying on her
front, in a dark blue dressing gown that had ridden up
to reveal pale bare legs, feet splayed. One fluffy slip-
per on, one off. Seeing no one else, I ran to the bed
and knelt by the body. She was facedown in the thick
carpet. Dark hair, tied back. Glasses next to her on the
floor, one plastic arm snapped off.

"Beth?" I said, touching her shoulder.

No response. I looked for blood and shook her very
gently, the smell of gun smoke hanging in the air.

"Beth?" I said again, keeping my voice low.

As my fingers touched her throat, searching for a
pulse, her eyes flickered open.

"Joe."

"Are you OK?" I whispered. "What happened?"

She turned onto her side, blinking slowly. "Ben?"

"It's me. Joe."

She tried to focus on me, eyes wide. "He's here,"
she whispered, gripping my arm.

"Who? Alex Kolnik?"

"What?" She looked confused. "I don't . . . I don't
understand."

"Never mind. Where's Alice? Is she OK?"

"Locked herself in her bathroom."

"Are you hurt, Beth?"

She shook her head once, quickly, her bottom lip wobbling.

I was dizzy, disoriented, like I'd stepped off a carousel and everything was still spinning around me. *No time to think*. I looked around the room, searching for something, *anything*, that I could use as a weapon. The room was a mess, with chairs turned over, clothes and framed pictures scattered across the floor. A large mirror next to the walk-in wardrobe was smashed in three places, spiderwebbed with cracks from top to bottom. Next to it was a pattern of black marks scored out of the wall, which I assumed was from the shotgun blast I'd heard moments before I broke the door down.

"Is there a gun up here?" I said. "One of Ben's shotguns?"

"No. They're all in the gun safe, in the dining room."

"Where did he go?"

"Downstairs." She gestured toward an open door at the far end of the bedroom. "That door is the study, and the workroom, and then the back stairs all the way down to the pantry. He went for more cartridges."

"For the shotgun?"

"Yes."

Shit. I went to the dressing table, looking for scissors, a knife, anything that I could use as a weapon. Nothing. My eyes moved to the big department store–size mirror again, cracked from top to bottom. Using my elbow, I hit it hard, three times, until pieces started breaking off and falling to the floor. I grabbed a T-shirt from the floor, wrapped it around the biggest

piece—a six-inch shard curving to a wicked point—
and gripped the makeshift dagger tightly.

Law of the jungle.

Beth grabbed my arm.

"Listen," she whispered hoarsely in the silence.

Someone was coming up the back stairs.

The wooden steps creaked, one by one by one.
Click. Not fast, not slow. *Click. Click.* Steady, measured, even steps getting nearer and nearer. Hard shoes
on old wood, like the ticking of some huge clock.

"Hide," I whispered to Beth, but she was already
disappearing around the other side of the super-king-
size bed.

I went toward the footsteps, taking up a position to
one side of the door into the study.

Click. Click. Click.

The footsteps reached the top of the staircase, and
I tightened my grip on the jagged shard in my hand.
Silence. Then more steps, muffled by thick carpet
now, getting closer. Closer.

I raised the dagger. This was where the madness
was going to stop. *Right here, right now.* I would do
what I had to do to protect what was mine.

The footsteps were in the study, calm and even,
just a few feet away . . .

A figure appeared in the doorway.

78

"Hello, Joe," my wife said.

Mel.

I opened my mouth to speak, but no sound came out. Indicating the weapon gripped in my right hand, she said, "You're not going to stab me with that, are you?"

I lowered the piece of broken mirror, still staring at her. Everything coming together, all at once. *Here is my wife. Not Alex Kolnik. Not Ben. My wife.*

Mel held her hands up, to demonstrate she wasn't armed. There was no weapon, just a cell phone. A white iPhone I'd never seen before.

"You," I said at last.

"Me," she said, lowering her hands.

I took a step toward her.

Beth's voice from behind me. "Don't go any closer, Joe."

I turned and saw that she had come out from behind the bed and was on her feet. All the fear had gone from her face. She wasn't wide-eyed or near to tears now. Instead, she looked energized, jubilant, like the female lead about to take a bow at the end of a show. She was pointing a shotgun at me. The gun was long and black, its two barrels like twin black holes sucking all the light from the room.

"Drop the broken glass." She thumbed back the hammers on the shotgun with a loud *click-clack*. She looked thoroughly at ease with the weapon, as if she was used to handling it.

I dropped the broken piece of mirror at my feet and noticed, for the first time, how different Beth looked today. Calm and in control. I remembered, with a sudden clarity, what she had studied at college. Another piece of the jigsaw slotting into place.

"Your phone," she said. "Put it on the dressing table."

I did as I was told.

"Sit down in the chair," she said, gesturing with the gun toward an armchair by the side of the dressing table. "Put your hands on the arms of the chair."

The barrels of the shotgun followed me as I sat down.

Mel picked up my phone and switched it off, then slipped the back off it and took the battery out, putting it into her pocket. She went to stand next to Beth, giving her a handful of pink shotgun cartridges before kissing her on the cheek.

I stared at them. Knowing, finally.

I'd gotten so spun around these last eight days, it had taken me all that time to work out the truth. To arrive at the only conclusion that made sense. But I still didn't want to believe the evidence of my own eyes.

"You and her," I said to Mel. "The two of you, all this time?"

She nodded, a tiny movement. "All this time."

79

Icy sweat traced a line down my rib cage.

I was the rat, and this was the trap. I had followed the bait, all the way in, and now the trap was about to close.

Beth said, "Do you know what misdirection is, Joe?"

"It's what a magician does."

"*Exactly*. The magician's flourish with his right hand—while his left hand is flipping open the secret compartment. Misdirection. You keep the audience looking at the wrong thing. We made sure you kept looking in the wrong place while we stacked the deck against you, and we made sure the police kept looking in the wrong place too: looking at you. We pushed your buttons and off you went, swallowing everything we sent your way. Everything."

I stared at them. Too many questions.

"The Facebook posts," I said, "the texts, the message on my computer screen. It was all you?"

"Both of us," my wife said.

Beth said, "It turns out that misdirection and improvisation will take you a long way in today's world. People put their trust in the strangest things—things they can't actually see with their own eyes—and then refuse to believe what's right in front of them."

"But I spoke to him on the phone," I said, thinking back to Sunday. "I heard his voice."

"You heard a *recording* of his voice," Beth said. "He used to record all his business calls at home and keep them on memory sticks. I just had to find a few of the right phrases to edit a little fifteen-second sequence together—got the idea from one of those recorded marketing calls where you think you're speaking to a real person before you realize it's a tape."

I shook my head, amazed at my own stupidity. I'd even seen those memory sticks myself, in Ben's desk drawer.

"You handed us the situation," Beth continued, "and we improvised like a couple of Oscar winners. We had our share of luck as well, but improv is like anything else, really—the more you do it, the more it comes naturally. And I realized, we're *really* good at it."

"Good at lying," I said. "Congratulations."

"Not lying," she said. "Acting."

"Your degree, at college. You did drama, didn't you?"

"Well remembered! Ben never let me finish my degree, never let me become an actress. He never let me do what I loved. And he never realized that I had actually been acting for years—acting like the faithful housewife, perfect and calm and *satisfied*, always happy in hubby's shadow. But this week has been the performance of a lifetime, don't you think? And you played along so well without even realizing what you were doing!"

"The stuff about Alex Kolnik," I said wearily, "what about that?"

"All nonsense. Never seen the man. Ben was going to get a restraining order to keep him at arm's length anyway."

"But you rented the black Range Rover to give the story a little bit of color."

"That was your idea too—you mentioned early on that you saw one at the hotel on Thursday night, and we thought there might be a chance to throw it into the mix. We rented it for a week and kept it in extended parking, then Mel drove it over when I met you at the park yesterday. And it came in handy today as well."

"What about the deleted email from Ben saying he was 'going home'? I might never have found it."

"We knew you would, eventually—you're a very easy person to read. Although Christ knows it took you bloody long enough to hack Mel's bogus email account, even though she'd used the most obvious password ever."

"How did you know I'd found the email?"

"A fairly basic piece of gatekeeper software told us which emails you'd opened. And, of course, you took the bait. You ran away up north just when the police were going to arrest you again. It made you look even guiltier, like you were fleeing the inevitable."

There had been no messages from Ben in Mel's email account from before Thursday night. My assumption was that she had deleted anything incriminating that dated back before their liaison at the Premier Inn.

But now I knew the truth: there *were* no messages before that day. Because there was no relationship with Ben. It had all been a fiction, constructed online, fed by social media and fueled by good old-fashioned suspicion and jealousy.

And I had eaten up every last word.

80

I sat up straighter in the chair, swallowing hard on a dry throat. "You said *was*."

"What?" Beth said.

"Ben *was* going to get a restraining order."

"Yes, I did, didn't I?"

"Past tense," I said, holding her gaze.

"Click-clock, tick-tock, and *finally* the penny drops," she said.

There was silence for a moment as I weighed my next words carefully. "So it was you all along. You did it."

"Did what, Joe?"

"You killed him."

"But how do you know it wasn't you, Joe? My poor darling husband—you hurt him and then you left him; you *abandoned* him. How do you know you've not been walking around as a murderer for the last eight days?"

"Because then there wouldn't have been a need for any of this." I gestured at her, at Mel, at the mess in the bedroom. "All these lies. All this misdirection. I would have gone down for it, and that would have been that. Justice would have taken its course."

"But instead you handed him to us on a plate. It's a lot easier to suffocate a man when he's unconscious, believe me."

She said it in a matter-of-fact way, as if she were talking about the weather.

"You were there in that underground parking lot when it all kicked off, weren't you?"

"Yes. Ben had asked to meet with Mel at the hotel, just the two of them. But I didn't trust him. I wanted to be nearby in case he tried to harm her."

"You saw Ben and me arguing."

"I watched it all. Unobserved in the shadows."

"And that's when you did it?"

Her face hardened at the memory. "You rushed off in a tearing hurry, and then it was just me and my bastard husband. I got out of my car, praying with all my might that you'd done the job for me. But you hadn't. So I fetched the blanket from the trunk of my car, thinking I would say I was making him a pillow if anyone drove down the ramp. But no one did."

"And?"

"I stood over him with the blanket for a minute. Perhaps two. No one else came in. We were all alone. And while I stood there, an idea came to me." Her eyes were shining with a dark light. "And then I smothered him."

Silence hung heavily between the three of us for a moment.

"It was really quite easy," she added.

"You called Mel back," I said finally, "and the two of you put his body in the trunk of your car."

"Yes. Then we went for a drive."

"And then you planted evidence in the trunk of my car," I said. "Suspicious searches on my phone. Planted my phone at the country park." I shook my head. "This is so screwed up it's unbelievable."

Beth laughed. "It's *completely* believable, that's the whole point! Cuckolded husband takes revenge on wife's lover—it's been happening for thousands of years. And the more you acted like nothing had happened to him, the guiltier you appeared to the police."

"I was the fall guy, all along."

"And a convincing fall guy needs convincing motivation."

"The pictures on that cell phone, the naked selfies of Mel—what about them?"

My wife said, "A very busy Saturday morning while you were out doing pools and parties with Wills."

I knew the answer to my next question, but I had to ask it anyway. "So there was never any affair between you and Ben?"

"He's not her type," Beth cut in. "She told you that on Sunday."

I was silent for a moment, trying to take it all in. Trying to make sense of my emotions. Disbelief. Anger.

Heartbreak.

"How could you do this?" I said to Mel quietly.

She said nothing.

"We didn't have any choice," Beth answered for her.

It was clear that she was in charge. She was the alpha female, and Mel, my confident, outgoing wife, was the beta. Just like her mum, Mel had ended up in thrall to a dominant, controlling personality, pulled along in her slipstream. Beth was calling the shots— serene Beth, the shy other half who had always seemed to be in Ben's shadow. Not anymore. Now *she* was the boss. Maybe for the first time in her life.

"I was asking my wife," I said.

Mel looked away from me.

"Mel?" I said again.

"We have to protect what we've got," she said, looking at the floor.

"And what's that?"

"Each other."

"And that's worth committing murder for, is it?"

Beth cut in, her voice hard. "Absolutely."

The last time I had seen them in the same room, one had been screaming obscenities and the other crying. More lies, all for my benefit—and for our friends and dozens of customers who could testify to the ferocity of a hatred between spurned wife and secret lover.

"How long?" I said.

"What?" Beth said.

"You two. How long?"

"Does it matter? What's important is that we lost each other for too many years, and then we found each other again."

"You had a fling when you were fifteen, the two of you."

"You spoke to Mark Ruddington, then."

"He told me about the party after the school play when you two first got together." Another piece of evidence that I had held in my hands—and failed to see what it meant. "But that was when you were teenagers. How did you get from that to this?"

"Teenagers are real," Mel said quietly. "It's adulthood when we get lost, forget who we are."

"Come on, Mel, you can do better than that. This

is me you're talking to, your husband. I know who you are."

"You don't get it, do you? Teenagers are honest. They're true—that's why they feel so vulnerable. It's easy to forget that with all the other junk that gets in the way as you get older. Work, marriage, kids, mortgage. I woke up one morning and realized I'd turned into someone I didn't recognize, someone I didn't even like anymore. And then Beth and I bumped into each other again at Charlotte and Gary's wedding a couple of years ago, and it all just came back, like being teenagers again."

"That was the party where you said you made the mistake. A drunken kiss that led to his obsession with you."

Beth said, "There was a drunken kiss, all right, but not with boring old Ben."

"That was where the two of you got back together?"

"Like waking up again after twenty years in a coma," Mel said quietly.

"This is not you, Mel. This isn't reality."

"I haven't forgotten what's real," she said. "Who I really am."

"Then what about our son? What about William? What about me?"

"You pushed us into this corner," Beth said. "If you'd kept plodding along like you've done for the last ten years of your life—good old Joe, head down, stuck in your rut—you needn't have been involved. But as it is—"

"As it is, you're framing me for a crime I didn't commit."

She jabbed the shotgun toward me.

"That was *your* choice. You got involved when you didn't have to, when you stuck your nose in. And then, almost like it was fate, you presented us with an opportunity that was too good to pass up. Gift wrapped and tied with a bow."

Now the shock was receding, it was starting to become clear: I needed to get out of this house, grab William, and take him somewhere safe. Somewhere far away from these two.

I needed to take the initiative.

"There's something you should both know."

"What's that?"

"DCI Naylor agreed to meet me here," I lied, checking my watch. "He's going to be here any minute."

"You called him from your cell phone?"

"At King's Cross."

"No, you didn't. You texted your lawyer, and then you came straight here."

"Naylor's on his way," I said again, a desperate lie that felt foolish in my mouth.

"No." Beth shook her head. "And do you know how I know you're lying? You thought you'd found the little spy inside your cell phone, didn't you? Thought you'd gotten rid of it and that your phone was safe to use again."

"The app you installed on my phone. System Track or whatever it's called."

"SysAdminTrack," she corrected me. "Best sixty pounds I ever spent. It's been on all your phones, by the way: the one you lost at the park, the replacement, and the one you've got now."

"I deleted the app."

"You *thought* you deleted it. It stays in the system memory, hidden. The only way to properly get rid of it—if you're not the one who downloaded it—is to do a full factory reset or get a new phone."

"You sound like an expert on this stuff."

"I installed it on Alice's phone last year when she started going to the park with boys after school. But I've always kept up with Ben's line of work. He never told me anything about what he did, about the industry that made his fortune—*our* fortune—so I made sure I kept up to speed. Waiting for the day he asked me to join him in the business." She frowned. "He never did, of course. Never thought I was worthy."

"Is that why you killed him?"

She ignored my question. "You didn't call your detective chief inspector, did you?" Her gaze was cool, unflustered. "You're a terrible liar, Joe. It puts you at a big disadvantage."

"I guess I'll bow to your expertise in that area."

"On the other hand, you made the perfect patsy—you're so predictable. Combine that with an app that turns your cell phone into a little tracking, spying device, and we knew exactly what you were doing from one minute to the next. We could switch on the phone's cameras and microphone remotely without you knowing, record video, audio, take pictures, access your texts and web browser, check your location via GPS, see what you were searching for on Google."

"Like a hotel in Sunderland."

"Yes! Or that awful casino. Or train times from King's Cross, or Fryent Country Park, or my little trail of bread crumbs to lead you to Steven Beecham—even though we couldn't figure out what the hell you were looking up STEB for at first! But yes, every single search. Sometimes it was like you couldn't even make a cup of tea without googling exactly how, when, and where you were going to do it. Even when you found out about the app, we knew that too—because you did a search on it."

I realized something else, another piece slotting into place. "You had it installed on Ben's phone as well, didn't you?"

She smiled. "For months. So we knew exactly what he was planning."

81

"What *was* he planning?" I said.

"A renegotiation of our relationship."

"Meaning what?"

"Two options. One—complete and utter humiliation, admit my guilt, capitulate, and grovel for another chance. Or two—divorce. But not amicable, nothing civilized for the sake of the child. That wasn't Ben's way at all."

"Not enough for him to win—everyone else had to lose, right?"

"Exactly. He was going to screw me over completely, either way—it made it worse for him that it was another woman, rather than a man. I would have been left with barely a fraction of what should have been mine. *Scorched earth*, he called it. All the sacrifices I'd made for him: my degree, my body, my freedom, my career. My life. All those sacrifices, to get screwed again at the end of it. But this way, my way, we get everything."

"He found you out, didn't he? He found out about the two of you."

"He was way ahead of you, Joe."

"It seems like most people are," I said, mostly to myself.

Mel added, "He asked to meet me that Thursday night supposedly for some off-the-books HR advice. But when I got there, he just showed me a picture of me and Beth together, said he knew everything, and gave me an ultimatum."

"Which was?"

"End it. End the affair and admit in writing to everything that had gone on. Apologize in person and in writing, to him and to you, apologize to his daughter, to his mother. Like Bee said, complete humiliation."

Beth cut in. "And I would then have to agree to dissolve our prenuptial agreement and sign a postnup in its place, with various clauses covering total forfeiture of assets and guardianship of Alice in case of further adultery."

"Using Mel as the messenger," I said.

"Yes. To show who was the boss."

"But you knew what he was planning anyway, because you were monitoring his calls, texts, and emails."

Beth said, "We knew it was coming; we just didn't know when. Turned out it was one boring average Thursday evening at a shitty little hotel off the North Circular."

No wonder Ben didn't want to talk when I saw him in that underground parking lot. He already had a lot on his mind.

I realized something else. "When he gave that ultimatum, you were listening in to the conversation, weren't you?"

She nodded.

"Every word, sitting in my car one floor below." She gestured at me with the shotgun again, the twin black barrels pointed at my head. "And then *who* should walk in at the end, right into the middle of everything?"

"Me."

"Good old Joe, walking into the game without even realizing it was already in play. But you came *so* close this past week to figuring it all out. There were a few times I thought you'd caught us, but you were never quite ready to make the mental leap."

"I got there in the end."

She looked amused by that. "So what was it that finally clicked for you?"

"The selfie on Mel's secret phone—the one with her topless in the kitchen. The one you showed me at the pub on Sunday. Something about it bothered me, and I couldn't work out what. It was only on the train back here today that I realized."

"What?"

"It wasn't *where* it was taken, it was *when*. All the date and time data had been deleted from the image, but the kitchen noticeboard was in the background of the shot, and William's Superstar certificate from school was on it. He didn't bring that home until Thursday evening, which meant that picture had to have been taken *after* she'd supposedly had this massive fight with Ben that sent him over the edge. So I knew Mel was involved in something, that she was still lying to me. I hadn't put you two together yet, but I knew the picture was a lie."

"Indeed," she said with a half smile. "Like all the rest of those naughty pictures. Pictures lie better than words, most of the time anyway."

"Then there was the escort agency. They were keen to get their repeat booking."

"Ah yes. Young Jules."

"They sent me his picture, just a head and shoulders. But as soon I saw it, I knew."

"You knew what?"

"He was the man I saw at the country park on Monday morning. Not Ben, but his double. Same height, same build, same hair. Put Ben's jacket on him and he's a dead ringer for your husband, or at least he was from fifty yards away."

"We were worried that he might not keep quiet after the police started searching the park," she said in the same matter-of-fact tone. "But it turns out that prostitutes are more easily bribed than most, and young Jules was no exception. Not really a surprise, is it?"

"All right," I said. "You win."

Beth shifted her grip on the shotgun slightly but kept it trained on me. "I could tell you were getting close this morning, that the penny was finally going to drop. I just *knew* it. So I had to get you here one more time, and I knew you'd do the full white-knight routine for Alice if you thought young Mr. Kolnik had turned up."

"So what happens now?"

"The finale," Beth replied. "Mel—you know what to do."

From a pocket, Mel produced a pair of surgical gloves and proceeded to put them on, the tight rubber snapping into place. From her handbag, she took a black-handled kitchen knife, a length of clothesline, duct tape, black leather gloves, and a black balaclava. I recognized it. All of it. The winter gloves I'd gotten last Christmas, the balaclava from a pre-William skiing holiday. The tape and clothesline had been in the bottom of my toolbox for years.

"What are you doing?" I said to my wife, a hollow feeling in the pit of my stomach.

Mel didn't answer me. The knife in her hand, she drew up Beth's sleeve to expose the skin. Hesitated.

"Do it," Beth urged her. "Go on."

Mel ran the blade down Beth's forearm, not hard enough to break the skin.

"I can't," she said quietly.

"Yes, you can. Harder."

Mel tried again, and this time Beth pushed her arm against the blade. A bright line of blood appeared as the knife cut a groove in her forearm.

"That's more like it," she said, blood starting to flow freely from the wound.

"Doesn't it hurt?" Mel said, her voice shaking.

"It's fine. Carry on with what you're doing."

Mel dropped the duct tape and the clothesline on the floor by the bed and the bloody knife on the floor about six feet from me. Maybe I could dive for the knife before Beth shot me.

I inched my feet wider apart on the floor.

Beth said, "A terrible thing happened here today, Joe. You broke into my house."

"I came to protect you. I thought you were in danger."

"Sweet. What *actually* happened was that you broke in downstairs, carrying that knife."

She indicated the black-handled boning knife on the floor. It looked familiar, and I realized why: it was from our kitchen at home. I used it to cut up lemons for Mel's G&T.

"You were looking to finish what you started a week ago," she continued, blood dripping steadily from her arm onto the cream carpet. "To get revenge on Ben for sleeping with your wife and ruining your career. And when killing Ben wasn't enough, you decided to get revenge in another way. By having his wife, just like he had yours."

"You're crazy, Beth."

"You tried to rape me."

"Of course I didn't." I sat up straighter, shifted my weight forward in the chair slightly. "What the hell are you saying?"

"You came at me with that knife—which only has your fingerprints on it, by the way—and tried to attack me. You cut me, tried to grab the shotgun to take it away from me, turn it on me. More nice clear fingerprints."

"I haven't touched the gun."

"You will have, in a minute."

"This is madness. Pure and simple."

"Is it? I think you'll find it makes a certain kind of sense."

"Stop it now. It's gone far enough. You've made your point."

Her eyes narrowed, and she took another step nearer, still leveling the shotgun at me. Her voice, when she spoke, was as taut as piano wire.

"Don't. Tell me. What. To do." Blood from her arm continued to drip in deep red drops onto the cream carpet.

I held my hands up, palms out.

"OK, OK." I put my hands down on the front of the chair arms, for leverage. Ready to make my move. *Protect the boy.* "You're the boss, Beth."

"That's right—for the first time in my life. I had eighteen years of my father telling me what to do. Who I should be friends with. Who I was and who I should fall in love with. Then another sixteen of Ben doing exactly the same. Telling me we didn't need to be careful, then telling me I couldn't have an abortion when he got me pregnant in our final year of college. Telling me to stay home and look after Alice full-time instead of pursuing my acting career. Then telling me he didn't want me working until Alice went to college. And then you, *you*, thinking you could take over from where Ben left off. Well, today it stops. For good."

I nodded toward the open door onto the landing. "And what about him?"

They both half turned toward the empty doorway, and I launched myself out of the chair, reaching for Beth, for the gun, for anything I could get ahold of to push those twin black barrels away from me. There was a split second when everything seemed to slow down: Mel let out a little shriek of surprise, Beth turned back, and I was lunging toward her, grabbing for the gun, my hand almost on it, the barrels dipping away out of my grasp, empty air, but I was almost on her, almost—

And that was when she shot me.

82

The blast hit like a sledgehammer and spun me face-first onto the carpet. I groaned and clutched my thigh, blood oozing stickily through my jeans. Mel threw herself on me, which was pretty much the last thing I was expecting to happen.

"No, Bee!" she said, using her body to shield me. "It was never supposed to end like this!"

"Your husband didn't give us any choice, Mel."

"No! He was just supposed to be a distraction for the police while we got everything sorted. That was what we agreed."

"He's our fall guy."

"But I thought that meant in court, with the police, lawyers, and everything! Not like this!"

"He took that choice away from us when he turned detective. As soon as he found your second phone and told the police about it, he was signing his own death warrant—you knew that. We both knew it."

In a small voice, Mel said, "I never wanted him hurt."

"We don't have any choice now," Beth said. "We have to play this out. All the way."

Mel didn't move.

"Melissa? It's time."

My wife turned to me, tears on her face.

"I didn't mean this to happen," she said to me. "Not like this."

"It hasn't happened yet," I said, my voice hoarse. The pain was excruciating, like a red-hot branding iron held against my leg. "You can still stop it. Stop her."

She shook her head, a tiny movement. "I can't," she whispered.

There was a dull void in my chest in counterpoint to the burning agony of my leg. My wife was here, next to me, protecting me, touching me, and I felt nothing for her.

It was clear that she had not loved me for months, or years. And now I finally understood, and the bond was broken. William and I were on our own now. I was his only hope. Beth snapped the shotgun open and dropped the spent cartridge, still smoking, to the floor. Blood from her arm continued to drip onto the carpet, the bedsheet, her dressing gown.

"Remember your choice, Mel. You know you've already made it."

"Mel, don't do this," I said. "It'll follow you forever."

Beth took two pink shotgun cartridges from her pocket—*Eley Hi-Power*, I noticed, trying to remember why this was significant—and reloaded the gun smoothly.

"Get up, Mel," she said.

Slowly, without looking at me, Mel got to her feet.

"Step away from him," Beth said.

Mel did as she was told, and Beth snapped the shotgun shut. "What you've got in your leg is bird shot," she said to me calmly. "This load I've got here, though, is a double-zero weight. For big game." She leveled the twelve-gauge at me again. "Enough for a deer, or a big cat. Or a man."

"Enough for murder," I said through gritted teeth.

"It'll be self-defense, Joe. You're twice my size."

We stared at each other for a moment in silence, the only sound the faint clicking of a bedside alarm clock.

"Where is he?" I said, trying to keep my voice level. "Where's Ben?"

She ignored my question. "You know our favorite topic of conversation, me and your beautiful wife, these last few months?"

"Apart from murder?"

"Our favorite thing was to invent stories about how we could be together. Without any men in the picture. But with our children, and our houses, our money. Without having a couple of messy, complicated divorces. And one night, we were both drunk, egging each other on, and I said maybe the best outcome would be if one of you died and the other one went to prison for it. It solved everything in one go. We would get everything, and you two would both be gone, and people would feel *sorry* for us all the time. The sympathy would be fabulous. Then a week ago—Christ almighty—you had your chance. I'm sitting in my car, watching you, thinking, *Yes, he's actually going to do it right here in this shitty underground parking lot. This is literally our dream come true.* But you couldn't even get that right."

"Where is he now?" I asked again.

"Same place he's been since Thursday night."

"At the country park?"

She laughed.

"No! We did drive out there, but there were too many people around, and he was just too bloody heavy to carry into the woods, even with the two of us. So we just left your phone there instead. Then I had a better idea. We brought him home."

"Home?"

"He posted a picture of his own final resting place on Facebook a couple of weeks ago. Spooky or what?"

I frowned, thinking back to all the posts on Ben's account from the last few weeks.

Building work. Excavation. Foundations.

"The new summerhouse in your back garden."

She raised the shotgun to her shoulder. "He loved this house. And now he'll always be a part of it."

"You'll never get away with this."

"We've been getting away with it right from the word *go*."

Got to keep her talking. Think of something. Think.

"That picture downstairs, of you at the end of a school show? The one that Mark Ruddington posted on Facebook?"

"What about it?"

"You played Lady Macbeth, didn't you?"

She nodded, lowering the shotgun for a moment as she recalled the lines. " 'What need we fear who knows it, when none can call our power to account? Yet who would have thought the old man to have had so much blood in him?' "

"And what about Ben's blood?"

"What about it?"

"Do you think you'll ever be able to wash that off your hands?"

She frowned, summoning another line from memory. " 'What's done cannot be undone.' "

I dragged myself toward her, my shattered leg trailing blood. Fear and pain. *This is it. You have to disarm her or kill her, for William to have a chance. Can you do it? Can you kill her with your bare hands?*

Yes. No choice. Bring her close.

"You don't have to do this, Beth."

She took a step forward and raised the gun to point at my head again. "Sorry, Joe. But I do."

"It'll be my word against yours, and you'll win hands down," I said quickly. "You're much better at this than I am; you've shown that this week. You win."

"It's the final act, Joe." She stared down the barrel at me.

"My word against yours, Beth. Think about it. Who in their right mind is going to believe me? No one."

She opened her mouth to reply but was interrupted.

A new voice—young, unsteady, fighting sobs—cut in from the landing beyond the door.

"Yes, they will, Joe. They will believe you."

This time there *was* someone standing in the doorway. Alice.

83

She was crying.

"Mum," Alice said, fighting back a sob. "How could you?"

Keeping an eye on me, Beth turned her head slightly to talk to her daughter.

"Go downstairs, sweetie. I'll be there in a minute. It's not safe up here just now."

"*How could you do it?*" Alice screamed from the doorway, pink cell phone in her hand.

Beth was unmoved. "You don't know what's going on here, Alice. Go downstairs now, please. I'm not going to ask nicely again."

"I *do* know what's going on."

"No," Beth said firmly. "You really don't."

"I know everything."

"How long have you been listening?"

"The whole time."

"That's not true, is it, Alice? Auntie Mel checked the landing a minute ago and you weren't there."

"I was in my room."

"So you've not heard anything, then."

"I heard what you said about Dad!" Alice screamed back, her voice cracking. "What you did to him!"

"I don't know what you think you heard, Alice, but you're confused."

"It's in your own words, Mum!"

"What are you talking about, sweetie?"

"You think you're so clever, don't you? So clever with your plans and your acting and, like, pretending to be Dad online? Well, you're not."

Alice came farther into the room, her face streaked with tears. She seemed to see my injury for the first time, the carpet around me stained dark with blood.

"She shot you," she said.

"Why will people believe me, Alice?"

Beth swung the shotgun back toward me. "Shut up."

Alice said, "Because of the recording."

Mel looked at her blankly. "What recording?"

"The recording I just made on your phone. And yours, *Mum*."

Beth was frowning, spots of color in her cheeks. The shotgun wavered slightly away from me as she turned toward her daughter.

"What are you talking about, sweetie?"

"Did you think you're the only one who can buy an app and install it on someone else's phone? Did you think I'd never find it when you put it on my phone, to spy on me? You think you're the only one who can listen in to a private conversation? Have you checked your phones recently, either of you?"

Mel picked up Beth's phone from the dressing table, unlocked it, scrolled through a list.

"SysAdminTrack," she said in a small voice. "It's on here."

Alice said, "Check the recordings."

"What have you done, Alice?" Beth said, her voice rising with anger. "What have you done, girl?"

"I didn't believe you, Mum. I didn't believe Dad would just leave. I didn't believe that he'd only send texts and not just call me. I've seen the way you used to look at him when you thought I wasn't looking. Like you wished he was . . ." She dissolved into a fresh bout of tears.

"Bee?" Mel said, urgency in her voice.

"What?"

"There's a nine-minute recording on my phone, from just now."

"Delete it," Beth said.

"Doesn't matter if you do," Alice said, holding out her cell phone. "I've already emailed the file to my phone."

"Delete it," Beth said again. "Delete it from both."

"No!" Alice shouted back, her voice cracking again. "I'm going to forward it to the police instead."

Beth turned toward her daughter, the shotgun swinging around all the way this time.

"Don't do that, sweetie. You'll regret it. We'll all regret it."

"People need to know what you did to Dad."

"I won't ask you again."

"I'm sending it to the policeman, Mum; I found his card in your handbag, with his email address on it. DCI Marcus Naylor." She held the phone up, her thumb poised over the screen. "The email is right here, ready to go."

Beth took a step toward her daughter, still training the gun on her. I felt a stab of fear at the thought of Alice getting hurt. She was just a child. Smart, loyal, brave, resourceful, for sure—but still a child.

"Put your phone down *now*, Alice!" Beth shouted. "Right now!"

"What are you going to do, Mum?" Alice screamed back. "Shoot me? Kill me like you killed Dad?"

Beth stopped for a moment. Turned the shotgun back toward me.

"No. But I will shoot Joe unless you do what you're told." Beth walked back over to where I was sprawled on the floor, stood over me, the barrels of the shotgun a foot from my head.

Alice lowered the phone but didn't put it down.

I stared up at the twin black barrels. This close, they looked huge. The fear was still raw and strong, but now there was something else, something more powerful, pushing against it: this had to end, and there was only one way the truth could come out. I had failed Ben, failed an innocent man, but I would not fail my son.

Only one way to make sure William didn't grow up under a murderer's roof.

Only one thing to be done.

Protect the boy.

"Do it, Alice," I said. "Send it."

Alice looked from her mum, to me, to her mum again. "I don't want . . ."

Beth pressed the muzzles of the shotgun to my forehead, hard steel biting into the skin. "Joe's death will be on your hands, sweetie."

"Mum, don't hurt him."

"I'll shoot him. I swear it."

I said, "She's bluffing. Send it."

"I'm going to count to three," Beth said. "If you don't put the phone down—"

"Do it for Ben, Alice," I said. "Do it for your dad."

Alice thought for a moment, gave a tiny nod, and pressed Send just as I grabbed for the shotgun.

THREE
MONTHS
LATER

84

The postmortem found that Ben was asphyxiated while unconscious.

Fibers in his mouth and throat indicated that a blanket held over his face was used to kill him that Thursday night. Suffocated as he lay on the concrete floor of the parking lot. His body was wrapped in the same blanket—from the trunk of Beth's car—when they found it beneath the half-finished foundations of the summerhouse in his garden. The postmortem also found that he had suffered a bump on the head sufficient to knock him unconscious for a few minutes, and a ruptured eardrum—but no fractured skull, no fatal injury from my encounter with him.

The knowledge that I didn't kill him doesn't ease the guilt that keeps me awake at night. I'm still *responsible* in a lot of ways. I don't suppose the guilt will ever go away. Guilt that I ran, instead of staying to help Ben that night. If I'd stayed with him, waited for him to come around, maybe he'd still be alive. Maybe it would have just postponed the inevitable. Maybe not. Maybe it *was* fate. Either way, the police opted not to charge me with assaulting Ben in the parking lot that night, in exchange for my full cooperation in building a case against my wife and her lover.

The police have since discovered a number of fairly elaborate plans—drawn up by Beth over the last year—to get rid of her husband. Mercury poisoning over a period of months. Tampering with the brakes of his car. Staging a botched burglary-turned-murder was another, in which Ben would end up killed in bed with one of his own shotguns. She also had a plan to spike his drink and push his unconscious body into the swimming pool. But she had never quite seen the right moment to turn any of those plans into reality—until I came along. Until the day William spotted his mother's car in traffic and we followed her to a hotel. I provided the opportunity by stumbling into the middle of something without any idea of what was really going on.

Alice saved me in the end. Even though she was the one with the most to lose. Both her parents gone. She'd tried in her own way to warn me of her suspicions that week—the emails from bret911—but I hadn't joined the dots. She's living with her grandmother in Sunderland now, but I'm trying to stay in touch so that one day I can start trying to repay the debt I owe to her. And me? I'm still in rehab for my leg. I don't suppose I'll ever run the hundred meters in twelve seconds again, but it's been a long time since I could do that anyway.

Trusting people is hard. Especially when I can't see them face-to-face, listen to their voices, and look them in the eye. So it's just me and William now, but we make a good team, and I've been relearning the joy of just spending time with him, giving him all my attention, rather than feeling I should keep one eye on my phone all the time. I feel calmer, clearer, more focused on what's important. I've avoided social media completely since it happened, gone cold turkey on my generation's compulsion to share every event, every emotion, every success, every random thought, every half-funny conversation. Because it's not the photographing and sharing and broadcasting that makes something what it is. It's the *doing*. The *being*. The *experience* of it. The wonderfully unfunny joke your son tells you, or the smile of a stranger on the street, the day out, the blue-sky Saturday, the unexpected kindness, or one of a thousand other things that makes it worth getting out of bed in the morning. That's the truth. That's what's *real*.

I bought William a pet in the end, just like he wanted. Not a hamster—a hamster is a prey animal. Instead we got a cat from the rescue shelter. A big black tomcat named Shadow. Cats don't need anyone; they can do fine on their own. They live in the moment and trust their eyes and ears, what they can see in front of them—I think we can all learn something from that.

William sometimes asks me when Mummy's coming home.

I haven't told him about what happened between us, or about her and Beth. I tell him that she had to go away for a while, with work, and I'm not sure when she's going to be coming back. I tell him that we'll be all right for a bit, just me and him, and that Mummy will be back one day soon. Back home so it's the three of us again, a family, just like before.

That's one lie I'll keep going as long as I can.

ACKNOWLEDGMENTS

Many people have played a part in bringing this book into the world. My agent, Camilla Wray at Darley Anderson, took a chance on me and has been a wonderful source of advice, guidance, and support ever since. I don't think I'd be writing these words were it not for her. I'm very grateful to Celine Kelly for her perceptive editing and forensic eye for detail. Thanks too to Naomi Perry at DA for getting it over the line (and sending my favorite-ever email).

Joel Richardson's skill, insight, and enthusiasm improved this story in more ways than I can recount here. Huge thanks are due to Joel, plus all the team at Bonnier Zaffre and Twenty7.

Thanks to Detective Superintendent Rob Griffin of Nottinghamshire Police for his expertise and guidance on missing persons and other police matters. It goes without saying that any errors or omissions in this area are entirely down to me. Special thanks also to my friend and fellow author Paul Coffey for putting us in touch.

I'd like to thank my brother Oli for many lengthy plot discussions in Devon pubs. One or more of those late-night ideas may have ended up in these pages . . .

although it's hard to know for sure, because I can never remember them the following morning (I should probably start making notes). To my mum and dad and my big brother Ralph for encouragement and interest over a lot of years—thank you. I also owe a debt of gratitude to Jenny, Bernard, John, and Sue for baby-sitting above and beyond the call of duty and many other kindnesses that gave me time to write.

Last but definitely not least, thank you to the home team. To my amazing kids: Sophie, for helping me out with my questions about social media; and Tom, who gave me the first line of the first chapter. Most of all to my wife, Sally, who was there at the birth of this story and helped bring it to life. Thank you for always believing. This one is for you.

Read on for an excerpt from

THE VACATION

by T. M. Logan

Available July 2020 in hardcover
from St. Martin's Press

SATURDAY

I

We drove north, away from the coast.

Through the outskirts of Béziers and deeper into the Languedoc. Vineyards heavy with fruit lined the road on both sides, ranks of low green vines marching off into the distance under a deep blue Mediterranean sky. Sean driving, his eyes hidden behind aviator shades, the kids in the back with hand luggage wedged between them, Lucy dozing while Daniel playing on his phone, me staring out the window as the scenery rolled by, the rental car's AC just about keeping the sticky midafternoon heat at bay.

If I'd known what was coming, what we were driving toward, I would have made Sean stop the car and take us straight back to the airport. I would have grabbed the steering wheel myself, forced the car off the road, and made him do a U-turn right there.

But I didn't know.

My instincts had been telling me for a couple of weeks, as we wound down toward the summer holidays, that *something* was up. Something was wrong. Sean had always been the one to look on the bright side, to make the kids laugh, to bring me a gin and tonic when I needed cheering up. In the unconscious allocation of roles in our marriage, I was the organizer, the rule-setter, the guardian of boundaries. Sean was the light to my shade—always open, funny, patient, the optimist of the family.

Now he was defensive, secretive, serious. Distracted, constantly staring at his phone. Perhaps work was getting on top of him—hassle from his new boss? He'd half suggested that maybe he should stay at home this week, because of work. Or perhaps it was his fear of reaching forty, which seemed to grow stronger as his birthday drew nearer. Some kind of midlife crisis? I'd asked him if he thought he might be depressed—if I knew what was wrong, we could tackle it together. But he had brushed my questions aside, insisting he was fine.

I flinched as he touched my thigh.

"Kate?"

"Sorry," I said, forcing a smile. "Miles away."

"How long until we turn off this road?"

I checked my phone.

"About another ten minutes."

He took his hand off my thigh and moved it back to the steering wheel. The warmth of his fingertips lingered for a moment and I tried to remember the last time I'd felt his touch, the last time he had reached out to me. Weeks? A month?

The fact that you're even thinking it means something isn't right. That's what Rowan would have said. The holiday had been her idea, two years in the planning. Rowan, Jennifer, Izzy, and me—best friends marking our fortieth birthdays with a week together in the south of France, husbands and children included.

"Grand," Sean said. "You OK?"

"Fine. Just want to get there, get unpacked."

"Have you heard from Jennifer and Alistair?"

He glanced up at the rearview mirror. "Since they lost us?"

"No, but I'm sure they're not far behind."

"I *told* them I'd lead the way and they could follow."

I turned to look at my husband. It wasn't like him to worry about Jennifer and her husband—he got along with them OK but had little in common with them, apart from me.

"You know what Alistair's like," I said. "He could get lost in his own back garden."

"Sure, I suppose you're right."

I went back to staring out the window at the lush green vineyards rolling past, dark grapes ripening in the summer heat. Off in the distance, the conical black towers of an ancient château stood out against the skyline.

After ten miles or so, Google Maps directed us off the main road and up through one tiny hamlet after another. Puimisson, St. Geniès, Cabrerolles- -sleepy villages of narrow streets and ancient stone, old men sitting impassively in the shade watching us pass by. We peeled off onto an even smaller road that climbed higher, winding back and forth up a hill where the vineyards gave way to dark pine trees, finally emerging onto the crest of a hill above the village of Autignac, a tall, whitewashed wall flanking the road. The wall ended in black metal gates tipped with faux spearpoints and my phone informed us that we had arrived at our destination.

Sean slowed the car to turn in and the black metal gates swung noiselessly open. Gravel crunched softly beneath the wheels as we turned onto the estate and headed for the villa, tall cypress trees, slim and straight and perfectly pruned, lining the long driveway like a guard of honor. On both sides were lush lawns of thick green grass, watered by sprinklers circling lazily in the midafternoon heat.

Sean pulled up next to Rowan's Land Rover Discovery, already parked in front of the villa's sweeping stone staircase.

I turned in my seat. Lucy was still asleep in the back, head tucked into her balled-up sweatshirt, long blond hair falling across her face. Since hitting her teens she seemed able to sleep anywhere, at any time of the day, if she sat down for more than ten minutes: she had slept on the way to the airport, and on the plane, and was fast asleep now. I had always loved watching her sleep, right from when she was a baby. She would always be *my* baby, even though she was sixteen now—and taller than me.

"Lucy, love," I said, softly. "We're here."

She didn't stir.

Her younger brother, Daniel, sat next to her, headphones on, absorbed in a game of something on his phone. He was her opposite in many respects—a little ball of energy who had never been keen on sleep, either as a newborn or now, an excitable nine-year-old. He uncovered one ear and took his first look out the window.

"Are we there?"

"Give your sister a nudge," I said. *"Gently."*

He grinned mischievously and poked her arm.

"We're here, Sleeping Beauty. At the vacation house."

When she gave no response, Sean unclipped his seat belt.

"Might as well let her have another five minutes while we take the bags in. Come on."

I opened my door and stepped out, stretching my arms after the journey, the air-conditioned chill vanishing instantly as the late-July heat enveloped me like a blanket. The air smelled of olives and pine and summer heat baked into the dark earth. There was no sound— no traffic, no people—except for the gentle swishing of the breeze high up in the cypress trees, the car engine ticking quietly as it cooled.

We stood there, stretching and blinking in the dazzling sun, taking in the villa. Rowan hadn't exaggerated: three wide stories of whitewashed stone and terracotta tiles, the parking circle shaded by olive trees, broad stone steps leading up to a double front door in dark, studded oak.

"Wow," Sean said beside me, and for a moment he looked happy, like his usual self—his old self.

I slipped my arm around his waist, needing for a moment to feel his physical presence as we stood side by side, admiring the villa. I needed to feel his warmth, the touch of his skin, the solidity of muscles beneath his shirt. To anchor him to me.

But after a few seconds he moved away, out of my grasp.

2

Rowan appeared at the top of the stone staircase, holding her hands out in greeting.

"Welcome to Villa Corbières!" she said with a grin. "Isn't it *marvelous*?"

She made her way down toward us, the heels of her expensive-looking sandals clicking on the stone. Since starting her own business she always looked immaculate, and today she was wearing a pale cream cami dress with Cartier sunglasses pushed up into her straight auburn hair. How far my slightly awkward student friend—who'd had braces on her teeth and New Kids on the Block posters on her wall—had come since we'd first met. I guess we all had come a long way, but Rowan definitely felt the furthest from her past self. She hugged me and I closed my eyes for a second, letting the smell of her expensive perfume surround me.

"This place is even bigger than it looked in the pictures!" I said, forcing myself to smile, watching Sean out of the corner of my eye as he ducked his tall frame into the car and checked his phone.

"Wait until you see the interior," she said. "Come on, I'll give you the tour."

Inside, it was all white marble and smooth stone walls, one exquisitely furnished room after another, full of light and beautifully decorated with discreet abstract paintings here and there. It was also deliciously cool, thanks to the air conditioning.

"It belongs to a client." Rowan flashed me a conspiratorial smile. "We've been getting on particularly well, recently."

"It's amazing," I said, and it really was: like something out of a coffee-table magazine. "Have you heard from the others?"

"Jennifer's crowd are still en route—they went the wrong way on the A9, apparently. And Izzy's flight from Bangkok gets in tomorrow morning. I'm going to pick her up."

We had met on the first day of university in Bristol, the four of us neighbors in the same hall of residence, then went on to a shared house until we all graduated. For a moment, I wished myself back to our shared house so powerfully that I could almost smell Izzy's weird and wonderful vegetarian cooking from those days, the perennial post-tennis Bengay smell of Jennifer's room, the heady cocktail of perfume and nail varnish and rosé as we got ready in Rowan's room for a Friday night out. Back then, it seemed like all four of us were essentially the same—same starting point, same university, same hopes and dreams for the future, just waiting for life to happen to us. We all wanted the same things. Then we had graduated and left our younger selves behind, like snakes shedding their skin.

For more than ten years after finishing university we had made a point of going away for a long weekend every summer, each year somewhere different:

Dublin or Prague, Edinburgh or Barcelona. We'd kept the tradition going despite everything—despite babies and work and other commitments—but then one year, when Rowan was heavily pregnant with Odette in the summer, we didn't get organized, and we just . . . stopped going after that, until we'd missed five years' worth of trips. I didn't really know why.

This vacation was supposed to kick-start the tradition again, doing something together to mark the year we all turned forty. *The big four-oh.* It felt as if we didn't do this all together now, we never would, so for the first time ever we were going to break with tradition by bringing all the children too, plus husbands, for a whole week rather than just a weekend. Spend some proper time together.

And so here we were, half a lifetime after we'd first met.

A little girl appeared at Rowan's side, holding both hands up to her. Her wavy red hair was tied in pigtails, her chubby cheeks lively with freckles.

"Pick me up, Mummy!"

Rowan scooped the little girl up and balanced her on a hip.

"You're getting a bit big to be carried now, Odette."

"I'm *not* too big."

"Hello, Odette," I said to the little girl. "You *are* getting big. How old are you now?"

She studied me with big hazel eyes, fingers gripping the strap of her mother's sundress. I realized that mother and daughter were wearing virtually identical outfits.

"Five."

"Daniel's around here somewhere. I'm sure he'd love to play with you."

"Don't like *boys*," she said firmly.

As if on cue, Daniel raced into the room and skidded to a stop in front of us, his pale skin flushed.

"Have you seen the TV?" he said in an awestruck voice. "It's *massive*."

Rowan gave him a wide smile.

"There's a gym, a games room, a sauna, and pool, too."

"Mum, can I borrow the camcorder later to make a house video?"

"Yes, but ask your dad first."

"Cool. I'm going to find the pool!" he shouted, haring off again.

"Be careful," I said to his retreating back.

Rowan opened the sliding French windows and led the way out onto a wide stone balcony. There was a long table and twelve chairs, all shaded by sun umbrellas, a view over a large vineyard on a hill sloping gently away from us. Fields and woods and low, rolling hills stretched out beyond.

"People have lived here since the first century," Rowan said. "There was a Roman villa on this site originally, then a medieval château which fell into disrepair, and now this. It's west facing so you get the most amazing sunsets."

I stood on the balcony, drinking in the French landscape. A rainbow of greens dotted with light brown terracotta roofs, villas and farmhouses spaced far apart, vineyards and olive groves, wheat fields lined with fruit trees. I felt a little ache inside, a feeling of *how the other half lives*: we could never normally afford to stay in a place like this. Not even close. Was that why Sean was acting so strange? Self-conscious because this place was so far out of our reach, so far beyond his salary—both our salaries combined?

"It's absolutely breathtaking, Rowan. Thank you so much for arranging it and having us all here—I dread to think how much it would cost for a week."

She squeezed my arm and followed my gaze across the perfect scene.

"Probably about twenty thousand in high season," she said. "But they don't hire it out to the public—it's just used for corporate events, jollies, schmoozing. You know the kind of thing."

I nodded, but in truth I didn't know: *jollies* and *schmoozing* didn't really ever come into my working life, and standing there with Rowan, the reality of how far apart our worlds had grown stung a little. I loved my job; I'd been a crime analyst with the Metropolitan Police for thirteen years now, collecting data and tracking patterns in crime, but maybe I only noticed everyone else changing because I felt rooted to the same spot—same job, same house, same path—as I had been for years. Maybe it was all about perspective.

Or maybe it was all about Sean.

"With the vineyard, the gardens, and the wall, we've got total privacy," Rowan continued. "All the vineyards inside the wall are part of the property, sloping down toward those trees." She put Odette down on the tiled floor and ignored her complaints, pointing instead to a thick line of trees about two hundred yards away. "We should all go down there later to have a look: apparently there's the most spectacular gorge beyond the trees, with a little path cut into the rock face so you can get down to the pools below.

Purest water you'll ever bathe in—comes straight down off the mountains."

"Sounds a bit cold for me." As soon as the words were out of my mouth I knew they sounded ungrateful, although Rowan didn't seem to notice. *What is wrong with me?* I needed to be happy here, in this remarkable villa, with all the people I loved together for a week.

"Over there," Rowan said, pointing at a church steeple, "is Autignac, ten minutes' walk away. There's a bakery, a little *supermarché,* and a lovely little restaurant in the square. On Wednesday mornings they have the most wonderful street market—lots of local produce, food and drink and crafts. You'll love it."

She pointed down at a tall, dark-haired man in a white linen shirt and chinos, talking on his phone, pacing by the side of the pool.

"Look, Odette, there's Daddy."

"Daddy!" the little girl shouted, her hands pressed against the stone balustrade of the balcony.

The tall man continued pacing and talking, raising a cigarette to his lips.

"Daddy!" Odette shouted again, louder. "Daddy! Daddy!"

He still appeared not to have heard, even as the echo of Odette's call rolled away down the hillside.

"DADDY!" she shouted again, her voice so piercing that I had to lean away.

Finally he acknowledged her with a half-smile and a distracted wave of his cigarette before going back to his phone call.

I instinctively reached out to touch Odette's arm, trying to calm her growing anger, but she batted my hand away and started pulling again at her mother's dress.

"Does Russ always have to be contactable for work?" I rested my elbows on the parapet, the smooth stone warm against my skin.

"Pretty much twenty-four seven," Rowan said. "Money never sleeps—or whatever Gordon Gekko bullshit his boss comes out with."

I was only aware of Russ's job in the vaguest terms: something high powered to do with hedge funds and currencies and city trading. I knew it involved lots of money, but none of the details.

Rowan's phone beeped with a message and she checked the display.

"Mummy! Pick me up again!" Odette was still pulling at her mother's dress, leaving little sweaty hand marks on the beautiful fabric.

Rowan began typing a rapid reply on the phone's screen with her thumbs.

"Why don't you . . . go and see what Daddy's doing?"

"No!" Odette stamped a pink-sandaled foot on the stone floor, her cherubic little face screwing up. "Pick me up!"

"Just a minute, darling," Rowan said, moving back into the house and the vast living area.

Odette shouted one last time and then ran into the house after her mother, her long ginger bunches bouncing with an angry rhythm.

I had to suppress a smile at her display of temper. Odette had thrown the most incredible tantrums from before she could walk, and she didn't show any sign of stopping. If anything, it seemed her outbursts were getting worse the older she got.

My own daughter wandered out onto the balcony, phone in hand, yawning and stretching.

"You're awake!" I said. "Oh, Lucy, come here and look at this amazing view. Isn't it incredible?"

She came to stand next to me, glancing at the landscape for perhaps a second.

"Cool," she said, turning to me. "Have you got the Wi-Fi password?"

3

There were ten bedrooms, split between the ground and first floors. Ours was off the first-floor landing, with a creamy marble floor and antique wooden furniture, gauzy mosquito nets tied at each corner of the four-poster bed. Sean heaved our suitcases up onto the bed and we began to unpack.

Daniel appeared in his swimming shorts, all skinny legs and arms and pale English skin. "I'm ready!" He put his goggles over his eyes and gave us a double thumbs-up. "Are you ready for the pool, Dad?"

Sean broke into a smile, shaking his head.

"Not quite."

"I want to be the first in!"

"J'ai presque fini," Sean said, putting a stack of T-shirts into the chest of drawers.

"Eh?"

"It's French for 'I'm nearly ready.'"

"Hang on, they speak French here?"

Lucy leaned on the doorframe, arms crossed. "Duh," she said. "That's why it's called France?"

Daniel pulled a face. "I can't really do French. Can you, Dad?"

"Sure and us Irish have always had a lot in common with our French brothers and sisters."

"Like what?"

"Neither of us can stand the English."

In spite of myself, I threw a towel at him, smiling.

"Just kidding," he said, catching it against his chest.

"Daddy's just being silly, Daniel," I said. "We get along very well with the French, that's why you're learning it at school."

"Can't really remember anything we've learned, apart from bonjour and pommes frites."

Sean found his swimming shorts in the suitcase, plucking them out from under a pile of shirts.

"That'll actually get you a long way, big lad," he said. "Hey, do you know why the French only eat one egg for breakfast?"

"I don't know, Dad."

"Because one egg is *un oeuf*!"

Daniel laughed for a hysterical moment, then stopped. "I don't get it."

"*Un oeuf? Enough?* An egg in French is—"

"Jesus, Dad." Lucy rolled her eyes. "That's literally like the worst joke I've ever heard."

Sean retreated into the en suite to get changed as Lucy turned and went back to her own room.

Daniel wrinkled his nose.

"Tell me it again."

Sean repeated the joke as he emerged in his swimming shorts, bare chested, tossing his jeans, shirt, wallet, and keys into a pile on the bed. He had started going to the gym and exercising regularly in the last few months and it was easy to tell—his chest and shoulders were broader and more defined, his waist slimmer. He hadn't been in bad shape before, but he'd definitely been putting the work in recently. I felt a strange pang of insecurity and something else—jealousy?—as if he'd been working out to try to impress someone else. Someone other than me.

Daniel was laughing again as he skipped out of our bedroom and into the hallway.

With our son gone for a moment, the smile on Sean's face faltered and died, and for a moment he looked grim faced and serious. Deadly serious.

I froze, a pair of shoes in each hand, not sure how to react. His expression was so unexpected, such a change from a moment ago, that it took me completely off guard.

He caught me looking and plastered his smile back on. "Just going to the pool with Aquaboy, then."

"Sure. You OK, love?"

"Grand. Never better."

"I'll finish here. Quick shower then I'll come and join you."

"Right you are."

I watched him as he walked out of our bedroom. He started in with the jokes again as they headed down the stairs, his deep Irish brogue echoing down the hallway.

I turned and went back to unpacking clothes into the wardrobe, a feeling of fear and sickness building so fast inside I had to sit down on the bed. I knew Sean better than I knew anyone else. I knew when he was unhappy, when he was telling jokes to hide nerves, when he was lying. And the look on his face as he'd said he was grand? I couldn't remember the last time I'd seen him like that. At his father's funeral, perhaps.

My phone beeped with a muffled singsong Messenger tone and I stood up, digging it out of my shorts pocket, unlocking it with my thumbprint.

No new messages.

I frowned and put it back in my pocket.

The beep came again, still muffled. Across the room.

I went to the clothes Sean had left on the bed, a short-sleeved shirt and jeans. Without thinking too much about what I was doing, I picked up the jeans and felt the pockets. A few coins, but no phone. I dropped his jeans back on the bed and listened to the silence of the villa around me. From downstairs, outside, came the faintest sounds from the pool. Splashing, laughing, Daniel's excited voice.

The muffled Messenger tone sounded for a third time.

Sean's bedside drawer.

From where I stood, it was close enough to touch. I put my hand out and snatched it back. Sat for a long moment, without moving. Then reached out again and pulled the drawer open slowly.

It was empty apart from his phone, facedown. He'd started going everywhere with it, as if man and phone were connected by an invisible umbilical cord. So much so that I'd started watching him these last few weeks, only half-deliberately, looking out of the corner of my eye whenever he picked up his phone, trying to see what was absorbing so much of his time and attention. Trying to see the unlock pattern he traced on the screen. Trying to see if I really was going mad, or if this was the start of something unimaginable.

I watched my hand reach in, pick his phone up.

Watched my thumb press the power button. Watched the screen light up with a picture of the kids from our last vacation together.

Just a quick look, I told myself. *To put my mind at rest.*

Before I could talk myself out of it, I drew his unlock pattern, my heart racing.

I know I shouldn't have looked. I *know*.

But I did.

And that was when everything started to come apart at the seams.